ACME

Artorian's Archives Book Five

DENNIS VANDERKERKEN

DAKOTA KROUT

MOUNTAINDALE
PRESS

ACKNOWLEDGMENTS

From Dennis:

There are many people who have made this book possible. First is Dakota himself, for without whom this entire series would never have come about. In addition to letting me write in his universe, he has taken it upon himself to edit and keep straight all the madness for which I am responsible, with resulting hilarity therein.

A thank you to my late grandfather, after whom a significant chunk of Artorian's personality is indebted. He was a man of mighty strides, and is missed dearly.

A special thank you to my parents, for being ever supportive in my odd endeavors, Mountaindale Press for being a fantastic publisher, Jess for keeping us all on task, and all the fans of Artorian's Archives, Divine Dungeon, and Completionist Chronicles who are responsible for the popularity for this to come to pass. May your affinity channels be strong, and plentiful!

Last of all, thank you. Thank you for picking this up and giving it a read. Acme is the continuation of a multi-book series, and I dearly hope you will enjoy them as the story keeps progressing. Artorian's Archives may start before Divine Dungeon, but don't worry! It's going all the way past the end of Completionist Chronicles! So if you liked this, keep an eye out for more things from Mountaindale Press!

CHAPTER ONE

<Artorian. I'll have you know that I'm called the Divine Dungeon now.>

Cal physically formed himself on the wreckage that his main Administrator currently lay uncomfortably prone on. After becoming Dale-shaped, he realized that said Administrator was clearly not in the mood for any of his nonsense. Something about the mixture of man-shaped-indent and the miserable expression that Artorian shot him.

"You made a skyland with illusory holes in it! People will randomly fall to their deaths and... *oh.*" Artorian stopped when he saw the tiny smile creep onto the dungeon-turned-man's face. "Those are *intentional?* You knew you weren't going to be able to house and keep all these people hearty and hale."

A terrible thought struck him. "Now that I think of it... your contract stated you would bring them back if they died, but I don't recall any mention of *when* you needed to uphold your end."

Cal wasn't used to speaking normally yet, but it would come. Dale's body sat down. With interest, he kneaded the dusty, ashen ground as if doing it for the first time. Likely

1

because he was. "Clever little thing, aren't you? I knew I liked you."

The old man harshly exhaled in his overlord's presence, flopping back down after trying to get up. He felt low on Mana, and that seemed to correlate with tired. Artorian needed a quick break from the serious, thinking to do that with some light-hearted banter. "I'm going to try to call you Cale from now on, just to sort out the 'who are you' mess. Like the cabbage. Since you are a combination of Cal and Dale."

The dungeon looked himself over, inspecting the body. "Right... I noticed the odd stares, but I didn't think it would be this incredibly jarring for people. I suppose I was wrong. Everyone who knew Dale thought I was some kind of possession demon. On a happier topic, how do you like Helheim? The nickname is 'Hel,' just so ya know. It's one of my few fully-solid landmasses."

The Administrator stirred. He stabbed a questioning finger down into the busted miniplanet he was now sitting upon; just for confirmation that the ground below him was what the dungeon-man was referencing. It would take less than ten minutes to walk Hel's full circumference. "This thing? Odd naming convention, but it's your Soul Space. Honestly, I expected it to be cold for some reason, but if anything, it just feels dead."

Cale flashed that creepy not-sure-how-to-smile smile again, but he broke it with a tone of elation at the opportunity to explain. "That's because it is! This honestly started out as my... uh. Waste pile of dead stuff? I turned it all into Corrupted ash. Some of it is dust, mind you, but I doubt it matters. You can't tell there's rampant Corruption because I'm siphoning the effects away, but you're sitting on the main source of infernal Corruption in my entire Soul Space. I plan on having it double as a gravity source for all the skylands to orbit around, once the rest of the gravity-Runes are in place. I do need a 'down,' after all. Expect it to become massive in the future. I'm going to use it as a night sky! *Somehow.*"

"But it will be *under* everything. Maybe put a reflection of it above the others?" Artorian pointed up at one of the highest islands. "Speaking of, the gravity on that one is highly unstable, does this plan have anything to do with that?"

Cale's pleasantry melted away to distasteful grumbles. "Noticed that, did you? *Sigh*. Fine. Yes. I am having some basic cosmology and layering problems. Currently, many of the visible masses are likely to bang into one another because the added mass of people is throwing the expected weight off. I'm going to try not to unfairly kill people, but I won't say there isn't going to be a significant number of casualties in the coming weeks. Stop glaring. I know about the… other issues."

Artorian did not, in fact, stop his glaring. With arms crossed, the grandfatherly admonishment continuously stabbed deep. "I trust Dani in all things when it comes to keeping you on task, my friend. However, I have the distinct impression that while you were prepared to some extent for people to live in your Soul Space, you weren't prepared to hold as many as you currently do."

Cale looked away, heavily considering being elsewhere and leaving the old man stuck here like a petite prince for a while. He wanted to, but that just wasn't fair. Cale in no way enjoyed having his weaknesses prodded at, but his new Administrator wasn't… wrong. "Alright. Look. To be honest, I have the Soul Space to tend to. I don't have the attention span to see and attend to every last little thing each person wants. If they want something, they have to earn it."

The dungeon didn't like how Artorian was suddenly and sagely agreeing with him, using a nod that felt suspiciously condescending. "That's a delightful idea, and what exactly is it that people can do to earn anything?"

Cale's next sentence didn't come. His hanging jaw snapped shut as convenient answers flew off like startled birds. After a long moment of pondering, he realized that even though this place doubled as his dungeon… there were no real traps. No monsters to fight. No mechanisms of loss or gain, save someone being stupid, and really no incentive to help him build this place for anyone who hadn't already promised. He had a reward system for existing tokens, but nothing that would allow people to gain new ones.

Artorian's ex-disciple slapped both of his hands against his face and groaned. "Celestial feces."

The old man knew he'd been right on the copper. Rather than say anything just yet to give the dungeon a way out, he let his overlord writhe in discomfort. Both to rub it in, and to give the dungeon a moment to reflect.

Cale took it hard. "Oh, I am not ready. I am so not ready."

Starting to feel guilty for tormenting the poor lad with silence, Artorian relented and pulled his sleeves up to his elbows. "Alright, alright. Enough introspection. My turn, then? I did say I'd help, and I have bucketfuls of solutions for you. I do know you have your own plans and focuses, so, how about this: You have all these people that will soon be both hungry and bored out of their minds. I know some have tokens for land and goods ready to go, but most don't."

Artorian leaned down, drawing in the ash with his finger since he didn't have the Mana to be fancy. "Select a few people that have deals directly with you to manage one of the continents. I suggest a small group of people for each, with only one person on said skyland that has permission to knock and come talk to you. That way they have to bicker and sort most things out between themselves. If that's too much, have a middleman they need to talk to before anything comes up the chain to you. Survival is foundational in people, and if you supply raw resources, they will try to do the rest themselves. Society builds best when it can grow uninterrupted."

After having drawn a basic diagram, he filled in individual segments to add some details. "After you have a hierarchy in place of who you want to talk to you, set a precedent on how you want that information delivered. For these first few months —if we can get a nice division of people to each skyland—all the supervisors of those regions need to do is inform you what basic resources are needed for the grand majority of people to remain self-sufficient. I understand delegating tasks creates end results that may have... problems, but I can help quash those. As a convenient bonus, being able to fuff about allows me very convenient transport methods. Which brings us to diagram three here: Providing people Essence and Mana."

Cale looked at it for a fraction of a moment to grasp it all. "Looks deceptively simple. What's that third section supposed to mean?"

The Administrator nodded, knowing it was oddly worded. He'd done so on purpose so it would get a prod. "In short, many people will want to cultivate. Currently, nobody can. All existing cultivators are on a death timer, and I'm not smooth talking that fact. My control over my own being isn't great, and I feel my remaining Mana siphoning away just from sitting here. Except that instead of it going out into the world, your hungry Soul Space is getting it all. I'm not excluded from having my **Law** connection hampered, but more on that in a moment."

Wasting no further time, he got to the point. "This section is specifically about you not wanting certain people to cultivate, or having them be able to. Turning on the possibility of cultivation for everyone, while *fair*... I'm going to be blunt, Cale. There are people from the Church and the Guild in your world that will *not* hesitate, not one moment, to replicate what they did out there, here. Currently the only thing keeping the status quo is your entire Soul Space being energy stagnant. I doubt you want those mindsets flourishing here? Unless you're fine with the Guild tromping around calling this place their world, as they have the most cultivators still alive and active."

This concept infuriated the dungeon, but Artorian thought it best to bring the possibility out into the open. Hel was starting to get hot from Cale's boiling emotions, and the reigning one was definitely bordering fury. Cale was essentially a big ball of ego, and would never give away what was his. "No. I don't. You had me intrigued, but now you have my *attention*. I was curious at first to see how you'd gotten down here. Still, you're not wrong, and I've got the time. What are your suggestions for improvement? And please stick to the big ones. If I remember anything from your memory stone, it's that you can talk a person to death. A point of contention: My guidestone will indeed always be Dani, and no matter what you say… if she says 'no,' the answer is no."

Artorian got right back to drawing in the ash. "Very well. Big things to tackle. Nice and even gravity, stable and real land-masses, more air, basic flora and fauna, and a task system for cultivators to gain Essence by pointing out errors or areas that need some kind of repair."

Cale understood. "If they're all too busy working to survive, they're too busy to plot overthrowing me. I know that's an abyssal and dark way to go about things, but I despise the idea of a ruling class made entirely of the Guild. One Barry was too many."

Artorian paused in his scribbles, but couldn't refute the matter. "You won't be able to slap down everyone. Though there will be those with zealous hatred that will squeeze the very last drop of Mana from their being to kill their age-old enemies, this deserves to be a fresh start for everyone. You're fair like that."

Cale bit his thumb as a gesture of grievance while thinking this through. Glancing at the diagrams, he disliked how inferior and temporary soot-scribbles were. Eventually, everything that was dead, or needed recycling, was going to fall down here. The notes here would be buried, and that wouldn't do. "I know what I'm doing. I have to run the order of operations by Dani for confirmation, or I'll never hear the end of it, but this is my tentative plan: Those Soul Space basics? You're right, doing those first. When the macro problems are tackled, we'll dig in deeper and look at the rest. Unlike me, you don't have perfect memories. So you're going to need a workspace for you to keep all these diagrams straight. We'll find something."

Cale considered the Administrator's diminishing Mana.

"For now, I need to not lose you to Mana deprivation. Sit and try to cultivate. We're sorting this out, right now."

Artorian wasn't about to turn down goodwill like that, and reached toward his spatial bag to pull out some pillows. When he grasped at air, he remembered he no longer had it. That made him hum out with some disappointment. *Mmm*.

Instead, he slotted himself into a rigid lotus position, just to stab at something he'd told Dale once as he sank down into his center.

<I always did like what you did with the place.> The Administrator was surprised when Cale could outright exist in his center when he arrived himself. Artorian shrugged it off and focused on the task; Cale could likely do a lot he didn't know about.

His gyroscopic cultivation technique spun up painfully slowly. Had it been metal, he would have heard the entire construct complain and groan since no Essence was being pulled in. It was like trying to make a water wheel work without the requisite river to provide that initial push.

Cale noticed, and adjusted the area to be plentiful. A torrent of unaligned Essence suddenly surrounded Artorian, funneling freely as it sucked into his much happier system. Unfortunately, when he quickly reached the critical mass that would force the gathered Essence to be traded out for Mana, nothing happened. Mere Essence wasn't enough to keep him alive and kicking as a Mage, but progress was progress.

Artorian helped Cale by putting it in words. "Alright. Hurdle one. I'm at the trade threshold. No activity; can't feel my **Law**."

Cale's body vanished from the surface of Hel. He didn't need it where he was tinkering, and he didn't like the idea of just letting it stand around without him in it. <Working on it. Ran into a snag. Those chains of chaos binding me have luckily not cut off my connection to *my* **Law**. *Phew*. Might have been in serious trouble had that been the case. It looks like it's just you all. I'm thinking because you're encased in my Soul Space?

My **Law** contains all of yours like subsets, so maybe I could be a chain link if you connected to me more… directly? I'm stumped.>

Hmmm. The Administrator had an idea, though his lack of information on how chains of chaos worked was kicking him in the shin. He knew that Cal, as a dungeon Core, had them wrapped around his physical being. They caused a litany of complications and inconveniences, and the 'chaos' bit meant that the rules on them weren't clear. That meant boundaries needed to be tested. Sadly, that also meant testing by throwing things at the wall and seeing what stuck. <I'm *not* stumped. Come with me; I've got something dumb we can try.>

Cal scoffed, following Artorian deeper into his center. <What, something dumb? I've never done one of those.>

The dungeon's nervous little laugh at the end was enough for Artorian to deduce sarcasm was at play. He zipped into his Soul Space without a second thought, and stopped when he realized Cal wasn't following him. <Well, get on in here!>

The dungeon didn't, inspecting things instead. <I have discovered the dumb thing and I'm feeling apprehension. I've never gone into someone *else's* Soul Space before, yet if I recall what happened when I tried putting a spatial bag into another spatial bag… the result wasn't pretty.>

The old man shrugged. <Look, I know it's a dumb idea, but what's the worst that could happen? It's not like there's some **Law** out there that states the worst thing that can happen, *will* happen.>

Cal decided to make a memory core duplicate of Artorian. Just in case. <Alright. Nothing ventured, nothing gained!>

Cal's mind entered the Administrator's Soul Space, and Artorian died on the spot.

CHAPTER TWO

<Welp. I've got good news, and I've got bad news.>

Artorian felt sick when he heard Cal's voice again. From initial observation as he opened his eyes, he wasn't on Hel anymore. Actually, was he under the Silverwood Tree?

He tried to speak, but his lungs ached as he took his first breaths. Like he'd never used them before. How did Mana hurt? He hadn't felt pain like this since his Ascension. Rather than trying to speak, he just mentally held onto the dungeonspeak connection, and used that. Dungeonspeak? Was that a new term? That wasn't important right now. <Cal? What... what happened? I'm hazy and, *sweet pyrite*, I hurt.>

Cal snorted at the turn of phrase. <Just remembered that you've been spending a lot of time with Dwarves. Anyway, you're back! I'm so glad that worked.>

Artorian didn't feel very secure, and movement of any kind was a mistake. <That *what* worked?>

Cal's silence did not bode well. He replied eventually, but only after Artorian bit through a lot of discomfort and got up from the grass between silvery roots. He managed a few staggered steps as he got used to his body again. It was *his* body, right? It didn't feel correct. No, the other way around. This body felt *more* correct, and that was throwing him off. He no longer felt the awkward tendency to lean forward and hunch.

<Looks like you noticed. You want the good news first, or the bad?>

The Mage grumbled, and remembered how to do basic stretches. His memories felt as if they were filtering in like pages being flipped in a book, rather than being easy to recollect. <Good first. I feel awful and want a pick-me-up, if you don't mind.>

The dungeon sounded delighted, excitement filling his mental voice. <I'd love to! So, the good news. You've got an achievement! I call it 'First to Die.' Out of everyone in my soul world, you somehow died first. Congratulations!>

Artorian narrowed his eyes at the patch of thickened Essence density, so Cal backpedaled. <I'm joking... Don't look at me like that! I mean, I'm serious about the dying first part. Anyway. Your **Law** connection is fixed. Altered. Mended? I don't know what I'm going to call it yet. Just... here. See for yourself.>

Ambient Essence spiked around Artorian with significant intensity. His cultivation technique spun up all on its own to absorb it, and that struck him so hard that he fell right back down on his butt. It didn't even need his desire to do so? What?

Artorian dropped into his center, and watched the magic happen. His refinement gyro had been upgraded with intricate Runes that lined many of the rings. Not a complaint, he supposed? His being swallowed up the free energy and, as he reached the threshold, it naturally traded in for Mana. Relief washed over him as it did, the pain in his skin fading.

Success! Kind of? <Cal? Why did it feel like the gathered Essence went to you? After which you donated back a drop of my Mana, that just *happened* to be of my type? Also, rather than mended, I like Cal-ibrated.>

Cal loved the term, but groaned that the old codger noticed

his workaround right away. <You killjoy! I was going to keep that in my back pocket and throw it at you as a surprise. But no~o~o, you had to go and be perceptive. Fine, yes. It's technically part of the bad news, but it *took* you dying for your soul to be able to connect to mine. I used your Seed Core to funnel your mind into a new B-rank zero body of Mana, with your specifications, and your soul just reconnected all by itself. I don't know how that last part works, but souls don't seem to like not being whole. The you that comprises you... is *you*. I know what that was supposed to mean, but I just confused myself.>

Artorian waved him off. <You're good, buddy. I understood. No soul would have meant my memories were in my body, but with a good chance of that person actually being someone else. My soul made it uniquely me. Common philosophy problem that turns out had a direct solution.>

An air of uncertainty lingered, and Artorian asked a question Cal hoped he wouldn't. <What do you mean, Seed Core?>

A nervous laugh once again broke out of the space Cal occupied. <Right, so you're not actually a dungeon, but we ran into a few... problems bringing you back. You're actually the first Mage we've managed it with. Before you ask, yes, there have been many casualties. Yes... you've missed a chunk of time.>

That last tidbit of information didn't sit well with Artorian, at all. A few weeks was doable, but if it was longer, he would have lost out on valuable family time. Cal audibly swallowed, and based on the way he conveyed the bad news, Artorian could tell a few others must have been glaring at him elsewhere. <This is part of the... bad news. A *minor*... twelve decades.>

Mana around Artorian turned the kind of hostile that made people grasp their children and escape the vicinity in a blind rush. Each one of his rage-controlled words were heavily enunciated. <Twelve. *Decades*. Cal?>

The dungeon cut him off before oaths were broken, or something equally disastrous occurred. <Before you get even angrier, I have very good news about your family. They're fine!

You missed nothing! They missed nothing! They're in the equivalent of stasis; have been since a few weeks after you entered. I was sure to get them prime spots. We've had a few... global mishaps.>

Artorian's furious air stabbed the surroundings, but relented as he internalized the promise that his precious ones were safe. His words remained controlled, but they hadn't lost a speck of built-up rage. <Continue.>

Clearing his throat as Cale solidified himself a body to speak with, he also made a table and some chairs appear for them to sit on. "Well, Dawn really didn't like hearing that, when she went to look for you, a day after being here, you were dead. Then she got Dani on her side and... *Eeesh.*"

Cale was in visible discomfort as he took a seat. "*Many* other problems happened. I know you're upset, but how about I talk for awhile and fill you in on the couple of catastrophes we've had."

Artorian sat, laced his hands, and exhaled strongly enough for a wind gust to blaze across a significant grassy plain. "Please do skip the catastrophes and start with what happened with me, then backtrack."

Rubbing his hands together like a salesman who thought he got out of a bad bind, Cale got to it. "I entered your Soul Space, and it popped like an overinflated balloon. We're thinking it's either because mine was bigger, or my **Law** tier was higher? Your space can fit in mine. Not vice versa. On the plus side, your death exposed your soul, and through our **Laws**, I managed to form a connection based on the Tower tiers. In short, I'm cheating by using the Tower as a connection source. With myself as the anchor of give and take. The good news is that it works! The bad news... About that Seed Core."

Cale leaned back in his chair, and pointed up at the Silverwood Tree.

Now that Artorian looked at it again, it was massive. The roots of it required a whole skyland by itself. Many glittering gems grew like fruit in its branches, and one in particular felt like... *him?* "Is... is that... me?"

Cale nodded slowly, but with a complicated grimace on his face. "Sort of? There is... a recurring problem, when using memory stones during reintegrating to a me-bound body. Specifically when the soul comes back to it. The first few times we pressed a memory stone to a body of your shape, the rock just shattered. The few times where it worked, you went insane and the body shattered shortly after."

Artorian was doing his best, but even his best made him look pale as Cale talked. "The soul-connection we're using to keep your cultivation a possibility has some side effects. Including a really nasty one on a layer I needed Dawn and Occultatum to actually grasp. Even then, souls are above my cultivation rank. The last century has been trial and error from lack of true understanding."

He amended his statement to try to clarify. "In short, specifically because your soul is connected to mine, something about the mind can't handle it. So instead of a memory Core, I tried one of the Cores up there."

Cale pointed at one of the glittering seeds in the Silverwood Tree. "We don't have a set term yet, but so far we're calling them Seed Cores. The entirety of your mind went into one. When we formed another body of Mana, instead of completely transferring your memories, it became more of a back and forth filtering. Your actual mind is in that Core, but your functioning one is in you. Explaining it is complicated, but the end result is that your soul merged with the body you currently have. It worked. No shattering, no insanity. You just woke up like it was no big deal."

Kneading his temples, Artorian groaned. No wonder he felt sick. They'd been playing paddle ball with everything he was. Cale continued to the next step, since this initial explanation had gone so smoothly. "There are some bonuses. You have a perfect memory now, we *think*. Memories sometimes do not make the trip between Seed Core and body. You don't have to worry about going insane over time, and if you get sick of life you can take breaks until time has passed. Everyone who becomes an Ascended is going to need a Seed Core for their mind, I think. Otherwise it's not happening. Like I said, you're the first one we've managed to get back. Let me give you the rundown of basic history."

Cale pulled up a map. Several, in fact, that hovered around their table. Each showed one of the continent-sized skylands. Now with fewer holes. "When we started, it looked like this. Millions of people. One island. We separated the races as much as we could, and that used up all the functional space at the time. As per your suggestion, I flooded the place with all sorts of random flora and fauna. I have functional rivers, and a mostly-working ecosystem."

One of the more fleshed-out maps enlarged. "This is the middle island. I named it Midgard for now. Humans and Wolfmen lived together on this one due to space constraints. As expected, most Mages, or people who used to have status and power, went nutso. Not insane, just tried to kill everyone they didn't like in the hopes of doing it a few times over. It didn't quite go as they planned, but Hel has gotten very large as a result."

The dungeon pointed at a very red statistic. "After a month, a few million people became a few hundred thousand. Also, there may have been a food shortage while I was busy mass-replicating memory stones from the endless flood of dying people that I promised to bring back. Oops."

Artorian had the suspicion that if Cale had focused on making food instead, he wouldn't have needed nearly as many memory stones. He hated that he was probably right.

Cale took a well-measured breath. "We may have also... run out of air, due to a fire that burned down an entire island of plant life. One of those fire mages Dawn brought in had an accident trying to overextend their Mana while still boxed. I was otherwise occupied at the time. When I noticed, I offered everyone a place in either stasis or a memory Core. That's where most all of your people currently are, sans hostile cultivators. I didn't do so good on the tasks versus rewards project."

The old man felt worse by the minute. "How... how many current survivors?"

Cale looked away and dismissed the maps. "It's... not great. Just most of the people who had direct deals with me. Everyone else is in stasis, or kept safe in a memory Core. Our S-rankers technically died to make a deal with me, but they're here. None of their S-rank energy could enter my portal; it all had to be abandoned for me to remake their bodies. Neither Dawn nor Occultatum had the soul reconnection problem, but their minds and their souls are like... the same thing? Occultatum is the new name for The Master, by the way. He prefers it."

Cale scratched at his head with both hands. "I don't understand it yet. No Seed Core needed for them. For the moment, I am the one supplying all the basic needs, food especially. Essence is currently being given directly, rather than through tasks. I need... I need an actual system in place before I can bring most cultivators back. This is not how I wanted this to go. Dani is furious with me, and while I haven't technically broken any promises or contracts, I don't feel too good."

Artorian squeezed his own hands together. "It sounds to me like what you need... is a good Administrator."

Cale slumped deep into his seat. "I don't want to tell you how long it took just to get *you* back. No, wait. Already did that. I can repopulate non-cultivators and cultivators up to C-rank with ease, but I don't want to. I have a mountain of tasks to begin, and more to finish."

The dungeon's facial expression was that of a living headache. "While I could run a dungeon, a civilization is not my playground. Luckily, now that you're back, I can pull up Henry and Marie. They should know things about kingdom building, people management, all that stuff. Come to think of it, I never did try assigning a group of people to a continent. I just asked my Bobs. A supervisor group just didn't seem useful when all they were giving me was raw material lists."

Artorian exhaled deeply and slowly nodded. He saw where the problems were starting to form a pattern. "Alright, Cale. Time for you to really stop trying to do it all on your own. Why don't we start with a group huddle of everyone still around, and we can delegate out from there? I have a solution for you, though I'm afraid I can't help with the math."

CHAPTER THREE

Lucky for all of them, Cale was fantastic at math.

The boxed A-rankers turned out to still be around as well, even if struck by a case of melancholy. With the way the world had turned out the first time, they weren't too keen on being social. As far as they were concerned, they too had failed.

Being a projection had downsides. Mages in stasis could experience the world, but not really act in it without grievous repercussions. As proven by a fire Mage who had gotten the tiniest bit over-enthusiastic. Watching an island of plants die, only to find out they couldn't actually stop the blaze, had not done them well.

They still all flocked to Niflheim when news reached them that Cale had finally managed to bring a Mage back. Niflheim was what Cale had named one of the in-progress skylands. While the innards of that continent were essentially one massive, foggy, root-twisted dungeon of mist and illusion, the otherwise inaccessible top of it belonged entirely to the Silver-wood Tree. Beneath its landmass-shading canopy, Cale emplaced a dome of abundant energy to serve as a 'safe zone' for those he was about to bring back.

The borders inside of the domes were lined with tables containing varied sustenance, as freshly reconstructed individuals were always hungry for some reason. Which was a nice way to say 'on the verge of starving.' As rebuilt people filed in via an unceremonious Cal-toss, Artorian just finished stacking himself a plate of food before he was tackled into the grass. His food went flying, turning to particles when it hit the ground.

"Sunny!"

Artorian gasped out his reply with a pained whine. "Nice to see you too, Dawn. Would you mind letting me up, dear? You're on my everything."

Snorted responses and snickers came from the peanut gallery in the background, but Dawn eased up and pulled Sunny to his feet before engulfing him in a heavy hug. She clearly was in no mood to let go. Right. It had been a short moment for him. It had been far longer for her. So Artorian kept quiet at her little sniffling shudders, rubbing her back to provide reassurance. "I'm here, my dear. I'm here."

A few people wanted to interrupt the reunion, but none had the heart. The few that took an uncertain step forward were stopped by a hand motion from Occultatum. Even though this new form of 'The Master' was no longer an S-ranker, the previous respect he commanded remained. With a nudge of his nose, most people awkwardly funneled by them to pick out their initial meal. Neither Henry nor Marie moved to do so, waiting for the moment to come to a natural close before wandering nearby to offer a welcoming hand as Dawn let go.

Dawn wiped under her eyes with the sleeves of her orchid petal robe, and finally managed a tiny smile. "I know. I know, Sunny. It's just nice to have *all* of you here. I was present for the first few… attempts, but that wasn't you. And then I didn't have the heart after that."

To the incredible confusion of Artorian, he could do little but watch the following interaction. When Marie spread her arms wide, Dawn walked right into them. Giving her friend a pleasant 'welcome back' squeeze. That was *Queen* Marie. How were they just casually hugging? Marie caught his dumb-founded expression from the corner of her eye, patting a recovering Dawn on her back while she filled him in.

"Hello, Artorian. It is nice to meet you. We have heard much about you from the days before the first breaking. Dawn here found me in those early days, and over the years you weren't around we became good friends. We didn't do very well with Mana deprivation, so we wanted to thank you for being the… test bunny? That helped us all get back. We also hear, to Henry's and my surprise, that you are going to be the main Administrator? As a prior King and Queen, we were hoping you'd spare us the time for a chat."

Artorian suddenly experienced a terrible thought, and checked himself to make sure he was dressed. Oh, thank Cale… simple grayish-white robe, definitely not naked. Clearing his throat to play it off, he strode in and shared a wrist shake with the famous duo. Dawn hung off his shoulder shortly after, just happy to see her people start off on a good foot as Sunny replied. "I would be delighted to speak at length on upcoming events. It was my hope that people would be interested in some ideas I had on how we could try again. Help with some worldbuilding? I can only hope there's less holes."

The surrounding figures nodded, and Artorian realized there was a small circle of people in his vicinity that were clearly listening in. Artorian was an unknown, but Occultatum—no, that was too long to say casually—*Tatum*, Henry, Marie, and Dawn were big names. Madame Chandra's projection joined their circle, staying in close proximity to Tatum.

Looking around, the Administrator softly mouthed an 'oh' when he deduced what the common denominator was here. "Dungeon Born strings. You all have a direct deal with our Overlord?"

Cale materialized in Dale's body, while Dani teleported in right after to settle on his head. "Overlord? I don't know if I like the sound of that. Maybe after I work some of this guilt off?"

Grace giddily copied her mom and appeared on Niflheim

with a spastic pop. She quieted and settled atop Dani when realizing there were a lot of people, making Cale look like he had a very comical head injury. Without even twitching his hand, Cale made a copy of Mountaindale's old circular meeting room rise from the ground. The round table smoothened itself without issue, allowing for cozy, plush-coated chairs to form around it. Enough were made available for the significant number of people present.

Ten feet outwards from the inner circle, a second circle rose slightly higher. Those without direct deals with Cale filed into that tier without needing to be prompted. Unlike the Administrator, this wasn't their first meeting. Artorian watched the artful display in respectful silence. He was about to mosey to the outer tier when Deverash the Gnome tugged at his pant hem, as he was going the wrong way. "Inner circle, funny man."

Before anything official started, those gathered whispered about how nice it was to talk again. Dev hovered over to the inner circle without any issues, tugging out the chair next to Dawn's. It seemed this round table had been used a few times before, as people were very specific about where they sat, with certain seats left purposefully empty.

When something underneath the translucent table went *click*, Artorian actually had a good look at it, and curiously noticed there was a considerably complicated-looking clock hiding inside. One of the hands spun incredibly fast, and he guessed that must have been the speed Cale had currently set his Soul Space to. Based on the myriad of hands, the current time-passing speed was as fast as Cale could make it happen. Based on Cale's expression, it was not as fast as he wanted it.

At twelve o'clock, Cale sat with his Dungeon Wisps in front of him. Each snuggled on their individual fluffy pillows. Most present knew Cale didn't need a body to be at a meeting, but it had been discussed prior that his physical presence was an appreciated gesture. It made them all feel like they were here to solve things together.

That earlier 'overlord' comment had stabbed Cale deeper

than the Administrator had realized, because the dungeon was being positively courteous. To Artorian's pleasant surprise, the usually zippy Grace remained very self-contained when she nested on her pillow, behaving like she was at a fancy dinner. More likely it had been made clear that if she didn't, she wouldn't get to stay. So the tiny wisp was on her best behavior.

Thanks to nameplates on the table, Artorian could figure out who was who. At one o'clock sat Bob Prime, Cal's most trusted and capable Goblin Mage from his Mountaindale days. Bob Prime was flanked by Tatum, and the seat next to him held the projection of Madame Chandra. She must have made a direct deal, but hadn't had her turn for a body yet. Next to Chandra, at the four o'clock mark, sat Brianna, the lady that had once been a Dark Elf princess.

In order, they were followed by Deverash, Artorian, Dawn, Marie, and Henry. An empty seat was kept open next to Henry, and the nameplate said 'Aiden.' The seat between an absent Aiden and present Minya was also empty. That nameplate plainly said 'Odin.' The loud lightning fellow from that initial fresh-entry meeting? Yes. Him. Thirteen seats total? He counted thirteen, so yes. Why did it have to be off by one? They almost had it even!

Artorian chose not to speak first. There was likely a way this round table talk worked, and he needed to learn the social status-quo. As expected, Cale had top-priority say. Though after that it didn't seem like there was any deep structure at play as casual chatter started slow. Hopeful tones, for the majority of it.

Cale gently clapped his hands together for attention, and the space quieted easily. "Hello all, thanks for coming to this decade's meeting. I know it's too early, but there's just too much good news not to call this one as soon as we did."

A slew of images in three dimensions sprung into existence above the table. A century of progress slapped the old man in the face, as this was the first time he had seen such refined methods of visualizing and showing concepts and ideas. He even felt connected to the information, certain that he could move, alter, recolor, or manipulate it if he wanted to.

Cale got right into it. "Big spots of good news. I can properly revive Mages, and I know for nearly half of you this is both very jarring and very new. I'd like to welcome back Artorian, Brianna, Henry, Marie, and Deverash. I'm going to flatly state that I chose not to bring in Odin or Aiden. You can likely guess the reasons."

Artorian would have been happier being told the reason, but he'd roll with the minor punches. He didn't need to know everything. From what he'd understood earlier, if forgetting was going to be a problem, that in itself wasn't too great.

Regardless, he looked around the table and reached over as best he could to shake some hands. They were all on the same team, after all. Bob looked scary, but what else could be expected from a Goblin bound to the **Law** of **Death**? Brianna was elegantly cordial, but there was something reserved about the handshake. Was Dawn silently glaring behind him? Probably. Minya's handshake went easier.

Cale motioned to each person in turn, giving them a chance to introduce themselves. Bob went first. "Hello. I am the Great Spirit's—I mean, Cal's—head Goblin. In the dungeon, I helped run major operations and contributed to Runes and research. I don't know what I'll be doing now; my memories are fuzzy and mixed. I am also not entirely certain of myself as I distinctly feel the awareness that my actual mind is not where I am currently sitting. I would prefer not speaking too much."

A round of nods went around the table. As they continued introductions in order, Artorian noticed neither of his sons were present. They had made a direct deal as well, but given there were empty seats at the table as was, he decided not to tackle this just yet.

Occultatum went next. "Hello, everyone, please feel free to call me 'Tatum.' I was The Master in my previous life, and would prefer if I was never referred to as that again. I'm one of the few people that has been around the entire time and, to be honest, I'm very spent and tired from seeing a lot of projects fail. I tried to help with making the original civilization, and because it didn't go so well, I would like to abstain from influencing the next version, in favor of just knocking some projects out on Hel. Thank you."

Tatum smiled softly as the projection of Chandra patted his shoulder. It wasn't tactile and couldn't be felt, but the intent went deeply appreciated. "I am Madame Chandra. Until recently, I have been keeping to myself with the other boxed mages. We have our own little community up and going, but given we can do little other than talk, we've been rather stagnant since Moonfall. Since I will be able to turn that around soon, I'd like to apologize for my current downcast state."

She paused, and allowed everyone to have a moment to remember how things had changed. "I assure you that once I can actually do things again, I will be in everyone's business. I am heavily into all things growth and nature, and having watched from the sidelines, I have a painfully good grasp on some of the basic ecological macro-changes that need to happen before we can give civilization another try. I would prefer to focus on that, rather than the dealing-with-people part. My heart isn't ready for it, and I would like to find myself in my forest before branching out. When possible, I would like to re-open my restaurant, and make all who sit with us into fast friends. It has been very lonely."

Another understanding set of nods followed, and the baton was passed to Henry as Chandra sat down. It broke the clockwork order, but that was fine. For a human who was significantly improved by Cal, he looked surprisingly nervous. "I don't know how to actually introduce myself other than that my name is Henry. I was a prince, and later King by default in the outside world. Here that doesn't hold true. I'm good at statesmanship, and the kind of tasks that a budding civilization requires to develop properly. When it comes to world development, I'm afraid I'm not going to be very useful. I... erm... Marie, could you please?"

Marie tapped his hip and Henry sat down, letting her pick up from the awkwardness. "Hello, everyone, I'm Marie, and I am in very much the same vessel as Henry. My skills are the same, and I'm aware they won't be helpful if there's nothing to fight and no people to manage. I would like to thank Cale for bringing us all back, but would like to say that I am so very unbalanced by seeing Dale just sitting there."

Some small laughs went around the dome, and a few people finally cracked a smile as Marie sat down. Rather than merely stand up, Deverash hopped onto the table. His stature might have been small, but his confidence was sizable. "A pleasant day to meet you all. If days are still a thing we have! I'm Deverash Neverdash the Dashingly Dapper, and I'm a Gnome from the ancient days. Unlike our dearest nobles, my people skills are not something that should leave an academic setting."

He cheekily winked at Artorian. "As such, before the breaking, my time was spent on figuring out alternative cultivation sources. I'm happy to report that I actually got decent progress when it came to pill refining, since the environment here does hold Essence. Turning that into something consumable was a topic I was very close to breaching. However, I would like to give that project to someone else in favor of being allowed study time on Runes, spells, wards, and the like. Anything that could be placed in the box labeled 'magic,' really. That's where I shine. Outside of academics, I do my best, but it's not my best."

When the Gnome hopped down, Artorian gave him a nervous look. Did it have to be his turn? He knew he had to stand, but he found himself inexplicably glued to his chair. Stage fright? Possibly. Dawn squeezed his arm, causing the weight of nervous dread to shed from his being. Her smile was soothing, and with a breath, he stood to speak.

CHAPTER FOUR

"Hello, everyone. Feel free to call me anything that strikes your fancy. Popular options are Artorian, Sunny, or 'Ey You! if you're a drunken Dwarf. Or really any string of expletives that makes you feel better after realizing you need to come talk to me. I'm a prior Elder and Headmaster, and my only real skill is to talk your ear off. I'm not half bad at delegating and administration, and I suppose my strength lies in the realm of obscure problem solving. When something makes absolutely no sense, I tend to be the codger you throw a pillow at."

He continued through the amused stares. "I delight in figuring the universe out, and I think that might be what I'm needed for. On top of being the first person to both die in Cale's Soul Space, and be revived, I'm also the first person to prod him about the holes in his world. I don't think he appreciated it, but that's what I do. I think we'll all get along wonderfully, and would like to cede my turn."

Artorian sat, and felt incredible relief when Dawn patted the top of his bald head while some laughter made the rounds. He wasn't a child! Well... that depended on how age was counted, he supposed.

Dawn had none of the oration difficulty the Administrator did. "As of my Incarnation, my name is Dawn. If you hear someone accidentally refer to me as Ember, that's fine."

The old man looked away, trying his best to seem innocent as he received significant side-eye.

Dawn continued her introduction. "I'm in the same trireme as Tatum. I've been here the entire time, both before the breaking and after. Most of my latent efforts have gone into working the **Law** problem out. My only skills have to do with war, military matters, and emergency triage. I'm an 'it needs to die' and 'get it done' problem solver. My skills lend themselves to actually field-testing all the Runes, spells, and odd creations that Cale, Bob, and Dev come up with."

She cleared her throat, adding a detail. "An entire continent is rubble from my work and, unless you need it for something specific, it's going to remain a broken landscape of sand with some oases sprinkled in. Blowing things up has kept me sane, and I apologize to the people I scared the life out of during some of my furies. I would prefer to keep testing creations, though if I can finally make some friends, then I would really, really like that."

Understanding nods followed all around. It had been stressful for the survivors, and the coming of the new age was a hopeful, bright new leaf. A fresh foundation that they all hoped to build anew from. *Especially* when it came to personal relations. With Aiden and Odin absent, Minya and Brianna silently had an entire conversation with one another using only their eyes. Cale made a minor motion that he was going last, so they decided between themselves that Brianna would go next.

Her words were silky in comparison to everyone else's. "I am Princess Brianna of the Dark Elf nation. Or so I would like to introduce myself. Brianna the Moon Elf is who I am now. My skills stay firmly in the realm of information, assassination, obfuscation, and material of such topics. Given a choice, I would like to build a home for my people when they return. Here, below the roots of the Silverwood Tree. Once the world is… settled, I would like to offer my services in keeping tabs on everything working as intended. We might have the ability to speak swiftly, but many thousands of people make many thousands of problems."

Silence reigned when Brianna sat. That was thinking a bit far ahead, but the usefulness couldn't be denied. As Minya stood and raised her arms to the sky, everyone could hear Cale mumble, "Please don't," while his face fell into his palm. Minya was stopped before she was able to go on a sermon on the virtues of their great savior, the most divine of dungeons, Cal.

Her arms dropped, body language visibly deflated. "I'm Minya, I'm a… procurement expert. I'm not sure how well that's going to work here, but getting my hands on items, goods, unique materials and the like is my specialty, on top of operating Cal's cult. Not that I have much of it left. I survived past the breaking for a very long time, so rather than request a purpose, I'm going to do the same as Bob and keep myself at Cal's disposal. I prefer being flexible, so I'll be doing what's needed as it comes up."

When Minya sat, Cale jumped up right away. His impatience was showing and it was finally his turn! Yes! "You all know who I am and what I do, so I'm going to skip that in favor of version two of the grand plan."

With an unexpected shattering sound, one of the three-dimensional screens winked away. Cale said nothing for a long moment, face forced into a flat expression as he was clearly doing something elsewhere in a big hurry. A new orb-shaped diagram of the plan came up, and this one was instead termed 'Version 3.' When he finally spoke again, it was accompanied with a nervous laugh. "Eheh, I may have accidentally dropped version two. So! Version three."

The diagram grew to cover the entire span of the table, and Artorian was incredulously surprised at how laughably massive Hel had become. It was dark as night! Had it not been on the diagram, he would not have physically looked away to see it was actually obscuring other skylands.

Cale excitedly rubbed his hands together. "So here's the way I want the world to work. In the center, Hel. It's both the main source of gravity, and half of my day-night cycle project. As you can see at the bottom right below it, I've got a moon planned. It's just a projection over a pebble for now, so, that's no moon. There is a pending projection plan for the sun, but we've got even less progress on that than we have with the moon."

Altering what the diagram showed, he made the overall scale smaller to show that all the continents were floating around Hel in a wide oval orbit. Some of the orbits made islands overlap dangerously close above or below one another, depending on their position in the trajectory.

The dungeon was proud of his ideas. "I have nine major landmasses under construction, Hel included. For eleven prospective celestial objects total, adding one moon, and one sun. Hel and the latter two are going to be stationary while everything else does the moving. Unless I need the moon for tides, but that's so far out, it's not going into the plans at this stage."

Cal highlighted a blueprinted section. "I've got other tentative ideas, but we'll cover those later. First, the big landmasses. There is a major problem that I'm going to choose to call a feature. Due to some difficult to control circumstances, and possibly when I made what due to my rank at the time, each skyland has a different attunement to gravity. We're still working on the Runes to gain some modicum of control over regions that large. Because there's a predetermined order to things though, I'm going to adopt it. The more gravity on a continent, the higher the Essence density that sticks around that area."

With a motion of his hand, statistics in luminous text and crayon drawings of rainbow bridges formed in convoluted fashion between the skylands. The bridges didn't at all go in order of numbered islands, and that seemed silly. Until they looked more closely at the numbers. Rather than the orbital order of skylands, the crayon lines were connected based on a smooth Essence density progression. Meaning the skylands were linked based on their relative gravity to one another.

After a few minutes of inspection, Cale started pointing out details. "As you all can see, Midgard, the skyland everyone portaled in on, has both the lowest density and the weakest gravity. Even if 'weak' measures out to what everyone was used to back out in the real world."

"It's the most stable because of this, so Midgard is where I'm thinking of decanting people when it's a good time. Additionally, I want to stick with the racial division we had going in the first version. It did help, even if it didn't turn out well. If Odin was here, I'd give him the credit concerning the naming convention for the landmasses. The next two skylands past Midgard have closely matching gravity, but it's a significant jump."

Altering some settings, cultivation equivalents became visible. "Based on the math that you can see, Midgard supports anything from G to D-ranks. The lowest pressure on Alfheim and Svartalfheim, on the other hand, begin at the bottom of C-rank. So in order to leave Midgard, I'm going to require that people are the equivalent of C-rank zero. Regardless of whatever system ends up working for us."

Silent nodding made the rounds, and Cale continued. "Since I have everyone stored, I spent some time taking a census. Based on the amount of people we have for each race, and what I have deduced based on average cultivation, the current plan is to decant humans on Midgard, Dwarves on Svart, and the majority of Elves on Alf. Brianna, I know you want nothing to do with the majority of the Elves, so you and yours are not included here. We have a deal, so you'll be settling on the Niflheim skyland. Just like you wanted."

Brianna crossed her arms with very pleased body language. She visibly relaxed in her seat, and the tension lifted right off her shoulders as she spoke. "Thank you."

With the Dark Elf leader significantly placated, Cale moved the diagram to the next section of the skylands. "I'm going to connect the C-rank bridge area between those two to Vana-heim, the low B-ranked one. Deverash, I'd like to talk to you sometime about a new Gnomish race. You're great for research, but more would be better. I'm thinking this to be the main research skyland, and I want you to pick a handful of people not in this first ring to help you with that. Speaking of. Henry, Marie, until I've got more done on my system, I want you two overseeing Midgard. I'll be adding Aiden only after you've had a chance to put things in place, to prevent round two of the all-out slaughter."

The nobles nodded; they'd figure it out. Deverash appeared pensive, but was not against starting a new version of his race. He gave a confident thumbs up when he reached a decision. Hopefully other Gnomes wouldn't share his hiccups in creating, and that alone would be incredibly helpful to have around.

Cale beamed. "Excellent! Vanaheim connects to Jotunheim. Artorian? I'd like you here. It has the most... odd problems. Not only does the gravity fluctuate for a reason I can't figure out, which really should not be happening in *my* Soul Space, I may have... released a few unintended experiments. The mid-B-ranked pressure skyland has been my test zone for critters and other things, and I expect some things didn't mesh."

The dungeon snuck in some extra work when he had a momentary genius thought. "I want you to find out what's wrong and fix it, while also being the middle-point for big, important news everyone else might have for me. Remember that lecture you gave about picking a person people could complain to before it escalated to me? Congratulations, you're it!"

Laughter barked around the table, and Artorian slapped his forehead at his own dumb hubris. He was going to be janitor to a bunch of B-ranked, crazy Cale experiments. While also looking for holes in the world, and serving as problem solver for odd issues everyone else had. He raised his hand to ask a ques-tion, and got a nod of approval. "Is there anything preventing people from talking to you directly?"

Cal mused it over. "Not yet, but eventually I would like there to be, and I'd like the network to be practiced before it's in place. If there is a problem that persists and can't be escalated, we can talk about it during big meetings like this. You may not remember, but I have the heavy penchant for getting distracted and losing track of time. Group gatherings like this are to keep me focused and on point."

With Artorian so thoroughly trounced, he dropped his hand and asked no further questions. He was just going to have to deal with it, and his Tibbins expression made the in-the-know section of the table smirk. He'd be expecting long-string expletives as names then. Delightful.

Cal joined in on the smiling, snickering to himself. It did make sense to give an administration job to a professed Administrator! "Well, that was fun. Jotunheim does have an additional difficulty. It's the only skyland that splits its rainbow bridge connection towards two different skylands. Mostly because both Muspelheim and Niflheim have similar upper B-tier pressure. Brianna is going to be in charge of Nifl, and protecting the tree. Unlike other skylands, people will be entering this one from below. I want the inside of Niflheim to be the big place to be. Topside is off limits to people not us, and if someone does manage to get there, then one of us here at the table will personally go deal with it, if not multiple. The tree being interfered with is one of the biggest no-nos of my Soul Space."

Agreement and assent went around the table. Mages especially felt very keen to protect their actual minds. Cale spoke again when he was happy with the reactions. "Dawn, I want to keep you on Muspelheim since you've been testing things there regardless. I'll also be sending Bob, the majority of my Goblins, and every variant of cat in my possession. C'towls included."

Dawn responded with a thumbs up, and Cale moved the diagram again. "This skyland I'm calling Asgard, and I am going to gate it so you need to do something at both Muspelheim and Niflheim before anyone can get in here. This skyland fluctuates in energy like they're mood swings. Asgard contains all the A-rank Mana levels, from minimum to apex. My deal with Odin requires me to place him there, so that's something I will be upholding. If my ability to balance pressure and gravity pans out, I am going to purposefully try to re-balance them to these current levels if they get wilder."

Tatum quirked a brow in query. "Does that mean I end up in Hel?"

Cale nodded, moving the diagram to the singular bridge connection from Asgard to Hel. "I liked your idea, and since I *do* plan on becoming an Incarnate, I am setting Hel aside for all things S-ranked."

Tatum was fond of this arrangement, and didn't have any complaints. It did cause Chandra to frown, as they were out of islands and she hadn't been mentioned. Cale noticed, and addressed it. "Chandra, I want you on Midgard. If flora has to be stable anywhere, that absolutely has to be in the place where the majority of people will be decanted. I want you everywhere to make sure the nature settings are working properly, and you have something that works. As for getting around… I will figure out how to make flight not as costly. Otherwise most of it comes down to personal skill and Mana control."

He sat back in his chair, thinking this talk was about wrapped up. "Until then, I'll see about a viable replenishment method. Speaking of, we should likely talk about your continued cultivation. I've got good news, and bad news."

The entire table's attention was deftly captured, and they leaned forward with interest at Cale's next topic.

CHAPTER FIVE

First, Cale made a hand motion toward Tatum to pose a question. "Would you mind telling everyone about that hiccup we discovered during testing? The one you knew about beforehand, but I really had to see to understand?"

Tatum squeezed his thin hand around his chin, contemplating just which of those instances Cale had meant. There was more than the sneaky dungeon was letting on, and this was probably an attempt at not letting people know just how often he got... distracted. He decided it was fine. Tatum always did love to teach and was now getting an opportunity. "Ah, you mean the hiccup with converting Essence into Mana, and why it works to raise your rank sometimes, but not at other times? Yes, certainly."

Tatum reached his hand toward a three-dimensional projection, willing it closer. The light construct zipped into his palm and reformed in his hands, becoming more of a flat plane with simple images displaying. Stick figures populated the lightboard, and people tried not to make amused sounds. He was ready for these reactions. "It's harder than it looks, and I'm not a dungeon Core that can cheat with reference frames."

The chuckling cut short, as he received some odd, questioning, and confused gazes in reply. Tatum had not been ready for their confusion. "Did… You understood what I meant by that, right?"

Cale shrugged and nonchalantly looked the other way. He didn't cheat. *Hmph*.

Tatum sighed and squeezed his fingers across his eyebrows. "Have none of you noticed we can't achieve Mage speed, and that we're essentially stuck at normal, mundane speed?"

He ended up wiggle-wagging his hand at his own statement. "We're *not* actually, if you look at the clock on the table. I know Artorian is a brand-new Mage, but I can tell he figured it out because he's not giving me the ridiculous look the rest of you are. It ties in with Mage tiers anyway, so I'll just explain."

The stick figures on his board started to move when Tatum paid attention to them, clearing space for more to be drawn. To begin, he drew himself as a stick figure and wrote his name above it. Tatum, B-rank.

He made his figure flex. "As a Mage, the energy you are made of qualifies as a category higher than a basic mortal cultivator. They use Essence, Mages use Mana. Because of this, your new body can do, sustain, and survive things otherwise impossible."

His figure stopped flexing, but suddenly found itself surrounded by much slower moving figures. "However, the basic threshold for what is normal also alters. While the world will always move at mundane speed, and Essence users can empower themselves to speed up or perceive more, Mages achieve that effect naturally. When they shift into the mindset to use their energy to the fullest, it does not feel like you speed up so much as everything else slows down."

Understanding followed with a round of nods as the stick figures managed to convey this. "Because we are in Cale's Soul Space, 'mundane speed' here is what Cale sets it to. Normally, Mages tend to only speed themselves up, thus everything else slowing down."

Tatum changed his stick figure to move at the same speed as everything else, and when it tried, it was unable to go any faster. "Cale has sped up the mundane speed of everything in his Soul Space. So while time passing looks normal to us, if an outsider saw us, we would be a blur. Our frame of reference functions differently. We are all already going so fast that our personal frames are stuck."

He pointed at his stick figure. Which was unable to go faster due to already going at a speed well above what it was capable of accomplishing without help.

Tatum had some numbers appear on his board for convenience, drew a stick figure to represent Dawn, and labeled her. "B-zero mage, tier *one* **Law**. This means her maximum new speed modifier is ten, because of a category difference. Plus, a part of her **Law** tier is bonus dilation speed."

He drew a second figure of Dawn. "At A-nine, if you don't count the new base bonus of what happens at A-rank, she would have a maximum dilation speed of eleven. Until that rank, Dawn is using fractions of that bonus 'one' that her tier provides. Now, once you reach A-rank, you can dilate and alter your frame of reference to a factor of one-hundred, rather than ten. So at A-rank nine, Dawn's *actual* maximum dilation is one hundred and one. Following so far? It gets messy from here."

People just remained quiet and listened to the explanation. This wasn't very useful if they were stuck in Cal, but not quite everyone had figured out why. Artorian still just wanted to know how Cale was cheating.

Tatum appreciated their willingness to listen. "This jump of ten happens again at the S-ranks, and again the step after, at double-S. Though, it stops mattering when you Incarnate. At that point, you have other problems. I'm not sure about the third-step rank, but I'm fairly certain it will be no different. Now, Cale, do you mind if I tell them about *your* tier?"

Cale raised an eyebrow and grumbled, crossing his arms. *Mmmm*. "Use Artorian. I don't talk about mine for the same reason we don't talk about yours."

Tatum raised his hands in immediate surrender. "Fair's fair. Artorian, would you mind sharing your tier with us?"

The old man looked around the table and saw only starving faces, hungry for knowledge. If these were to be his friends, he didn't see a reason to cause a roadblock now. "I don't mind, my friend. I went to the top. Tier seven hundred and twenty. I am bound to **Love**, all affinities."

Dawn and Cale were the only ones that didn't break into laughs, gasps, or total disbelieving silence. To the outer ring of projection participants, this was either a joke, a ridiculous lie, or, worst of all, true. When the old man remained calmly seated with his fingers laced, and Dawn began to get irritated, it occurred to the rest of them that… oh dear. That *hadn't* been a joke.

Henry leaned forward in his seat with a heavy expression. "Did… But how? Did you discover the secret of Ascending through the Tower to upgrade your **Law**?"

Chandra scrutinized the old man with a glare. "I doubt it, he doesn't have the time spent, and that *all-affinities* part makes me suspicious of outside involvement. Isn't that right, Dale?"

Cale once again whistled softly while looking the other way.

People intrinsically understood he'd been the culprit, as Chandra's mention of Dale made it clear to Artorian that someone else had received that same top-tier treatment. Cheating rascals.

Tatum cleared his throat, recomposing himself. "Let's get back on topic. Alright, Artorian. So. At your apex of A-rank nine, your maximum time dilation would be one hundred, plus seven-twenty. For a total frame of reference difference up to eight hundred and twenty times mundane speed."

He let that sink in a moment, then pointed at his own stick figure. "Even if you went this speed, you would still be stuck at the speed we are currently going, as Cale is *still* making this world go faster. The 'floor,' so to say, is above your maximum."

He then pointed at the clock on the table, causing people to start inspecting and doing math. Deverash the Gnome was the first to understand. "Oo~o~oh, I get it."

When nobody else aside from him and Tatum seemed to properly be able to read the clock, they all shot expectant glares to the Gnome. Deverash delighted in deluging them in the details.

"Cale is around A-rank four. Has a tier equal to or above Artorian's, and — the 'and' is big here — has tapped into some kind of sub-**Law** source that lets him multiply that number even further. Based on the fifth-deep layer of cogs in this clock."

Cale just smiled, and took the opportunity to show off. "**Time**. I'm tapping into the **Law** of **Time**. Same tier as Artorian, and yes, I'm higher. Please no further questions on that topic. I'll tell you when I'm ready."

Dani gave him a look, so Cale quickly played nice and got back on topic. "**Time** doesn't actually let me do a whole lot. Going backward is a big no-no. Forward only works by speeding up the time you yourself travel at. Which is that frame of reference thing we've been on about. The difference is that, unlike normal frames, you don't suffer the problem where you're doing bonus damage to the world because of how fast you're going. Go at ten times the speed as a Mage and you'll blow the camp down with a wind gust just passing by. Going at ten times the speed with the **Time Law** causes no side effects to the environment whatsoever."

Cale made his own diagram appear, just to give people a visual comparison. "I'm not very adept at it yet, and I will forewarn you that the dilation will ramp up as I do. Currently that **Law** is letting me go another *category* of speed faster. So, one hundred, plus my tier up to A-rank four. Then multiply that number times ten. That's the *current* mundane speed my Soul Space is set to."

He shot Tatum a wide smirk. "That's what Tatum means when he says I'm cheating. While you are stuck in this time-frame, I am not. I can slow back down without affecting the rest of you. Resulting in me having easily a thousand days to play with, compared to the span of your single one. That's a lot of time to make pretty diagrams in."

Tatum rubbed his eyebrows again. "Exactly. This is also a nice segue into our initial topic. You all know that our **Law** takes Essence and converts it into Mana? How we thought that this 'trade,' for lack of a better term, was a way to increase the tiers of our **Law**?"

Nods followed, at which Tatum unpleasantly groaned. He was hoping at least one person aside from Dawn or Cale might have known. "Turns out that's wrong. The Essence converted *refills* the Mana in what I'm going to call our 'bucket.' Said bucket is larger depending on two factors. One: the number of ranks you have achieved as a Mage, as it indicates how well connected you are to your **Law**. Essence trades don't make a Mage's Mana bucket larger — they just refill what's been used."

Tatum looked around to make sure that people were paying attention. Good. "Since most Mages are all leaky buckets until they can control themselves and their effects properly, this is a fairly constant process. If you're currently losing Mana, it's because something about your body isn't completely in tune, and your energy is trying to fix it. Unfortunately, because we are in the Soul Space, it's instead going to Cal. We get nothing back, and I mean nothing. The bubble we're currently in is, at best, a temporary fix."

Marie paled a little at the realization. "One moment. Doesn't this mean that every cultivator in this Soul Space would eventually be guaranteed to die from deprivation, unless they were perfect in their self-control *all* the time? Nobody can do that!"

Brianna smirked pleasantly, and raised her hand. "*I* can do that. I made a deal specifically not to be stuck in that situation. The Dark Elf faction saw it coming when everyone else dropped like flies. I banned Mana usage our first week here, and set the focus to full preservation. I had to run a gamut of inspections to make sure nobody was leaking. If they were, then they ditched any other duties and were required to go straight to practice. Also, if any other Elf thought we were going to give up protecting the Silverwood Tree with our lives, they were mad. No offense to our ancestors."

Dawn made an appreciative nod of her head when Brianna made a cordial mention toward her, and immediately forgot the earlier distaste. Right afterwards, Dawn clenched her jaw. No, no. She should not become pride-stricken like those damnable tall ears. Still, she appreciated the diplomacy, though the explanation needed to move on. "Occy, please continue."

Tatum nodded, and many people arched their eyebrows in surprise at Dawn from the nickname she'd just used. Dawn just shrugged. You couldn't be around someone for a century and *not* find a nickname. Tatum just kept talking over their stares. He'd expected today to be revelation-heavy. "Back to point one, the bucket analogy. Some people can naturally replenish more Mana when they're at B-zero. Their bucket seems to be larger. In short, the higher your Tower tier, the larger your bucket. That's factor two."

He drew two identically-sized buckets on his board. "The problem is, when inspecting a Mage, the bucket never really *shows* that change. Instead, we describe it as the Mana being of a higher purity, because somehow more Mana has fit into a bucket of the same size."

That received some understanding in return, so he kept lecturing. "This has caused a lot of confusion in the past. Artorian and Dawn, if they were both the same rank, would *appear* to have identical Mana pool maximums. Even though the pressure coming off Artorian would be much, much higher than Dawn's."

He scribbled some numbers above the stick figures. "One bucket of full Mana for Dawn compares to seven hundred and twenty buckets of that same purity for Artorian. Since we see the buckets as the same size, the 'pressure' we feel from someone is very subjective. This made it horrendously difficult in the past to measure correctly. You never know if someone is controlling, or hiding, or using some other thing to change what you can see. If your ability to see and inspect is even something to write home about. Knowledge from our world on the topic is very messy, and correctly discerning 'oomph' between Mages came down to guesswork unless they got into a fight. Those fights rarely ended as expected."

Henry's hand went up; he was visibly confused. "What makes our Mana buckets *actually* larger, if trading Essence just fills us back up to capacity? Also, I have seen Mages from my old court use far, far more Mana than they could personally hold."

Tatum nodded sagely, as that was true. "You can personally contain Mana in your being, your body of Mana, up to your rank maximum. The rest will have to be stored in your Aura, or be used rather quickly since you can't hold onto it for long."

He created a new stick figure to showcase energy flows. "A Mage has to decide if their Mana is going into their Aura or body. Adding it to your body also triggers the dilation effect. This adds significantly to your body's strength and durability. You can safely hold, *maybe,* up to the next rank of Mana in your Aura if your body is full."

Tatum made the stick figure explode. "Everything else you will lose fast if you don't use it immediately. Trying to hold onto excess Mana a long time causes overflow burnout, and blows you up. As does attempting to take it into yourself when you're already stuffed to the gills. We haven't had a lot of chances to make sure of that since we've been here. Can I explain the problem with how we actually improve our rank now?"

People went quiet and sat back down, realizing they'd been interrupting him a bit much. Tatum exhaled sharply through his nose, and altered his diagram. "It works like this."

CHAPTER SIX

The diagram floating near Tatum changed to show a chart he was in the middle of working on. Several ranks and tiers showed as imprecise overlapping graphs, and there was a note in the top right that said 'measurement results number five-fifty-five' An irrelevant detail.

"There's a considerable, major issue when it comes to increasing your Mage rank. That being, it's not quantifiable. I have tried method after method and measurement after measurement, and the best I have is: The more you understand your **Law**, the higher your rank will be. Which is so useless that it sounds like common sense, but it's what I have to work with."

Tatum pointed to a specific bell curve. "A rank B-zero Mage knows nearly nothing of their **Law**, and an A-nine Mage knows just about everything. It becomes exponentially more difficult to increase your rank each time, as what you need to know to increase from one rank to the next is… esoteric. All I am able to recommend is to read books, discuss your **Law**, contemplate it, study it, meditate upon it, delve into it, and act on it. That's about all I can suggest."

Another eyebrow rubbing made them look positively bushy.

"It is impossible to know how much knowledge there is on a topic, and there are neither guidebooks, nor manuals. The higher of a tier you hold in the Tower, the *worse* this is going to be. Cale is going up as fast as he is because he never has an Essence shortage, and has endless time to meditate. Until he gets distracted."

Dani snickered, so glad others weren't unaware of certain bad habits. She took silent joy from the table becoming more comfortable with making stabs at their 'overlord.' Good, she thought. He needed to be kept on track and would be poked in the sore spots until he got it right.

Artorian raised his hand for a question, and Cale motioned toward him in approval, glad for a diversion of topic. "Would you happen to know how initial ranks are decided? I want to think the Node we are connected to checks our knowledge somehow, but that doesn't seem completely… reasonable? I easily reached B-rank two without any extra time in contemplation. Yet B-rank three feels unreachable. Is meditating and mulling a topic over sufficient, or is it necessary?"

Tatum wasn't sure, but Chandra cut in. "I know this one. When Cale was still the Mountaindale dungeon, I underwent a rank-up in my tower tier. I went from a plant Mageous to a nature Mageous. Initially, my rank dropped. I don't know if that was the Mana 'bucket' evening out, or the fact that there is more to know about nature than there is about the subset of plants. But, when I thought about it—and I really mean introspective connection-making—my mage rank shot up several times."

Cale grumbled, recalling the unpleasant event. "Yes. That hurt. You sucked so much Essence out of the Tower path floor in my old dungeon that I felt it, and shortly *after*, you destroyed an entire line of my golems. Just by tapping them as you shot by at what is now a casual run. You show off."

People snickered. Chandra was all smiles.

Artorian pensively rubbed his beard, asking a harmless question. "Is this area sufficiently Essence dense?"

Cale didn't like something about the inflection his Adminis-trator had asked that with. "Artorian... no~o~o. What are you plotting? There's plenty of Essence but why a— Oh sweet fuzzballs and kittens! *Yee~eowch!*"

Cale squeezed his arms around his chest and bent forward so fast that his face loudly bashed into the clock table. It caused a resounding gong as he droned out a very unpleasant *ow*. "Why...?"

Ding.

Artorian's expression turned bright, wide, and showed many of his teeth from how happily he was smiling. Dawn threw her head back when she saw, laughing with the full breath her lungs would allow. Her hand slapped her knee so hard that it caused a thundering rumble. Nobody present suffered any side effects, but it got people's attention when she spoke. "B-rank three! Just like that! What did you do?"

The old man felt pleased as punch. "What was suggested! Our dearest master chef said she contemplated a topic. There-fore, I take that the bar is one of necessity. It is not sufficient to merely *know*. It is necessary to invoke and evoke the knowledge."

Artorian tapped the side of his nose. "I figured there has to be something the Node is doing to track our progress. Knowl-edge that sits still is likely invisible, but surface thoughts are likely *not* off-limits, based on Chandra's story."

He gave credit where it was due. "When she ruminated on the topic, that was the point where her Node went: 'Ah! Yes! I see you do know this. Let me update my spreadsheet.' Which is what I tested. I know a decent amount concerning the Node I am bound to. Of the many aspects and schools of thought, I contemplated a single one. I have heard it be called 'Storge.' It refers to the natural or instinctive affection from a parent to a child."

He moved his palms upwards. Some playful, light feathers clouded off from his hands for effect. He knew it was a waste of Mana, but ah well. "Poof! Just like that, my **Law** marked a checkbox. My Essence was converted up to where it could, and available Essence in the environment was forcibly drawn in. So I'm rather glad it was of a safe type. Or at least, so I think from this one test. More information over time will help us understand this better. The results speak for themselves."

Artorian tapped his finger on his lips. "I can probably just… do it again."

Cale groaned, head still pressed, defeatedly, to the table. "Please don't. Give me a break and let it be my turn to lecture."

Amused snickering went around the table, and they sat back, assuming Cale wanted to actually explain his rank-up system, since he was preparing something of the like. People settled down, though Cale had to continue flooding the area with copious amounts of Essence, as both Henry and Marie ranked up in short succession when they gave the concept a try.

Cale cried out, pretending to be a whiny child. "I hate you all…"

Dani landed on his head. "That's what you get for not doing things properly. People are going to experiment. I'm sure you know a thing or two about that."

Cale whined back. "But *Dani…*"

His wisp was brisk and firm. "No buts! Explain to them the silly game idea you couldn't stop rambling about to me when I was busy trying to teach Grace. I am *so* glad you finally have more people to talk to. Go socialize! Actually put some of the plans in motion. Focus your efforts!"

Cale winced, and sighed in defeat. "Yes, dear…"

People held their giggles, taking this reprieve to eat from their plates and get comfortable in their seats. Cale spoke in hushed whispers to Dani for a while longer.

Their overlord got to business when she told Grace to come with her, and they both whisked away. "Right. So. I still abhor giving people something they didn't earn in some way. I vividly remember that not having a good mechanism for cultivators to progress really just ended up hurting in the long term. Mostly hurting me. So, before we get started, I wanted to put some things on the table. Minya, can I rely on you to spread this around when it's time?"

She nodded without question. "Of course, Cale."

Cale smiled. "Thanks, Minya. I'll skip right to it. I asked you all to oversee a chunk of a region so I would have some particular task you could be doing. My plan doesn't have a quantifying aspect yet, but since you're helping me, I'm helping you. Easy as that. Those of you with a stipulation in their deals that I have to help with your growth or something... we'll talk after."

He winked at Artorian. "As a general announcement. If you can rank up, I'll make sure you have the Essence to do so. You're helping keep this Soul Space in shape, and to be honest, there might be a great number more issues than I have let on."

Nobody was particularly surprised. Cale was trying to make an entire world from scratch, and so far mostly on his own. Of course it wasn't going to work according to what they in particular had hoped for. There would always be a way that a fresh perspective could help.

The explanation continued. "Not all regions have a supervisor. Mostly I did this on purpose. I want Alfheim and Svartalfheim to develop with minimal oversight for... testing purposes. I'm not decanting anything there until the environment can support the Dwarven and Elven populaces. I also wanted to run something... problematic by you all."

Cale needed to compose himself. "It's harsh, but at the same time I think it will be necessary. When I decant people, they get their memories and cultivation back."

"*Once.*"

"If they die again, they're starting over as a baby without memories. Should they reach the point they were at before, I will re-grant their old power and maybe their memories. Given the problems we encountered with sanity, it's come to my attention that an eternal life leads to problems with... psychology. So expect the first decant to be another cluster-cluck. Everyone will remember their old alliances, hatreds, and the like. They'll even have the power to act on them... for a while."

His inner circle had no response. They were on the fence on how to feel, and all chose to finish hearing their overlord out before adding their own commentary. This was directly messing with people's lives, and that sat well with none.

Cale seemed aware of that fact, ready to address it. "I am doing this because of a snag that Dawn, Tatum, and I found in trying to mend Artorian. We... have a finite amount of people. I can't duplicate, copy, or really do much of anything with souls. I can make a body with a mind in it, and... it doesn't work."

His expression turned sour. "The popular theory is that people without a soul or a center don't have Essence access, and that Essence in fact mutates them. Doing incredible, wild, chaotic harm. The attempts on people that didn't have a center, found their lives were... short. The moment they were in an area with even a smidge of ambient Essence, it went paws up. So while we have several million people stored, that in some way is also *all* we have. If all the souls are used, no children can be born."

Chandra placed her hand over her mouth, and Marie wasn't far behind. Henry looked stricken, and even Brianna expressed a deep frown. This was harrowing news.

Brianna closed her eyes a moment, and cut in. "You are saying that unless we have a way to keep the population cycling, civilizations will die out purely because they cannot grow further once they reach a certain point? Can I make the guess that this is why your initial decant includes their old rivalries? To ensure they will attack one another and begin a history of conflict that future generations will uphold?"

Cale just pointed a finger at Brianna, his expression flat. "I don't like it either, and I have even worse news. I will be phasing out the current cultivation system. It won't be something that's allowed entirely as we get the world in order. For now, this excludes you. Until the time comes where it is absolutely necessary that you fully integrate into my new system.

You won't lose any of your progress, but it will completely change how you gain power on the path of 'cultivation.' There will also be a new power track to keep hold of, and that brings us to the 'game' I could not stop telling Dani about."

Pulling all the diagrams to him, Cale made a colorful visualization of his world. It showed all the rainbow bridges between skylands, and the names of the people he wanted to attend to particular ones.

Feeling like being fancy, Cale altered their local space. It was meant to be entirely visual, but it gave those who didn't expect it a fright. Even though his inner circle sat in chairs, they no longer saw them, or the table. They only saw each other as the diagram enveloped them all as it quickly gained size. Letting them see and experience it from within, as if they sat in an oversized planetarium.

Henry, Chandra, Aiden, and Marie's names hovered on Midgard. It needed the most attention, and thus got the most supervisors to tackle developing issues. The 'wildcards' Alfheim and Svartalfheim had nobody. Vanaheim was assigned to Deverash, Jotunheim went to Artorian, Niflheim to Brianna, Muspelheim to Dawn, Asgard to Odin, and Hel to Tatum.

Cale made the moon larger. "Minya, I'm going to coat the moon in clouds and make it the place where new life reformation happens. I want you there to make sure things work out well as we build it. Bob, I changed my mind, I'd like you here as well."

Altering the diagram, new explanations formed around the moon. "In addition to solving the tidal problems if I add oceans, the moon is for a different long-term project. It's going to contain the physical representation of the grand majority of everyone's memory stones. Mages not included; those go in the tree."

He highlighted the Silverwood Tree on the map for comfort. "Since a **Law** is bound to a soul, even a reborn person, or creature in the event of a non-humanoid or something, will have an inclination toward that aspect. Even if I set them back to fishy rank."

A smaller diagram appeared within the larger one. "We already partially tried it. Someone bound to the first tier **Law** of **Water** will only ever bounce back to that Node when that person goes through Ascension. They don't even go through the Tower; their connection is instant. I have plans for the sun, too, but I can see I'm getting distracted again."

Cale replaced his new diagram with one labeled 'goals.' "The game. No name as of yet. Starts from the premise that we've been trying to quantify absolutely everything. Which is why Tatum had such a headache earlier. Personally, I haven't made a dent of worthwhile progress. The amount of time I need to get something right is pretty maddening. Worse still if I'm going to explain it with actual numbers. Much of the universe just wasn't designed to be quantified, so we'll do what we can and will fix errors as they come up. The system will likely change several times before we have a working model that sticks."

He pulled up what could only be described as a stack of statistical sheets. Numbers as far as the eye could see. "I'm going to do my best to condense everything a person *is* into understandable numerical values. When I can monitor this data, I will implement ways it can be changed based on things you do. Thus increasing or decreasing some of these numbers."

To the mental agony of some, papers started being laid on the unseen table as Cale kept talking. "Increase a number past a certain threshold, and I increase your game rank. Eventually, a higher game rank will translate to more cultivation help. Like I said, I hate giving things away for free. I also need to know everything you know about your own **Laws**, to make progress in mine. So, up to a point, I'll be able to get you through the B- and A-ranks. That's far away, but that's par for the course."

The model of a person materialized into being. "Since I can directly influence all factors in a constructed body, as I am literally making every aspect of it, I can also change how strong, durable, fast, or smart someone is, just based on what the 'number' of that particular feature reflects. I can easily make Mages bodies now, and while I don't have the numbers yet, I will. Does this make sense so far?"

There was a painful silence. Deverash raised his hand with caution, his voice full of hesitation. "I'm... I'm going to need you to repeat that. Slowly."

CHAPTER SEVEN

Several days' worth of time went by as the meeting dragged on and on. There was too much to talk about, and a break was finally called when the inner circle understood what Dani had meant about Cale simply not stopping. Even as Mages, they still suffered severe headaches. They slept on provided beds just to give their minds some rest. What the Mages were most thankful for in that moment was that they still *could* rest. Sleep remained blissfully helpful.

Most had nightmares about spreadsheets full of numbers. They didn't want to be *reduced* to mere numbers. They wanted to have lives, which was something that seemed increasingly less likely as time went on.

Artorian woke up groggy, an odd thing to wake up as. He meandered to the eternal table of sustenance, picked himself up some fresh-squeezed fruit juice, and chewed on a shank of spiced meat. He wiped at his eyes with his sleeve, and just looked up to lazily zone out and stare at the other floating skylands.

<How are you feeling?> Cal's voice popped into his head, and Artorian didn't have the energy to send back a deep and

taxing sigh. But apparently thinking it was enough. <Was my game talk that harsh? Eeesh.>

Artorian kneaded at his forehead, mustering up some willpower. <Cal. Let me... provide perspective. You had a group of people that had been 'alive again' for a day. A few days now. Their lives, and the manner in which they were used to leading said lives, are gone.>

He waited a moment for that thought to linger. <You sat these people down at a table, and told them that not only is everything they know *not* going to be recreated, but that they have to be responsible for an entirely new world of people that will repeatedly have no clue who or what they are. You have isolated us by giving us power, and while I know that wasn't your intent, we all feel terrible in the knowledge of what we must knowingly do to people. For your Soul Space to stay functioning.>

Lacing his fingers, Artorian sat cross-legged on the grass and just tried to keep his spirits up. <Then, after telling everyone that they are forcibly complicit in some very problematic psychology, you tell us that not only are we breaking people down into separate parts for them to start over, but that you are planning to permanently alter the entire method and manner in which we have lived our lives.>

When he looked up to regard Cal's perspective, Artorian's eyes looked old. <I remember eighty years of life, Cal, and I am a *young* Mage. I am fresh and new. On top of that, I specifically have a mindset that eases me in accepting this kind of information to process it. Those that think with their emotions first are not any lesser for doing so, but they will certainly not take what you say as easily as I will. Then... you showed us the numbers.>

Artorian squeezed his hands, trying to figure out how to word this next part. <We are... we are people, Cal. Also, yes. *Cal.* I remember you when you were separate, and what you told us had no Dale involved. I think somewhere along the way you forgot that.>

Artorian tried to smile, but it was visibly difficult. <Seeing

the world in terms of statistics is a way to pick the world apart, but as someone not particularly math-inclined, I can tell you that I was fairly sickened. Remember, my friend, I began as an external cultivator. I relish concepts and ideas and big problems. The waves of the universe are where I swim. To tell me: 'By the way, buddy, everything you are can be quantified and broken down to the most specific number, and that's what I'm going to use to measure everything by.' Cal... I... I don't want to do this.>

The old man felt like he understood Tatum just a little more as his fingers attacked his own eyebrows. <I know I promised I would in my deal, but pyrite, my boy, not like this. I *cannot* look at a person and go, 'Ah, number thirty-three, welcome to evaluations.' *No*. People have names, personalities, intents, desires, movements, and inclinations. An entire mess of emotions and beautiful differences that make them the people they are.>

Cal remained silent as Artorian physically restrained his anger. <The methodology is cold. The methods are cruel. You made me feel like I was in a cold room with white walls. No details, just glass panels that I am supposed to believe are people. There was no **Love** in it, Cal!>

Ding!

Artorian broke into B-rank four. The air around him rumbled, and a chunk of Essence vanished with a pop as Cal was backhanded by the **Law** of **Love**. His immovable defense of the importance of his **Law** had been in itself a necessary part of the concept. One that does their utmost to fight for what they **Love**, and see to its utmost fruition, was a core aspect that the Node was fully on board with. The Node had heard Artorian's declaration, and slammed its mug of ale down on the table in visceral agreement after a hearty drink. **Love** in all things! Hear, hear!

Cal groaned. <*Aaww*! Why does that hurt. Every. Single. *Time?*>

<**Love** hurts, sometimes.> The old man's response was monotone. <Probably because your soul is the conductor of

energy that you are directly tied to. My **Law** should not be much lower than yours, and I'm guessing that because the energy purity causes an intense cost, you actually feel it. Speaking of, you've been putting off a conversation with me for well over a hundred years now. You keep saying we'll talk later. It's later. What are you avoiding?>

Cal wondered if the universe had something against him. The amount of clapback he was getting was leaving even him with a sore cheek. Artorian's **Law** had literally slapped him! Straight to the Mana. <I... okay. I'm going to give you some Essence for a teleport. You'll know where to go. Let's talk there. No disembodied voice.>

When the Essence was provided, Artorian felt the pull toward... the sun? Wasn't that just a projection? He'd find out, now that his Mana was fueling back in as the Essence traded out. Couldn't Cal just give him Mana directly? There was likely some hiccup.

Fuff.

Artorian popped into existence on what was very much not a projection. His feet stood solid on a permanent construct of hard light that lacked any illumination. It was see-through, and explained why it couldn't be seen from the skylands he'd been on. The design confused him, until he saw the similarities between this and his solar cultivation technique. None of the rings spun, and a temporary walkway constructed itself beneath his feet as he moved to its center, following the direction of the pull. "Cale?"

Cale sat behind a desk in the very center of the solar construct. A copy of Artorian's house on Mountaindale easily fit within the innermost ring. There was even space for several sizable additions. The current design on the inside, while incomplete, was identical to what he knew. "I'm here, Artorian. Just reminiscing a moment. I really did not want to have the talk until this was done. That seems to be the norm with you, so I will just roll with the punches. Speaking of, your **Law** has one abyss of a backhand."

Artorian chuckled softly out of amusement, and pulled a chair out. He didn't sit as his eyes caught the memory stones glinting on the wall, the names of his favorite people listed underneath them. Not just one or two, either.

The wall held his entire adoptive family, including close friends and other people he was fond of. His five grandchildren and their respective families. People from the Fringe. Skyspear students and colleagues. A Bard's College. The entire Modsognir clan, and several more from others. Decorum and Blanket's Beast Cores were both present as well. Unharmed and untarnished.

His grip on the chair loosened as he mindlessly meandered over to the wall.

"What…?"

Cale inhaled slowly. "I call this place… *Artorian's Archives.*"

He motioned to the general surroundings like a showman. "It holds a copy of everything you've ever done, written, experienced, and the Cores of who you hold closest to your heart. It was going to be my introduction gift during your big welcome as Administrator."

Cale managed a wavering smile. "Now it's more of an apology, and guarantee that I keep my promises. Your people are safe. All of them. Every last one. There is a copy here of everything you have ever created or read, including a copy of everything I know of that you didn't. The space we're in looks treacherously small."

He motioned to a fake door on the wall. "When the library wing is done, I thought to wake Alexandria up. The way in and out of the archives is currently impossible without my direct help. As soon as the rings start up, you will need to teleport to get in or out."

Artorian staggered back, and fell butt-first into the chair. His eyes still glued to the wall of his life. "I… yes. Certainly. Teleporting. Of course."

Cale waited a moment for the old man to get his bearings. "I told you that you needed your own workspace that first day on Hel. In my old dungeon, I mentioned that when we talked about the specifics, your circumstances would be very favorable."

The dungeon made a ledger appear, dropping it on the table. "You and your people brought in enough samples for two full skylands, in terms of things I can plant, test, and the like. I planted that Morovian grass all over Jotunheim, which caused unexpected problems. I was at a loss until I checked up on some of your memories. I should have known better, really. Now we have monster-sized rabbits in the mid-B-ranks roaming around in packs. Fighting other monster-sized B-rank... things, for area superiority and nesting space. There's also a few bugs."

The Administrator stared at Cale. His gaze bored right through Cale's head as he pretended he hadn't just heard the workload that had been foisted upon him. Again.

Cale defensively put his hands up. "Every skyland has its own unique set of... *problems*. The different supervisors will help take care of most of them, while I take care of macro issues. I still have holes in my skylands. Since they are all getting very big, pinpointing problems is becoming more difficult. I can still only be in one place at a time."

Artorian pressed his hands together. Fingers to his lips. "Why a game, Cale?"

The sudden cut in conversation made the dungeon take pause. "Oh. I... Hmmm. I'm much older than eighty, Artorian. If I count only mundane speed years, I'm well over a century, but my dilation changes all that. Feel free to add a zero, or two. I don't keep a good track."

Cale tapped on the ledger. "Not only do I frequently get distracted, but worse, I get *bored*. Boredom kills me. The game is to keep myself sane; to have a constant stream of information to look at. Something to have fun with. I didn't think it would come off so clinically cold when I told the inner circle."

The old man nodded slowly, eyes still locked on the over-lord. "I can't fulfill the tasks you've put forth for me. I don't remotely have enough Mana to fuff between skylands and check up on people."

Cal shot a finger to the air with a wide grin. "About that! When it comes to Mana costs for teleportation for work purposes, yours are free. I will be refueling all the fuffing so long as it's for doing tasks I need you to do. I know that's going to be most all of them, but you should never be drained down to your death plane or approach deprivation burnout. Ever. Not from transport costs."

He quickly made a note somewhere in a place he was sure he wouldn't lose it. "For now, you will be receiving a portion of the Mana of creatures you kill. Directly upon problem solving. I'm going to tell the others as well. It's something new I'm trying. No pausing in cultivation needed. You solve a problem? You get reward energy to refuel. Maybe not up to capacity of what your rank can hold, but enough to make the task feel worthwhile. Personally, I like Tatum's bucket example. He explained it to me while face deep in alcohol as he hung onto a bar the first time. Ha! Hmm. Bar... Mana bar? I like that."

By the time Cale was done talking, he noticed Artorian was no longer sitting at the other end of the table. He had instead walked to the far wall, and was inspecting copies of the weapons he'd used over the course of his life. "Ah! Yes. I made duplicates of those too, in case you needed one to help prob-lem-solve."

Artorian nodded slowly, picking up an ancient-looking bow at the end of its lifespan. He felt the details and the gnarled marks of long use. Even if it was a copy, it felt identical to what he remembered. "Alright, Cale... I'll bite. Let's talk shop, and then let's try round two on the topic of your game."

Returning to his seat, he kept ahold of the nostalgic bow. Just to feel the texture and familiarity of it between his fingers. A small comfort as he thought about how it was all so surreal. A century of time. Living in a Soul Space. Worldbuilding. It was a lot to take in.

"I don't actually think I know what to ask for anymore. This room alone is a shock. The contents have my heart in a vice. I'm surprised I'm not more emotional? I thought I would be. Instead I just feel numb. I also feel odd being the only one who can teleport, save for perhaps Dawn? Why not just create some teleportation shrines people can freely use? Keep the energy local and save some trouble."

Cale lit up at the suggestion. It was clearly filed away under some to-do list. "I would need someone to suggest a good place for it, but that's doable. I hadn't given thought to letting others erect structures, or alter the landscape. I... I might do that. If all the issues on the skyland get resolved, I'll give the supervisor of the place the ability to play around as if they were in a sand-box. That will lessen some of my burden."

He pulled away from his thoughts before he got distracted. "Back to you. You specifically have a deal concerning your growth, so growth you will have. I have made a rudimentary 'quest list' of all the problems I'm aware of on a skyland. When that's fully crossed off, we should talk more about it. You can access it just like you pulled that light-diagram to yourself, and it will de-luminate when you no longer need it. You're sure there's nothing you want?"

Artorian placed the bow on the table, lost in deep contemplation as his face furrowed. "You said all the creatures on the skyland I'm supervising are B-ranked. Does the island ranking reflect the monster strength?"

Cal affirmatively nodded. "It does. Very directly. That ambient Essence pressure due to gravity is a big deal, and the experiments I littered around the place changed to match. It's why every skyland above the C-ranks has a direct supervisor. I will be taking care of Asgard myself until I feel like bringing Odin in, and giving him the rundown. No idea when that's happening, but I suppose you'll know when he contacts you in the forum. Speaking of, thanks for that. Wood Elf techniques are pretty awesome. I'll be putting our own senate together shortly, so we don't need to physically go far to meet in a hurry, if necessary."

The old man glanced at the wall of weapons. "Well, buddy, I think it was a kind thought, but all the weapons on that wall put together aren't worth a grain of salt. They belong in a museum. You're tossing me into a pile of B-ranked monsters around and above my current rank. These mundane weapons won't do zip. I'm also rusty when it comes to actually fighting a serious threat. I may need Dawn's training. If you have any *Mana* tools I can use to fight the detritus and clean up, that would be helpful. I would buy one, but, you know... you took all my money and there aren't any stores."

Cale snorted at Artorian's sly little smile. His attempt at pleasantry. "Ha! Right. Shopping was a thing that happened nonstop on Mountaindale. People really liked it. You know what, I will add a store to get items. Some kind of prestige shop. Problems solved or tasks completed will give out energy, or a token, or a resource you can trade for goodies."

An idea struck him. "Speaking of, I would say you do have some favors to spend. If you were walking around and shopping, what *specifically* would you want to buy?"

CHAPTER EIGHT

Cale proudly rubbed his hands together. "And… done! Rosewood can chew on her own branches; this is easily just as good. Better than petals too!"

Artorian stood still with a flat, tired expression. Rosewood indeed; she might have even been faster. "Speaking of, are my Wood Elves around? I didn't see them on the wall."

The body Cale inhabited partially discorporated when he appeared on the cusp of answering. That was… new. Artorian rephrased, more calmly. He thought it best to check on his overlord instead. "Cale?"

When Cale's body properly reformed, his expression was downcast. The surprise question had struck him harder than expected. "Are you… up for hearing more of that bad news?"

The old man replied with a stoic nod.

Cale needed to sit. "No, Artorian. The majority of them didn't make it. We could only take the ones whose entire tree could fit through the portal. Which was less than they hoped, but I was assured later on that those who remained behind were content with their choice. They were of the earth. They would stay with the earth on whatever course it traveled."

Cale did have some positive news. "We have combination saplings, and a handful of memory Cores of those that could get their mind to me in time. They didn't *want* to do that, but a few of the more responsible ones refused to let seedlings go without a parent, even if it left them empty and powerless. As an example, Mahogany and Birch are here directly, while Hawthorne's offspring is present in stasis as a sapling."

Artorian failed to keep standing, falling back down into his seat at the information. Silent at the revelation, he held his mouth and chin. Some had made it, but that didn't make coping any easier. Many of those that didn't make it, he knew. Losing Rosewood was a hard blow. "I am going to need to sleep on that for a few days, my friend. I would like to distract myself. What did you just make around me?"

Cale moved to the old man's side, fully in agreement that a distraction was needed. He spoke with a grin. "I call them neon robes, because the days of fuchsia passed."

The old man's face remained lackluster. Artorian didn't appear to catch that masterful pun, so Cale sighed and just continued on with more familiar details. "I used Rosewood's design base, and included my own armor-type improvements. They look like the robes you're used to, but the material is mithril that I've run through a new refinement process. It may have a heavy violet tint with a silver sheen, but it's tough stuff! They can also glow, because I felt like it."

The back of the crafter's knuckles rapped against one of the squared patches that made up the design. "Interwoven in the robe are actual solid panels. Added protection in places I've noticed people take damage rather often. I had plenty of research time in Mountaindale to make good armor. I would have made you a set similar to Henry or Marie's, but I don't think you like body-coating full-plate."

Artorian looked himself over, inspecting the details. "The robes are excellent, Cale. As for the full plate, I avoided it in the past because I could never have a custom-fitted set. The stock variants take forever to get in and out of. Since Ember's set, though, my opinion on heavy plate has shifted. Besides, you're trying all new things in your Soul Space, right? So, why not? Let's try something new. If I'm going to be a janitor, I should wear the correct attire. What's the most insane full plate armor you can make? Consider it a crafting challenge."

Cale stopped to stare at his Administrator. "You know something? I know you're saying that just to push my buttons, but it's working. Tricked out full plate? Fine. What weapon am I matching to it? I know you like spears and the like."

Artorian tapped his chin, and smiled. "Something new… as a Mage, my strength is fairly ridiculous. So, since I'm no longer restricted to *sensible* weaponry, and Mana use is prohibitive… *plus*, you're trying to do things with numbers. What's the biggest khopesh you can make? One that I can still swing around? It doesn't seem like I'm going to an area with confined spaces, and my opponents are sizable buggers from the sound of it. With dilation locked, both I and my enemies can only go so fast."

Cale pulled the long sleeves of his shirt up, his mocking voice one of a mad elder crafter with a chip on his shoulder. With heavy chest-puffed fanfare, he performed some dramatic and wholly unnecessary huffing. "*Oho!* You are a thousand years too late to think that's a challenge for my crafting skills, grasshopper. Some oversized version of a simple sword, and measly full plate? Mountains shatter to the fall of my hammer as the nine heavens shine upon my work. Hoo! Ha! Grandmaster-crafter. Maximum anvil."

They both devolved into dumb laughter at their overdone theatrics, slapping the sturdy table at full strength from how ridiculously dramatic that display had been. The table received some serious new dents, but overall survived the onslaught of good cheer.

Cale wiped a tear of laughter away from his face. "*Ahhh.* I will… I will just make stuff and drop you into Jotunheim. We'll go from there. Who knows, maybe backhanding a few murderous rabbits will help make us all feel better. If you need a city somewhere, I suppose let me know."

Artorian firmly shook his head to decline. "No, no, I don't believe I want to have cities in Jotunheim. Minimal structures. I want it to be a place we can go to really let loose, and not be concerned about collateral damage. Since all the enemies are B-rank, and massive. There's some catharsis to be gained by defeating challenges like that. Plus, it sounds like unless you're a B-ranker, the place itself will just turn you to paste."

Cale nodded sagely to confirm Artorian's suspicions, letting the Administrator talk.

"I'd say that's a nice threshold to stop people that aren't supposed to be there. I think it was Dev's skyland that bridged before mine? I wish travelers luck. In Jotunheim you might be dealing with giants, but in Vanaheim you're dealing with what-ever warmachine or living Runestorm Dev comes up with."

The dungeon grinned to show his agreement. "I know where I'd rather be, even if his area is difficulty scaled to B-minus. I saw the weaponized version of that trireme he designed. *Eeesh.*"

Artorian considered it. "The entire skyland seems like a brutal battle royale?"

Cale nodded again, as that was currently correct. "Many skylands currently have a 'the strongest prevails' theme going, but due to the introduction of crazy sizes on Jotun, it's entirely different there. The massive weapon would not help you in a dungeon setting such as Niflheim, but I see it working where you're stationed. You might need more than a sword? Abyss, it might even break. I'll prepare an assortment of weapons up here. You shatter one, pick the next one from the wall. It will be good material- and Rune-testing for me!"

The old man didn't deter the crazy crafter, and stood back up to be a mannequin. "Suit me up, tailor. We've got a skyland to suss out."

Cale rubbed his hands together, and cackled madly. "One experiment, coming right up. I'm going to knock you out for this so... nighty night!"

Bonk.

A full day later, Artorian woke up. He didn't recall going to sleep. Or dreaming. Why was he so heavy? His vision was fine, but when he looked at his own right hand, he saw a full plate gauntlet coating it. Something about the sizing was wrong? It was significantly larger than his hand should be, given the comparison to the table he'd slapped before. Pressing his hand down, his armored palm covered its entirety. Whatever he was wearing, it was far bigger than any armor he'd ever seen prior.

He flexed, and his right hand moved without issues. The oddity was that the armor felt like his real hand. Strange. Was he wearing a suit of armor, or *was* he a suit of armor? Golem? Construct?

"Cale?" He spoke, and it sounded no different. Before, with Ember's armor, his voice had been modulated. To not have that happen here was unexpected. On closer inspection, his right gauntlet was covered in Runes. Those probably all did… something. Finding out what they did might even be fun. He should show Dawn!

Fuff.

Fuff? He shouldn't have gone fuff. He didn't fuel any Mana into tel— *Thunk*! Artorian went tumbling across a landscape of heat, pressure, heavy gravity, and endless sand. "Ow!"

He'd been struck without warning by something powerful. It sent him barreling through a few dunes, half an oasis, and a structure of some sort that probably used to be a pyramid. The impact deeply indented the center mass of his chest, and the suit he was wearing siphoned his Mana to fix the protections up. What the heck had hit him? "A searing fist? Isn't this armor supposed to be damage resistant? That's a massive dent right away! That isn't just going to buff out with some elbow grease!"

He got up and brushed a small river of hot sand off his being as a very confused voice resounded. The owner of the voice stopped short of punching him through the rest of the pyramid, her voice allowing him to become centered once more. "Artorian?"

Dawn hovered next to him, dumbstruck with her blazing fist

mere inches from the side of his face. She looked like she'd stopped mid-flight on a copper. Dawn's mouth gaped open in disbelief, and she looked incredibly taken aback. "I thought I heard some weirdness, and the faceplate of that Sphinx Golem *looks* like you, but I didn't expect it to *sound* like you. Are you in there? Or… *Cale*, if that is *you*, I am tearing this thing to chunks all the way to the scrapyard. You have been dropping annoyances into Muspelheim all day, and I will not hesitate to wreck this one too."

Artorian just put his hand up. "Dawn, it's me, Sunny! Is it not… am I difficult to discern? I know I'm in armor, but still."

Dawn squinted her eyes, checked something, then looked off in the distance. "*Mmm*. Sunny is there. Not here. I am having a hard time with tracking ever since the Soul Space… Niflheim just always grabs the attention. Tell me something only my Artorian would kn—never mind. Cale has all his memories. *Ehhh…*"

"Incarnate fire bees."

Dawn stopped short. She smiled wide, then frowned deep and slapped his helmet hard upside the head. Leaving a trail of finely-controlled burning Mana. "Get out of that iron bucket. Out!"

That brought a conundrum to light. "I… you know, I don't believe I know how to do that. Also, I too had the issue that I'm not sure if I am in the suit, or if I am the suit. When you punched me, it didn't hurt as much as I thought it should. Then again, I remember being a D-ranker when you gave me the run around the first time."

Dawn's response was flat. "You are fifteen feet tall. Easily. I think you're the suit, and Cale pulled one over on you. As far as I can tell, your mind is in Niflheim, and your last 'Artorian' body is there too."

She motioned her hand up and down his form, her attire of interlaced metallic golden cloth straps reflecting ambient light. "This thing? It's a Sphinx Golem with your mind in it, I think. I'm not sure. I could hit you really hard to find out?"

Artorian frowned, but his face didn't copy the motion his mind wanted it to. It didn't have that function. "I'm not entirely sure that—"

Thunk.

Artorian awoke on Niflheim in his actual body, a cold sweat beading heavy on his forehead as he patted himself down. Yes, *yes*, this was the real one. Real as it could be, he supposed. That was… awful? Odd? He just died! He should go back to Muspelheim and check on what happened to the thing Dawn hit. Yes, he'd do that. Immediately.

Fuff.

This time, his fuff was intentional. His aim, however, wasn't perfectly on the mark. He popped in a good ten feet above the sandy ground and fell with the full weight of heavy gravity dragging him down. When he smash-hit the ground, the sand tasted like potatoes and asparagus. That… probably hadn't been intentional. <Cal! Your sand tastes like vegetables and your armor is garbage!>

Spitting out a mouthful of sand, he coughed and brushed his mithril-lined silver-violet robes off. *Blehhh*.

With a sharp pop, Cale popped in next to him. "You broke my Golem. Already? *How*? At least the gravity pressure finally seems to be working as intended."

"I punched it, and it died." Dawn strolled up with hands in her pockets. She'd been adamant that her strappy outfit needed pockets. "Wasn't even difficult. Gave it a love tap. I knew it was another one of your dumb trash experiments you were trying to bury in the sand so nobody would see. Honestly, you spent all that time getting Sunny's face detailed and right on the faceplate, and you make it a hulking bruiser? Come on. Sunny didn't even notice his left arm was essentially a thirty-foot khopesh."

Cale whined loudly. "No, *you* come on! I got the mind safely tethered and everything. Not even a test run? He asked for something new!"

Dawn's furious finger pressed hard and deep into Cale's

chest, making his clothes sizzle. "If you want to change some-one's race, or body that they inhabit, you *ask* them first. Or I will tell Dani about some of the mistakes you've tried to sweep under the rug here."

His hands shot up in surrender. "I yield, I yield. Dani is almighty. Yes, I tried having a little fun, but alright. No more unsanctioned body tests. I'll make a sign-up sheet. Kill my fun, why don't you?"

Dawn's grumble made Cale discorporate. She spun on her heel in the sand after, only to prod the same burning finger into Artorian's chest. "And *you*! What was that pathetic taking it in the chin tactic? What happened to dodging? I thought you knew how to fight!"

Artorian scratched the back of his head, a bit embarrassed. "You said that sentence in past tense. Which is why it is correct. I *knew* how to fight. I no longer do. It's been a very long time and what I needed was only of use in large scale, strategic battles that only involved people. I have no *idea* how to fight monsters. All my weapons training is useless against the foes of the size I'm expecting, and even then, everything I strike will have at minimum a Mana body. I have minimal experience in handling those, and most prior experiences I have skated by on via luck. I can't rely on that here; I need actual skills, and I have no idea where to start."

Dawn stopped poking him as hard. She knew he wasn't wrong, and Ancient Elven military training sprang to mind. "What kind of fighting style are you looking for? Before you go off adventuring, I will teach you."

She reflected on the topic for a second, and then held a hand up. "Actually, don't answer. There's probably only one style that's going to matter from this point."

Artorian quirked a brow with interest. "That being?"

His friend grinned wide; arms proudly crossed. "*Mine.* You are going to learn a style called Pantheon. Because when someone fights you, that's what they should feel they are up against. The style is geared toward having to fight multiple enemies that are stronger, faster, and more skilled than you. All at the same time."

She glared at him a moment to chastise him. "I know that you too have been cheating with dilation, and you don't have that here. We'll start right away."

Dawn grinned wide, effortlessly stepping back into the same teaching-mode that Artorian had become so very used to during those early days of being a D-ranker.

"Lesson one! *Run.*"

CHAPTER NINE

It was hard to tell if Muspelheim was hot due to the specific circumstances of the pressure problems it had, or if it was simply due to the inhumane amounts of flame Dawn threw around with a level of control that made Cale jealous. Everyone in his Soul Space had Mana leakage issues. Everyone except a handful of people who came in with several centuries of control training and practice. Any S-ranker had phenomenal control of their Mana by the time their Incarnation occurred.

Dawn was a fresh Incarnate, so her reversion to a form of Mana was manageable. It only took her a year to re-acclimate until she wasn't a danger to herself.

Tatum... Tatum had been stationed on Hel because not only did it currently have the highest Mana density and pressure, but he had not had nearly as easy a time with the reversion. The pressure on Hel wasn't even enough to support him, and it was about time for a safety stasis again. Cale filed it away and looked back to Muspelheim when a mountain-sized explosion of heat scorched the landscape.

He dared say... she was cheating?

The Goblins he'd been transferring to Muspelheim had all

taken to hiding underground, out of sheer fear of the angry fire goddess raging upon its surface. Granted... he *had* been using that massive sandland to neatly dispose of a few problems. Anything dumped would slowly get buried, crushed, and return to usable Essence. His influx made that not so necessary, as his ley lines gave him plenty, but there was nothing wrong with a *little* greed. Also, if someone removed the sand dune one of his mistakes was buried under, it had a good chance of waking up and attacking anything in the vicinity. *Heh heh*.

Double-edged buried treasure! Cale loved it. There was also some slight enjoyment to be gained from seeing a tiny silver-violet dot zip around to avoid pillars, orbs, cones, cubes, and other shapes of twisted fire.

He was glad he'd made the mithril-lined robes the colors they were. It really helped him see the victim of Dawn's 'lessons' against the lemon-honey backdrop. While she rather angrily ran him through drills from above. How was she not suffering Mana drain from her particular hover method? He could... sneak a peek again? No, best not.

That would turn the ex-S-ranker's ire upon him. He probably should apologize to his Administrator about the body thing... <Hey, Artorian.>

An explosion thrummed the mental connection as real sound transferred through from its sheer reverberating intensity. Somehow Cale even felt that the flame was deep violet in color. <Kind of... *busy*, Cale! I don't know what I did to upset her this time!>

Boom.

The connection shuddered like a door panel in heavy wind, a distortion blurring the sound as a plume of burning spears descended from the sky with the brutal intensity of vengeful rain. Chunks and pieces of words filtered through the connection, but it wasn't until Cale broke and reset the link that they heard each other again. <Sorry about that. I've accounted for Mana distortions now. I just wanted to apologize about the golem thing. I thought it would have been fun!>

Artorian was thinking to himself, hidden in a dark alcove created by an errant blast. <I'm hidden. Pretty sure I'm hidden? Oh, you can hear me. I would have been happier if you'd told me more first. What were you even testing, or do I not want to know?>

Cale sent the old man some images. <No, it's alright. Here. I was trying to see if I could safely move a mind that already had a body elsewhere into a new body. I based it on a successful concept from my Mountaindale dungeon. Dani used to body-hop floor bosses back in the early days. It was good times!>

He got back on topic, trying not to fawn over Dani too much. <Anyway. Once my bosses were defeated, that was sort of it. That got stale! So, I thought, well, what if my boss turned into a second version before the floor was complete? Meaning the adventuring party has to defeat that as well before they can get to the reward? I know it's cheap padding, but in Mountaindale, too many people were getting to my depths *far* too easily.>

Artorian filtered through thoughts containing advanced versions of Snowball, including a humanoid version possessing the head of the animal in question. The amalgamation was rather feline in appearance, but easily a foot taller than the average man. He also noted they were twice as strong by design, but if anything, the details started getting glossed over. Causing his mind to wander to other critters. <That just makes me miss Blanket and Decorum.>

The dungeon understood, but there was a snag with executing the reunion. <I can't decant the sugar glider until the exact time I also decant his cultivation partner. Jiivra and Blanket come as a package. I can send Decorum over to Jotunheim, but he may not do as well as you might think. Out of curiosity, why *are* you still on Muspy? You've got things to do on Jotun.>

Panic rose in the old man's mental voice as the connection shuddered from a concussive heatwave. He was once again on the run. <She found me! Cal, you overestimate what I can do.

None of my common survival and combat methods work in your Soul Space!>

Dawn had known at a glance, but to Cale he'd have to confess the painful truth. <As soon as I had it, I relied on the time-dilation experience to carry me through fights. I have, throughout my life, abused circumstantial situations to turn my near-losses into wins.>

He dodged something perilous before hurriedly rushing his explanation. <Being in your Soul Space is like being in Mountaindale. I can't extend my Presence even a little bit. So I can't finely control my external abilities, or any effects that I've become accustomed to. I don't have the Mana control to create effects that don't cause loss, and in case you forgot, my method is to *Invoke* effects. It was wasteful to begin with!>

Boom.

Artorian again dodged something that sounded unpleasant. <Abyss! Just getting around is difficult! I may recover the Mana for teleportation expenditures, but teleporting *once* costs a big chunk. Since recovery happens slowly and over time, I can't just throw those out one after the other.>

Boom.

<One second of flight drains easily a tenth of my current rank. My toy box of escape options is so small that unless I learn new things, I am just going to get eaten by an oversized flufferbun. My weapon training is for use against *people*. My psychology tricks work against *people*. My training is for weapons completely classed as 'mundane,' which is useless against anything B-ranked. The technique knowledge I gained from the Wood Elves is almost *all* utility. Or so deep into a specific tree of knowledge that I don't understand enough of the basics to even try using them without years of practice and reflection.>

Boom.

A rolling tumble down a sand dune staggered the connection, but Cale fixed it while his exasperated Administrator stole a breath mid-rant. <Bows and arrows aren't going to do a thing against something with a hide stronger than an iron house.

Spears and polearms help with range, but that's only tactically sound until the enemy breaches a certain size. My armament options are toothpicks to fight mountains.>

Artorian dove for safety as a wall of flame colored the landscape with variants of rolling red behind him. <I have a Mana body, but I don't know how to truly use it. As a Mage, I'm not fit to be called a novice. This robe helps, but it's just that, Cal. *Help*. I originate from Morovia. I grew up surrounded by beasts that ignored you because you weren't worth the effort to eat. Too small of a snack. I *never* learned how to deal with them. Instead, I was thrust into the world of mallards and morons.>

Dawn's attacks only increased in intensity since Sunny was doing *so well* splitting his attention. To the surprise of them both, she cut in. <You realize I can hear the both of you, right? Stop distracting my student, Cal! Get out of this forum. Sunny, every time you talk, I can pinpoint your position. Stop giving your opponent information to work with. Since you can't die and lesson one is too easy... time for lesson two!>

Boom.

Cal reeled back as a distortion forcibly cut off his communication line. He remained still and in place for a long moment. Why were all ladies so abyss-blasted scary? No wonder matriarchies worked so well. Could he do something with that?

Cal's machinations were lost on Artorian. Dawn's student heaved in rushed breath after breath while running across a sandy landscape that didn't seem to have an end. As a B-ranked mage, he was fast. Even without dilation, the amount of force he could endure and press into the world to propel himself forward was incredible.

Fully empowered C-rankers had nothing on a B-zero Mage, and the effects only became increasingly profound as one's rank went up. So long as you fueled your body properly. His real problem was this abyss-blasted gravity! The pressure in Muspelheim slowed him by a factor of at least half, and he had it on the nose that the current pressure was meant for B-rank eight to apex people.

<What is the first lesson?> Dawn slapped him from his musings with a pointed question. She was keen to continue up her rain of heat if he got it wrong. Luckily for Artorian, he was a clever cookie.

His response hastily resounded mid-stride. <Never stop moving!>

<Correct!> The avalanche of burning weaponry that currently chased Artorian formed into orbs, shooting back to Dawn's current position for her to re-absorb the spent and shaped Mana. The sky cleared of roiling orange-red clouds, and Artorian stopped his mad dash across the sands to just press his hands down on his knees.

He caught his breath as Dawn descended in a controlled hover. There were other things living on Muspelheim? No wonder they hid underground.

Pant. "Emby… that was… rough." *Pant*.

"I didn't even know Mages could run out of breath, or that swiftly." Artorian needed long moments to recover, though it happened faster than he thought as the Mana in his form balanced out evenly.

Dawn studied him. "You did well. How did you catch on to the patterns of my attacks so swiftly? I did my utmost to change them up with frequency, and yet you rolled out of the way before any of my slashing blades, piercing lances, or cleaving axes divided the space you occupied."

Her hands were surprisingly soft as she helped him stand up straight. "Also, the explosions. I was sure I was going to get you more often even if I was going so easy."

Artorian pressed his hands to his hips after accepting the help to get upright, and just stared off into the distance. "I thought of cycling Essence to my eyes to discern heat in a given area. Instead, the Mana present in my eyes just shifted to the configuration that would let me see the pattern involved, but it achieved the same mechanical effect. I think that because you are reliant on a fire affinity channel, heat telegraphs your attacks. I used the same trick in Phantomdusk when you made that series of spears come out of the ground."

He motioned around to all the unfairly hot sand around them. "This environment didn't do me any favors if you kept the attacks soft and contained. Those were the ones that grazed or struck me. When you overdid it, the difference became clear enough to see before you ever initiated the attack. By just managing my internal Mana in a way that doesn't cause expenditure, I am trying to overcome my current issues. As, since you heard my vent, I'm in a pickle. I need to increase my being-a-Mage proficiency."

Dawn paused and held her chin. That was… interesting. It wasn't her preferred method, but if it worked for her best friend, she might need to alter her lesson plans. "I… don't know of people that manage to just do that on the fly. It sounds like you're fighting an information war rather than a ground skirmish. Depending on what you can glean, you might render your opponent's abilities moot. Maybe my style isn't the best here after all."

She snapped her fingers in revelation. "I get it now! '*No*' style. Ha! It's a denial maneuver!"

Artorian frowned. That was a piece of information all the way back from the Fringe. How did she get her hands on that? His expression betrayed his concerns. Dawn smirked sweetly at him, but didn't feel like withholding. "Alexandria keeps some impressive records, dear. I read everything I could that involved you; I'm part of your fanclub!"

Her cathartic grin grew as the old man threw his head back and groaned. Burying his face into his hands. "Not the fanclub nonsense again. No~o~o."

He thought he'd escaped such topics, but it had *survived?* "Biscuits! Doesn't that mean you should be taking it easier on me? Your Gran'mama'd half the skyland chasing me!"

Dawn grumbled a moment at the reference, and shook her head. "Sunny, you're my bestie. That means I am going to be *harsher* on you. Because I want you to do well, and half-assing it isn't going to cut it in this Soul Space. You missed a chunk of time, and you haven't seen some of the maniacal nonsense Cale tried to put us through."

Her warning was dire. "This place might look like a cute duplicate of a planet in progress, but make no mistake, he is running this place like a dungeon. That's what he knows how to do well."

She half-turned her exposed shoulder, pointing up at the continent currently in orbit high above them. "The people he's put on each continent are supposed to help with the 'civilization' aspect. Lots of tiny things that all move independently are difficult to keep track of when you're repairing the mechanics of your universe. You think gravity is the *only* thing that's busted?"

Dawn dramatically pouted at him. "Sweetie... Hel did not get *that* big because things went *well*. It didn't come up during the decade meeting, but we have attempted far more than just two or three versions of Soul Space Management. This isn't our third start over, like Cale wants you to believe with that show of his. It's our *two hundred and seventy-seventh*. Cale just called it version three in the meeting to make all the newly decanted people think things have gone better than they actually have."

She scowled in the direction of Asgard. "I think when we first entered, there were seven continents, mostly unfinished with gaping holes in them? We are now on nine continents, and we got those last two entirely due to trying to repair problems."

Dawn snapped her wrist at the artificial night sky. "Tatum got latched to Helheim for more than his personal issues. It's so he can take care of all the abyss-cursed swans and geese. The place is crawling with them, and each one is some A-plus-ranked monster of a thing. Cobra chickens and Hydrageese are *no joke*. They have given *me* a run for my copper, and every last one of them is *immune* to the natural elements. Which includes the basic four affinities. My fire doesn't do anything unless I draw on my celestial affinity to augment my attacks, and even after all this time I am terrible at it."

Artorian said nothing. Dawn looked like she'd needed to get this off her chest for a very long time, and only her bestie was someone she actually wanted to vent and expose her heart to. She kicked at some sand, creating a sonic boom. It caused the old man to cover his ears as the particles accelerated with bright ignition. A half-standing pyramid was instantly reduced to a cute pile of crumbly rocks. "Do you know how Muspelheim quadrupled in size overnight about fifty years ago? Did I tell you already?"

The old man didn't. To act as Dawn's opposite, Artorian acted with pure calm as he slowly shook his head. The Soul of Fire huffed, then drew a deep breath. "Oh, I'll show you. *Jorm!*"

Nothing happened at first. Then the landscape seemed to shift ever so subtly. Artorian squinted. Yes, yes it was indistinctly moving. Or it was at first, until the ground under his feet rumbled with earthquakes. The problem wasn't his sudden vertical movement, but the landmass that *experienced* said movement.

His brows shot up high at the scale of what he saw. Artorian's eyes were full of stars, and they grew wider and wider as the largest crystal cobra in history rose from beneath the sands. Hot gravel rained down from avalanches of change as debris rolled off from the beast's indescribable, lumbering size.

The cobra stirred slowly as it woke from a nap. Jorm had shifted when Dawn called, and his head turned toward them laboriously. The very air swirled with dust devils from his minor serpentine slide. Leagues of sand were displaced as Jorm's head rose, the cobra barely needing to move the rest of his coiled-up mass. His snout closed the distance to hold position above them, blotting out a whole sky of ambient light. There existed rivers smaller than Jorm, but that was an unfair comparison.

Dawn reached up with her Mana, and fondly rubbed his nose. "I booped his snoot! He's *precious*. Just very tired. Meet Jorm, our world serpent! Cal's little experiment to see what the maximum size of a living creature could be. So you know: Jorm *wasn't* the largest, he's just the one that survived."

CHAPTER TEN

Jorm was a sweet baby. He didn't do anything except sleepily rumble and taste the air with a flicking tongue the size of twenty triremes. Artorian's jaw was still solidly buried beneath the sand. That was the size Cale had been toying with? Just how massive were the things in Jotunheim going to be? He'd been expecting house-sized creatures; castle or cathedral-sized even. Not this colossal walking landscape. Never this! Jorm was a landmark in and of himself!

Weapons? Forget weapons. Nobody not at minimum A-ranked could do a thing to this cobra. They would be a fly, bashing their head against a Dwarvencraft ingot. The Mana density Jorm was giving off alone was affecting the overall gravitational pressure of Muspelheim.

Dawn nudged him tenderly, and he finally shut his gaping mouth. They watched the world serpent return to its nap cave after basking in Dawn's warm and loving attention. It burrowed beneath the sands like it was sinking through water, sliding under without a speck of difficulty. The rest of the world around Jorm just... *moved*. Solid rock might as well have been cotton puffs as it broke against Jorm's scales.

Dawn was pleased as a mother hen. "He's such a good boy. Uses the cave system under Muspelheim for the majority of his mass, and is happy as can be to just nap in the hot sand. It keeps him warm. If you're curious about what he eats, it's anything and everything. Cale mostly keeps him sated with raw Essence. As a snake baby, he's content to just stay put when he's not hungry, so that works out for everyone.

She winked cheekily at him. "He went hunting for food, *once*. Ate the entire tenth continent. Swallowed every last one of our accumulators."

Artorian kneaded his temples. "I don't want to know."

The response elicited a whole gaggle of giggles as Dawn enjoyed that response dearly. "Oh, it gets worse. His insides count as an entirely separate region with all the crystal in there. All the enzymes needed to keep him healthy are copious; he's an ecosystem all on his own. Cale keeps him around as a case study; Jorm was used as a basis to make some of the other islands work at all."

She pointed down at the sand. "Also, you can't see it, but the entire bottom half of Muspelheim's interior is nothing more than an island-dotted water reservoir. In addition to hot sand, Jorm likes baths. The cavern has a fake sky, and doubles as a tropical paradise. I heard you were the one that brought back the majority of the samples for that? Nice going. Shame I can't put my city down there. Cale mentioned something about a pirate theme a few decades back. Nobody has been willing to bite."

The academic just sat on the sand, kneading the bridge of his nose as he needed a moment to take all of this in. "Sounds relaxing."

She smiled. "Well, we have training to do, but I would love to show off what I've done down there so far!"

Artorian returned her warm expression. "I wish I could see it."

Dawn perked up at his request. Curling her arm around his to pick him up, she *vwumphed* them without further prompting.

Artorian's exposed feet slid into much cooler, more pleasant sand on arrival. His eyes and senses took a moment to adjust to the much less oppressive surroundings than that of the sands above. This grotto floor was even colored differently, and the sight of all the shimmering wet blues was far more comforting. Now this he could get behind!

As far as he could see there were islands of gentle sand, palm trees galore, greenery aplenty, and Goblins. *Goblins every-where.* They panicked at the very sight of the feared fire goddess and ran blindly for the safety of their cobbled-together tropical fortresses. There was an entire Goblinoid clan war happening down here! Amazing!

Artorian's glee was so heartfelt that he clapped his hands together and did tiny little jumps in place. "*Eeee!* I love it! It's so beautiful! Oh, I could just pull up a chair and lounge here for years. Are those coconuts? I always wanted to use one as a drink container again. That year at Mayev's Spire spoiled me."

A nearby slithering sound stunted his excitement, and without a second thought he bounced to the safety that was Dawn's left shoulder.

She snickered hard and smiled wide, her arm protectively sliding around his shoulders. "You bunny. Hopping around all scared. You should know the buns on Jotun don't have that trait anymore. They got fat. They're still some scary monsters ever since Cale decided he needed more than fancy Bashers to test things against. Also, that sound is just a Lamia. Or Lizardman? Yuan-something, I don't know. It's been getting busy down here. Half-snake, half-person."

A twelve-foot-long, feminine-looking snake holding a palm tree spear hesitantly approached, wild fear in her eyes. Artorian could not look away. She was just so *interesting*.

The majority of her body *was* snake-like, but she had humanoid arms, and the face was nearly all the way there. The strange thing was that she looked terrified. So why was she cautiously advancing with a pointy stick? Artorian glanced around without moving, and noticed he was less than five feet away from a clutch of buried eggs. When he moved to look straight down at them, the Lamia's hood flared in anger and panic.

He didn't like that, and slid into old habits. "Can you understand me, dear?"

Artorian's question was soft, and while the Lamia's upper body shot back a foot as she remained balanced on her tail, she neither fled nor responded.

Dawn just closed her eyes and shook her head no. "No language to speak of. Not yet. No more than the most basic of grunts, hisses, and pictograms. Sorry, Sunny, I thought I moved us to a place that wasn't yet populated. It was barren the last time I came to this exact spot. I guess the bonfire I left behind was a popular place for warmth; looks like it's a Lamia tribe-fire now. They're also fighting with that local Goblin tribe from the sound of it. Equally not as smart."

The Lamia hissed at them, and it returned their focus to the topic at hand. Dawn released her bestie and floated to the now extra-terrified creature that froze in place. The Lamia's spear broke against the sheer press of Dawn's body as she moved against it, splintering the weapon. As it fractured, the creature was forced to drop the remains before cowering in intense fear.

Dawn spoke, but it was directed to Artorian. "Because Jorm is creating an imbalance with his Mana density, the pressure isn't harsh down here at all. So even though the burning sand-realm above is upper B-ranked, the demands of it are far less taxing inside of Muspelheim. So creatures like this that are *maybe* low D-ranked can exist without being crushed. I'm not supposed to *allow* them to exist… but I have a fondness for them. Cale can fight me."

She placed her warm hand against the Lamia's cheek, and her gentle expression caused the creature's abject terror to slowly turn into apprehension. The threat wasn't harming her, nor her clutch. Her weapon had become useless, but she felt in no danger as the motherly touch brushed across her cheek.

The warmth of kindness spread through her being, but something else did as well. The Lamia rippled in bulk as her pale scales sizzled to glow a deep, vermillion red. Drawing a heralding breath, the now C-rank one Lamia shuddered with a sudden influx of power—an influx that had occurred *just* because Dawn touched her.

Newfound clarity blossomed in the Lamia's eyes, and her fear slowly faded further as she found herself ever so barely pressing more and more into Dawn's warm side. The fire goddess no longer felt like the single most threatening embodiment of death. Now, the Lamia felt soothed by her very presence.

Artorian was all smiles as he watched Dawn copy his Auric signatures. The soothing effect from her Aura made it easy to leapfrog to the realization that the imbued Essence she was transferring over was of his method.

She was invoking her Mana lovingly, and he could get behind that. Fostering care, soothing, growth, and affection. This was what Invoking was best for—to just act freely and without restraint as it fulfilled the given objective. For all her might, Dawn was such a caring sweetie at heart. The Soul of Fire cupped the Lamia's face and kissed her forehead, touching noses a moment before the creature was let go.

The Lamia made a hesitant half-reach toward Dawn, but what she instead felt against her fingers was a weapon that the fire goddess willed into being. Cale wasn't the only crafter in this Soul Space, and tools of war were Ember's specialty.

A longspear that matched the Lamia's vermillion coloration formed in her hand, and at her beckon, flame flared into being across the glimmering ruby blade. Dawn let go as she handed the haft over, causing the Lamia to stare in bewilderment. The duo of gifts freshly received didn't fully register until the Lamia saw her reflection in a pond of still water. She touched her own face, and when she turned to try and communicate with the goddess to somehow ask why, Dawn booped her nose.

"Your name is *Surtur.*"

Lacking language, the Lamia still understood her naming process on some fundamental level. New capacity for thought roiled in her advanced brain, and Surtur recognized Dawn for what she was as new insight and ability to reason graced her senses.

She was in the presence of something greater. Something *more.* A person or thing so far above her that only another of her kind could ever be her equal. Ancient and all-powerful, an entity no force could topple.

Surtur also knew that this Ancient *loved* her. For it had blessed her with both might, magic, and a *name.* Not knowing what else to do, Surtur did the only thing she could think of, and bowed deeply; her head dipping down in deference.

**Vwumph*.*

When Surtur rose from her bow, her divine was gone. Vanished in a puff of heat and flash of fire. She felt strong, clever, and blessed. Instinctively, she knew that she was now the best choice to lead the future of her tribe.

Was this what she had been blessed for? Surtur did not know, and did not yet think to question further. If she had been blessed, then the divine must have prepared for her a purpose! In devotion, she would see to it that her people lived long, and spread far.

With her blessed spear in hand, she gathered her clutch of eggs. Setting off to take dominance of her tribe, ideas kept populating in her mind, with one in particular rising to the top: The goddess of fire must be known. Knowledge of her presence must spread. Shrines would be erected, and the people would pay tribute. For Surtur, First of the Flame, had come.

At a different bonfire in the expansive underground, the cultivator duo popped out on a similar-looking island. This one still remained devoid of Goblin life. Artorian felt contemplative, sitting in the sand as he mulled some of Dawn's words over. "Is that what you meant by our plight to build civilizations? I take it that's what you did there?"

Dawn let herself fall into the sand before she snuggled into his side, stealing his right arm with both of hers. "It's taxing, but yes. Cale may want us to stick to 'focusing on creatures meant for our continent,' but I don't dislike them. I don't see them as nuisances."

She sighed, resting her head on his shoulder. "I just feel guilty. Guilty and full of pity when I see them. Their lives are short compared to ours, and I know that when I meet one, it will be the only time I ever do. This has caused a few Goblin tribes to live in service to me, interpreting what I do for them in entirely different ways. The Goblin I actually helped is already long gone, though the tribe's fantastic tales persist."

Dawn nudged her nose in the direction where they'd been earlier. "That was my first Lamia meeting. She was beautiful."

Artorian gently curled his arm around Dawn to be there for her. "You did wonderfully. You took a creature of fear, and gave it a future. She, in turn, will see to the future of others. Life will turn as a great wheel, and you will be remembered for it. Did you also see how much *more* beautiful she became after you empowered her? Many of your own features became hers."

He was softly punch-nudged in the shoulder for his cheeky comment. Dawn was plenty aware it was meant as a compliment. "You're sweet, Sunny. For a scared bunny."

Dawn giggled as she got a retributive soft punch to the shoulder right back. This erupted into a childish back and forth, the two slapping the other's hands away before settling down to stare at the fake sky of the cavernous ceiling.

Sunny broke the silence to bring up something she'd mentioned earlier. "You mentioned you didn't want your city down here. Why not?"

The Soul of Fire just pointed up at an illusory cloud. "Mostly because I had a silly little idea, and I wanted to try it before defaulting to more sensible options."

Artorian leaned over on his side to quirk an eyebrow in interest. It was unlike the old Ember he knew to not do something efficiently. For her to indulge a straight up fancy? He would admit to being a curious cat, and listened.

Dawn moved her hand like a boat breaking through the waves. "I already talked to Cale. I want my city to be a conglomerate of interconnected triremes, upon which a castle is built. I'm still designing it, but I don't have the Gnome's skills. So, it's taking a while and most of it looks like a youngling's charcoal scratches."

For a precious moment, she was lost to the world and spoke with her dreams. Her expressive hands doing just as much of the talking. "I want each of them to look like a favorite fort from my childhood. I want the fleet to skate around in the clouds. Able to disconnect into separate fortifications and seamlessly sail in the sands below."

A thought of reality brought her back, though it also ended her expressiveness as her mood visibly dropped. "I've been a terror up there on Muspelheim, and I want the Goblins to start populating those sands. Goblins are surprisingly crafty tinkerers. I need to let them be. Besides, my C'towls are bored. They could do with a sporting hunt."

Artorian supportively held her hand.

She liked that, and kept close. Momentarily back in her land of hopes and dreams. "I love boats. Always have. I want to theme my personal abode around them somehow. I don't know what I want living up in my fortress yet, but I think it will be popular with the C'towls? When I got back in touch with the pack that nestled in my shadow and let them roam, they took to the desert like a second home almost instantly."

Dawn visibly appeared more comfortable after getting that off her chest. They were quiet for a while longer before Dawn realized that she was rather fond of this. "This is nice. I could build a little retreat down here. If you ever wanted to just get away?"

Artorian smiled, patting her hand. "That sounds nice, dear. Could you give me a primer on lesson two in the meanwhile?"

Dawn's sudden smirk unsettled him. He'd just stepped upon

a boobytrap, and it was going to explode under his feet. He just knew all sorts of devious ideas were building behind her eyes.

Without warning, she tickled him. Artorian shrieked before rolling around in the soft tropical foliage to get away. Dawn cackled and chased the escapee.

"Lesson Two: *Never stop attacking!*"

CHAPTER ELEVEN

Muspelheim suffered indigestion.

The plume of sand that burst from the ground blasted away several C'towl. They sprung from their napping places and hissed, bristling their owl wings at the threat as their bodies puffed up in thick swaths of fluff. A projectile had burst from the ground, and had not stopped on its way up until striking something else that was solid.

Krathunk!

Artorian's head struck one of the prototype triremes hanging in the cloudy sky above Muspelheim. He crashed right through the glimmering lightframe hull, levels, and top deck until his momentum finally evened out. Then Muspy's gravity took hold, causing Artorian to slam into the translucent deck floor. Luckily the hard-light was solid enough to catch him, preventing Artorian from crashing back through the other way.

He rolled across the deck, but caught himself on the edge of a sheet when the one next to it turned out to be fake. So on top of being discombobulated, Artorian realized he didn't know which chunks were solid, and which were not. It had Cal's handiwork written all over it, complete with impossible to discern holes in the world. He grumbled at having no way to figure out which panels were fake and which were not.

Staggering to his feet, Artorian realized that was incorrect. He could absolutely figure out which of the blueprint panels counted as solid and real! The Mana in his eyes altered to account for that discrepancy, but he didn't like the trick it played on him. All of it was real? Well that's pleasant progress for Cale but *terrible* for him. It didn't make some of the panels not-solid!

How had he gotten up here again?

Artorian recalled watching Dawn perform some truly elegant acrobatics. A dance of movement that ended with the back of her heel traversing upwards. It connected to his chin, closing his mouth shut. The strike then, with that same motion, launched him skywards from the tropical grotto. Sending him barreling upwards like some gravity-hating reverse meteor.

He'd burst through what counted as the ceiling, several tons of rock, and chafed against Jorm's side through a cavity. Jorm then hip-checked him, causing him to be redirected. He'd then burst through the topsoil. Topsand. Layer of sand? Didn't matter. Artorian roughly recalled spiraling through some clouds, then finally he'd head-bonked the trireme. How high *was* this thing?

Rubbing the back of his head, he waddled to look over the edge and leaned a hand on the ledge for support. Oh, Muspy was small. No! Muspy was *massive*! It only looked small because of how high up he was, but his mental image of the landmasses shattered.

They were all so much larger than he'd previously conceived.

Sure, '*continents*' had been mentioned, but he'd solidly been holding on to the thought of skylands as *islands*. Similar to small, country-sized landmasses. Roughly like it had been when he first arrived and could still fly and teleport freely. Oh, he could teleport freely *again*.

Right. His head hurt.

On further observation, Artorian decided he was very much

wrong. When they'd said 'continent,' they had meant it. Muspelheim had mountains, lakes, rivers bordered by the occasional oasis dots of green. Craters galore, and one very suspicious rolling landmass in the form of a serpent. Which was terribly easy to discern while this high up. Even a small movement from Jorm caused one abyss of a change to the general region. Whole dunes shifted and rivers realigned at his passing. He'd likely woken the lad up by bumping into him, and Jorm was now looking for a cozy spot to fall back asleep in.

Artorian moved from starboard to portside to check out the landmass. If he'd been C-ranked, it would have taken him and a caravan of supplies two or three years to travel from the eastern edge to the western edge.

"Admiring my region?"

Artorian jumped and pressed a hand over the place his heart was, staggering back a choked hiccup of surprise when Dawn just *appeared* behind him with a **vwumph**.

He felt out of sorts and off-balance. Was that what it felt like when someone just showed up out of nowhere? No, something else was wrong with him. His continued stagger made Dawn worry. "Sunny? Come now, I didn't even hurt you. I just initiated a launcher. Sunny?"

Artorian recovered slowly, but there was a point where he'd felt significantly more stable as his Mana senses reeled back in. When the world started making sense again, Dawn was holding onto him tighter than he realized. That was a boon while his mind caught up. "I'm alright. I think I'm alright, Emby. My head felt strange, like everything was filtering in too slowly. It's passing now, and my thoughts are normalizing."

Her frown didn't disappear, her words soothing. "I think we should postpone lessons."

A determined hand waved it off. The old man wasn't having any of that. "My dear, I only look old. I'm spry, and with a Mana body I can handle this. Just getting used to things is all."

Dawn smirked. "Oh, I know you just *look* old. Planning to change that in the S-ranks? You could just ask Cale to saddle you with a body from your prime. I wouldn't mind seeing that. Even before the Soul Space, I was easily a millennium older than you. Yet here I look like a twenty to thirty-year-old. Personally, I am quite pleased to not look like a grandmother, even if the Ember in me still holds to that truly not mattering."

Artorian smiled, nodded, and did some stretches. Only a second or three afterwards did he realize those were entirely pointless now. He paused, then stopped awkwardly.

Dawn was suppressing a snort and giggle. Her hand curled in front of her smirking mouth as she was doing her best to hold her tongue. "You're adorable. It's like you *know* you're an energetic being now, but you haven't walked the walk yet. It's always so cute to see newly Ascended struggle. Don't worry, honey. I'll help. I'm going to remind you of something I think you've forgotten. Give you some hope."

Dawn opened her hand, and reshaped her Aura directly, forming a blooming set of rose-lilies in her palm that burned with icy-cold fire in bright teals and blues. "Presence is our mind-being. So long as I am referring to myself as a *Mage*. The 'being an Incarnate in an Ascended body' is odd, and comes with... problems. They break, you see. I switch out to a new one fairly often. Tatum goes through one every few days. As reference, being double-S ranked in an A-ranked Soul Space has caused real headaches. Regardless. Presence might be forced to adhere to the body-shape while in Cal's Soul Space, but... you never lost the ability to shape your Aura, and it retains all of its innate features. Try it."

Artorian opened his palm next to hers, and considered the shape of a cube. His Aura extended from his body, which it was currently tightly glued to. On his palm, it formed the shape of an invisible cube.

He didn't want it to be invisible, and considered the teal light of Dawn's flowers. Interesting that they were cold. His cube flooded with iridescent color, and while it in truth remained connected to his Aura via a fine thread, he could toss the cube up into his hand and catch it. A Nixie Tube lit up in his mind. "This is how you've been retrieving your constructs!"

Hehehe. Dawn nudged him in the shoulder, then poked at his cube. "Bubble texture? Interesting choice. Remember that you can mimic many things, and that it will take on the weaknesses and strengths of that concept."

Artorian considered his history for a moment. "Sword Aura?"

Dawn groaned, her face squinting as she looked away in disgust. "Why is everything always so dumbed down? Tell me you didn't get that from some other Elf."

A forced smile bloomed on the old man's face as he tried to deflect. "My disciple! It came from... watching my disciple! Yes."

"*Uh huh.*" Dawn's eyes drilled into him from the side, seeing through his charade even if he was being partially truthful. "*Mhm.* Know what, it's *fine*. Speaking of. You're *fine*, right?"

Artorian grew... concerned. Was there a... problem? With learning from other Elves? He learned from many books to understand a topic, surely it wasn't any different when learning... live... why did she look so angry and why was it so oppressively hot? "I... yes?"

A tiny, wicked smile graced Dawn's lips coldly. "Oh? Good. Let me show you the origin of that tiny little derivative currently called 'Sword Aura.' That you absolutely *didn't* learn from a Dark Elf. That theme and being underhanded is *their* shtick."

"Crackers and toast." Artorian leapt full-force off the edge of the trireme before the light-construct exploded into finely sliced frost-burning chunks. He didn't stick around to see the original technique showcased when *he* was the target.

As a secondary thought, how did she make fire cold? A problem for later. First, not falling to death! Luckily this part he'd done before, and with similar methods as well. Dawn's reminder was blissfully helpful, and as he fell from the sky, he hurriedly reshaped his Aura.

A silent but furious Soul of Fire peered down from her mid-air hover, watching while the discarded trireme wreckage fell to the ground around her. She saw a pair of C'towl-inspired luminous wings envelop, then spread out from Sunny's back.

"C'towl wings?" When did he have the time to put something that intricate together, and why had his foolish butt not used it before? Her voice boomed from above. "Use your entire arsenal, you scared tulip!"

With wings extended, Artorian's freefall turned into a smooth glide. Even better, this did not count as Invoking! Cal's Soul Space devoured free Mana like a starving animal, and while he wasn't great with techniques, the drain on his Aura felt surprisingly minor.

Aura didn't extend his awareness like Presence did, so fine control was more difficult. However, it didn't seem to be subject to the same limitations while in this space. Unlike Presence, formed Aura was allowed out in the world. He loved loopholes! Excited, he did a barrel roll just for the fun of it. *Whee*.

Vwumph.

Dawn's sudden appearance staggered him, ending his rolling. "It is entirely odd how you can go from running for your life to having a good time in the span of a few moments. Lesson two: Never stop attacking."

The baker's dozen-worth of fireballs hovering around her reminded Artorian of important life lessons. One: Do not anger the miss. Two: Dodge!

Goblin-sized fireballs launched from Dawn's hovering cylinder in sequential order, and even though he dodged the first three, the first one had turned and caught him right in the stomach. "*Oof!*"

It bashed the wind right out of him and knocked him off course. That hurt! Fireballs were hot! As a testament to Cal's crafting, on the other hand, the neon robes held up. They even brightened with a flare as they ate and dissipated the energy.

What was he supposed to do? A fourth fireball whisked past his ear, answering his question as he twisted himself into a dive.

Flight was fantastic, but he was no skilled bird and Dawn without doubt possessed the superior flight-type. Was she missing on purpose just to toy with him? There was no way she should have missed a single sh— *Oof*!

"Sunny! Attack! You are failing this lesson and the longer you keep failing, the more of these orbs I will send after you!" The snarl in Dawn's voice did not go unnoticed. He had such doubts about how to proceed. He was under duress!

Well… when in doubt. *Fireball?*

Dawn was about to send the fifth homing projectile at her favorite fool, but held off when it looked like her technique was being copied. Three orbs of sunlight formed into being around the gliding old man. They started small, like peas. Then they grew, larger and larger, until she had to squint in order not to be bothered by their cumulative brightness. What was… *Oof*!

She received a taste of her own medicine as a solar hexagon slammed into her chest at Mach one. The sonic boom clapped before it struck her. If Dawn did not have A-ranked defenses, that would have knocked her off course. Instead it just winded her for a moment.

Her hand reflexively grabbed hold of the hexagon, and Dawn squeezed the formed attack like a balloon until the owner of the Aura whined out an 'ouch.' Still. Progress. "Your Aura can be *harmed*, Sunny. Do not give your opponent an opportunity to attack it! It is a Mage's weak point."

It was likely she should not have given that particular bit of advice this early, but in her own experience with hindsight, she preferred that new Mages knew it sooner rather than later.

Bursts of light flashed from the remaining two hexagons around Artorian, who took the advice and set to testing it right away. Streaming luminous beams erupting out of the hexagons missed Dawn entirely, but struck her orbiting ammunition. Her cylindrically-stored fireballs were shot out of formation, while the feeling of her Aura taking some harm forced her hand to let go. The beams didn't last for more than a flash, but it was enough to free the trapped solar hexagon from her grip as she whined out a surprised groan.

"Oh, oh, that's how it's going to be? Straight to the practical? Fine." She slapped her hand down in Artorian's direction to smack him with a sheet of gravity, but she was prevented from finishing her attack. The hexagon she had just released poured out a lance of sustained light right into her shoulder, causing her sheet of gravity to go wild and collapse into itself with a *vwop*.

With Dawn's attack interrupted, the air screamed as her heels dug into the surrounding space. A liminal field of Mana appeared where her feet ground to a stop, momentarily thickening the air. When she came to a standstill, the wavering field faded shortly thereafter as she got control of the situation.

All her flaming orbs burst, breaking their formations and flying away to autonomously attack her opponent. This time without holding back or purposefully missing. As she homed in her attacks, Artorian's brightness faded enough for Dawn to see a suspicious change as the cause. With a flick of her wrist, her flaming attacks spread to form shielding umbrellas. She could launch her attacks with ease, but just eating whatever hot-hatched plan Sunny was putting together without any protections ready was folly.

The umbrella shields bought Artorian the time he needed. All his Aura-shaped hexagons merged together into a ball that had more sides than Dawn could count in the two seconds she had.

From the multi-faceted construct, a rainbow laser of condensed sunlight pierced the sky in Dawn's direction. The beam impacted her shields, shattering them one at a time as the blast just kept punching through them.

This time, rather than the line of light lasting for but a flash, its power remained sustained for several seconds. Several more of Dawn's shields veered to intercept, preventing the line from reaching her before its energy ran out.

Dawn blinked to clear her vision; she'd never seen him put a technique like that together. Not even once. "Sunny! What was th—"

She didn't get a chance to finish her question as Artorian took lesson two a little more seriously. The next beam lacked that pretty, rainbow quality. What it gained in turn was a foot in beam diameter and one imposing sound effect. This refined laser cracked through the air with a resounding *bwaap*.

That howling klaxon lasted the entire lifecycle during which the beam fired. The attack stuttered to a stop only because Artorian was the one who forgot to defend. Dawn twisted her wrist, closing up the umbrellas to send the burning orbs forward.

Instead of being able to concentrate, Artorian got pummeled with thirteen near-sentient fireballs that cheated at pinball. That neon robe of his lit up like a flickering firework. He did his best to knock them away and load another beam into his Aura construct, but by the time the second *bwaap* tore through the air, Dawn had devised a counter.

Artorian thought it was a clever counter.

Before the beam of condensed sunlight struck her, Dawn had formed the Aura construct of a mirror that flat out redirected his attack right back at him. He was reminded of a certain fight against Cataphron. "Mirrors, huh? Two can play that game."

When the beam nearly struck him, the counter had been countered. Artorian made his own mirror with a thought, and redirected the attack sideways and upwards.

An orb of heat about to smack him upside the head instead received a full-force assault. The impact and damage of the condensed light was enough to make Dawn wince and lose her concentration. When her attention shattered, so did the Aura mirror she was sustaining. Dawn had time to make a face of surprise before she was shoved off into the distance as the beam punched through its original path.

The burning auto-attack orbs faltered, then vanished.

Vwumph.

Artorian wheezed, breathing heavily when the teleportation sound distorted nearby. Dawn's hand squeezed tightly on the disco ball that was essentially an omni-directional light-cannon, preventing its use. "Well, you sure caught on quick. Since you've gotten a handle on things, I suppose we can stop with the warm-up? Time to combine lesson one and two. You got me good with that attack. *Interesting* configuration with your Aura, that beam. After this, you're going to tell me how you got *kinetic* energy into an attack that should have been pure light."

Artorian rolled his shoulders, gently licking his lips to relish the upcoming challenge now that he had a general, most minimal, handle on things. He was feeling confident! An incredible mistake, but he felt it regardless.

Dawn recognized the sudden ascent of foolishness. He learns that tiny bit of control, and he thinks he's ready to go toe-to-toe with a Blade of War? Okay.

Dawn's enjoyment overtook her anger, the change in demeanor noticeable via the resounding pressure that rippled through the air. Sunny had rarely shown signs of succumbing to the cultivator's curse of power obsession, and here he was showing the first traces. She was going to enjoy drilling those inclinations out of him. Dawn's eyes blazed bright nova orange.

Her words were sharp and deep, indicative of a tournament announcer.

"Round one. Fight."

CHAPTER TWELVE

The sky exploded.

Multiple concussive booms with matching effigies of light and pressure repeatedly flashed in the airspace above Muspelheim. The kerfuffle was so loud and so distracting that other inner circle members came to see what the problem was. The issue, it seemed, was identical to a lover's quarrel.

Brianna tapped her lips at the spectacle, watching the immense aerial ballet of adaptive Mana shapes, clashing ideas, dodges, and interacting attacks to create mostly destructive effects. Good thing there was nothing else except for in-progress triremes to destroy up there, and Muspelheim was nothing but sandy craters anyway. "I was sure they were best friends. Best friends do not fight like this."

Queen Marie just shook her head in reply, willing to dig deeper. "Dawn is the one that says that; I've never heard her opposite ever mention it. I think it's a case of 'her will goes.' Our Administrator doesn't seem like the kind of person to make Dawn do anything she does not wish to, and in the event she ever changes her mind, I expect their dynamic will be a conversation that happens then."

Marie sighed. "Otherwise… Yes, I see it too, and I wish Dawn would be honest with everyone. Still, that's not really something for us to get involved in. It's not like I *forgot* she's actually an Incarnate, plus her age was accidentally let slip by Cale when she wasn't around. So… I'm not saying a word."

The noble duo sported matching outfits, Cal's new idea to try to make everyone feel like a team. Spotless, fitted, regal, mithril-lined snow robes adorned Marie and Brianna. Though they, rather than the robes, were the reason they looked good. While the attire didn't fit their particular theme, it did fit their current positions as supervisors.

A few people had so far been excluded, but nobody was going to make Dawn or Tatum do something they didn't want. Marie cocked her head lightly. "How are they *not* Mana drained?"

Cale stepped out of the ether, holding two shrubbery branches in front of him. He'd been hiding nearby, possibly not with the most effective camouflage. "Two factors. One, I'm cheating. Two, they're using their Aura to retain most of their Mana. I was originally going to chastise them, but after watching that first interplay, I changed my mind and decided these count as 'testing.' Those new techniques are being made on the fly, and I am *so* curious to research how they work. Those are *all* Aura constructs up there."

One of his branches pointed at one of Artorian's disco balls before it spectacularly exploded, marking his point of interest. "I am recouping their expenditures by making the area they're in Essence dense to keep them fueled. I don't think either of them even noticed their cultivation techniques are slurping up the surrounding energy. Probably because their ranks are staying exactly stable, and they're very distracted. Where's Henry? He should see this. Ah, found him. Arriving… now!"

Pop.

"Oh, *abyss*, that is jarring!" Henry was forcibly teleported in. Collapsing to the ground until he found proper footing, he managed to get to his knees twice before stumbling around on

Muspelheim's sands with all the dexterity of a clumsy fawn. "The pressure here is… Oh, that's *harsh*. I hope I don't have to be here long. Midgard is a paradise in comparison to this crushing weight. What's going o—"

Boom.

Henry's attention was rapidly drawn to the spectacle in the sky, his question answered. His hands pressed to his hips, he meandered next to Marie. "That… Wow. Is that Dawn and Artorian? They're really going at it. Those are some massive expenditures they're throwing out. Is that a literal rain of flaming Mana spears, being countered by… are those pillows of light and water?"

Cale nodded. "Nice to see you survived my new feature, also that it worked this time. Yes, it's very interesting in that section of space. The methods and manners in which they are changing and altering their Auras on the fly, upholding multiple effects in multiple places, and how they are tactically trying to out-do one another is excellent. I'm getting a lot of ideas here. I especially like how they are both trying to exploit the adage of 'adjacents interact' when it comes to the extraneous effects of their Auras. Dawn clearly has the upper hand in experience and skill, but our Administrator has creativity out the wazoo."

Brianna was still contemplatively tapping her lips. "He's going to lose."

Marie sternly agreed. "Oh, absolutely, but I think this is supposed to be a lesson. Based on several of the attacks, it looks as though… If she truly wanted to, she could end this fight in a heartbeat. So, it's not a matter of victory. More that she's working through some things, and teaching the Administrator a thing or two while she's at it."

She pointed at Artorian. "I mean, you can see him adapt and improve on the fly. As he does, she exposes more of her arsenal. Eventually he's going to reach an adaptation limit, and it's probably coming up. She has had the time to practice what she's doing, and he has not. Of course he's going to lose."

Brianna agreed sagely, her hand supporting her elbow.

"He's *terrible* at being a Mage. Meanwhile, Dawn is a work of art. Her body control is immaculate, and even without Aura her energy does not leak, nor go anywhere she does not wish it to. I can see traces of Dark Elf skills, but far more refined and whole."

Brianna's feet shuffled beneath her as she tried to copy a set of steps. "I can infer the way she is moving at certain times to be the source of the Moon Elf stealth methods. Only my mother ever flowed through space with such refinement. Dawn does not appear to occupy space, so much as she is moving through it as one with the air. Artorian, on the other hand, is a floppy toddler. Look at that inefficiency."

Cale shrugged. "He's not a dungeon fighter. His skills, while decent, aren't much when you compare them to the living legend he's fighting. I have a full copy of her memories, so she can have whatever she wants as far as I'm concerned. Ember... I mean, Dawn, is going easy. She has attacks that could wipe Muspelheim out of my Soul Space, even now while compressed down to an A-ranker. She hasn't even used her Soul Space attack, so... the comparison gets a shrug from me. I'm just glad to see the practical version in action. I hope our Administrator can hold on a little longer, just so I can study more of Dawn's shaping in action. Did you know that 'Rain of Spears' isn't actually her Aura? That's a proper technique with near-zero loss."

Brianna whistled, impressed. "I wouldn't mind some of those lessons. Assassins always welcome more tools in their belt."

The group watched the spectacle as the odds were clearly turning against the Administrator. Cale smiled at a sudden stroke of genius, just a little before he decided to test something. <Hey, Artorian. If you weren't so horribly frightened about Mana loss and running out, how much... *more* could you do?>

Artorian's reply made Cale giddy. <Do you like light shows? >

<Show me.> When Cale told him to go ahead, Artorian felt

an odd connection against the back of his head. Roughly where his spine ended. This was… new? It didn't feel like cultivation. It felt *direct*. <This is untested, so if you go *pop*, I'll make you a new body.>

Artorian drew an empowering breath. The wings on his back vanished as a platform of hard light formed beneath his feet. It was wasteful. Horrendously so. Yet Artorian felt no drain on his rank, and the Mana connection to the back of his spine fueled his expenditures smoothly. *"Oho-ho. I could get used to this."*

Dawn glowed like a blazing hearth fire, her frame wreathed by heat. Easily a hundred illusory heat copies hovered around her as she finished her latest technique. They each independently prepared their own attacks. The options were many. Nitroglycerin pockets in the air to serve as mines. Phosphorous arrows that would explode and shatter into shrapnel if they so much as neared their target. Hundreds of homing darts that drilled through barriers. Clouds of crimson lightning that would periodically strike at anything with the wrong Auric signature.

A slew of these attacks brewed, and the enraptured smile on Dawn's face could only be described as intimidating. For her, this was fun.

Practicing her own lessons, she'd never stopped moving. Her attacks had either built or endlessly roared toward him, and she'd twisted the environment to her favor as much as she could. Without needing to call it out, she could tell Artorian already knew that was the third lesson: *Location, location, location.* If you couldn't pull the fight to an advantageous position, make your position advantageous.

An odd sensation pulled her senses to reality.

Dawn paused a moment as her environmental control felt invaded. Swapping her vision back to the mundane, she saw her student was no longer sporting his wings. Instead he was just *standing there.*

No. Sunny never just stood still in the middle of battle. Not with lesson one being what it was. She shot a blazing spear at his form, and it went right through him. He didn't even dodge! Dawn frowned hard. The form she'd attacked wavered slightly, and she realized what was wrong. Her Mana had not gone through him. More… into? Then she'd lost it entirely. What new trick did he just find in his pocket?

Cale shuddered. <Oh. *Eesh*. Hey, uh… Artorian? Maybe don't do that again? There is a limit to the amount of Mana you can safely hold. Clever absorption trick, but really. Please no; you will guaranteed pop.>

The Administrator hummed, and Cale had to guess it meant assent. From Artorian's actual position, a five by five foot cubic frame formed. The lines keeping it together were nearly illusory. Anyone could move through them without breaking them. Just as if they were normal light. With plenty of Mana at his disposal, he invoked his new idea. "I call this… 'The Grid.'"

From Artorian's initial cube-shaped frame, more cubes multiplied out in every direction. In all three dimensions, a luminous, harmless grid formed. Miles of it. Satisfied with the visuals, the back of his hand hit air.

Wub.

The thrum moved through the grid, and for just a moment, each light line was no longer harmless. Every attack, effect, Dawn copy, or environmental hazard that intersected a line was *absorbed*.

The wrenching Mana loss jerked Dawn to the side. She caught herself and snapped her head away from the edge of a line she was near. Now that she knew what it did, she knew not to touch it. Unfortunately, her copies didn't have her reflexes. Half of her preparations were wiped out in a moment.

"Sunny, no! That much energy would expl… oh… *oooh*." Hovering above Artorian's right palm, an impressively-sized orb hummed loosely, thrumming against the air as all the stolen Mana was funneled into it to prepare an attack. One that was not hampered by the grid. In fact, the grid was directly feeding this new disco ball.

Artorian wasn't even touching the excess Mana. He knew

better than to store it within himself after playing janitor in the Ziggurat. The orb chunked and clicked. Creating strangely… kinetic noises, for an energy ball. The Mana construct shaped into a tube as it formed some kind of lens at the end. A design similar to a stargazer?

Dawn wasn't about to let him launch whatever this attack was. She snapped her fingers, and all her offensive methods went off. She held back herself to watch the interplay, being cautious with her approach. If an attack touched Artorian's grid, then the attack went away. Absorbed to be fuel in the growing stargazer that aimed for her real form like some sort of Dwarven cannon. As it did, she could see the dozens of amplification lenses slotting into place inside.

That explained the kinetic noises. He was making an amplifier via Aura construct! When had he ever gotten in close proximity to a fully-functional stargazer? The only one she knew of was at the old Skyspear— ah. Yes, that would do it. He'd plenty of time to inspect it once it was taken down from the mountain, but that was a reminiscence for later.

Right now it was time to focus.

Her dozens of attacks neared the impact zone, but a clatter of glass shattering made Artorian vanish from the spot he occupied. Dawn halted her personal advance immediately, forming an iridescent jousting lance solidly in hand. She'd been hoodwinked! His actual position was elsewhere, and she'd been using mundane vision this whole time. Literal mirrors and a lingering Mana signature had befuddled her senses. That was lesson four! It was too soon for that!

She altered her sight to something more useful. As she did, Dawn noticed that the mirrors were everywhere. Easily a third of the area around her was obscured, or showing a scene not actually there as angled mirrors filled the cubes. Almost as if it were boxing in the entire… *"Abyss!"*

Bwaap!

Artorian's finished stargazer was nowhere near, but it didn't need to be. Without kinetic involvement to the beam itself, the five-foot-tall and wide energy blast shot in a clean straight line. The beam neatly engulfed the entirety of the cubic grid square it passed through, making the follow up calculations rather easy. As the beam collided with the first mirror, its line angled and veered off with minimal to no loss in potency. Any loss it did have was swallowed right back up by the gridlines, and fueled back into the original attack.

End result? There might as well not have been a loss, because it just wasn't noticeable as the entire grid lit up on the inside. Angled mirrors made every available spot within the grid a zone where the beam was eventually guaranteed to pass through. There was nowhere to hide.

Artorian couldn't help but ask for feedback. <How's that for a lightshow, Cale?>

Cale snorted. <You might want to pay attention.>

<Wha...?>

Thunk.

The entire grid shattered all at once as a *vwumph* sounded right behind him before Dawn unceremoniously knocked him out. "No skipping lessons!"

She caught Artorian's unconscious form, having discerned where his actual body was by having seen the flash of where the beam attack began. She'd chosen to end the cute little trick in the event something went awry, or he'd missed a mirror somewhere.

Dawn fussed, even if Sunny could not currently hear her. "That beam could have easily erased a chunk of the continent. That was a light emanation filled with A-rank Mana! *You fool!* Where did you even g—"

Her unspoken question of where he'd gotten all the Mana from was answered when Cale called out to her in the incomplete forum. <Hey Dawn! Nice match! I'm going to dial down the ambient Essence up there. You also might want to let him go. I'm transferring his mind. That body isn't going to last more than a few seconds after an expenditure like that. Don't worry,

he'll wake back up in Jotunheim. I made him a spot. Thanks for the practical tests!>

Grumbling, Dawn checked Sunny over first. Sure enough, the body Cale had made for him did not hold up. There was an obvious injury to the back of his neck as the source of the problem, and she had no choice but to let the body go as it discorporated into particles from excessive burnout.

The overburdened form felt weightless when his mind left it. Dawn breathed with relief when Artorian's actual presence was once again on Niflheim, likely getting a new body constructed. Zipping away, she joined the rest of the inner circle. Cale remained silent as he was busy re-absorbing all the energy up there. Rampant Mana storms were a big no-no.

Brianna and Marie applauded. Henry said nothing, too busy digging his pride back up from the depths of the sand it had crashed through. His thoughts were rampant. These people were insane! Essence techniques like those existed? What kind of academic madman comes up with an attack like that? Henry swallowed, and convinced himself he needed help. "Someone please tell me what just happened."

CHAPTER THIRTEEN

Artorian awoke to being licked in the face.

A large mauve liger was lapping him awake, but he didn't want to be. Rolling over to sleep for another five minutes only left him with a face full of grass. His eyes opened slowly as his senses began picking up details. It smelled earthy? Damp, like freshly-crushed foliage.

Exerting himself as he pushed up, Decorum meowed in protest. The fat cat flopped on him as if he were a pillow. *Oof*! "Dec... Decorum! You oversized little... ah what the Cal... It's fine. Wasn't I just... kickin' Dawn's keister? Did I win?"

A familiar Dwarven voice told him off. "Nah. I saw the replay. Total whoopin'. She wiped the floor with ya."

Artorian shot upright, sending Decorum barreling off with a loud set of unhappy cat noises. His pleasantry grew threefold as a younger-looking version of Big Mo was seated nearby. "Mornin', sunshine. How ya feelin'?"

With a blur of action, his arms surrounded the Dwarf immediately in a big hug. How good it was to see another familiar face. "'Ey. 'Ey now... Come now, Sunny. Really, how ya feelin'? I'm in charge of ya for a day. I gotta submit a report."

The Modsognir patted him on the back, sighing as he just supported his old friend a moment. Artorian let go soon enough. Not soon enough for the Dwarf's liking, but he wasn't about to gripe as the not-so-old man checked himself over. "I feel fi... why am I young?"

Artorian felt himself over. What was he, thirty-five? He had hair? He had *hair*! Short fluff rested upon his head when he formed a mirror to see. His beard and lengthy mustache were gone. Well almost. His facial hair was trimmed, just a bit longer than week-long stubble. His entire build reminded him of when he had been in his prime. Actually, that seemed to be exactly what it was like... so why did he hate it?

Seeing himself in the mirror, his smile faded fast. This wasn't him. This was not a 'him' he wanted to be. This hurt. Seeing this face... hurt. "I... appear to no longer be alright. A moment, please."

Artorian did not mince words. <Cal? Change me back. Change me back right now.>

Cal's voice popped into his head. <Oh, come on. I know Dawn was fairly adamant about asking you first, but I really thought you might appreciate the—>

Artorian wasn't having it. His mental voice bordered on pain. <No. Not one iota. Change me back. I never want to see this face again.>

Cale was silent for a moment. <I... I see. Sure thing. Close your eyes a second.>

Artorian did as instructed, and his mind was whisked away. When it returned, the shape it was in felt comfortable. With all the wrinkles that entailed. <All set. Back open, please.>

He opened his eyes and saw himself in the mirror he'd created. Same spot in... wherever he was. He was bald once more. Both the well-kept beard and honorable long-hanging moustache were back in place. <That's... that's much better. I know you meant well, Cal. That person... it's just not me anymore. That face belongs to a man who lived in the Phoenix Kingdom, and died at the precipice of a house that

should not have been empty. I... I wish you hadn't taken everything in my spatial bags. I put some very personal items in there.>

Cale understood. <When I took your spatial bags, I moved them elsewhere so I could upend them to get all the items out before absorbing everything. I will go and sort your things. I think I know what you'd like. It may take me awhile, but I'll materialize a gift box in your place. When you decide *where* you actually want it. You're currently on the southern edge of Jotunheim. I'm giving you a token. Just throw it on the ground where you want your abode. I'll put what I find inside.>

Artorian ran his hands down his beard, wistful as he recollected himself to a state of comfort. Away from bristling anxiety and unwelcome memories. <I appreciate that, Cal. You have a good one. I will... I will figure things out here. I suppose I've been skipping out on actually cleaning the place up.>

There was a feeling similar to a nod, and Cal vanished from Artorian's awareness.

Big Mo exhaled deeply. "That's tough to watch. Ain't used to any of this yet. Just watchin' yer form change in front of me like that. It ain't natural."

Artorian shrugged. "It's the new normal. Why are you here, my old friend?"

The Dwarf hopped off his rock, and that made it clear that he wasn't properly here. There was a see-through nature to his being. "It's temporary. The dungeon thought it would be best if ya saw a familiar face when ya woke up after getting' yer butt kicked by the Incarnate. I just have a message really, but I think ya just talked to the big man upstairs himself. All me message says is that it would be nice if ye could focus on your region for a while. Was told ye've been doin' anythin' but."

The academic stared off into the distance, where he watched a rabbit the size of seven houses hop on by. "That... That isn't wrong. I arrived and went off to do my own thing. I was convinced I needed methods. New methods, to actually survive on my own continent. Well. The skyland I'm supervising. It's not mine. I think I would not want it to be, even if that was an option. I'm no king. I don't rule well."

He rubbed at his face, and honestly didn't know where to even start. He was supposed to... do what, exactly? Clean the place out of B-ranked monsters. All of them? Did he have an underground like Muspy? Did he have a sky region like Dawn's triremes? It was too big a job for one man. "I... don't suppose I could persuade you to stick around and help?"

Big Mo heartily laughed, and shook his head no. He pointed at himself. "Look, I'm already some kind of half-ghost that's losin' physicality as the hands tick by. I was told it's like this because I couldn't survive the pressure of this place. If yer not a Mage, don't cross to Jotunheim. Very simple rulin', an' I'm not keen on gettin' squished. Ya got that confused quirk on yer face. What's eatin' ya?"

Artorian sat, folding his fingers in his lap. "Well. I left because I needed a problem solver. I have my problem solver. So... why do I feel so oddly lost? I woke up and don't know where to begin."

The Dwarf pressed his hands to his biceps. "Focus, ya wee sod! What are ya fightin' for? *Who* are ya fightin' for? Why anythin'?"

The academic formed a list so he could reply. "I would like to see my family. Spend time with them. See them grow. See them flounder. See them just... live. I want to be a part of that process. I want to see the children play, stumble, and learn. I want to see my originals from the Fringe have a second chance at life, in an environment that doesn't rip their happiness from them."

A difficult thought struck him. "Yet... I don't want to see them go. I'm going to outlive them, Don. I'm going to outlive them all. What do I do when the day comes where I must bury my Lunella? My Wuxius? My Grimaldus? What will I do when I hold Astrea's hand as she peaks a hundred, seated in a rocking chair with spun yarn on her lap? Making sweaters?"

Don didn't indulge Artorian. The Modsognir snapped at

him, fully in the role of a Patriarch taking care of a friend. "Focus! Yer making assumptions. Yer takin' life for granted and seein' only the endpoints, ignorin' the myriad of things that can change as a pebble becomes a mountain. First things first. They're all interred. What do ya need to do to even get things started?"

Artorian broke free a nearby stalk of six-foot-long grass. He coated it in his Aura, increasing the rigidity so he could write with it in the ground as one would a paintbrush. He put the unpleasant thoughts away for the moment, and got to scribing. Scribing made him feel better. "I need to make a place for them to be. I cannot do that for them while I attend Jotunheim. To begin creating a place for my family, I must finish my allocated tasks so there are no further distractions. Nor grumbles from… I suppose the higher-ups. I can't make a place for them here, as my family cannot survive the Jotunheim pressure. As you say, avoid the squish."

Don was nodding along, making the hand motion for him to continue. He was on the right track as far as the community-minded dwarf was concerned. "Don't be concerned with how long it'll take. From the little I've gathered, ye've got an awfully long time to work with. Let us all out into the world when the world can handle us. I can tell ya from experience that the Modsognirs alone aren't pushovers. We'll tear a mountain right up!"

The academic was amused, and agreed with the claim as he wrote further into the dirt. "Correct. Then my to-do list is as follows. See all of Jotunheim. Improve my cultivation. Set myself up a local connection-point. See to errors and allocated tasks. Make a list of what to do with the place. When I finish the Jotun list, I can talk to Henry and Marie about a spot on Midgard where I could install my family and friends."

Hmm.

Don smiled. "Thought of somethin'?"

Artorian scratched at his chin. "Well, it just occurred to me that I'm here, yet not squished. So if perhaps I could assist my family with Ascensions, settling them all on the area I supervise could be a possibility. I'm sure I'm overlooking many possibilities, but my head just isn't in the game at the moment."

The Patriarch sat down next to him. "Want some suggestions?"

Artorian lit up at the offer. "I would love some suggestions!"

Don counted on his thick fingers, occasionally glancing up to the academic to make sure he was still on topic. "That sort-of house sort-of midpoint? Tallest mountain, all the way on the top. No better vantage point. For yer family… this is going to be a hard pill to swallow, brother. Wait as long as ya can, so that when they wake up it's in the best version of this world that it can be. Take it from a friend. It doesn't hurt bein' a memory rock on a wall. We're not aware of the passage of time. What *really* bothered me was when the dungeon pulled me out and explained how different everything was. This incomplete place was the worst thing to be told about, and honestly, I hate it. If ya get the chance to patch the place up, make it so real that when yer kids run out, they can't tell the difference. Much easier on the mind. I sure would've been happier."

He moved on to his other hand to keep tallying points. "Yer head lives in the clouds. Focus on what ya can do here and now. For every here and now, as they come. I don't know yer tasks, but I don't think it will take ya anythin' other than time. I just saw yer body get reshaped in front of me, Artorian. What's death, to ye? Would the dungeon really let ya be if one of those oversized fluffer hoppers got ya?"

Artorian squeezed his thumbs together. "I didn't think you were so cerebral, my friend. That is excellent food for thought. Though I would still prefer to avoid the experience. Speaking of fluffer hoppers, I should likely go see what kind of problems they actually cause. Based on what I saw on the other continent, we're to impose some kind of sense of balance? I know there's 'mistakes' out and about that need tending to, though I don't know if I'm sure what that means until I see one."

Don Modsognir walked around the scribbling on the

ground. He saw Decorum in the distance, rolling around on some minty grass. "Sound like yer less lost. Listen, brother, I would like to go back to sleep. Think ya can handle it from here?"

Artorian pushed up his sleeves. They fell back down right away, but he posed in a silly manner, like some faux hero. "Fear not! Here comes I, inkblot!"

Big Mo smiled toothily. "There's that troublemaking spirit o' yers! Go on now. Go meddle. Destabilize some regions, like the clever old man I know that hid from a whole clan of Dwarves in pyrite-blasted full plate. Ya wee rascal."

His Dwarven friend winked out of being, and Artorian turned to sit a moment longer before patting his own knees and getting back up. That was what he did, after all. He got back up. "Right... to work then!"

CHAPTER FOURTEEN

The top of Jotunheim's tallest mountain didn't reveal the entire landscape. Muspelheim was big, but it didn't hold a candle to his skyland of all things giant. The landmass itself matched the needs of that which lived on it, but mostly because of a rather sinister omnivore cycle. Every creature was food to every other, given it could be bested.

It was easily going to take him a few centuries to go over every square inch of it. That was fine. He had the time. He had the plan. He had the checklist.

Artorian rolled his shoulder as he stood at the edge of his courtyard, gazing down while scanning over the northern side of Jotunheim. Turned out Basher bunnies were pushovers. Big fluffs? Yes. Big dumb-dumbs? Also yes.

The size alteration had removed the advantage of pack tactics. While strengths had been added, advantages that used to be benefits were now weaknesses. He'd never go hungry! Not that he ever would, but eating every day was a reminder to himself that he shouldn't deviate too much from the idea of humanity. If he veered too far from that path, it would cause problems.

Unfortunately, Cal had also been correct about other matters. Decorum did not have a good time. He had been transferred to a lower-ranked area for now, until he could build himself up to be a natural Mage-ranked creature. The attempt by Cal to place Decorum directly had been a nice touch, but fruitless in the end. Decorum wasn't used to hunting Mage-ranked prey, nor used to a B-ranked body, and that had ended poorly.

No worries. There would be more chances for the Morovian liger. Until then, it was Artorian against the world. As far as Cal knew.

A fire bee nested in his beard, pleasantly resting as it formed a sneaky communication connection. <Dawny, how is today?>

A buzzing sound replied at first, voice following. <Well enough. I'm having more trouble with unity than I am with discord. The majority of the gobbo tribes are jumping on the 'worship the fire thing' bandwagon, and it is making keeping the clans separate troubling. I think this time I'm just going to leave it and see if they can actually cobble together an empire. Some of the newest generation turned out to be horrendously smart. How about you?>

Artorian groomed his beard, still looking northwards. <Turned out that the rabbit problem wasn't much of a problem. I finished removing the last group of them early yesterday afternoon. Today I'm spotting some peculiar activity now that the rabbits are no longer around to trample everything underfoot. I may have to go bug-fixing. Are we still good for dinner in the grotto?>

Dawn's reply came smoothly. <Bring some more rabbit, I have the ice cellar up and running with perpetual cold fire. My favorite few Lamia are still putting the roof together, even though they don't understand why one is needed. They don't complain, and I'm generous with food. Thus why the extra rabbit would be appreciated.>

The connection buzzed for a moment, but came back clear. <I cleared out an island for incoming goods, I'll send

you an image and geolocation shortly. That last rabbit was so large it crushed a few things. Have fun hunting down those bugs.>

<Alrighty. See you at dinner.> The connection winked out, and the fire bee cooled. It recharged slowly, but it let them talk without needing to use the forum.

Cal was always listening in the forum.

Artorian had found out the hard way when relaying Big Mo's mention that death wasn't something they needed to worry about. Their overlord did not agree. They would be brought back, but the cost would be that their return would not be immediate. They would lose time. They may have plenty, but as nobody knew just when the chains of chaos would no longer bind Cal, time wasn't something any of the inner circle actually wanted to lose.

Progress would be delayed. Personal projects would be delayed. Time with short-term work would fail or be interrupted, and they would need to start over. Each skyland had its own particular quirks and slew of problems, depending on what the planned purpose of that continent was. In comparison to some of the others, Artorian had it easy. He wasn't trying to establish a civilization on his.

Taking Muspelheim as an example, Dawn had four core races to deal with, separated within three divisions of her particular skyland: The tropical interior, the desert top layer, and the trireme fortress in her cloud-layer. While it would have been convenient to divide those between the Goblins, Lamia and Lizardmen, and C'towls plus variants, that just wasn't how it worked out.

Jotunheim had different problems.

There was an underground but, unlike Muspy, there was no land. It was the equivalent of a giant well. Just an endless lake of water the entire way through. It too housed oversized troublemakers, but they tended to be of the shell, scale, or fish variety. It was the same as up top, just with swimmers instead of walkers. His sky space didn't do him any favors, stuffed with the worst annoyances. Flyers. He was going to call the darn things Magpies.

He'd fought for a year to claim his mountaintop, after traveling for several just to find one he liked. They were a popular nesting spot for those that liked to play above the Jotunheim cloud layer. To make matters unpleasant, being Mage-ranked had all gone to the monsters' heads. They all thought they were the apex, and it was infuriating. All the infighting between the native species turned out to be a boon, but 'the fittest surviving' ended up causing more issues in the end.

Artorian had not yet discovered a convenient method to induce weakness cycling so some creatures would always be vulnerable to some others. He'd suggested it to Cal, but the dungeon was too busy with other things for specifics like that.

Some heavy earth-affinity birds were the worst culprits. How birds even managed earth affinities... he didn't want to think about it. Better to focus on the agenda. Today was about bugs. Honestly, it felt like he would get rid of one and suddenly there were a hundred more. Ah well. He might as well get started. *Fuff*.

Since work teleportation was 'free,' he used it precipitously. Cal had stopped being so generous, and now had a few Bobs installed as a monitoring service in the moon. What had been constructed of it, anyway.

If the supervisors went over the allowed Mana budget Cal gave them, it would be taken out of their personal cultivation instead. Cal had termed these 'Mana costs.' They could get it back via the established and agreed on methods. They got some from vanquished foes. Some from finishing a task.

That left Artorian at a solid B-rank four again, having smoothly stepped back into it after a few years of playing catch up. Odd to think it had been several years already. He was under the firm impression that his **Law** had cheated specifically to smack Cal.

Artorian snickered, and didn't mind. He was going to be forced to pay the extra catchup costs regardless. Reaching the fifth rank would take all the effort it should have taken him to reach four, plus the rest to actually breach it.

That was fine. That was fair.

An air- and earth-affinity praying mantis jumped away as Artorian fuffed into existence near it, accompanied by swiftly disappearing down feathers. "Hello, hello! Don't suppose I get lucky today and you can talk?"

The mantis jumped forward and swiped at him, as if to catch prey to eat. Its mandibles chinked against a hard-light shield, and its claw sizzled loudly, starting to melt where it kept squeezing. Checking the damage, Artorian noted a sizable crack in his egg-shaped dome. Honestly, Mage tier beasties were real go-getters.

He sighed. "No luck today. Crackers. One of these days I'm going to encounter a Mage rank with actual intelligence, rather than having specced further into apex survivalism. You're all so darn low on the tier list without it."

The mantis didn't understand him. It was just injured, and that part it registered. Mana made or not, these oversized bugs were no different than their small, squishable versions. Maybe he should have left some mountain-Basher-bunnies? Their jumping around had sorted these bugs for him.

No, no. It also left the bugs inclined to remain underground, and he had to find 'the broken one.' He didn't know what else to call it yet, but of the few species he had cleaned up, at their centers there was a variant that the rest seemed to originate from. It always had some peculiar features that it shouldn't reasonably have.

The broken mountain-Basher had Runes all over its horn. Runes that it was most certainly not supposed to have. It allowed the bun to double its velocity on a charge, but through some fluke, the Rune didn't properly register what counted as a charge. So instead the bun moved at double velocity all the time. While this wasn't a problem for the rabbit, it was a drain on regional resources as the Rune endlessly sucked in Essence to remain active and empowered.

This was the kind of problem he was supposed to fix. The mantis in front of him did not appear to be the broken one. As it sprang forward again to lash out with its still-functional bladed pincer, it jerked and dropped dead before reaching Artorian. The Administrator had his finger pointed up at the bug, and a sharp line of his Aura had stabbed it right through the brain with enough force to crack through the Mana shell. Mana or not, if an attack would reasonably kill the normal version, that constant held true.

Artorian walked by the house-sized body as it collapsed. The mantis twitched helplessly before discorporating into particles. Some of which moved as a clouded swirl, and whisked into his being. His 'cut' of the energy as the Soul Space auto-absorbed all the dead things. It had been B-rank three. A lower-end monster for Jotunheim. Likely just a scout? The highest ranks he'd encountered so far were B-six. Those being the broken ones. B-rank seven turned out to be the lowest rank in Muspelheim and Niflheim, while this B-rank three he'd just encountered was the highest rank you'd find in Vanaheim, Deverash's spot.

Reportedly, he was having so few problems with the wildlife that he could focus entirely on 'experiments.' Of course he could. How convenient. There was also an entire gaggle of Gnomes running around there now, and on some days, you could hear one of said experiments explode. Gnomes were *Gnomes*, after all.

"Found it." Artorian looked down into the dark soil. A deep hole was hidden under a mushroom grove, each the size of a full-grown tree. Odd to consider a hole so large 'hidden.' When he flickered on his Aura, it illuminated his surroundings with not-so-friendly emanations of crackling light.

This version had air and earth Essence heavily-infused, making it an electric display to anything living that came close to him. Sure enough, another mantis leapt from the hole when the light removed its stealth. No longer hidden, it pounced at him only to receive a concussive zap!

The curled arc of lightning fried its gooey insides. Charred and sizzling, the dead mantis flopped to the ground and discorporated. Artorian was pleased to see this Aura configuration do what it was supposed to. "Bug zapper seems to work. Shame the range is so short."

Artorian hummed loudly as he moseyed his way down into the cavern. As he did, echolocation information began to flood back. The reverberating sound visualized the layout of the hive he was walking into, which was mighty helpful. He'd found he could either keep the map 'in mind,' or use a sight wavelength to 'see' the layout through the world. Insects made some elaborate nests, and that made what he was seeing odd. No mantis could have dug this.

As he got further inside, a worker ant blindly rushed at him. Another bright arc of teal turned it into charcoal. He stared at the remains until they became particles. "A worker ant? How strange. I don't recall them being too hostile."

One B-rank three didn't feel like a big threat anymore, not now that the bug zapper was up and running. Artorian figured if it was a creature his Aura didn't immediately turn into a puff of dead dust, then he'd put some effort in.

Today's trip was meant just for scouting, but when the ground began to rumble, he felt some concern. "Perhaps... best to find another way in."

As he turned, he found an unexpected company of insects waiting for him. A mix of mantises and ants blocked his way out. They'd trapped him in? Since when were bugs that smart?

His eyebrows shot up when the bugs jumped out of the way, and it rapidly got rather dark. Something larger had been lured close, and it slammed down right where the insects had gathered. The rumbling weight caused a complete cave-in, the opening slamming shut as the ceiling tumbled down and followed suit.

Artorian turned and bolted deeper into the ant's nest.

He could still die from being stepped on! He outran the cave-in, but his mind didn't linger on the collapsed passage behind him. This was behavior that was definitely too smart for some insects. That entrapment maneuver had been tactical, planned, and executed with precision. Someone was pulling the strings; that trap felt like it had been put together for *him*. "Abyss! Those sneaky buggers!"

CHAPTER FIFTEEN

When the tunnel behind Artorian stopped collapsing, the deafening rumble died down with it. The sound of a few rocks still tumbling down the passageway echoed through the pitch-black space, but that was the last of the cave-in.

Artorian's run dropped to a jog, then to a stop as he realized that he was covered in soot. He'd thoughtlessly zapped a few things on the way, but the expected insectoid resistance had been minimal. That bothered him as well. It was as if creatures had purposefully been vacated from the expected cave-in zone? He didn't like the idea of some higher bug-mind directing an entire hive. It reminded him of certain arachnids.

He shuddered. Arachnaes he never wanted to see again.

Point of order.

His way in was gone, which was far more important than the consideration of him being dirty. Studying the way he came, it was clear he wasn't leaving that way. The earth was packed too thick to just break through if he wanted to go up, or it would take him an unacceptable amount of time to dig. Artorian guessed that he'd been trapped on purpose, but if he had to connect the dots further, then the enemy had hoped the cave-in would kill him. He mumbled to himself in the dark. "Either way, there is definitely something fishy at play here."

He wished he wasn't alone.

Oh right, he wasn't! Artorian mentally entered the forum, becoming present as a mote of light in a bright landscape of white marble construction. When he spoke, it was with the intent for anyone to be able to hear him. <Excuse me, does anyone have any pointers on underground survival? I got myself stuck in an ant nest.>

Brianna's deep violet mote appeared, but her voice remained unchanged from her usual cadence. <Ant nest? Ah, right. Jotunheim. Well, there are always multiple surface connections to any nest, so try to find one of those. Airflow should lead you. If it is stagnant where you are, you're in the wrong place.>

A bright green mote popped in next to Brianna, and Chandra's voice joined the fold. <Sounds interesting. My addition would be to try to find a root system. The thicker the roots, the closer you are to the surface. It is easy to get twisted and lost in a cavern system. As for the ants, if you had any crushed eggshells or diatomaceous earth, I would be able to help. Otherwise you may just need to work your way through them the hard way. Expect great numbers.>

Artorian's teal mote bobbed appreciatively. <Thank you very much, I'll give it a whirl and see if I can't find the exit. I'm hoping giant ants won't be too much of an issue.>

Brianna's mote bobbed back with a sassy question. <Well don't be too sweet down there, that's how you *get* ants. Why not just teleport out?>

The teal mote dejectedly shook from side to side. <Not work related. It counts as an escape, I believe. Or so Cal's abyssal *fine print* said, the last time I talked to Bob. So, I would like to avoid just fuffing out unless it's truly dire. Honestly, you run away from an overgrown rabbit *one* time, and the joke chases you around forever.>

The green and violet motes both bobbed, understanding.

That was reasonable; a teleport could be very costly, and they were never going to let 'the rabbit incident' go either. Especially recently, while Cal was implementing many background changes to his soul world that just caused more frustration. Something about more numbers. It was hush-hush for now, but they were sure it was going to come sooner rather than later.

Artorian checked up on them. <How are things in your regions?>

Chandra's mote face-planted on the white marble ground in response. <Nobody likes my Dryads! The Treants keep being corralled back to a forested area, and people keep picking at my Wood Nymphs. I'm just going to keep all my creations close and focus on my flora tasks. Speaking of, how is air quality where you both are?>

Brianna's mote brightened to a warm mauve. <Excellent progress on my end. I have managed to create a haven for my people, and several dozen of my kin are already present within my domain. The air quality underground could use assistance. If you have anything that would help with that, please do send over a box. We will get to planting.>

Artorian's mote spun in place when it was his turn to answer. <Air quality where I am is terrible, but I also just survived an indoor landslide, so perhaps I'm not the best judge at this moment. I may just have the same problem as Brianna when it comes to inner-skyland quality of life. Above, Jotun's breathing quality is excellent. Those plants that provide air are massive in size here, so I've few issues to report. I'll box you a few samples when I'm topside.>

Chandra's mote got up off the ground. <Thank you. I am going back to making more optimized grass. Come back to the forum to chat sometime.>

The green light winked out, and Brianna's followed shortly after. She offered some advice before she went. <You should really reconsider a civilization, Administrator. It significantly lightens the workload.>

After her message, Artorian was alone in the forum. He

hovered for a while to see if anyone else might visit, but none did. So, he just left. He was in for a serious surprise when his mind returned to his body in the ant tunnels. Lightning arced out as he regained awareness, and another ant he hadn't been aware of burned to crispy cinders while he came to. "*Wow!*"

Sweet mercy! He'd been under attack while in the forum, and hadn't realized it! His bug zapper Aura was cleaning the house! He was suddenly very glad not to have lingered too long, as what seemed to be an endless, ravenous horde kept charging his position. Ants came for him relentlessly, one after the other. The electricity boiling from his Aura struck without pause, and the expenditure was starting to tax his actual Mana stores from the sheer frequency of defensive bolts that lashed out.

The ants were literally crawling over their own dissolving dead to get to him, and there appeared to be no shortage in their supply.

Artorian had the thought that his all-affinity channel deal was one of the smartest investments he'd ever made. Access to an earth affinity was just so darn crucial. Having the direct affinity connection turned out to be whole categories more optimal and cost-efficient than having the Mana compensate and glue the effect together. Perhaps he could try out an actual technique for a change? He *had* been practicing with Cal's machinations these last few years.

Taking an appropriate stance, he let his electric Aura continue to discorporate the sea of advancing ants as he went through the motions. Strands of crackling Mana formed between Artorian's fingers. The frayed end of a lashing strand kept attempting to latch onto an ant, but they perished too swiftly from the bug zapper as they came close. A convenient problem to have, he supposed? Being more aggressive in the attempt, Artorian twisted energy through his earth and air affinities.

He uttered and 'spelled' the words in the way Cal wanted him to. As he did and performed the motions, the effect shaped into being. The 'spell' then unleashed when he willed it to. "[Chain Lightning]."

In his half-dance, he kept one hand behind him, then stabbed two fingers forward as a powerful thunderclap resounded through the tunnel. Between the tips of his fingers, a tear-sized dot of cobalt liquid lightning formed. From it, a blast of teal electricity furiously cracked forth.

The bolt struck the foremost ant between the mandibles. As that initial ant exploded, the bolt chained into the ant next to it. Then the next as the second ant vanished in a shocking flash of teal gradients. The afterglow string of bright Mana visibly lengthened each time it bounced to the following adjacent target faster than the old man could keep track of. He missed dilation options.

The crux of the technique was letting the 'chain' freely bounce between enemies. Artorian had needed some time to understand how Cal's 'targeting' concept worked. In this chain lightning spell, enemies were currently designated as 'living things not the caster.'

The Mana he invested merely stretched as the chain spread. When several hundred ants had been zapped to dust in the span of maybe a few seconds, he pulled the invisible chain back. Reclaiming a solid amount of spent Mana! "Seventy-ish percent? That's great! Better than the *nothing* I'd get if I'd tried Invoking the same effect."

That spell cleaned up the minor ants well!

Artorian even recouped the lost Mana from the technique just from all their deaths alone. Woo! Cal had initially gotten that idea from the interlinking effect of Artorian's higher **Law** functions.

Artorian also wanted to play with those, but merciful Cal were higher functions expensive. He waved his hand around, his fingertips hot and sizzly. Artorian blew on them just to get some of the heat off, and accidentally caused a gale inside of the cavern system. Oops?

Additional Mana was granted. He must have killed something by accident? Bonus? Bonus! Speaking of, best to report the success as requested. <Cal. I did that thing you wanted. Did it work?>

Cale's response came a little slow, like he was digging through records. <Which thing?>

Artorian sat down on a pile of dirt, taking a breather for a moment. <I used [Chain Lightning] as the spell function. Rather than Chain Lightning as the Invocation.>

Cale flipped through physical papers, or that's what it sounded like through the connection. <Oh, you triggered my Spell Stone. Nice going, that gives me damage numbers to work with. Strange, that's high. That's way too high. You got *how much* Mana back? Oh no, that won't do. That's far too efficient for the beginner rank that you're at. It was even a dual-affinity effect! Why didn't my penalty Pylons trigger properly? Dangit, Bob! I have... One moment, Artorian, don't go anywhere.>

The Administrator burst out laughing as the connection broke. "Don't go anywhere? Ha! Good one. You'll also need to tell me what 'penalty Pylons' are!"

He got up and started to wander down the tunnel right away. His humming came back in full-swing as he re-mapped the underground ant nest. More areas and dead ends had collapsed or suffered a cave-in, and it looked like the suggestions from his fellow supervisors had not been needed. He found the exit.

There was a downside to said exit, as it went through a rather sizable open cavern. Large and open underground areas were always suspicious. The movement there was serious. So copious that he could not discern what kind of creatures were there.

He walked for a good few minutes before he found a dead ant and a fallen mantis that he had not killed. The ant had pincer marks raked down its side. Harm from mantis bites? Yes. Mantis. Were they *not* working together? This damage seemed very recent. He almost walked by the corpses before stopping dead in his tracks.

Dead things discorporated.

A body lying on the ground meant *not* dead.

These things were playing possum! Blading his Aura, he sliced down and cut both bugs in twain. A gash formed in the far wall from his Aura extending out too far, but that was fine. Both bugs discorporated as a result. Had that been an elaborate trap? Would it have sprung had he aimlessly kept walking?

His humming continued, but his feet didn't. The ceiling had *moved*. Shifted. Specifically, a warrior ant shaped space on the ceiling had minorly shifted to the left. "Oho… clever. Pounce down upon the prey, ambush from behind?"

Tsk tsk. Artorian clicked his tongue, and prepared a cavitation bubble with Mana. He shaped the attack location, so the bubble occupied space identical to the shifted warrior ant. The bug burst from within as a *wub* thrummed through the tunnel, ant guts raining down from above. While the front and hind… paws? Hooks? Alright, he didn't know what the name for an ant leg was and dropped it. Parts of the ant remained latched to the ceiling. He'd blown it in half with sound, which was very messy, much loud.

Ow. Artorian rubbed his ears. "Sound in confined spaces is not the way to go."

Chittering sounds reached him when his hearing became functional again and that infernal ringing eased. Had he walked, he would have fallen on his butt from the soundwave's backlash. His Mana restored, more energy than he expended once again making it to him. That soundwave must have killed other things deeper in. Odd. What *was* he accidentally killing?

Bugs should be more resilient. What kind of bugs were weak against both sound and harsh movement of air? *Hmm*. "Eggs perhaps?"

If he was near a nursery—hatchery? Whatever it was called —that would be cause for deterrence. If that was true, it made sense why the nest was throwing soldiers at him. Speaking of, here they came now. Looked like just two of them? Why was one blue?

Lightning arced out from Artorian's Aura, and it did bupkis. As the mandibles of the big blue creature closed, he dropped to the ground and rolled away as his Aura flickered. It repeatedly struck out against the aggressor, but unfortunately without avail. The soldier ant behind it was of the common polka dot variety, but it was hanging back.

Jumping to his feet, Artorian slapped his hands together toward the ant. A soundless, forward-facing wave of cutting air slashed outwards. While it partially indented the blue ant's exoskeleton, it completely failed to slice through. "Crackers! This critter has earth and air resistances!"

The next bite did not get dodged in time. The blue ant struck forward again, and this time Artorian suffered for it. The pincers enclosed around his middle, painfully squeezing together. His robe prevented the slashing damage, but the crushing force was a serious problem as his hard-light protections immediately cracked to pieces.

So much for his fancy shielding! Had he been fleshy, this would have been the part where his ribs would have shattered. Instead, nasty cracks appeared on both of his sides as the Mana body took harm. It bloody hurt, too!

"*A~a~auw!*" Artorian shrieked out from injury and pain. He grasped the pincers in an attempt to pry them apart, but luck failed him. The ant was stronger! Plan B! Fire engulfed his left hand, and infernal coated his right. The blue insect shrieked out an awful sound when its left pincer burned enough to crack away in Artorian's grip. The middle of its right mandible outright disintegrated, allowing its prey to fall free.

The blue ant panicked and skittered back, clicking in distress at the other soldier. Artorian wouldn't have believed it had he not seen it. "Communication?"

The ant which had been hanging back recklessly jumped forward. Fortunately, it was *not* lightning resistant. Meaning that it was dust shortly thereafter as an arcing flash struck it, vaporizing the polka dot ant in a misty teal cloud.

Grumbling as he staggered, Artorian shifted the fire effect

on his hand to celestial, and swiftly pressed it to his wounds. Reaching out with his other hand, a chain grappling hook of infernal power shot from his palm. It pierced into the ant's face, causing lines of infectious black to surge into the beetle's form as Artorian called out.

"*C'mere!*"

The ant was violently reeled in and caught by Artorian's open hand, which crushed down while coated in raw infernal might. The beetle spasmed, then fell still to discorporate.

Artorian fell to a knee, one eye closed as he groaned from exertion. He didn't know why that helped with coping, just that it did. He almost laughed when he heard the voice in his head. It just hurt too much to try. <Alright, back to you, Artorian— Why are you injured? I told you not to go anywhere!>

CHAPTER SIXTEEN

Artorian sat down on a lightcube that he haphazardly framed into being. Rather than respond right away, he mumbled his dissatisfaction as his healing wasn't working properly for some reason. <Yes, well, you have a habit of 'getting back to me' later than you tend to think. The last time you told me to stay put I didn't hear from you for a month, and you continued the conversation as if it had been on pause for perhaps a few seconds. Make a timekeeper! Now, why am I not healing?>

Cal metaphorically bit his tongue, and assembled some timekeeping devices behind the scenes. Which, if anyone asked, he'd absolutely had all along. <Mana body! You're just channeling energy through your celestial affinity. That's not enough. Mending to your body needs to match the affinities of your **Law**. Celestial works great for restoring fleshy bodies. *Not* energetic ones.>

Considering the knowledge, the Administrator just tried it. To his delight, he found the cracks in his sides began to slowly mend. "Oh, what a relief!"

Artorian continued his reply in the forum. <Appreciated, old sport. Back to the topic then. What's this business with the

words that makes it feel like I'm talking in brackets? I still don't really get it.>

Cal was giddy. *Too* giddy. <They're spells! Okay, well, they're spells in Rune format that I've embedded into Pylons to make sure their effects are both consistent and measured depending on how the limit p... *what?*>

Artorian had materialized a plate of hard light, and was currently *thunking* it against his forehead as the dungeon chattered on like an excited bird. <I don't understand the words that are coming out of your *mou~u~uth.*>

The dungeon felt pensive for a fraction of a moment, then sighed at the realization. <I never gave you the breakdown of terms, did I? I just sort of... threw words at you. The whole 'spelled' thing. I'll explain it properly, one piece at a time. The 'brackets' feeling is a transference.>

Cal made Artorian some temporary visual aids. <You're initiating an effect that doesn't entirely come from *you*. You're fueling the intended effect and the cost, but the actual A to B is being done by the Pylon. Speaking of, I have to construct more of them.>

An informative wall of text in the form of a dome surrounded the old man, who hoped it blocked incoming attackers, since it also completely blocked his senses. Cal just kept tweeting. <Explaining a 'spell' requires I go through the gamut. Anyone else I would tell to hold onto something, but you'll be fine.>

Artorian closed his eyes and took a steadying breath, but said nothing and listened.

<It all starts with the idea of the pattern. A pattern is the intricate design that makes everything in the universe. An inanimate object has a far less complex pattern than a living being. That box you're sitting on is easier to form than your feathers, for example.>

Artorian rolled his wrist, indication to go on with the collegiate lesson.

<The flows of Essence generated by living creatures, which

surround them and hold their pattern, are also called Aura. In the sense of it existing.>

Cal made a point of differentiation here. <Not the manipulated version cultivators use, even though the word is the same. When someone becomes a Mage, their pattern Aura and their manipulatable Aura merge. This is what is called True Presence. I saw from your memories that you attempted this early. That should have killed you, by the way.>

The old man just smiled at him, very much alive and kicking. <I'm following, Cal, and yes, I'm aware. I was told so *repeatedly* by many upset voices. I'll slate my less-than-stellar version in the dictionary as Primal Presence. The Mage variant is smoothly unified in comparison, and I have a shambling theory that it's part of why my C-rank improvement, erm... well. *Stalled.* Can confirm. Do not recommend.>

Cal hummed a derisive *mhm*.

<The point is that everything, if you want the 'effect, being, or thing' to remain consistent, has a set pattern. Everything. I have called the method of making a single effect act consistently the same a 'mold.'>

Cal showed an image of an anvil. <I understood that via the reference of casting a mold, like pouring hot metal into a cast so you always get a similar product again and again. People without molds tend to rely on pricey Incantations, but even then, *some* knowledge of a pattern is involved. To the best of my information, only a few are foolish enough to throw Essence around without *any* pattern. Know anyone like that, Administrator?>

Artorian shrugged and innocently looked the other way. <It suited my purposes, and everything turned out fine. Even if the whole debacle was grievously expensive. Invoking guides Essence toward an effect via imbued identity and directed will. It then forms its own patterns to do so, which is one of the reasons for the high cost.>

Cale's visage appeared nearby, and nodded. <Correct. At first, I thought Invoking was a derivative of the Incantation, but

DENNIS VANDERKERKEN & DAKOTA KROUT

it turned out not to be. That method of yours is going the opposite way of where my Pylons are headed.>

The anvil image changed to a pyramid. <The first patterns that cultivators are able to figure out are always the *temporary* ones. Essence patterns like this, that create temporary effects on the universe, are called *Enchantments*. So, for a minute, you could walk on acid, or repel it from your feet, or something similar. Releasing all the power of an Enchantment at once, using gestures and words, is called an *Incantation*.>

The dungeon rubbed its invisible hands together, the image of the pyramid filling in with building blocks. <That's the springboard to the good stuff! From Enchantments we go to *Inscriptions*. Rather than being temporary, these are *permanent* patterns that create the same effect on the universe as the prior version. Sadly, just like their origin, there are nasty consequences for getting it wrong.>

Cal filled in another building block. <Inscriptions are almost always the precursor to Runes, usually after going boom a few times. A Rune is also a permanent pattern of Essence, but better! It is the name specifically given to a *completed* Inscription. Much less chance for it to go boom, to the point where it nearly never does. You really do need to get the pattern precisely correct, or the boom will be bigger.>

Artorian kneaded the bridge of his nose. <Then, is 'spell' by chance the next form of a completed Inscription? Sorry, Rune? I'm doing my best here.>

Confetti burst into being and fell down around the old man, the mention celebrated along with the squeak of a rusty horn. <It is! For all these processes, what you're *actually doing* when evoking a technique is moving your Essence through your meridians to create the intended pattern. Chain Lightning, for example, has a very specific pattern and design. Getting the pattern you make within you mostly right makes it work, but that's just step one. Since that's not useful for a Mage, I'll skip this bit and move on.>

Cal moved the nearly completed pyramid to the side, and

brought up a map of meridians in a body. <As an Ascended, shaping the technique pattern happens with Mana. Given the meridians aren't a big deal anymore at that point, the *whole* of the body can be used. That lack of forced limitations lends itself to far greater creative freedom, as you've got a less restrained canvas to paint on.>

The meridian map vanished in favor of pulling the pyramid back. <After observing and testing for a long time, I came to the conclusion that what people are doing is creating, or trying to create, a Rune. Anytime a Mage attempts to cause a specific effect, they convert their Mana into the type of Mana or Essence needed for the Rune to work. That particular tidbit was an important puzzle piece that I'm very glad to have.>

Cal visualized some Runes on the inside of the dome as an example, including their lesser forms which led up to this point. Artorian's eyes went wide. They were so easy to understand once he was actually looking at them!

Cal noticed his attention skyrocket with a sly grin. <The detail work is why not everyone can use every type of technique, and why they need to have a certain amount of 'affinity' for success! Don't tell Dawn, but I've been observing her Mana flows. The majority of her abilities make her trade out that fire affinity Mana for 'the rest.' Great to have confirmation.>

The top of the pyramid happily pinged a light on and off. <A '*Spell*' is a *completed Rune* that has the correct ratios and affinities included in the pattern! No guesswork with what Mana or Essence you need to convert, or how much. The spell does it all! Experimentation on people has been great... though still no luck on adding Runes to flesh. I haven't had the time to dig into Northmen knowledge on the topic; I'm sure they have something. It distorts the natural meridian pathways below the skin and... why have I not tried on Mages?>

Cal grew suspiciously quiet, and his attention turned elsewhere. Artorian heard the conspiratorial mumbles regardless, paling slightly when he overheard the dungeon's question. <Where are Henry and Marie right now?>

Clearing his throat, the Administrator cut Cal off from his train of thought and pulled him back into focus. <Speaking of them. I know Henry and Marie gained their titles by default when their Kingdoms fell. That was a heavy talk... But, I don't recall the King and Queen being Mages before they entered your Soul Space? When did that happen? On that note, if you can make bodies from Mana at will, why didn't Decorum's work?>

The dungeon paused when its attention wavered on which direction to go, but turned back to Artorian as Cal removed the information dome. There were no ants waiting in ambush! Bless. <Both of them Ascended before they entered my Soul Space. I know it's a faux pas to ask that of them, but you really could have. When it came to their early days in my Soul Space... They lasted a while, but burnout took them in the end. I'd rather not talk about it. That conversation is as unpleasant as new C-rankers trying to enter the Tower while they're here. There is a lot of help involved from my end. Ascending normally is difficult, doing it with me as a medium? *Yeowch*.>

Cal paused his lecture to make a snap decision, considering the side effects of the C-ranker Ascensions he currently had in mind. <I will personally be overseeing every single Ascension from this point on, because without me I don't think it's a survivable affair.>

The dungeon sounded irritated. <Those I have helped so far did not start on floor one, they started on yours! Seven-twenty. They didn't climb to find a **Law** that suited them; they had to descend to find a **Law** they could *handle*. The first few hundred floors were all blanks to most of them, not one **Law** they had all the affinities for. With going down just as costly as going up, those are draining events for me. I've resigned myself to knowing that from now on, each Ascension will be just as pricey as yours. Just because people have to go in the opposite direction. I don't even know why.>

Artorian shook his hands like they hurt, but it was a

phantom pain. That was a good amount of Essence! <I take it they all have debts, as well?>

Cal energetically affirmed it. <Oh, you bet they do! As for Decorum, he's a sweet kitten. Those massive claws and one-pounce neck snaps? *Ahhh*. So good. It wasn't the Mana body that really ended up being the problem. It had limitations, but mostly the issue came from Decorum himself. Having never been a Mage-ranked beast before, he just didn't know or under-stand why nothing he did killed anything. His mind's hardwired to kill fleshy things, and that knowledge just doesn't translate as soon as you're dealing with Ascended. So, he got his keister kicked. It did make him far more cunning to constantly try, but in the end it was fruitless.>

A map appeared before them, with a dot shining on that mind's current location. Artorian was intrigued. So, Cal could track any of them, at any time? Good to know.

<I've put him in Alfheim for now, so he can naturally grow to the apex of C-rank in Beast Core terms. When he breaches, he'll go to Vanaheim and likely stay there unless we manually move him back down. Jotunheim just... isn't a good fit. Which is odd to say for a creature that's used to being the largest threat on the board, but his version of largest is optimized and stops at a certain growth level. Decorum's biggest form will just never beat the smallest form of some of the other critters you're supervising. Well. *Maybe*. We'll see, he's got far to go. Who knows, Decorum might surprise me!>

Artorian laced his fingers. <I appreciate the clarity. Pylons and bracket words, then?>

Cal had seemingly forgotten that was the purpose and point of the topic, and scrambled to pull information back up. <Yes! Right. Pylons are crystals that I grow, which can hold a series of spells. Specifically as a series, because even with spells, there is variation between the specifics. So, I just figured, I'll add every variation! Adding every variation let me find that some spells are just *better* than others. Even if the patterns they have are *mostly* identical. I've started ranking these from Beginner to

Sage. I may change my naming scheme, but I'll probably just add to it.>

Images returned around Artorian, showing several variations of [Chain Lightning]. He scratched his head at the sight. Some of them didn't even rely on the air and earth affinity combinations! Peculiar. <Cal, some of these... How did you get this?>

A specific image illuminated, showing it required an *elemental* source of air? That was impossible to get! <This one I have from Odin. Like Dawn has an elemental fire channel? Odin has the air one. He got it by getting stuck in a nasty Mana storm while nailed to the sky. In your words: do not recommend. Back to the topic. When you use the specific way I want you to say it, or 'talking in brackets' as you so eloquently refer to it, the Pylon reacts and inserts its spell pattern in place of the one you would have otherwise used.>

A different set of two spell patterns lit up. <I am testing adding numerical values to... everything. So, when you used the spell, you should have activated *this* Pylon.>

The low-ranking example-pattern of [Chain Lightning] activated with a glow, the one Cal's system referred to as the example, before veering off toward deviations to follow Cal's attention. <Through interconnection to other Pylons to check for your specific variables, it should have ramped down the list and selected pattern twelve over here. Instead, it chose a random pattern, and you ended up with seventy-two. Which, as you likely guessed, has around a seventy-percent Essence and Mana recoup rate. This is in addition to it outright being objectively better in output than its lower numbered variants.>

Artorian squeezed his chin. <Interesting. Why did you want me to use pattern twelve?>

Pattern twelve lit up, and some golden words illuminated around it. They looked like notes? Cal filled in with an explanation. <I have this semi-functional tracker in place that keeps tabs on how much you are all using a specific Essence channel. The more energy you funnel through a type, the higher the

tracker ticks. The Pylon currently checks the tracker, and depending on your usage, your mastery, and a slew of other checkpoints, it is supposed to select the pattern that matches that 'skill level.' Because your earth affinity use is close to nil, and your air use is decently high, it should have balanced out and struck somewhere between ten to fifteen. Instead, some of my Pylons outright didn't activate, and I still don't know why.>

Artorian smiled, but did his best not to show it. <Alright, alright. What other bracket words do you want me to test while I'm stuck down here?>

The Administrator's smile could not be contained any longer, widening as literal lists started appearing before him. All those beautiful spells! Pre-molded, pre-shaped, pre-tuned! He loved this. If he could memorize them, his efficiency problems were as good as solved!

All hail Cal!

CHAPTER SEVENTEEN

Ants didn't understand the frightening nature inherent in giggling. Or rather, they didn't at first. When the first warrior ant assaulted the last known position of the invader, it imploded. What the observer aphids heard and relayed back to their equivalent of central command was [Cavitation].

More of these mysterious panic-stricken and fearful communications were sent back to the central chamber occupying the Unified Insect League. The Hivemothers didn't understand the spoken tongue, so communicating with their aphids wasn't easy. Instead, they communicated in colors and vibrations; vague impressions and vivid memories connected primarily to scents. They received images of what should have been a nigh-dead invader making many unnecessary jump-bounces. Making loud, continued noise in varying vibrations. Even when there was no warrior to slow the antagonizer's descent toward them.

The Unified Insect League had many things that worried their enhanced insect minds, and all their near-mindless counterparts. The league's leadership did its best to contain the damage, and that in some part was helped by how their hierarchies functioned. Only the Hivemothers could uphold the connection that allowed communication with their particular hive.

In the U.I.L., there were five factions that banded together: The Manti, Beetle, Ant, Aphid, and the Arachnae.

Mandibles clicked in concern as to how the invader-thing knew which paths to take that led directly to them. The Ant Queen assured the others with calming scents that her worker caste had dug appropriately, and many dead paths leading to death-traps were ready.

The invader simply did not take them.

Instead, she and Beetle Queen were staving off the invader's progress with expenditures of troops. The Ant faction had, as a result, suffered significant losses, and that forced the U.I.L. to rethink their plan of attack.

The invader was in their home. Was even here no longer safe? Here, with all of them together? Aphid remained quiet, focused on logistics and keeping the more mindless members of the U.I.L. faction fed and hydrated. It had little to no say in the affairs of the league, but also suffered the least casualties as the other factions were all reliant upon the aphids for one thing or another. A prestigious mushroom seat, they could not be denied! Still, they remained quiet.

Ant and Beetle were in an uproar. No amount of calming scents from Ant was hiding her deep and innate displeasure that her colony wasn't able to keep this single, measly annoyance at bay. Beetle had been amused at Ant's failure at first, but after losing some of their clan hybrids, Beetle was no longer so judgmental.

She had sent some rhinoceros beetles. They had hard shells, curved horns, and were strong! One scarab had been sent along to allow the Beetle Queen better endpoint communication. Her wishes could vibrate to the antennae of the scarab with ease and, more importantly, the other way around. Observer aphids were difficult to believe given what was currently happening.

Beetle didn't like sending one of her higher-ranked family to oversee what should be a small 'contain and conquer' task. However, if it got the threat removed by her family, she could claim great credit! It was thus to her great dismay that the informative vibrations from her scarab… silenced.

Wub! Artorian was wrong, applying sound in confined spaces was fantastic! *When directed*. This escapade had turned from a slog and grinding endeavor into something genuinely fun. A cadre of hard-light instruments hovered around him, each playing their own little tune. The spell [Instrument] was a little broken, and he loved it! Of course, it would be fixed and specified when the time came, but for now he was a dancing, moving orchestra of sound and good cheer.

The air distortions he made himself were accompanied with thick drumbeat drops. Those aside, he hopped and bounced, then jumped and leaped through the confined tunnels with glee.

The laughing old man danced through the caverns, keeping them well-lit with his Aura as he tested one spell form after the other. It was driving Cal crazy that he couldn't discover the Pylon limiter problem, so he'd saddled himself with firing off one spell after another! Just to 'help' each time some bug came into view.

Artorian was sending constant feedback to the Pylons with his spell use, and that signal should be trackable to let Cal find where the problem was. Until then, he was a one-man pa~a~arty. He shimmy-shuffled his way sideways in accordance to a steady beat. Head-nodding and skidding at significant speeds. He hip-checked some lesser ants, juggled aphids, and color-seared ceiling threats to add a bonus light show to his merriment.

"[Rainbow Beam]!" A random assortment of multi-affinity beams struck out from one of the instruments hovering around Artorian. It burned, then shocked, then transmuted the target. The ceiling crawler was visibly confused at being alright, clicking as it wondered why it was now a caterpillar. It then perished, exploding from the inside out from an overabundance of bright, vivacious energy that overhealed it to death.

"[Earth Lance]!" Outstretching a finger, a replica of a heavy jousting lance formed from the surrounding earth and stone. The lance balanced its handle on Artorian's finger, then launched forward. The drilling strike skewered the first large red-colored beetle he'd seen right through the cortical synapse. It died on the spot. When the earthen lance lost the energy keeping its solidity together, it crumpled back into a pile of rock as the beetle discorporated.

"[Rock Burst]!" The stilled stones on the ground shot forward, bursting to form shrapnel. The blast directed itself into the oncoming mantis-wave as Artorian recycled the prior attack. Perforating his enemies in a randomized conical pattern as ever smaller flechettes pinged off the tunnel walls, reflecting further. "The Mana gain is fantastic!"

The Pylons were clearly severely malfunctioning. It turned out that he simply never got a spell formation under the seventies! Artorian was going to ride that mistake until it was repaired, and he giggled the entire time he skipped further down the tunnel network.

Pylons made it so easy, though they weren't perfect. Having specialized in higher functions, he realized that even though the mold was one of spell quality, there were bits and pieces within the spell forms that still remained unfulfilled. He was easily able to use his usual identity and shaping tricks to add on a further layer of complexity. Which did not escape Cal's notice. The dungeon was fuming that there was another quality level to go beyond 'spells,' but Cal wanted to have the knowledge too badly to be upset.

Artorian couldn't remember the last time he could throw out abilities and have this much fun! He was just making up words at times, and it still worked! Spells were a playground, and he was the hellion wild child.

Chittering was heard ahead, and a very sizable armor-plated beetle trundled forward, with compatriots! Oh joy! He could scarcely decide what to try, and bumped his side-checking hip toward the vanguard.

"[Gravity Trap]!" Bounced backward from being hip-checked, the foremost rhinoceros beetle staggered as it stepped over the location where Artorian had placed the trap. Its legs skittered for grip, then ceased touching the ground entirely as it slammed into the ceiling at instant terminal velocity. It shrieked! Beetles being able to do that at all was still odd. The damage from the trap wasn't really enough to kill a B-ranked creature. Unfortunately, their invader had only begun with spell testing.

"[Steel Guillotine]!" A blade of metal sliced down from the exact segment of ceiling which the beetle was forcibly plastered to, and smoothly cleaved its head from the rest of the body. Thick, viscous green fluid splattered out from the severed connection, but it flooded upwards to stick to the not-floor due to the forced direction of gravity. Neither lasted too long as the beetle discorporated, while Artorian received most of his spent Mana back. He hopped in place, taunting the next beetle in the row by throwing fake punches at it from afar.

The second rhinoceros beetle thought the way forward was clear, and charged toward the foe. It found it was mistaken as it too slammed into the ceiling at sudden terminal velocity. The guillotine blade currently embedded in the floor shot back up, and in but a moment it suffered the same fate as its brethren. Artorian squeezed his hands into joyous fists, shaking them at the sky. "So, spells *can* be sustained? This is aweso~o~ome!"

Further down, in the Unified Insect League's antechamber, Ant Queen chittered and ordered her elites to attack. Soot fire ants. They had been effective against almost everything else, and should be here as well. She said nothing about her colony severely dwindling in numbers. The majority of her warriors had fallen. The Midas and Majors were kept in reserve in the closer chambers, but it was looking bleak. Fear pheromones were pouring off from the Ant Queen. It unsettled those around her, and spurred the Manti to proper action.

Artorian had stopped his merry little taunt dance to inspect a scarab he'd pinned to the wall. Each of its limbs were perforated by a drill-spike, keeping it solidly screwed to the cavern rock even as it struggled. It should be able to break the rock wall just fine, but not the hidden hard-light Mana wall behind it that the screws connected to. It struggled, but in vain as the academic opened its back plates to inspect the scarab wings. The movement forced the entire left side of the wing to unfurl. "Well, aren't you pretty? I think I'll not squish you, and instead give you to Dawn. I bet that exoskeleton of yours would glitter majestically in the sand."

Artorian reached behind him and fiddled with a mundane pouch. He pulled a small cube out from it and clicked a button at the top, then waited a moment as Cal appeared in all his dramatic majesty. <I, the Great Spirit Cal, have been summoned! Tell upon me your wishes three!>

Artorian snickered. <Sorry for the interrupt. I hope the Pylon business is going well. I found a critter I'd like to box and have sent to Muspelheim. I think it will thrive there.>

Cal looked the scarab over. <Well, that's pretty. One box to Muspelheim? Can do. I'm glad to see you're finally using my boxes properly. My spatial bag experiments aren't working well, so this is a nice intermediary. Let me just...>

Winking away the pinning effect, the scarab condensed to the size of a peanut, neatly fitting into the box Artorian held in his hand. The box then clicked shut, whirled, and settled with a ring of light around it. <Good ol' Dev and his machinations. These box balls are great.>

Cal agreed with Artorian's commentary, and the box promptly vanished. Added to Dawn's inventory rack at her temporary base. When she got back to it, the box would be waiting for her in the to-do pile. <One box, delivered. Eventually I'm going to automate this. Unfortunately, I'm still working through the Bob-limit, and they're starting to get antsy on the moon. Ha. Get it?>

The old man nodded, then gave a salute. <Thanks much, I'll get back to it.>

Cal paused before leaving. <Speaking of: [Gravity Trap]? You somehow managed to light up both the 'gravity' and the 'trap' Pylons at once. It just worked. I don't know how, and I'm still stuck as to why your limiters aren't properly triggering. That [Steel Guillotine] in the logs? Pattern seventy-five. You should have gotten maybe up to pattern five. This is ridiculous!>

The dungeon popped out, his attention needed elsewhere. Artorian burst out into deep laughter, slapping his knee from the jolly time he was having. Multiple Pylons? So, these spells could be *combined*?

Oh Cal... the one person you should not have told that to was the meddler. Artorian was all smiles, and pulled his sleeves up as the hovering instruments began their music once more. The ground trembled, indicating large numbers involved in movement. Echolocation told him it was more ants, except that these had some nasty front-facing pincers and mandibles. Best not to get nipped!

Rubbing his hands together, he had himself a think until the first of the soot ants came into view. *Oho*! "Fire immune! Venom-coated pincers." *Hmmm*.

Were they truly fire immune? Or was that just their outsides? Making the motions swiftly, he reached out a hand and made a violent crushing motion. "[Blazing Cavitation, Crushing Gravity]!"

Nothing happened. Instead, it sounded like something exploded in the background. The muted tones of which then fizzled out. Cal's roaring, upset voice, on the other hand, was back with him in a flash. <Artorian! What did you do! Three banks of my Pylons just went up in... *Wow*!>

The effect triggered late, but *oh* did it trigger. Rather than be contained in the foremost soot ant, the effect anchored itself to Artorian's intended point in space. The coruscating force then remained at those coordinates as the rest of the functions activated.

Artorian felt punched in his cultivation at the brutal cost he was paying. The Mana this amalgam spell took as fuel could have easily paid for three full teleports! But that was nothing in comparison to the chunk it took out of the Jotun underground. Noticing what was happening, he turned tail and fled the way he came.

Cal and Artorian had seen the initial patterns of the wombo-combo activate, and did not want to see the rest as they booked it.

The effects didn't activate in the order he'd vocalized. Conflicting events were trying to trigger, and the coruscating force built as it tried to figure itself out. The spells for Cavitate and Crush looked at one another, decided they were mostly the same, and went off simultaneously.

The issue being that Crush moved matter inwards, while Cavitate added pressure that forced an opposing reaction, and forced matter back outwards while that happened. Gravity then decided the intent was to squeeze everything to the space-coordinate point the spell was anchored to, and smashed all the matter Cavitate tried to rebuke right back down.

This occurred while the prior clashing forces remained at play, creating the visual of an orb that flickered between states of expanding and contracting at astonishing speeds. The strobing alone caused epilepsy in all the bugs that survived long enough to see it up close.

Blazing looked at this mess, shrugged, and just jumped in to set the entire area affected by the combination spell on perpetual pressure-fire. Colorless heat surged as the gravity ball sucked in everything it could and munched it down to particles.

Artorian just screamed out a spell and positioned it behind him. "[Unbreaking Net]!" When he was sucked off his feet and pulled back toward the epicenter of doom, he slammed into the netting of his panic barrier.

It was surprisingly costly as Omni-Mana—his temporary name for when all affinities were used at once—was used to power it, since he'd foolishly not used an affinity descriptor.

Rock and dirt poured past him, pushing through the holes in the net in neatly cubed shapes. The pressure pulling at him made it feel like he was being grated into fine cheese by his own catching mechanism. Luckily, his Mana body held.

The rest of the hive was... not so lucky.

CHAPTER EIGHTEEN

Chaos reigned in the Unified Insect League antechamber.

Beetle and Ant were gone. Just gone. Mantis remained. No, Mantis *arms* remained. Specifically, latched onto the remains of her prestigious mushroom seat that now looked clawed to pieces. The force of the yawning pull originating from the tunnels had ripped Mantis's body right off her limbs. Aphid was paste. Nothing but a long green smear along the left side of the wall.

The Arachnae was not faring much better, but well-spun webbing had saved her hide. She was missing several legs, but those would grow back. She'd survived the... whatever natural disaster just happened, and she feared that her suspicions of what was coming for them were true. Pained, she first untangled herself from her web. Then limped off to the chamber of the *great secret*. She needed the special shiny. It was all that could save her family now.

The Arachnae hadn't let the others know, but she was a *little* smarter than them. She had a unique trait that other queens lacked. A superior memory. She did not forget old events in favor of the new. She did not know why she had this gift, or why she always seemed to inherently know the location of anything any of her webs touched.

It didn't matter. It had saved her today.

Where Beetle, Ant, and Mantis had sent forth their families to deal with the looming threat, she had ordered hers to retreat. To flee far and hide deep.

For what was coming… was the thing of dreams.

Panicked and hurried, the Arachnae recalled the nightmare of a hand, tightly clasped around her face. The hand left her powerless. It left her at the whims of the wielder. She didn't know what a hand was, exactly, save for that it had five mini-mandibles that did not bite. They only squeezed.

Making it down the hidden passageway, she felt welcomed elation. There it was! The special shiny. The trinket was responsible for their unity. This small, strange object of power that she did not understand.

It was soft, and tender. It did not live, and it did not speak. Yet it held the sights, sounds, and smells of… togetherness. With it in her grip, the connection to her children grew a hundredfold, and she could sense them even from far away. She hastily told them to flee. Flee further. Flee faster.

For the thing of dreams comes.

Could the trinket protect her? Likely not. She was weakened, harmed, and still leaking hemolymph fluid. Damaged legs were ceasing function as they coiled inwards, the Arachnae now unable to claw her way back out of the hole which kept the secret-thing safe. She watched in growing terror as the strings of her web plinked with vibration. It heralded the coming of the dream and, at the same time, the end of a nightmare.

The invading creature moved through the antechamber and stopped.

Was it inspecting? Was it learning? Would it turn around in the hopes it had finished what it had started, so long ago? Where Ant and Beetle had not paid attention, Arachnae had listened to Aphid's observations and stories. She took in the sights even Mantis considered foul, and unbelievable. Yet believable they were, for the sights and sounds were true.

Her Beast Core turned cold as the walking dream continued down the path, turning a hidden corner leading straight to the trinket. Her special shiny. Again, she mentally screamed at her offspring to flee, and she clutched the trinket hard to her chest while she shivered, cowering in a dark corner. Perhaps it would not see. Perhaps it would think her dead. Perhaps it would not find her.

"*Oho?* What have we here?" Artorian illuminated the confined tunnel space he occupied. He'd passed through the desolation he'd caused, and was feeling downright remorseful and guilty. While he had capped out his current Mage rank with all the energy gained from a full hive-wipe, he'd also broken several of Cal's toys, and would be 'penalized.' Artorian had agreed that in recompense, at some later time, he would test drive a 'monster body' for Cal. One that would haunt him until he got it working right. A tough sell, but a deal struck nonetheless.

When he moved through the remains of the antechamber, he inspected the mushrooms that were positioned much like council seats. Yet survivors he did not find. Only the casualties and what was left of them. Such as the colorful smears on the wall.

It honestly wasn't much, and even the smears discorporated if you looked at them too hard. He'd abyss-near sucked the entire cavern into that burning death ball. At least Cal had renamed it, and that combination of effects was now called [Demon's Maw]. *Scary.*

Humming to update his map with echolocation, he pinpointed the source and current placement of 'the broken thing.' Since it wasn't moving, he figured it wasn't a creature this time. He dismissed his silenced instruments so as to not cause unwanted interactions, and wondered what to expect this time. Twisted space? Twisted gravity? Intolerable heat for no reason? Visions that became real? It had been a chaotic rollercoaster anytime 'the broken' were involved. This time it was… a large spider? That couldn't be right.

It looked *so* scared.

Artorian pressed his hands to his lips after questioning the air with his spoken words. He hadn't really expected a response, and he still wasn't any fonder of spiders. He could have killed it then and there. But he did not. His hand stayed because of what it was clutching ever so tightly to its chest.

This Arachnae had found it. *His* recovered Phoenix Kingdom pillow. The one he'd picked up from the crib. The one Cal had so far failed to retrieve. Could things that were broken not be located by Cal? Was that why he needed the supervisors to comb the land?

Again, Artorian noticed that the creature looked absolutely terrified. Well… could it be blamed? Once more, pangs of guilt wrecked his stomach. He approached, and the Arachnae twitched and wormed away from him. It attempted to chitter? Even that was difficult. Such a familiar sound, except scared, rather than furious and angry. He eased down to a knee, and extended a hand. "Hello there. I'm not sure if you can understand me, but could I have that? It's very important to me."

The Arachnid didn't respond; it merely wormed away further. Artorian just about slapped his forehead. Not human! No vocal cords, nor Mana-copied ones. Still, it seemed intelligent. Perhaps this was one of the minds that had kept the hive in such a unified state?

The Arachnae's chittering rose to clear panic, becoming louder as her mandibles clicked. Though, not at him? He glanced over his shoulder, seeing that several other spiders were slowly crawling toward him. Why was this Arachnae warning the approaching ones? The realization of that thought lingered with Artorian. How did he know that this clicking was a warning for them not to approach?

He certainly did not speak 'spider,' but perhaps to 'speak' was the wrong concept? He intuited the meaning, and he felt it as it brushed across his Aura. The Arachnae was speaking with… vibrations, clicks, perhaps smells? Fueling Mana directly to his **Love Law**, he decided he had to know more.

His senses widened, and he saw the strings that connected the Arachnae to her children. They were greatly amplified by the crib pillow, and the inherent power within them screamed of unity. How… touching. This spider had feelings?

How… unprecedented.

He'd never considered the possibility before, and was now faced with first-hand evidence that she, definitely a 'she,' was sending images and warnings. Thoughts of apprehension and calls of retreat to children that sent back only soothing waves of support. The children would ambush him, and take him down. Then their mother would be safe.

Such depth. From… Arachnaes?

No. It couldn't be true…? Yet his **Law** did not show him lies, and he knew it. Well, his **Law** actually showed him lies too, but more in the sense that it provided him the ability to tell if something was one or not. Here, in the communication of this hive, there was neither hidden meaning nor subterfuge. They were just sapient creatures trying to look out for one another.

Fusing Mana into his Aura, he copied the patterns the Arachnae used to convey messages, and outright hijacked the communication thread. When he thought he'd about gotten it right, he translated his words into… spiderspeak? "Fear not!"

Across the communication network on which the spiders conveyed their meanings, the loud thrumming paralyzed them all from the booming mental force alone. Facing a physically threatening foe was one thing, but one that could invade their minds? All was lost. The message itself was lost, obscured in the sheer volume and power that cascaded over their network. The **Love** connection reached far and wide. No spider on Jotunheim was safe, and they all froze in place. Suddenly acutely aware that they should have heeded prior orders.

Silence reigned as Artorian rose, his calm steps bringing him to the paralyzed spider queen. He reached down, and took the crib pillow from her… claws? Why did they look so much like hands? Now that he inspected her, humanlike features were mid-formation on the black widow's body. Was it evolving into something else? Would it have gotten the chance to, had he not interfered? Stowing what was his, he once again took a knee. This time, right in front of the spider queen's face.

Artorian felt such a mixture of discomforts. He recalled Dawn, and the Lamia. He so disliked spiders, he thought that he feared them. Always had. Yet did he always… have to? Was there not a better way? A more… **Loving** way.

His hand gently pressed behind the Arachnae's frozen left mandible.

The Arachnae could not move as the shiny had been taken from her claws. Her body remained completely locked up, and not from lack of fluids. The mental pressure remained strong, bearing down on her consciousness like a great weight.

The dream thing was going to kill her.

She felt the hand close the distance to her synapse cord. Had she been able to close her eyes, to not see her impending end, she would have. The terror in her soul screamed loud and strong as 'the hand' touched her. She knew what it was now. She saw it, and felt it, and once more the night terrors of being controlled took her.

No such control took her mind. The hand lingered, but it did not take. Instead… the pressure on her thoughts lifted, and a soothing warmth bloomed within her. Extending from behind her left mandible, the effect spread into her synapses. Heat rushed through her being where previously it was so very cold. Where she ached and ailed, that pain faded. She heard a clicking, saw an image, and understood a smell. It was 'spoken' rather than felt, but she felt the question all the same.

The thing of dreams asked gently, "Show me."

So, show she did. Images, sounds, and experiences flooded the connection easier than they had ever before. Previously the Arachnae had been moving information up and down a single string, but now it felt like the string was the size of the nest, and there was room for everything at once.

The Arachnae's memories showed her awakening, and the understanding went as such: First there was the *them* and the *they*. The nameless who were plenty, and came from nowhere.

The visuals Artorian interpreted were vague, seen by eyes that knew nothing of concepts, and saw the world as it was new. In time, he understood and made sense of the images as the Arachnae showed the crawling and the calm, the mushroom and mantis, the ant and aphid. To the spider: 'They' were 'us,' and only then did the arachnids understand that they were that 'us.' Their sense of identity grew slow, the lesson a laborious one.

The Arachnae's memories continued showing Artorian a first-person perspective as the spider learned that: 'We' came with the flower and the pollen, the dew and the succulent. We dug our homes as halls of earth. We found caverns and crags, the wet in the waters, and the untouchable above.

To hail the untouchable above, we grew wings to greet it. Yet were rewarded with the snatch of furious air. The above descended, and ate us whole. So, we abandoned the above, and remained on the top.

The Ancients remained, and kept watch.

Establishing ourselves on the top, we grew hooks to climb, and legs to walk. We were rewarded by crush and flatten. From nowhere, the tramplers came. Because of them, we were kept underfoot by the deadly tremors of great leaps and bounds. So, we abandoned the top, and remained in the below.

Again, the Ancients remained, and kept watch.

In the below, all was damp. We grew balance and fin, buoyance and breath. We were rewarded by swallow and bite. The below things came from the everdeep, hungry, and in great masses. So, we abandoned the below, and remained only within.

Once more, the Ancients remained, and kept watch.

Then the aphid watchers sent stories. Visions and uncertainties. Smells strange and profound. For something *new* had come. They called it the sun that wandered through dreams, for it was bright, and went undaunted. First, the wanderer came for the wet, and made them weary. Defeated in their waters and doffed of their scales, they ceded their domain.

Then the wandering sun sought the sky, and tamed the furious air. Neither claw nor peck, swoop nor slash could oppose this dreamer. Defeated in their heights and felled of their feathers, they ceded their domain.

Then the wanderer claimed the mountains. Burning bright for all to see as the great tramplers were vanquished from the top. Those who leapt and bounced were removed. Made anew as formless dust, the ground no longer pounded with their being.

Without the shaking earth, we thought then that it was safe to once again seek other paths. We were mistaken, for now the wanderer comes for the burrowed and hidden, the small and silent.

So, we swiftly prepared the trap and coil. The league planned cave-ins originally meant to swallow tramplers, and formed paths obscure to delay invasions. The Arachnae knew now the identity of her dreamer. The cloudy creature of her nightmares. This dreamer was the wandering sun, and the wandering sun comes for all.

When it did, it would *take*.

The Arachnae would cry, if she could. With her fading will, she ceded the domain of the Unified Insect League. They were defeated, and conquered. She was ready to die, and hoped one of her children would take upon themselves the mantle of leadership.

For she understood it now. While to her, the day this dreamer came was the most important day of her life, to the dreamer, it was but another in a long, meaningless series.

A moment more of life, and the Arachnae felt confusion. Why did she live still? Why did these thoughts come easier, and easier still? What were words, and how did she suddenly know so many? Their meanings, their intentions. She knew them, but knew not why as the warmth broadened her synapses and fueled her Beast Core. Unknown strength came to her, and rather than merely look off in a daze, she turned her attention to actually see.

Her form was altering!

The dreamer held her by the cheek, but it was not the cheek of a spider. Even if her black chitin remained the same, the new form had things called arms, and she too now possessed the mystical things known as hands. Two, even!

Her upper body remained connected to her spider form, while her legs regrew thick, and plentiful. She gazed toward the dreamer as her vision sharpened, and observed his eyes as a bright rainbow burned within them. The light coating the dreamer flared outwards, illuminating the cavern of the trinket as glittering sparkles hung in the air before adding to her frame. Healing it. Improving it.

The dreamer was not killing her. It was mending her. Making her better. Making her something... *more*. It was... blessing her? She did not understand. She did not grasp the words. Only the meanings as she finally understood that 'he' had told 'her' not to fear.

The dreamer spoke. "Perhaps this is easier, now. Hello there, my dear. Are you well?"

The Arachnae swallowed through her new throat. She understood the words, but had never used any of her own. Her jaw trembled, and even as it moved, she could not form the sounds. The dreamer merely performed a facial twitch known as a smile.

Was he pleased with her? Was he not upset? Confusion rooted deep within her, but the very presence of the caring hand on her cheek was just... So nice. It didn't hurt at all. Instead, the hand felt warm and welcome.

A visual flashed in her mind. Some part of her sat blanket-bundled in front of a fire, cozily bobbing back and forth in a rocking chair on a chilly evening. She felt the feeling, and understood.

The dreamer was not here to hurt her. It was here for the trinket, and they had all simply attacked him on his journey.

When the hand pulled away, the Arachnae's new arms rose in panic. *No, no, do not go.* She did not wish for the warmth to go. The revelation that her dreamer and fear, the hand of control and terror was nothing of the sort, unsteadied her. She swallowed again, and did her best to copy his words so the dreamer would stay. She tried to click as if she had mandibles, but instead more throaty sounds came out. "A... Am. W... Well."

Artorian couldn't contain his good mood. He felt so pleased! He'd thought his ramshackle idea had not worked. "Oh, well that's just swell. What was I supposed to do next? Right, I believe I was supposed to name you. There's great power in a name. Too many start with 'A' these days; I'll start at the other end for a change. I know! I name you Zelia!"

Zelia the Arachnae Queen felt a surge of incredible power. All of that... from a name? She was going to try and formulate a question, but the dreamer was speaking. "Now let's see. I'm supposed to give you an actual blessing? I think I'll give you: [Blessing of Argent]."

Zelia felt her body lock up again. Her synapses thickened further, and even more information and senses were able to freely stream and develop. Silvery streaks replaced the red on her spider body, and her irises equally took on the color as the black widow symbol on her spinneret altered to that of a silvered sun.

The heat inside of her was no longer borrowed, it was now her own. It had been granted, and the hot bioluminescence translated through her silvery markings. How strong they glowed.

Her cheeks were cupped, and Zelia received a tender kiss on the forehead. "My fear. It feels... abated. Live well, my dear Zelia. I will come check on you now and again. Help me clean up, if you'd like? I sure would appreciate it."

The connection to her mind ended smoothly, softly, gently. The dreamer said something that sounded like the word [Teleport]. The meaning was beyond her reasoning, but a kinship manifested with the word as the wandering sun brightened. The dreamer condensed into a speck of light, and vanished. Leaving only her and her still-paralyzed children in the hall of the lost trinket.

When the dark set back in, her silvery glow rebuked it. New spider limbs found their foothold as her form reverted to that of a common arachnid once again. The 'advanced' form was difficult to uphold, but the method was not forgotten.

Thoughts trickled in calm and clear, and control of her form tingled to life. She lived, and felt mighty. The wandering sun had come, taken only her fears, her nightmares, and had left. Rather than accept her domain, he had returned it to her claws. 'Help me clean,' he had asked. A strange bond of loyalty to the being that saved her life made her feel... like that was the least she could do.

Her new power roiled through her network, and all over Jotunheim unfrozen spiderlings stopped their fleeing scurry to acquiesce to her new demands.

She was Zelia, and for her dreamer, all Arachnae would *zealously* cleanse.

CHAPTER NINETEEN

"You're late." Dawn drummed her impatient fingers on her upper arm. The dinner she'd made was getting cold by the time he finally showed up. Artorian looked harried when he tele-ported into their little hideaway under Muspelheim. Dawn decided it wasn't actually a big deal. A wave of her hand returned their meals to optimal temperature.

She shoved a bowl into his hand, and flopped next to him so she could finally eat. She'd worked hard on this! It was even something other than dumplings of bear flank, bear jerky, bear steak, bear… something.

Artorian came alive at the first bite. *Mmmmh*. "It's marvelous, dear."

Dawn beamed, because of course it was! Having it acknowl-edged was the thing she'd wanted to hear, and that made her own dinner taste all the better as she cracked a coconut in half to drink the milk. They ate in silence. Pleasantly taking in the serene, calming view as confused gulls flew around above. Occa-sionally, the noisy birds *thunked* into the ceiling. It at least shut them up for a minute.

Neither of them talked about work here. This was a place

for much-needed relaxation and downtime. The lounge chairs they climbed into afterwards were meant for naps, but said attempts were interrupted when Surtur slid over. Artorian and Dawn shared a look, but some minor motions of nonverbal communication led to the decision that Dawn would rather check on it. She handed Artorian her coconut. "A moment, dear. My named one needs me."

The chosen remained a good distance away until Dawn approached and acknowledged her. Surtur still carried that burning spear, but there was an obvious feeling of deference and respect in the vermillion Lamia's body language.

Artorian nodded and took the coconut, trying a sip. *Phooo*! It was milky alcohol! His eyes burned from the vapors it gave off, and his tongue curled while his face twisted into a wince. "Oh, why is it so sour! Is this a coconut or a thousand squeezed alcoholic lemons? Sweet Cal, this is strong."

His stomach hurt, and he needed to put it down. Glancing over, Dawn was giving him a despondent look from all the embarrassing faces he'd made, and the vermillion Lamia was snickering. Her hand covered her mouth as she clearly tried not to laugh, which only made it worse.

In Surtur's perspective, even the Divines needed rest. If the Divines rested, then so should they. Many of her greatest influences and lessons were drawn from the limited interaction she had with her Divines. Their actions laid the groundwork for how she changed and led her own tribe.

Dawn did not mind. She did not know how to teach them. So it all worked out.

That the Lamia came in person was cause for concern. That didn't happen too often, but Artorian knew Dawn was glad to see her. The Fire Soul's blessing had given Surtur longevity far over and above her peers. Not to mention the might.

Artorian took his nose from the equation and butted out. Cozily laying back down in the lounger, he watched the tropical waves brush up against the sands of the island they spent their downtime on.

When Dawn returned, she downed the entirety of the coconut without so much as blinking an eye. That monster! She could drink Dwarves under the table if she could keep that swill down. Artorian winced just from watching, and quickly changed the topic. "Is all well in sandland?"

Dawn mumbled incoherently, exhaling hard enough to blow a gale up at the ceiling and send whole flocks of gulls into whirling disarray. On the top layer, certain patches of sand exploded upwards from the sudden air pressure.

They didn't see it, but they knew. "The Goblins and their empire are doing so, so much better than expected. Surty is worried about border friction, but didn't want to go attack them without my permission. I told her to do what she wanted; I trust her. My confidence in her really helps her mental state, and she feels validated. The uncertainty was eating at her, and I wasn't going to let her suffer like that."

Artorian nodded; that sounded lovely. "Is she your favorite?"

Dawn confirmed with a proud nod. "She is. The Goblins are all too zealous and that causes so many dumb problems. If you ever get around to blessing a creature rather than playing eternal janitor, make sure that whatever blessing you give it does not include zealotry, or any of its affiliates, in any way. Absolute headache."

The Fire Soul inherently knew something was wrong when Artorian shot her the 'Tibbins face.' "Sunny. What did you do?"

Artorian hastily drank from his own water cup, and spoke with all the intensity and squeaking timidity of a mouse. "*Nothing.*"

She blinked at him, believing that statement about as much as a Goblin stayed out of trouble. "Okay. Know what? When you want to tell me what you broke this time, I'm here. We're going to have another inner circle moot soon, by the way. Oh, and we all heard Cal cursing up and down the entire length of the abyss for what you did to those Pylon banks. Honestly,

Demon's Maw? Do I even want to know what you combined for nonsense like that?"

Sunny choked on his water, coughed, and wiped his mouth clean while entirely pink in the face from grievous embarrassment. His voice was even squeakier than before. "Oh... y'know. Nothing major."

Eeee! Dawn poked Sunny in the ribs, right in a ticklish spot. He bolted upright from his lounger and accidentally launched upwards from the exertion, sticking to the ceiling above like a spider. Just his feet remained attached as he stood 'up' while upside down. He cautiously rubbed at his sides. "Fine!"

Rather than hovering, he released his hold on the ceiling and just fell. Dawn took two steps and caught him in her arms. She grinned wide, teasing relentlessly. "Isn't this supposed to be the other way around?"

When Artorian was put down on the ground, he sat on the side of the lounger to explain to Dawn the entire kerfuffle that he was now responsible for. He knew that this place wasn't for work, but it was unavoidable now. Getting it all off his chest, he told her everything.

Dawn listened nonjudgmentally. Not what he expected, but it was nice. The tail-end of his story was interrupted as they both felt a sizable shift in world speed. Their relative frames of references had doubled just now. No, a category increase? Not doubled. Cal had just added a zero behind their current dilation frame speed. Dawn and Artorian looked at one another for confirmation that, yes, that did actually just happen.

<Hello everyone!> Cal popped into the senate-space loud as a town crier. <That was less subtle than I'd like. Could everyone gather in Niflheim for a meeting? I may have pushed go on a few changes I did not yet mean to. See you soon!>

Dawn's grip squeezed Sunny's wrist. She was visibly calming herself before her chin tilted upwards. Her eyes glared angrily at a spot Artorian could not see, and he knew clearly something was wrong. "He broke them. He abyss-blasted broke them. I was working on those triremes, Cal! Sunny, I'm taking us. Ready?"

Artorian brushed his robes off and took her hand instead of her wrist, which was enough for Dawn. *Vwumph*. They arrived near the moot-circle as several other supervisors popped in. Brianna's teleport was seamless and soundless. She appeared from nothing, as if walking out of thin mist.

Marie didn't pop in so much as majestic gates swung open from thin air, with trumpets heralding and tooting. Mystical illusion knights crossed swords above a rolled-out carpet as Queen Marie stepped forward. Artorian knew that the thematic teleportation effect was tied to your **Law**, so just *what* **Law** did she have that caused this?

A question he was dying to ask as they took their seats.

The sounds of the inner workings of a clock clicked and ticked, and with the chime of a major hand Deverash 'clicked' into being. One second he wasn't there, the next he was. The sound lessened and blunted for a second or two more, but ended thereafter as he took a seat and high-fived Artorian with a big smile. The old man winked and whispered to the Gnome's ear. "You've got ash in your teeth, my friend. Were you smiling while near a furnace?"

Deverash cleaned his teeth with some Mana, and nodded vigorously. "Oh yes. Our latest Vanaheim contraptions are true marvels. Putting them together takes some doing, and we essentially live in a scrap heap of our own making. We all love it though. I've never seen a happier hobnob of Gnomes. It's a little strange for everyone else to turn our failed machines into the equivalent of clockwork housing, but it's homey!"

Dawn also high-fived Dev, and then shot finger crossbows in the direction of Marie as she sat down. What an odd way to show affection. Eh, Dawn could do as she pleased.

Artorian leaned forward, and pointed to the teleportation effect packing itself up. "Marie, what is your **Law** to make *that* happen?"

Marie looked splendiferous, her hair in majestic curls.

"**Glory**, Administrator; my **Law** is the concept of **Glory**. I am fully seated in my role as a Queen, and just like Henry I am going to try to make my part of Midgard a proper civilization. When both our regions are up to snuff, we're going to merge them. Our plans were rushed with the *surprise decanting* today. Something I really want to ask Cal about."

Henry joined shortly after, except that he burst from thin air with a roar as some sort of Phoenix-Lion. Artorian had no idea what **Law** that could be either, but it was flashy and nostalgic. Sadly, asking would have to wait.

Cale was finally here, guided to the inner circle moot by a very upset violet Wisp, who bobbed and dragged him to his seat by the ear. "Now *sit* down and tell them what you did!"

"But *Dani~i~i.*" Cale was unapologetically hurled into the seat, and the body of Dale promptly popped into being in time to bounce and cling to the chair.

"No buts! You tell them, this instant! You cannot assign people to help do your dirty work if you only ever *add* to their work. Do you know what I found *hidden away* in the Muspelheim sands? Do you know how dangerous it would have been if Grace had found any one of those? You tell them everything, and by the time I come to pick you up, you'd better be done. Momma Wisp, out!"

A copy of the Silverwood Tree sprouted from the ground in the direction that Dani angrily bobbed toward. The branches formed a welcoming portal gateway, and Dani silently zipped through it. Not long after forming, the portal closed as the branches moved away. The silver root descended back into the ground as if it had never been there. Artorian filed that nugget of information away, and a glance at Dev told him he wasn't the only one that wasn't going to forget that visual. The Dungeon Wisp could make instant portals anywhere she wanted? Nifty!

Cale defeatedly held his face, waiting for the entire menagerie to shuffle in. A crack of thunder later, and Odin was present. A howl to the moon, and Aiden was here. The growth of underbrush opened up into an oversized rose, and Chandra stepped from the opening petals. Space warbled, and Tatum stepped through. When everyone was present and seated, Cale deeply inhaled. "I should start with an apology."

The supervisors of the inner circle crossed their arms, wondering what Cale had broken this time. Cale didn't leave them in suspense. He just wanted it out and off his chest. "I may have... accidentally... triggered a Pylon; which triggered other Pylons, that were linked to the decanting and randomization processes. A few... *things* have been added to each continent that aren't supposed to be there. I'll just, uh... I'll list off."

Cale swallowed, and made several floating lists appear. Reading the contents made the supervisors hold their faces. "Midgard, congratulations! You've got people! A small... *one million* of them. *Eheh*. Hope that ecosystem is ready. The census says half wolfmen, half humans. *Erm*. Good luck?"

Aiden was elated and howled in victory, but the royals were not ready for people. Chandra looked plenty confident, as her plants were ready to go. She had also gotten those Jotunheim samples, though she went to pluck them herself given some troubling news that had come down the grapevine. Artorian just didn't have the chance to send her the box in the timeframe she wanted. She doubted he would complain about less work.

Cale continued with the news update. "Svartalfheim has a good number of Dwarves, and some... Aether technology Deverash had to scrap. Alfheim now has Elves that weren't ready in the slightest, and all of Deverash's pill-refining goodies, tomes, cauldrons, plants..."

Deverash looked horrified, but kept dreadfully silent. He knew it was his turn next. "Vanaheim. *Erm*... the Mana accumulators we've been keeping in the depths sort of all... *popped*. You've got Mana storms that I'm not sure I *want* to absorb. Preferably, I want to shove it back into accumulators, but until then it's... y'know. Doing its own thing and giving me indigestion."

The Gnome slowly placed his forehead against the table, saying absolutely nothing as Cale kept going.

"Artorian, you have an... uh... I'm going to call it a *Kaiju*? Jotunheim has big critters, but now you have a really, *really* big critter. One of the Pylons keeping Jorm-size limitations in place popped. You've got crabs. One of them is... especially girthy. It's inside of Jotun, and it would be really bad if it broke out. So... yeah."

Artorian joined Deverash in silently pressing his forehead to the table.

"Brianna, there *may* be an entire horde of steam and mist-based creatures specializing in trickery, guile, and deceit loose in the Niflheim depths. Plus... one massive floating eye with a lot of tentacles, where each of those tentacles copies functions from my old assimilators. I call it a Phosgen."

Brianna squeezed her lips to show her sincere lack of amusement. If Cale could be assassinated...

"Dawn. I—"

Dawn cut him off, her gaze leveled judgmentally. "You broke my triremes, my entire sky fortress, and basically anything else I had up there. You also added cat people. Anubites. Bird people. And other half-and-halfs that I am going to have to discover *names* for. My desert is a war zone right now, as people remember who they were *before* they were those creatures. Yet now they're *that*."

Cal fell silent, swallowed, and moved on. Best not to poke that hornet's nest. Speaking of *hornets*... "Odin. On top of all the Golems and Elementals we already had in Asgard, we... *erm*. Well, we figured the mixture out! Which I suppose is sort of good news? As a downside, they come in swarms, have a great plethora of affinities and abilities, and they are very pissed off at everything for no good reason. They are also all immune to lightning and thunder."

Tatum already felt miffed, but Cale got to him regardless as Odin got up to stomp around and curse thunderously.

"Occultatum, Hel has a bit of an undead problem. Except that they don't really count as undead?"

The supervisor of Hel held his hand up to request a pause. "Cale, there is a copy of every animal, ever, walking around on Hel. Except that it is *only* their skeletons doing so. There is no meat on them, and yet they behave exactly the same as their living counterparts. Save that as you said, they're not dead. Those are living creatures, limited to being only bones. Each and every last one of them are the *highest* A-rank things you can reasonably hold inside of you. One higher now, after your very recent rank up. I want to say congratulations? We all felt the speedup, and there's no new **Time Law** modification on the big clock in our inner circle table."

Cal nervously laughed, and scratched the back of his head. "Yeah, about that. There is *one more* tiny issue that affects everyone."

CHAPTER TWENTY

In the depths of Jotunheim, Artorian scribed notes studiously. He sat on a platform of hard light long after the meeting had concluded. After taking sufficient notes, he just watched the chaos as several thousand species of crustacean had an all-out wild war. Rubbing at his brow, he held his head with his fingers as the crustaceans devoured their fallen. They grew and adapted some of the features of their felled, then continued with the cycle.

Adaptive crabs were one thing. The real problem was the oversized monstrosity. The spiky boy that towered over all the others. He was going to call it a 'King Crab.' Because in this brawl, it ruled. Its heaving left pincer alone was easily the size of... a hundred floors of the Skyspear pavilion. *After* the Dwarves had remade it. Jotunheim was known for issues with girth, but this was a Jorm-sized problem.

The shell on the creature was so thick that even stealthily attempting piercing attacks did jack-nothing. Artorian mulled the Kaiju over, his attention focused on it. The King Crab snatched up large prey, devouring it. As it did, its shell slightly grew. Unlike ordinary crabs, this one did not appear to shed its exterior layer, which was when some of the smaller ones seemed to become vulnerable. The King Crab simply grew, and grew, and grew as it ate. For now, the inner space in Jotun could easily contain the beast.

For now.

Artorian tallied issues. Major problem number one. The abyss-blasted thing possessed an inherent Mana-repelling effect, and it outright absorbed free Essence. Every Mana-fueled attack that he'd thrown at the Kaiju had either done nothing, or worse, reflected the heck back at him. Pyrite, he'd dodged his own attacks and some of them were exceptionally speedy. The end result left him with a spent repertoire, holes in his robe, and an unscathed self-designated 'World Boss.'

He threw a pebble down at the grand grotto lake, the water now anything but still and silent. It plunked right in. Not one single bounce. "How in Cal am I fixing this?"

Sunny rubbed his eyes and cycled vision methods to ascertain weaknesses, but as he cycled and cycled, he found none. That was frustrating, and while he sat there being useless, the crab went along its business unopposed. "Dangit, dangit." <Dangit!>

Artorian had not realized his last, frustrated outburst wasn't physical. He strummed a string, and a new voice returned to him with a cautious question. <My... Dreamer?>

Sunny perked up. What? Who was he talking to? This wasn't one of the other supervisors. <Hello? Who am I speaking to?>

The response came with a sense of awe. A feeling, before the words came. <Zelia, the Argent Web, my Divine. Are you well? Can I be of service?>

Artorian was honestly surprised he had a mental connection to the creature that he named. Dawn had never mentioned this. One of those things he was supposed to find out on his own? Aw Hel, no loss to find out now. Someone to talk to was good, though he didn't know how to feel about the title she'd addressed him with. He didn't pry for now, more concerned about the chosen instead. <Nice to hear from you, my dear. I'm well enough; stuck in a pickle I'm not yet sure how to handle. I'm afraid I'm not certain how you'd help with this one. Let me ask you the same question. Are you well, and do you need anything?>

A deep-rooted feeling of pleasant happiness returned. Zelia's demeanor felt less deferential, and peppier. Excited, even. She was trying to control herself, but Zelia was clearly happy to have this conversation. With it being mental in nature, she didn't even have trouble speaking. <I cannot ask of my Divine. I am well, your grace, merely minor scrapes.>

The Administrator frowned, and that gesture translated over their connection. Zelia was clearly about to apologize, but Artorian didn't let her. He didn't know where she'd picked up those words, but he was incredibly uncomfortable with their use. <Please, none of that. I do not like to be called your grace, or any such titles. Sunny is just fine. At least that's close to my name. What's this about *scrapes*?>

Zelia's response wasn't... quite what he'd hoped for, but he wasn't going to correct it a second time. She was doing her best. <As you wish, my Sun. Please do not be concerned over my state, it will heal. I am here as an instrument of your will.>

Artorian kneaded the bridge of his nose. *Aii*. He didn't like that. The whole 'Divine' business sat terribly in his stomach. Maybe naming a critter had been a mistake?

He sighed. "Too late now. Responsibility ho!" *Fuff*.

Zelia jumped when Artorian fuffed into existence next to her in a cloud of fluff. Her nearby children dropped what they were doing, swarming to defend their queen. Preparation was the limit of their action, and they found themselves unable to approach. Their queen did not wish it, and so they could not. <My Divi—!>

Her actual voice was not yet able to form the words, and only her thoughts could reach out. That was fine. She'd get there. Artorian pressed his hands to his hips like an over-concerned grandfather. "Zelia, I am not amused, please tell me more about these sc— *Zelia*! What in Cal's name! You're all torn up!"

He rushed forward and pressed a hand to her slashed spinneret. A scratch? This was near-lethal damage! A scratch, his foot! "Young lady. You tell me this instant what you have been up to. This kind of harm is unacceptable."

Zelia's form shuddered as it was coated in Artorian's Mana, the high-purity energy quickly restoring the Arachnae back to good health. It made him squirm a little to watch, but being so close to the passive spider was making it a little easier to cope with his arachnophobia. It wasn't so scary when you knew they didn't want to hurt you. Zelia stammered, too stressed to speak as her somewhat-human jaw opened and closed in jabbered attempts to form words.

Artorian just held her reformed chitinous upper half, easing his hand against the back of her head. Concerned, he pulled her down so the spidergirl's non-human face rested on his shoulder. "There, there, it's alright. You're going to be alright. Take a breath for me. A nice, big breath. Then another, and another. Yes, good. That's a good Zelia. Now stay put."

Zelia felt her Divine's hand softly rub and stroke the top of her head. He was petting her? She didn't mind one bit. If one of her children or allies would dare attempt this, she'd eat them whole! But not her Divine. Her Divine was allowed. She spoke with her mind, since her mouth was unable. <I... we... we have been cleansing. Trying to cleanse. The big things on the outside are many, and strong. We do our best, but our webs cannot hold them all. Our fangs cannot penetrate some hides. Our nitrate venom cannot reach their synapse. We are stomped. Pecked. Stabbed. Slashed. We go to cleanse again anyway; it is our cause.>

Guilt knotted in Artorian's stomach. Why were his words taken out of context so often and so easily? "You did all that because I asked you to help me *clean*? My dear, that's not what I meant... but. *Good job*. You've done very well and I'm very proud of you. Could we maybe talk about something else you could do? The harm you've taken is… it's no. Just no."

Zelia lit up at the praise. Quite literally. She shone a bright silver and the space around her warmed. That she had misunderstood her Divine was brushed over. She had been praised, and complimented, and he wanted her to do something different now. Zelia suddenly realized she was rather tired. So very tired from unceasing cleansing. Her head naturally came to rest on his offered shoulder, and she slowly transferred her weight as she stopped holding herself up.

Sunny didn't have any issues supporting her. He could see it in her face that she was exhausted. Zelia had no concept of what certain expressions on a human face meant, but it was easy for him to recognize her stress from being overburdened.

How much time had passed for them? Their meetings went a little faster than the rest of the Soul Space. Something about the **Time Law** being held in their inner circle table. It didn't matter. He'd check her work later, and just be a supportive adoptive parent for now. This *Divine* thing was not for him, but family? Family he could do. "Come sit with me, my dear."

The Arachnae didn't fully understand how she was supposed to do that, but her Divine was creating heaps of floof with minimal effort. Grand pillows! Oversized equivalents of the soft trinket! Except that they were outright massive, and plushier in touch than her own spider silk.

Her pride felt dented. Something dared be softer than her silk? This was a personal challenge. Settling on the pillows, she felt soothed. Each pillow creation radiated a tender copy of Artorian's starlight Aura, and that did wonders for the mind and body. It was so cozy, Zelia had to actively fight to stay awake, and her children chittered and clicked at her in worry. She sleepily clicked back that they should stop warring, and focus on hive and nest building. So, they did.

Zelia wished to speak, but found her head falling into a very welcoming lap. Her eyes were heavy, and as a hand brushed over her attempt at hair, she dozed off and fell asleep without a fear in the world.

<Well, that's precious. I thought you didn't like spiders?> Cal's voice resounded in Artorian's head, and he responded calmly.

<My misunderstandings and personal faults are to blame for many things, great spirit. That does not mean I have to hold onto them. Her name is Zelia, and she is my first named Beast. I'm not fully convinced you didn't have a hand in it, given the 'broken' object I found clutched in her grasp. What do you need?>

Cal was to the point, but his tone carried a hint of worry. <Any progress on your Kaiju quandary?>

Artorian didn't see a reason not to take care of two minds, while he was at it. <None. I'm a bad matchup. My current abilities rely on Mana techniques and spells, and the blasted thing is something worse than immune. It's *repellent*. The bigger the effect I throw at it, the higher the chance my attack gets reflected. Being hit by your own abilities is awful. I'm checking in on my named one while trying to strike at my confounding and conjure a solution. The Earth Lance had the best results, but that exoskeleton is mad thick.>

Cal pondered it over for a moment. <So, if you had a solid enough item, moving at significant enough velocity. You could crack it?>

Artorian thought that was actually quite reasonable. <I tried that. I applied my Rail Palm to a rock held between my fingers. It sped off, but the rock just shattered on the shell. Not a dent, just a stone that became powder. My current musings are on higher **Law** functions. It's costly, but if it does the job, I'll pyrite-blasted do it. I'll go full-on Gran'mama's slipper on that crabby Kaiju! As a random question that's suddenly nagging at me: Why do **Laws** eat up Essence at all?>

Cal answered the nag first. Oddly enough, that was the easiest. <**Laws** actually need Quintessence, which is the original form of Essence. Also known as Raw Essence? I'm starting to think it's a more refined, purer version of said raw Essence. It follows the opposite path of cultivation everyone else we know is going down. Still, I think that for the Heavenlies residing in the Nodes in the Tower, Quintessence is needed for some reason. So, they get some Essence together, reverse-refine it into Quin, and that's as far as I have gotten with my guesswork. On second thought, not a great answer.>

The dungeon scratched the back of its head. <I've got an idea involving totems to tackle the Kaiju. I may have to tie you to the power source for them to be effective, but that's speculation. Oh, totems are things I used early in the necromancer war to extend my dungeon influence out to places where I otherwise didn't have any. I figure if the crab rebukes overt attacks... Being surrounded by a Mana field might break it down.>

Artorian quirked a brow. <Totems. Why ever would you make something like that? Seems awfully wasteful for a war. Useful, but costly.>

In hindsight, Cal was in agreement here. <It was back in the days where I fully relied on my Presence, or my dungeon influence, to break down another dungeon Core. I had to invade its space with my totems, surround it, then contain and conquer. It's a good thing I did, too.>

A thought bothered Cal. <Considering it after all this time, I don't think I ever told anyone... but I made the totems because I deduced that the only type of threat that could offer my enemies the certain advantages they had at the time, was another dungeon. I think to many people—allies included—it may seem odd that I simply had these totems ready before ever being aware we were up against another dungeon. Honestly, I just figured it out and forgot to mention it. Likely should have done that.>

The dungeon shook it off. <Anyway, I have an idea. Come to the sun. It's about time we got that bad boy operational! Well... When you're free. I've got enough ladies mad at me and I don't want *her* added to the mix. Named ones are fiercely

loyal. Dawn's Surtur hates my guts because I tried to steal her away. That was one *angry* snake lady. *Eesh*.>

Cal winked out. <See you in the sun!>

Zelia's eyes were open and looking up when Artorian glanced down to check up on her. <My Dreamer. Your thoughts with the great spirit are *very loud.*>

Artorian snorted as he suppressed his laugh. <Yes, yes, I suppose they are. Terribly sorry, my dear. I didn't mean to wake you. I didn't know you were in the conversation. I take it you did not wish to interrupt.>

Zelia made tiny nodding motions with her face, and purpose shone in her silvery eyes. Oh dear. Oh no. What was she scheming? It was fine. He was sure it was harmless. What was the worst it could be? <My dear, are you well enough to let me go and get to work? I have to get the sun started with our great spirit.>

The Arachnae smiled innocently, and nodded again. She got up from his lap, took a prideful stance, and then gave a slight bow that she held until her Divine *fuffed* from the current antechamber.

All the pillows went with him, but her strong, healthy glow once again bloomed the chamber with silvery light. A few of her children skittered over. She had orders for them. Her voice was cutting, full of purpose, and reached them all at the same time.

"Cleanse the Kaiju."

CHAPTER TWENTY-ONE

Artorian fuffed into his sun-space living room.

It looked just like he remembered it, without a single speck of dust. His family and friends, students, and personal acquaintances remained safely stored on the wall. The separation from the main network must have kept them safe from the surprise decanting. *Good.*

Cale sat slumped at the table, looking so very tired and taxed that Artorian couldn't help but see Dale. Rather than sit across from his old disciple, Artorian dragged a chair across the floor and set it down right next to the haggard dungeon. When he sat down, he put his arm around Cale's heavy shoulders. Cale blinked, coming back to his senses. "Wha...? Why is your arm ar——"

"Hush." Cale stopped talking when the grandfather's gaze bored into him like a drill. "Do you have any idea, my boy, how exhausted you look? You haven't been taking care of yourself, and I don't need to be told that you took the backlash from that last hiccup particularly harshly. Just like Zelia, you're just not used to facial expressions. You don't seem to be aware when your face is drooping so much that it looks like it's melting. Come here, put your head down."

Artorian tugged his old disciple's head against his shoulder. Staying right next to Cale as he held the back of the youngster's head. Or what was currently a youngster, as far as the old man was concerned. A youngster that had been yelled at by all his peers, and his favorites. Over some mistakes. "Artorian, I really d—"

"Hush." Artorian wasn't having any of it. "No excuses. No deflecting. You can pretend to be peppy and energetic as a squirrel of lightning, but under no circumstances are you immune from things you think yourself invulnerable to. Even you need rest. The bubblier you get, the more you're trying to cover up something else that you're feeling."

Artorian's other arm went around Cale, softly rubbing his back like one does to console a stressed child. "Work can wait. Take the minute. You can have the minute. I'm not upset at you. I'm not mad. Stay in the physical body, and close your eyes."

Cale indeed felt significant fatigue, but he couldn't stop now. Stopping was bad. Stopping was inefficient. It should be go, go, go! "My feelings aren't…"

"Are you going to tell *the* Ascended to the Node of **Love** that feelings aren't important? No, my boy. Close your eyes, you'll feel better. I promise. Even you can't hide stress from me. Close your eyes, and listen."

Cale grumbled. This was embarrassing. A soothing hum expanded from the person he was laying on. An Auric shift? It felt so… soothing. As a dungeon Core, this kind of effect didn't really get to him. As a mind in a real body however, he felt what it was like to have prickles rush across his skin. The pleasant sensation of soft warmth encasing a form when it wakes in the morning, as the person realizes they don't need to get up yet. The experience of being just too comfortable, and no longer wanting to move. He felt sleepy. He couldn't sleep though! It was all… so important… to finish.

Cale's heavy-lidded eyes were a positive sign to Artorian, who thought Cal was burning himself out. Trying to do too much, too swiftly, and without proper care. He was glad Cal had showed up in Dale's body. He could only reason with Cal, but Dale?

Dale was human, with very human limitations. No amount of time makes one immune to feeling attacked when your core social circle is upset with you. Dale would need at least one person not upset with him. How could he deny the lad a haven?

"Everyone makes mistakes, my boy. Everyone. There is nobody and nothing that does not stumble. Everyone feels at times that they are not doing enough, or not doing well enough. That's not a slight on your efforts, that's just life. You try so hard to be perfect, my boy, but perfection is unattainable."

The *humm* gained a melodic quality. "It is a trap of thought, for once you have something that is perfect, it is either innately no longer, or you have found something else it could improve upon. There are no endpoints in the journey of improvement. Even if you find the exact, perfect thing for any given end, it is *merely* the most correct thing. The best way something can be for a single given purpose."

The melody was soft, becoming the background tune of a lullaby. "If you seek perfection, you seek folly. The most correct way something can be is more than good enough. Just like you, lad. You are also more than good enough. Your people will settle. They will forgive you. They will welcome you again, and this will have been but a bump in the road. You rush when you should rest. So, rest, my son. Rest."

The soothing effect from Artorian's Aura engulfed his old disciple, and he altered the combination to add in a pinch of the sleeping concept. His lad did not speak. Cale was just breathing softly, passed out in his supporting grasp. "Good. Good. Even an infinite mind requires interludes."

With but directed will, fire flared in the hearth of his home. As if they were eating wooden logs, the flames licked, popped, and crackled in the fireplace.

He dimmed the ambient light in the house by absorbing some of it. Wanting something to do while he played pillow, the academic surrounded a book on the shelf with his shaped Aura. With some effort, he pulled it close so it hovered open in front of him. Artorian flipped the pages without ever physically touching them, and read patiently just to create a little background noise as the fire crackled pleasantly.

A good while later, a Silverwood root broke up from the floor and formed a kaleidoscopic portal. Grace, the youngest Wisp, zipped around. She was curious and in full on search mode. She was looking for... There! She found her daddy napping on the thick robes of grandfather, and the old man had no intention of letting him up while Cale sawed forests down with each snore. Grace hovered nearby while his calming, slow, sleep-inducing tones read from the open book. It made her drowsy, and her zippiness wavered as she stopped flying in a straight line.

Her descent was caught by a platform of fuzzy light. It felt like solidified fluff while it carried her over to deposit her on Cale's head. Just like her papa, the littlest Wisp nested in place and fell asleep. She'd come to play, but naps were always good!

Dani burst from the kaleidoscope portal shortly after, panicked and stricken. Why had she ever taught Grace how to portal-form? Now she could lose track of her anytime!

Artorian knew she'd arrived. *Shh*. "Up here."

Dani hadn't exactly been making much sound, but her energy and activity was gently hushed as Artorian picked back up from the line in the book he'd been reading. Dani would have snapped with a physical voice, but the serene effect of the scene was profound. There was something nice about seeing Cale actually take a nap, with Grace nested peacefully. <Artorian? What... how did you make him sleep? He's immune to... oh. Real body. Oh, you clever, scheming old man. I should be so mad at you right now. He has work to do, but...> *Sigh*.

Artorian winked gently with a sly, scheming smile. Just to prove her right. <Hello, Dani, it's lovely to meet you under

circumstances that don't require immediate action. I do apologize for nicking your people, but even a halfwit could see the strain and need for sleep. I don't know if Cal ever slept, but Cale does need to. If he wants to spend time in that body, he is *not* free from its limitations. I'm not sure if the other supervisors notice, but I am aware of many of the visual changes he makes to his soul world. I try to limit my vision so I don't poke my nose in, but I'm not unaware just how much it is that he does. He needs a few *years* of snooze, let the world just turn.>

Dani settled on the table. As a Wisp, she had perfect movement in any direction. Her tone was half-joking. <Are you going to sit here for a few years and let him nap there?>

Artorian considered it. <Yes, if I must. I'm more likely to tuck him in, but I'd prefer to be nearby when he wakes up so I can make him some breakfast. Couple eggs, some savory meat. Couple vegetables. *Mmm*! A potato! If I can get my hands on one. Some tea. Ooh, tea. Love me some of that quality hot leaf juice.>

The violet Wisp stifled her giggle. <That's sweet, Artorian. I… I may have been harsh recently. That big Pylon problem might have been a few years of work where you're concerned, but he's been working on it at normal speed. He's been carving those Pylons for millennia. It's not uncommon that he speeds back up and doesn't at all have a solid grasp of how much time has passed for us. I know for a fact he's been sulking. He just threw himself at his work with people upset with him, and this is… this is nice.>

The old man nodded empathically. <That is what it is meant to be, and I appreciate your perspective that it is so. Why don't we get this lad into a nice bed, tuck him in, and take care of a few things while he catches those Z's? I'm pretty sure I can get this sun up and running… somehow. The ambient light is nice, but a natural day-night cycle can't be beat. The circadian rhythms of creatures need to stabilize; they're all stressed all the time.>

Dani looked around, saw past the walls, and inspected the

plethora and great mixture of Runes splattered all over the sun's rings. <How much do you know about Runes?>

Artorian was looking at the exact same thing, and his head cocked from side to side. *Mmmm...* <Whole lot of nothing. You need esoteric? I'm your man. Nitty gritty woodworking details? I couldn't put that cabinet together unless I had both help and was staying out of the way of the person actually working. It has been far too long since I've practiced those skills. Then again, if I have a few years while the great snorer over here is resting his spirit, consider my sleeves pushed to the elbows, and I'll figure it out. What's the worst that could happen?>

The violet Wisp stopped all movement. <Do you know what a jinx is? I think your tally must be fairly sizable. Know what? Sure. Go ahead. If it *blows up*, Cal will just have to make a new one and then he'll feel better for not being the one with the biggest mess up. A win either way. Now arms up, I'm taking my two children to bed. I'll be there when they wake up, you just make *progress* on this sun thing.>

<You got it, boss lady.> The book moved in place of his hand, saluting the Wisp. Dani formed a field around both her babies and widened the kaleidoscopic portal, hovering them both through before going herself.

<Good luck. Try not to set the world on fire?> With a wink, she was gone. The Silverwood root retreated back beneath self-mending floorboards, and just like that Artorian sat alone in the stilled sun. He drew a deep breath, and leaned back in the chair. The book landed on the table with a clap, and he rolled his shoulders pensively.

When the root was entirely gone, a tiny smile curved upward on the edge of his lips. He spoke to himself, but it was wistful, and not entirely without plotted enjoyment.

"Well... Sweet mercy, Cal, your Wisp is *clever*. She saw right through me. Progress, you say? Alright, Dani, I'll make some *progress*."

CHAPTER TWENTY-TWO

"Bright, too bright! Hold! *Ho~old!*" Sparks flew copiously as the heat pushed him away, rebuking Artorian all by itself. The solar rings spun so fast they not only caught fire, but caused full on electric waves of some kind. Artorian's hair bristled, entrenched in a heavy static field. Everywhere his face wasn't obscured by borrowed Gnome goggles, it was sooty and sunburned.

Artorian's ordinarily snow-white beard was peppered with ash. The ends were frayed and split, but his smile shone undaunted as he used every ounce of his Mage strength to keep this *one* cable in place. He laughed maniacally, for he was close to success!

Deverash screamed at him over the mental connection, and even that loud of a message was barely audible over the wretched screeching of rings that weren't properly spinning on their own yet. The resulting thudding struck deep, and each clang was both a gut punch and an instant headache. <Slow it down. Slow it down! You are seven-hundred percent over capacity! The construct can't hold this! Artorian. Artorian! Slow it down! I have blown up my fair share of war machines to know this isn't going to hold!>

The old man hollered back with all the confidence of a blind faithful. <She'll hold! Now add more power, turn those Runes on! More power, Dev! *More power*! Bahahaha!>

Deverash felt stunned. More? What did he mean *more*? The entire thing was rigged to blow. When it did, the fallout debris hurled at blinding speeds was going to eat entire chunks out of the surrounding continents. People were screaming at him in the senate to stop his madness, and several of the supervisors were already scrambling toward him to halt this catastrophe in the making. <Fine! You want more? Here's more! Flip the breaker, boys! Slam that accumulator until it's tapped, and if she goes boom, then we'll make it the biggest boom!>

A horde of other Gnomes near Dev cheered, hooted, and fist pumped to the sky in unison as several of them jumped to hang from an oversized lever. A good thirty of them piled on the switch, and their cumulative weight and strength was finally enough to drop the sturdy lever. With a gnarly click, even the lever seemed to dispute that this was a good idea. Cracking loud as thunder, the full torrent of captured Mana from Vanaheim's storms poured through the semi-ethereal cable Artorian was keeping steady with everything he had.

Deverash couldn't even figure out what the cable was, and all he had gotten out of the old madman was 'Higher **Law** function!' Whatever that was supposed to be. As the power blew one capacitor, then two, one of the accumulators outright shattered into dust. That very matter was sucked up and slammed into the cable. Pouring into whatever batty, convoluted contraption Artorian had set up in his house.

The center of the sun was now so bright that Dev couldn't even look at it. Even with his specialized goggles and Mana shielding.

Wild screeching from interconnected rings pitched louder, tearing and ripping the very air around them as some rather upset *clunk* sounds clicked into place within the complicated-as-can-be solar contraption.

Dev again tried to make his voice heard. <Sunny! Your cable! It's siphoning directly from the Mana storms in Vanaheim! The transfer Pylons can't handle this! You're eating up a continent's worth of Mana! Stop!>

"Artori… aaah!" Occultatum arrived first, but had to immediately turn away from the sheer blinding brightness. Even his A-ranked body was rebuked by the raw pressure this sun-in-progress was putting off. Rather than try to yell at the old fool a second time, his mental voice lurched toward the others. <Don't port in, do not port in! Not safe!>

<We figured, Tatum! That's why we're flying over.> Chandra snapped at him through the senate, but her upset venting was interrupted by a most pleased cackle as Artorian yelled at seemingly nobody. For whoever the recipient was supposed to be, couldn't be here.

Artorian's words thrummed with power. Intoning deep, primal, connective might. His **Law** was present in full force, and whatever designs he had in mind were materializing.

<How do you like that, you ancient crafters and self-righteous know-better-than-thou's? No sun Node in the Tower? Fine! Scaredy-cats! You go through all the trouble to make an Ascension track and you forget *the sun*? Do you know who you're dealing with? Hey, *five hundred and fifty-five*! **Acceptance, Accept** this! *Hiyaah*!>

The Glitterfold was shaking, and floor five hundred and fifty-five wasn't doing so hot. On the contrary, actually. As it was very, very hot. Specifically, the first all-affinity **Law** on that floor wasn't having a good time as a **Law** about one hundred and sixty-five levels above it was very **Lovingly** suggesting an… alteration.

The only Ascended of **Love** was trying to apply some tough **Love** to a higher up that he would otherwise have no say over. When prompted why her Ascended would even attempt such a thing, all Artorian did at the merest brush of the question was show his Node the memory of his interaction with the **Accep-**

tance Node. The self-entitlement **Acceptance** displayed made **Love** realize just how full of itself that Node was. **Acceptance** should not be contingent on a conditional, nor by devious intent. **Love** was furious, and with the full memories of what her Ascended was scheming.

She smiled as only a livid mother could.

Artorian's own smile did not fade. For while the sun construct was definitely straining, the actual goal of pouring oceans of Mana into his **Law** for this particular bit of vengeance was the most savory and cathartic thing he'd attempted all decade. He'd have to thank Dawn for the secret formula later. Like she'd said when he hung in outer space: A physical object, a nonphysical object, a metaphysical object, a **Law** connection that fits his theme, and an Essence signature. Intimate knowledge sympathies made things work!

It was even easier this time, as several of the requirements overlapped! The sun Core in Cal's Soul Space outright covered the first three, his own **Love Law** connection for the theme, and his memory of the **Acceptance** Node for the Essence signature connection. All bundled in a nicely-wrapped package of intent.

Dawn had said talking to him out in space was costly, but that was fine. He had experience with oversized and unruly Mana storms, and if the previous one could cross out every A-ranked demon and down from the planet, it would surely be a nice snack for *his* **Law** as they, together, enacted this unified improvement to the tower. It was, after all, just a matter of energy.

The other supervisors were taking shelter behind Tatum's darkshield as they arrived. Rebuked by the sheer clashing intensity of forces as the sun Core made the kind of noises even A-rankers didn't want to be around. They didn't see the truth behind the interaction, and only the prior S-rankers could feel something deeper was afoot.

When Dawn arrived, she threw up her own shield to absorb rampant heat and brightness. That did much to make this encounter bearable. Now she was hungry. She missed jerky. She'd steal a bear from Jotunheim just for this.

Deverash ran for his life, and the other Gnomes followed him as the noise reached the kind of crescendo that told even the most amateur of crafters that events had deftly entered the realm of 'not good.' An inner ring cracked loose, shattered, and the other rings pulverized and mulched it to dust. <Sunny, she's falling apart! Abort, abort! Get out of there! I've gathered all the memory stones like you wanted. We got the whole wall. We're moving them to Vanaheim! Run!>

Laughter was all they heard at first. <Good! Get them out of here. We didn't need that swivel-section! Just a little longer! It's working. Dev, it's working! Enough energy *just* got through! It's done! The Node! It's do—"

Pop.

The explosion was so intense that it was entirely soundless. The shattered sun threw chunks of itself all over the Soul Space. As expected, fractured ring sections impacted every continent like falling meteors. Devastating and rearranging the landscape here and there. Anything that had previously been in those spots was solidly dead or demolished, and the burning fragments sizzled with impossible heat as they remained embedded in the landscape like some shrine from an age gone by. Bits of the runic construct were littered everywhere.

Those that had gone past the acceptable bounds of Cal's Soul Space decided to be cheeky, rebounded, and hit something anyway. Leaving the undersides of a few continents with some truly inspiring new decorations.

Artorian died with a smile on his face.

Being point-blank right next to the origination of the blast made his end spontaneous, accompanied by the most spectacular cultivator-caused explosion in history. He became particles, his mind automatically snapping to his Core in the Silverwood Tree.

The entire Soul Space curled in a wave as if someone picked it up like a blanket, and dusted it a single time. The movement allowed a single deep ripple to carry over the entire area. Unfortunately, that was also enough to finally wake Cale up. Whose first wonder was why he had such an intense stomach ache, and why it was so bright. The dungeon took the equivalent of a breath, and asserted control of his entire space. Smoothing it out like a map laid on the table. <Dani?>

Dani bobbed nearby as he, still in Dale's body, lay on a bed on the surface of Niflheim. <Yes, dear?>

Cale blinked and, for a moment, really did not want to get up. Though only for a moment as he rose slowly, knowing something incredible had just gone wrong. <What did I miss just now? I know I was asleep, as strange as that is, but something really hurt a moment ago. It's gone now, and everything feels fine aside from a gaping hole in… oh no.>

Dani hummed and dropped a plate of eggs, veggies, meat, and a potato in his lap. <*Mhm.* I'm sure it's very important, but before you do anything, you're going to enjoy breakfast. Eat up.>

He considered springing to action, but knew better. Cale looked down at the plate, picked it up, and did as he was told. It was so tasty! He didn't know Dani was an utter and complete master chef. What the him! <Dani, this is amazing! It's so good!>

Cale scarfed it down, and then awkwardly paused mid-bite, a piece of bacon sticking out of his mouth. <Are you trying to distract me from what just happened, and possibly the reason my entire sun-in-progress is over there, and there, and there?>

Dani dropped an extra serving of cooked eggs on his plate. <*Hmm?* Don't worry about it. Someone went through a lot of trouble to make sure that when you woke up, you didn't have a reason to feel so bad anymore. Also, I'm fairly certain that cleared all those jinxes off his plate. It was a little forced, but if they were going to slot in anywhere, that was a great place for them to go. It's like he could calculate his luck, or something.>

Cale cautiously ate the eggs, wanting to ask more. However, his supervisors all popped in to visit Niflheim together, preventing him from doing so. All of them? Oh wow, all of them. Except the Administrator? Why would he be miss—*Oooh*.

"Cale. Cale! Are you feeling alright?!" Marie, Chandra, Brianna, and Tatum were all bolting toward him while the rest dawdled behind with more of an unsteady meander. Dev, for some reason, was doing his utmost to hide behind Odin's left foot.

The person in question, with his mouth still full of breakfast, gave a solid thumbs up. He swallowed as he was surrounded, using the offered napkin from Dani to wipe his mouth off. "Hey, all. It's not inner circle time yet. I feel fine! I think? Woke up with some indigestion, but aside from my sun project being mysteriously missing from where I last put it, there doesn't feel to be a big disturbance. My Essence intake is proceeding without issues as normal, and... oh... ooooh, that looks like it hurt. Wow, am I glad I was asleep. Something used my **Law** and soul and an intermediary for a *whole bunch* of energy and that would not have been pleasant to be awake for. I think I can go ahead and guess who was responsible, given the easily observable facts."

The supervisors were still stricken with worry, but if Cale said nothing further was amiss... well, then nothing further was amiss. Instead, he seemed extremely happy about something. That it was that none of them were in the slightest upset at him, and all came running to check on his well-being and care, they did not know. To him, it meant the world. "Why don't we bring our sun destroyer back and ask what happened?"

Dawn crossed her arms and raised an eyebrow. "No time penalty?"

Cal shrugged. "Oh, there will likely be a penalty, but I don't think I will need to impose one for there to be one. From the look of the new architecture on all the continents, and several wrecked personal projects, you all will have plenty to say. I'm just going to clean up some, when breakfast is over. Besides, as far as I can tell, he took a lot of energetic mass, and played around just to drive it home. Look at the giant hole in Jotun-heim. He's going to have fun fixing that."

Hmmm. "Mass Driver? Now those are words that I like. I think I can do something with that. Hey, Dev, quit hiding and come over. I've got an idea for a little project."

CHAPTER TWENTY-THREE

Nobody had a chance to get a word in until Dawn was done shaking Sunny down. She had him by the front of the robes like a wet rag pressed to a metal washboard, and was berating him up and down the entirety of existence to scrub him of foolishness.

How dare he pull nonsense like that! What if his mind had been irreparably damaged! He should be happy it was just his body that had atomized. If he ever got such a foolish idea in his head and went through with it again, she would skip the line and atomize him herself for sheer idiocy! "You will apologize to Jorm before you fix your mess. Your wreckage caught the poor baby right at the end of his tail. It's all sore and swollen! When the others are done with you, you *will* come right over and take care of him."

Artorian held the back of his head and apologized profusely, but it wasn't enough. Each supervisor read him his rights; and Cale slurped delicious milk from an oversized coconut in the background. It was loud too, and he didn't bother hiding the sound in the slightest. It was as if he was slurping up catharsis.

Even Dani sat nearby, wearing a pair of sunglasses that covered her entire Wisp body.

When the last of the supervisors returned to their respective regions, Artorian fell back and collapsed on the grass, laid out and tired. It was even a brand-new body. Didn't matter. He was *so* tired. Cale looked at his coconut with sudden disinterest and chimed in. "So, my turn?"

Artorian slapped both of his hands to his face. Hiding it from the world as he groaned. "Not *you* too."

Dani snickered, but Cale got up and walked over. "Of course, me too! You still broke my sun project; made off with quite a chunk of Mana, solved a Vanaheim problem that really wasn't yours to tackle, and if my soul had a tailbone it would be sore. You also aren't taking the timeout penalty, so I'm assigning something else to Jotunheim instead."

Artorian groaned more, still flat on the ground and unwilling to move his hands away. "That being?"

Cale mused with entertained delight. "People! I am adding *people* to Jotunheim. I have a bunch of B-rankers that were decanted in the C and below regions, and I was wondering where to plop them, temporarily or otherwise. There are also some people in the lower regions that don't belong. As you're also one of the few supervisors that doesn't have a proper civilization working, why not? Unless you were planning to do it all with your beloved spiders."

The defeated old man mumbled from behind his hands. "Do what you want, Cale."

Cale nodded with a smile, checking the vicinity to make sure everyone else had left. "Oh. I will! Now that that's out of the way, what did you actually do that taxed my soul so much? The real reason I'm not as upset as I am, is that, *somehow*, you got me part of a rank. Not a full rank, but a chunk. I think a portion of it is from what you were saying as I was falling asleep. The perfecting thing? Finding the most optimal method and best way something could be does sound more plau—"
Whoop!

The Soul Space thrummed, and for a moment all the supervisors stopped what they were doing. All of them wore the same expression on their face: they didn't want to be bothered, and yet someone was at their door. They were going to… ignore this. Cal had just ranked up.

Cale shook his head. "Well, that was a rush. I guess that's the other half? What did you do to my sun for it to blow? Because it really shouldn't have done that."

Artorian dropped his hands from his face, sighed heavily, and got to it. "All that problem Mana from Vana? Well, the Gnomes were trying their best to stuff it all back into accumulators before it tore more of their civilization to shreds, and glassed the rest of their continent. So, I offered a solution. Using my **Law**, I leaned heavily on the connective aspect and formed a cable from Vanaheim to the sun when they were geophysically close to one another. Your whole 'rotating around Hel' bit came in useful there."

He scratched at his beard. "I knew it was going to take a lot of juice to get that sun working, but I also knew I probably wasn't going to be able to do it without a full working knowledge of what every Rune did, or where to start. I figured that out at the exact moment where I realized I had gotten started and there was no real going back. I wasn't going to get that sun to start up as intended. So… I had a *different* idea. Who said I had to start the project from *your* end?"

The old man sat up, needing to hold the side of his head to cope. "You are Runes, and facts, and nitty gritty. Honestly, Cale, you've got that covered without me. So, I thought, what is an idea so ludicrous that Cale would need me for it? That's where I started rubbing my hands together. For I had a plan! A devious, impossible plan! Do you remember Ascending in the Tower? Every single Node that you met? I can tell you I certainly do not, but there were a few that stood out. Some good, some bad."

Artorian was starting to smile. Coming to the full realization of what he'd hopefully accomplished. "One of those bad eggs was the first all-affinity **Law**, with a strong focus on acceptance. Push comes to shove, turns out that it's a greedy, self-centered **Law** focused entirely on its own merits. While it espoused 'acceptance,' it did so under dubious conditions. It always struck me as a thorn in my side how a concept without strings could have so many of them. It hid them well, but it could not hide from my philosophy."

Dani bobbed over and gave the old man some water, which was certainly appreciated as he talked. "So here I sit in your Soul Space. With a **Law** that puts emphasis on connections, a vast energy source free for the taking, a **Law** that's a pain in my keister, and *this sun* that's not working. So, I think to myself. Wouldn't it just be *grand*, if there was a **Law** in the Tower that actually, directly had to do with the sun? Not the empyreal stellar formations, not the moons. The sun. Direct and pointed. Then I thought to myself, why yes. Yes, it would be, and that would be such a help for getting an actual sun in place here."

Cale remained silent; his face twisted with concern at what he was being told. The wily old fox continued with newfound energy, his hands clasping together as he acted out the revelation with additional drama and show.

"Oh look, would you look at that? I found a spot! Now, I'm no buffoon; I knew I couldn't possibly affect the Tower of Ascension, much less the Nodes in it. Especially if the theory 'that's where the Heavenlies are' holds water. However, I know for a fact that the Nodes up top—the ones we are tied to—have some serious personality. Their charisma and magnetism are otherworldly. Unlike me, I believe they can most certainly affect something in the Tower, especially when it ranks below them, with a convenient bonus when they have a nearly direct thematic connection. So, with all the components in place, I got started. When my Node came knocking with a 'what in the Cal are you doing' …I recalled certain memories."

Snap. Artorian snapped his fingers with a luminous grin. "Just like that, she was onboard. All we needed was enough raw energy and power to get it done. It was down to the wire, and I knew I'd be obliterated. Yet it was as you said, that the sun project didn't look like it could break. So, I used that factor as an additional anchor, and poured on the Mana! I would say it cost easily a planet's worth of Mana, but uh… You should try to conjure up an image of a sun's pattern. Just saying."

Cal remained a statue of apprehension. He turned to look at Dani for approval first, and only when she nodded a 'go ahead' did he raise his palm and attempt to discern a sun's pattern.

His eyes went wide as the constantly-evolving deep core emanations of a sun moved and twisted. The living pattern blazed into being on his hand. He was awed, silent at the sights before him as his **Acme** Mana filled in the blanks and grew the diagram. This was it! The pattern of a sun! Straight from a repurposed Node in the Tower that was delighted for its knowledge to be put to immediate use. It just about rushed to hand over the pattern, and **Acme** traded delicious Quintessence for it.

Cal didn't even notice Dawn teleport in with the swiftest hurry of her life. She was intrinsically drawn to the pattern of anything fire, and this one screamed for her as the **Law** of **Fire** craved the knowledge of such a high-tiered pattern. Her black hole supernova eyes took the pattern in, and if her Incarnate rank had been able to increase at that moment, it would have. Since Dawn could not… Unbeknownst to any of them, a different conversation began in the Tower of Ascension.

Dawn too, stood in awed silence as Artorian fell back down on his butt. He finally had the full headache, eating the mental backlash of being atomized. Something he'd rather not do again. Materializing a cornucopia of pillows around him, Artorian snuggled up and got cozy. *Ahhh*. "Much better."

Dawn nudged a mesmerized Cale in the shoulder. "Are you all done with him?"

Cale remained enraptured by the sights. Fascination

pouring from him in the form of bubbly enthusiasm. "Oh yes. I have completely forgotten what other penalties I was going to apply. Forget my first sun. I did it all wrong! This is— Oh yes. Oh. *Ohoho*! We're in business, boys!"

Dawn smiled at him. "Good! Don't mind if I take this!"

Artorian had momentarily been comfortable. Unfortunately, his pillows discorporated as Dawn grabbed him by the collar of his robe, and snatched him away. *Vwumph*!

His butt hit a pile of sand. Alright, pile wasn't fair to say where there was nothing but sand. The air was heavy, and hot. The increased gravity of Muspelheim hit him like a ton of bricks as it stacked onto his shoulders, but still he forced himself upright. "Yes, yes. Jorm's tai—"

His sentence was cut off as Dawn squeezed her arms around him and tackled him into the sand dune. She said nothing, and just held tight for dear life. Was… was she shivering? It was a little warm for… His Aura picked up the sense of lingering dread. Without another thought, he replied in kind and just held the sweetheart of flame. "I'm fine, dear. I'm fine. Didn't go anywhere. See, right back where you can hold me. All fine."

She thumped her fist harmlessly onto his chest, biting back words to get out the important ones. Her eyes were watery, and she looked up with gritted teeth. "Don't do that again. You promise me, with Mana, that you will never idiotically blow yourself up like that again."

Artorian grit his jaw back, and pressed his forehead gently to hers as he took her hand. "I promise, my dear. I won't idiotically blow myself up like that again."

The Mana tightened around his being, holding him to a new oath that would obliterate him fully if broken. The Keeper of **Oaths** kept an extra close eye on certain individuals now. He whispered softly, just to ask. "Is Jormy's tail actually hurt?"

Dawn pouted, and shook her head no. Jorm was fine. "You make me watch my most favorite person blow up and you think

I'm going to let you off easy? I don't care if your body can be remade. I was worried sick. I felt my heart drop all the way into my stomach, and if I didn't feel you appear back in Niflheim, I think I would have tried to tear the whole Soul Space apart. Just hold me, you idiot."

Artorian smiled, nodded, and sighed. "I love you too, dear. I'll be here as long as you'd like, until someone lights a fire under our butts to make me go back to work."

The Soul of Fire felt flushed, but didn't correct anything. Her voice mumbled, "Pillows. The sand is coarse."

By her request, sand was vacated to make way for a tiny paradise of pillows. It was much softer and less annoying to lay on than sand. He even added a tent roof for style points. Honestly the difference was minor for a Mana body, but if Dawny was happy, that went a long way.

Her voice cracked. "Do you really?"

The academic just nodded to her continued mumbling. "Of course, I do. How could I not? If you're wondering why I haven't mentioned it? It is because I don't feel it right to throw one's feelings at another mind. Not without their assent and acceptance. The smoother ones such as minor grumbles, and worries, and complaints. The soft feelings that do no real harm save but inform. Those are fine. The large, heart-reliant and life-turning decisions?"

He shook his head. "No, those are either mutual, or not mentioned. To impose one's feelings on another without concern for their side is... Just no. It's not me. It doesn't sit well. You have called me your best friend for decades, and if that is where you are comfortable, then that is where I shall stay, and be no fussier for it. It's not a limitation, merely the place I am happy you are willing to spend time with me."

He snickered a moment. "I must admit that I do also feel a little odd about being a rather old man hanging around a very, very pretty Fire Soul. Yet that in terms of age, you so vastly have me beat. *Ow*!"

"Don't poke at a lady's age, youngblood." She was leering at him through her lashes, but it wasn't a damning one. Merely some playful jabbing. "It's... difficult. I am Dawn, but the majority of me remembers life as Ember. The new bonfire perspective? It lets me act and *be* in a way I would have never felt comfortable before. I have gotten to be bratty. Selfish. I have had the opportunity to truly live for myself rather than some endless warring cause. I liked it because it was so new, and freeing. Yet as the decades roll by, I feel myself slipping back to Ember. The stability is profound, and as much as I try and cling to the Dawn perspective... The Incarnation is changing."

She squeezed his hand back a little, enough to feel the comfort as she got a worry off her chest. "Not having an S-ranked body here is causing some problems I haven't wanted to talk about. One of them is that without that form—our souls and minds being one—we are malleable and extremely subject to change. If I wanted to become Ember again... I could. Easily, too. I just don't think I want to. I... I heard about the joke Cal played on you. He gave you a body from your prime, yet you rejected it instantly? I was told that it was because 'it just wasn't you anymore' and hearing that helped me in some way."

She half-flopped into the pillows, just to get snug. "As an Incarnate, that's so important. Knowing oneself is the cornerstone of your being. I asked Tatum, as he's been one for so long. Unfortunately, he doesn't know what happens if your core values move around after you've Incarnated. Apparently, it doesn't happen? Yet, it is happening. The solidity that was supposed to ground me doesn't exist here. So, having you around helps. Do you know how lost I was as Ember? Entire centuries of my memories are hazy clouds of blood and death. That forest? I woke up there."

Dawn continued, and Sunny listened quietly. "Ember had three phases of life, of which two counted: The beginning, and the end. The entire middle is a muddled mess. At the end, when I woke up... Yeah, you were old for a human. Regardless of your age, you could be such a child. You're petulant, tempestuous, stubborn to a fault, and you can't help but stick your nose into trouble. You look old, yet even through loss and labor you had all the energy when it came down to having some fun. Like an endless well you cheated into existence. It was so appealing. This idea that the old, and weathered, and bordering the end of life could still have such a heart filled with splendor."

Dawn rolled over, and lay on her back to look at the sky. "You didn't judge me. You didn't play to the stereotypes. You asked what I needed and kicked the rest to the curb. You were such a pain at times, and yet you did it because it would help me. There were days that I wanted to skip you over a lake like a rock. Then there were days I just sat there with my hand against my cheek and watched you work magic with words. Some days I watched you explode, and sometimes, perhaps even on that same day, I watched you pull the pattern of a sun out of your pocket, just to *give it* to someone."

She looked at him softly, and had difficulty speaking. Her bashful side was back. "I think that's why I love you. I thought ill of you those first few years, for it seemed that so often that you took a topic, and made it about you. Then the punchline came, and you've got the answer in hand for *someone else*. With that dumb little so-proud-of-yourself smile on your face, like it was no big deal. You just atomized yourself to give Cal a single pattern, for crying out loud. Don't think I didn't notice that you got all of the heat off of him at the same time. I will be gossiping with Dani about that later."

She swallowed once more. "Thank you. For… just letting me be me, and not putting your foot in front of my pace. I like best friends. Just… don't be upset if it might be true that you mean a little more to me. Okay?"

Artorian softly patted her hand in support. "Do you mind if I get another hug, my dear?"

Dawn just smiled and squeezed the life out of him. "You're the best, Sunny. Who knows? Maybe when you Incarnate, you'll form a body that isn't a geezer. Maybe you'll feel better then."

She snickered, and Artorian smiled pleasantly at the jab. "I think geezer is just right for me. Let it be. I'm having a good time lying around in the desert with my bestie, and no, my dear, I don't mind one bit. Proud of you for being able to get your feelings out. *Ow*! Why did I get hit that time?"

The Incarnate was leering at him again. "Did you even notice that you ranked up when I said it? B-rank *five*, boy."

CHAPTER TWENTY-FOUR

Deverash was waiting for Artorian in Jotunheim.

He heard the **fuff** of arrival, and slid off the statue of the Administrator. It was a new addition on the pathway leading up to the multi-tiered pagoda on the top of the tallest mountain.

The old man himself hadn't even noticed Cal's practical joke yet. The dungeon had a knack for making statues come out of the ground of embarrassing events that should be remembered. Sunny's voice came from within like a tired grandfather who was expecting company. "Come in! I'm aware you're there. Door's unlocked."

The Gnome opened the door just by pushing.

The entry level of the pagoda was all comfort, no business. Artorian lay sprawled out around a buffet of food. He'd just flopped down to start shoving it all into his mouth. This body had never eaten before, and everything tasted new, even though he knew the flavor. Experiencing something for the first time again could at times be exquisite. Dev pointed at some grapes. "Mind if I…?"

The old man gave a wave of assent as he tore chunks out of bear brisket. He was clearly too occupied with eating for such trifles. If hungry, eat! Gnomish culture had changed over the last few years, but declining a free meal was certainly not in the rules. The duo of old friends ate until their bellies were big.

The more human of them released burps, but Deverash waved that silly little emanation away as some paltry oddity. His own belch scared house-sized birds away from the mountain, and Artorian waved his hand to open the windows for ventilation. "Pyrite, Dev! How did you even get it that loud! Never mind, my ears are still normalizing. I take it you're not here on a social visit."

Deverash daintily wiped his face off, the picture of dapperness once more. "The Jotuns have been decanted and are running free, but that's not my part of the business. I'm here to finish a special project that your sun-splosion started. It actually wasn't that hard once we had all the components. Do you mind if I explain the concept?"

The academic gave a pleasing thumbs up. "I am all for not moving, and listening to concepts. That's my jam."

Gnomish contraptions spilled out from Dev's sleeve. "I've been developing a ton of goodies. I call this one a 'projector.' Can't do the free-floating images Cal does, but I can project a static image so long as I have a flat surface. It's on your ceiling."

They both looked up, and Artorian was quickly interested. "One of the functions Cal was trying to get out of the solar spin research was to solve that Kaiju problem. Particularly, borrowing spin from the sun, in order to slingshot a projectile down at it. Like a sling, except exponentially larger. In pursuit of that idea, us Gnomes gnomed around some. We ended up with fully-functional Runes pertaining to magnetic matter acceleration. That static field you formed around the sun was a big help."

Dev altered the images he was projecting, and shoved the flat version of a Rune on the ceiling. "This is what we're calling the [Mass Driver] spell Rune. It can propel any material ferrous enough at the same velocity you broke that sun apart with. Additionally, while Cal discovered that you could not put Runes on flesh because it would distort meridian patterns, that is not true for Mages. No meat."

Artorian no longer liked where this was going. "I see. Where, then, are these Runes supposed to go?"

The Gnome clicked his contraption to the next slide, and an image of a hand showed; with arrows and descriptions of what was supposed to go where. "On the touching sides of your middle and ring finger, in a fashion so that when your fingers press together the Runes overlap near-perfectly. If you charge these linked Runes with Mana, it will build what we're calling a 'charge' that transfers the built-up energy into the ferrous projectile, causing it to propel forward. The heavier the material, the better. So, with some help, we've prepared a pouch of Iridium Li. Those old Morovian coins of yours? Was a fun joke down with the development team."

The academic deeply kneaded his brow. "I take it I don't have much of a choice in the matter of being a guinea pig?"

"Nope!" Dev beamed, hiding some secret enjoyment to get back at his friend for one of those rampant sun shards, that may or may not have wrecked a particularly sensitive project. "It's probably also going to hurt when applying them. Remember that we have to redo this every time you get a new body."

Artorian groaned. "Great."

The explosions of Mana from the decanted were getting awfully close by the time Deverash was done a few days later. While the Gnome worked, Artorian winced and tried to distract himself.

They listened to the new 'Jotuns' make a right mess of things outside. For some unknown reason, possibly because the pagoda on the tallest mountain was the only real building on the whole continent, the Mages were fighting their way toward it. Who knew why they were doing that, but it was a trend all the decanted seemed to be in on. They had also discovered that killing creatures refunded them a chunk of their Mana. Delightful.

On the upside, Artorian's cleaning duties had severely lessened. On the downside, they were hoarding 'broken' items and creatures rather than destroying or containing them. Dev had also not lied about the pain involved in the Rune carving process. They literally had to go *in* his Mana form, and had to be added in a way so that healing didn't make them go away. Nasty business, but that was the fate he'd picked.

Best to just roll with the punches. Lots and lots of punches.

When Dev was done, he put his instruments away. The front door of the pagoda blew inwards shortly afterwards. Mostly in splintered form.

"Oh, come now, I just repainted last year. Is cyan not popular anymore?" Artorian threw his hands into the air with an immediate complaint, as some B-ranked Mage with singed and frazzled short black hair burst shoulder-first into his pagoda. The man was flummoxed at first. Wasn't... what?

He collected himself, righted, and threateningly pointed his finger. "I am Quan Chilly! I challenge the master of this place for ownership of the domain!"

Artorian blinked, and looked to Dev for a moment, who equally had no clue what the B-ranker was on about. <You might want to think of something, Sunny, I don't think you're in a state where you can fight. Not after a multi-day procedure like that. You need to rest and let those Runes normalize unless you want to start all over again.>

Nodding slowly, the old man wrested himself from his seat with a grunt. "Excellent! I've been waiting so long for someone to show up. Unfortunately, my boy, I am not the master of this mountain, I am its caretaker. My role is to await the one that will become the master of this domain. Since you are here, I take it you've brought the key so you can take over right away?"

Quan looked unsteady, peering about suspiciously at the pillow-laden hotspot. "What... key?"

Artorian frowned, and looked to Dev. "Did we not put up a ton of signs? I could swear we littered instructions all over the place."

The Gnome nodded sagely, as if he was completely right.

"Everywhere. Couldn't have missed them unless you did something dumb like blindly run up the side of the mountain. But nobody would do that."

They both over-the-shoulder glanced at Quan, who, based on the rock and dirt still clinging to his pants, had done exactly that. Artorian just shook his head gently. "You're in the right place to become master of the mountain, but in order to actually get that done, you need the key. You know, the one that the big crab in the depths below is guarding? I even made a giant hole for you all to enter through. Bring the key to the pagoda, you become the master of the domain, and I can go home."

Quan said nothing, still suspicious as the duo chattered again. Artorian rubbed at his chin. "We should put up a sign outside the door. What if more candidates miss it?"

Dev nodded. "I'll get a panel; you get the ink."

Artorian agreed. "Good call."

Quan didn't go anywhere, his stance still prepared for full combat. Ready to throw blows when this strange ruse came to a close. More Jotuns showed up, and they argued among themselves for a while until it became clear that none of them had actually found these 'instructions,' and that none of them were actually certain about this 'becoming a master' business. Save for the new sign the old caretaker and his assistant were putting up.

The instructions were clear once the panel was properly erected.

Hello, candidates!

Welcome to the pagoda on the mountain. If you've collected the key from the King Crab down below in the depths, then you are in the right place to become master of the region! Please do not keep destroying the front door. It's open. When you have the key, the caretaker will take you to the floor of mastery, where you will be granted the title that allows you regional control. If you do not have the key, it's in the direction of that gaping hole in the distance. We made that specifically to help guide you.

Thank you.
-Management.

Deverash cleared his throat after the Jotuns ran off. <Say, is there actually a key?>

Artorian's face was flat and guarded, but his mental voice was giddy and giggling. <Nope! Not at all! Just one pain in the keister crab I couldn't defeat. It's sneaky, but I will gladly throw them at that problem all day every day while I do my actual job. You know, testing the Mass Driver. Want to port over to the cavern and see what it does? I know it's not ready, but if it works, great. If not, that will be one angry Kaiju when the Jotuns show up.>

Dev zipped over and held onto Artorian's sleeve. "Speaking of, I had a look at it. It has an Immaculate Beast Core, so it could be A-ranked."

That was answer enough for the Administrator. *Fuff*.

The King Crab was even bigger than last time. Of course it was. Why would it be anything other than bigger? Dev let go and hovered a short distance away, while Artorian formed a hard-light platform to step up on. The platform needed to be nice and stationary as he held the wrist of his left hand, stretching fingers out at a target miles and miles off in the distance. "I see no reason to waste time."

Slotting an Iridium Li between his digits, he took aim and initiated the spell form. "[Mass Driver]." Artorian didn't realize he was propelled backward until he broke through a few columns, and Dev caught him. The cacophonous *boom* that shuddered through the space and caused tall waves made the old man's ears ring. His Iridium projectile had sped off at Mach five! Deverash cheered at a successful firing test. The arm didn't blow up either! Best not tell the old man about the control group. "That was awesome!"

Artorian shook his head, hearing a complete garble. "What? What was awesome? It didn't work, I just flung backward."

Dev was bouncing with a grin. "It worked! The static gathered around the sigils, and after you poured some truly insane Mana into the formation, they linked up and fired off that Li at somewhere around one thousand seven hundred and fifteen meters per second! You dropped an entire rank from that one shot! The electricity and sudden light show were incredible! There was a *pziouw* sound and the surrounding air tore, caught fire, and wavered where your ferrous projectile passed. They need some tweaking, but those Runes are devastating! Let's go back and see what it actually did to the——" *Crash*.

King Crab, now vehemently upset, smashed his colossal claw through cavern columns as it gave chase to what was, at best, an irritant. For a tyrant that had gone entirely unopposed in this space so far, possible threats were not acceptable. The rock-lobber would be crabhammered. For something so massive, it moved deceptively fast. Dev just squeezed his lips together until they were flat. <Not a dent. You made it angry, hit it with the force of a tiny meteor, and it's not *dented*. We should get out of here!>

Artorian grabbed Dev by the shoulder, and *fuffed* as the hammer blew through the space they previously occupied. The King Crab didn't understand why it didn't feel like he'd just killed something, but the annoyances were gone. Good.

"There it is, there is the crab. Kill it and take the key!"

The King Crab turned to the sound of the redirected decanted arriving. More annoyances? It was already angry. Luckily for them, they were right on time! Hammer time!

CHAPTER TWENTY-FIVE

A Cal-season later, Artorian ate sand as he got tossed through another dune. *Bleh*. Lessons with Dawn had continued, and according to her, he was still just as rusty and terrible. "Are you even trying? We're doing that again. From the top!"

The academic shoveled himself free of the sand dune, brushing the excess from his robes. His attention was captured by the callous jeering in what accounted for makeshift bleachers and stands.

From the palm trees below, tribes of Goblins had set up observational arenas. For some reason, fighting lessons with Dawn always took them through some part of the sprawling Goblin empire. Maybe just because they were everywhere on Muspelheim now.

The Goblins, in turn, had learned that these random occurrences involved their fire goddess tussling with a Divine from another land. Endlessly supportive, they cheered only for Dawn. The spectacle was so grand and observed by such numerous Goblins that Dawn had taken to moving their battleground path along certain arenas where they could be watched. In her opinion, being judged by bystanders put extra fire in the hearts of students. Direct, screamed feedback pushed them to improve and continue to get better.

Artorian was no exception, not the least bit interested in being called weak and sloppy by a crowd of Goblins. Snooty little buggers with their fancy clothes and fancy accessories and functional government system. How had Goblins managed to keep an empire running steadily? Goblins! They were even accepting of the other races, and had a place for them within their society and structure.

Humans had failed at doing that, and they were being shown up by the abyss-blasted locals. How was this not humiliating? In the upper echelons of the Muspelheim government, the Lamia were in charge. Surtur's very direct connection to Dawn made her an important hierophant.

Artorian was outright jealous of her civilization's success. Meanwhile, he was sneakily sending his Jotuns to deal with overgrown seafood. That Crab was still King down there. Given the losing streak he was on, he cycled up his predictive eyesight trick. "Dawny, this is really not—" *Whoop*!

He dodged the quickfire lightline prediction when it informed him of possible incoming trajectories. He ducked to the ground like he was sliding forward under a rope, and a flaming leg whirled through the space his stomach had been. Dawn's attack passed harmlessly overhead instead, save for the extra tan. The Fire Soul snapped instructions at him, though he still hadn't grasped the pattern of what they were supposed to teach. Just like Ember, Dawn was a very 'learn by doing' teacher. "Elbows up! Deny your opponent's avenues of attack!"

The second kick was identical to the first, but Artorian simply wasn't fast enough to dodge in time. He was punted along the sand, up the pyramid's stairs, and *thunked* into the topmost chambers only to break the peak.

Surtur held her glass teacup with bewilderment as she looked up, watching some sizable carved slabs become suspended in mid-air. The crumbling wreckage that should have squished her was surrounded by radiant glowing light. With a grumble, Artorian tossed the rubble away from the souls not involved in this lesson, leaving Surtur with a brand-new hole where her ceiling used to be.

"Surtur, are you alright, my dear?"

The Lamia in the room blinked, nodded slowly, and Surtur only remembered then that she was holding tea. The visiting Divine became a line of light and *panged* off back to one of the arenas. He was knocked skywards on arrival, his lightline bending away from a straight trajectory. Dawn's voice angrily boomed at him to not so obviously telegraph his attacks and movements. Lessons by learning indeed. How would one even knock a line of light away? Dawn's method appeared to be: 'just do it.'

Hanging out in the space between continents from how hard Dawn had punted him, he sighed, crossed his arms, and just rubbed his temples. This wasn't working. He wasn't learning the fighting style; he was just getting knocked around. It was best to just tell her. <Dawny, this isn't working. I'm not learning your fighting style. I'm just your bouncy ball. We need to try something else. Would it kill you to try classroom style?>

The reply was huffy. <Sunny, we're no longer trying to teach you Pantheon style. I know that didn't work. What we're doing now is… Fine. Since you don't like the way I do things, and you clearly aren't noticing your own improvement, I'll think of something. Go play with your civilization then.>

Artorian mumbled halfheartedly. <I think I'd rather get knocked around more.>

<What was that?> Dawn's ear twitched, but Artorian *fuffed* and arrived in the Jotunheim pagoda before she could chase him out of the sky, and drag him back sandside for further Goblin gabs.

The Administrator excused himself swiftly. <Nothing, dear! Working on Jotun! All's well. Thanks for the lesson, even if I don't see the progress you do. Are you sure I'm getting better? It really doesn't feel like it.>

When he walked down the circular flight of steps to reach

the ground floor, he was surprised to find a crowd. <Yes, you are. It's a little annoying that the person whose **Law** is all about sympathies isn't picking up the things you keep doing better on. It's fine, you'll notice if you get into an actual fight that isn't against me. Just try not to do that too soon? Good luck with Jotun, Sunny. I'm going to spend some time with my named ones.>

The connection ceased, and a great number of eyes turned to Artorian as he stood on the stairs looking lost. Jotuns? Yes, it certainly seemed like it. "Did... did someone finally get the key?"

One of the B-rankers shoved a finger in the Administrator's face when he'd made it the rest of the way down, the long Elven digit as accusatory as the voice of the High Elf himself was. Oh, joy. *Long-ears*. How had they gotten here? Cal, please stop decanting... "You lie! There is no key! Only that monster of a thing down there. We tried hunting it for months, but abilities either do nothing or bounce back, and getting close enough to strike it just turns you into paste."

Artorian looked around at the easily thirty B-rankers here. "I'm not following, why are there so many of you here? I expected one or two people to complain about the difficulty. Not thirty."

The room exploded in complaints. Each Mage was trying to yell over the voices of the others, and Artorian motioned for his windows to open just to safeguard them from breaking. The sheer volume alone was a threat to his prized colored glass. It had taken much work from Muspelheim to get glass that beautifully made!

A Dwarven water Mage muscled forward. It was nice to hear the accent again. "'Ey, you. Yer the caretaker? Well then how 'bout ya take care o' yer guests!"

Artorian was clearly about to ask what they'd like, as he wouldn't mind a drink himself, but the Dwarf was pulled back as someone else took his place to yell demands instead. That Mage got punched in the knee and collapsed, and not a minute later most of the B-rankers were breaking the ground floor of his pagoda. Like it was some cheap backwater bar.

Not interested in the concept of engaging in diplomacy of the dumb, he found himself a corner and just started knitting. A tall B-rank eight that was likely not supposed to be here pulled the brawling crowd off each other. Artorian already didn't like the man. He had that smell. Guild smell. That particular way of talking, too. Oh, this wasn't going to fly.

"Break it up! You all agreed we'd talk first and brawl after! You, old man. Caretaker, right? We're doing things differently than what that sign says outside. We're making our own ruling system, and that crab of yours can drown!"

Artorian's ear twitched. The knitting material vanished, and a document with an accompanying quill popped into his hands. "Well, why didn't you say so? What shall I be writing down?"

The ex-Guild leader smirked wide, arms crossing his substantial chest at such an easy victory. "As it should be! The new rulers of this place will talk, and when we agree on something, you will write it down."

Artorian smirked back, deviousness hidden under a facade of helpfulness. "Sure thing. Let me provide some seating."

With a snap of his fingers, pillows populated the half-wrecked ground floor. Giant bean bag type things. People took seats after some poking and prodding, but once they sat, they didn't want to get back up.

The high B-ranker cleared his throat. "I am Ellis Henaren, Deputy of the Adventurer's Guild, though I'm aware it's no longer around. I started in Midgard, passed some kind of numerical threshold, and received an option to be transferred. I took it, and now I'm here. Midgard didn't offer further cultivation opportunities, but here there are plenty! I put forth that we commence a monarchy, where I shall be in charge. You may now all give your opinions."

Starting a meeting by sowing dissent was not the best way to get something done. Ellis was imposing his rules because he believed he was currently the strongest man here. Artorian slowly tapped the pages on his clipboard against his forehead.

Ellis sneered. "Dissatisfied with my ways, scribe?"

"Oh no. Merely had an itch. All good now." Artorian shook his head, but paused as silvery lines originated from the right side of the B-rank eight. The incoming silver vectors slowly turned golden, and Artorian didn't fully understand why he was seeing this until Ellis's right hand solidly formed a fist.

Wait. Prediction was active? Already? Sure, he'd forgotten to turn it off, but this current version only worked against quantitative threats. It should also be giving him maybe a few seconds worth of heads up. This was far more.

When the lines converged into a single, guaranteed possibility, they blinked bright gold. Artorian moved his head to the side and countered, effortlessly dodging the B-ranker's blow as Ellis swung to crack his skull like a soon to be smashed melon. Ellis was fast, but not Dawn-fast. She was relentless. Ellis was a slug in comparison, especially when it came to deciding his actions. Sweet Cal, they were straight and simple. Oh... She'd snapped at him for that. Was this why?

The high B-ranker smashed into the ceiling rather than connect with the scribe like he'd expected. He didn't even realize he'd been counter-struck until he had a moment to notice he'd gotten plastered on the ceiling somehow. Also, there was a gaping dent in his chest. His Mana body was not doing well in the slightest, and he forgot he could fly before coming back down and smashing into the floor. "H-how...? I'm higher ranked."

Artorian inspected his fist, honestly confused. Smoke was rising from his knuckles, but as he flexed his hand, it didn't feel harmed in any way. He had forgotten that his Mana purity was around seven-hundred times higher. Was that why Dawn ravenously gave it her all, all the time? If he ever actually did hit her, would it do more than he thought it would? Or was this development recent because of the combat practice? He didn't actually know for sure, and put it on the list of things to test.

For now, he cozily leaned back and scribbled something on the clipboard before replying in a flat, bored monotone. "If you have a complaint, take it up with the crab. No amount of rank or power will give you the upper hand here. Unless you're master of the region, or mistress!"

He pointed his quill at one of the ladies in the congregation with a smile. "The rules don't discriminate. Now, I believe you gathered for an interim leadership and rulership type? Please do continue; I'm scribbling."

"I'm leaking Mana. It's not stopping!" Ellis winced and whined, unable to get back up off the ground. The man's body exemplified a visible outpouring of misty opaque energy. "I'm an eighth tier Mage! There's no way. No way you're stronger than me!"

Artorian glanced up over his clipboard. "Unless you're about to patch yourself up, would you like that on the epitaph? You seem like a person who is used to having doors open for them. Perhaps we could put that on a door?"

A Nixie Tube flickered. <Hey Cal. Quick question. Can I make someone be a door? Just a door, but able to open and close as if it were smart. I have a… convenient test subject.>

Cal's response oozed interested amusement. <You had me at 'door.'>

CHAPTER TWENTY-SIX

People present on the pagoda's ground floor went pale. Even the darker-skinned folk altered their Mana forms to show active discomfort. They didn't like what they'd just witnessed. Some nobody had just floored—or in this case, ceilinged?—a Guild B-ranker, and then... how would they even describe what happened next? First, the caretaker had ripped something from the man. Then the body of the Mage was dragged to the entrance, and forcibly morphed into the shape of the broken-down door. The original remains of which became particles.

When the new door was formed, what the caretaker held was shoved into the construct. Taking a step away, they all watched the door rebel, slamming open and shut. Unfortunately for Ellis, that was the only thing he could do for the moment as his Mana body was, by a higher authority, stuck as a 'door.'

Artorian giggled. "I'm going to call you portc-Ellis! Oh, we should add that feature, I'd love a portcullis for the pagoda. Maybe Port for short? It rhymes, I like it. Cool off by being a gate for a few centuries, Port. When you learn how to behave and not be such a power mongering snob, we'll let you be a person again. You best be a good door now! Being a bad door will swing your evaluations poorly."

Strolling away and back to his seat, everyone present understood that not only was Ellis that gate now, but also grasped that he was there as the item itself. When the caretaker sat and picked his quill back up, they didn't feel so good about this hostile takeover anymore. A High Elf even meekly raised his hand. Artorian waved the quill at him. "Yes, my boy?"

"I… I am Grand Elder Wa Nong, of the Wa family. I hail from the land currently known as Alfheim, and I wanted to ask if it's too late to go back." A few other hands raised to join that particular notion, mostly all Elves that seemed to be related.

Artorian scritched something on his paper. "I'm not certain, my boy, did you not choose to come here? That's my understanding of it. Also, Grand Elder? What's that about?"

Wa Nong eased out of his seat, sporting the same simple starter robes as everyone else. He didn't move comfortably in them. It was highly likely his possessions had been stripped and replaced upon transferring to a new continent. "On Alfheim, the system of ruling has changed a few times. Currently, territories are owned by families rather than any sort of government. Each family has a hierarchy of their own making, but certain popular trends keep recurring. Each family has a Patriarch or Matriarch. They are the founders or heads of the families, and have final say on anything the family goes through."

Nong motioned to himself for the next part. "Below them are the Elders and Grand Elders. Elders are trusted individuals in the family, each assigned to a specific duty to help oversee the workings and needs of the family. They end up just running everything. Grand Elders are problem solvers, and we are generally sent out alone to quell an issue. The power difference is usually so vast that it results in this. The family branches out further, but that hierarchy can be erratic. What is mentioned is the only true uniform similarity between families so far."

Easing his arms behind his back, Nong wistfully looked out of one of the many windows. "I did choose to come, at the behest of my Matriarch. She wished to conquer higher lands in the hopes I would return with powerful spoils. Unfortunately, all my weapons were stripped from me on arrival, and the pressure to exist here was harsh even for me. In Alfheim, I am a mighty, nigh unstoppable force. Here I feel fresh and naked as a babe in the hungry wild. So, I would wish to return, if possible."

Artorian touched his quill to his lips, pondering it over. "I have good news and bad news."

Alfheim residents inched forward on their seats as the care-taker spoke. "The good news is that there is certainly a way to go back. The not so good news is that you need the key. It's the same key one needs to become master of the region, but it can also be used to return. I just take you elsewhere for it. I'm afraid I can't help you acquire said item, but I can tell you that the Crab has it. Which I believe is the dilemma that made you all end up here in the first place?"

Elves groaned and fell back in their beanbags. The Dwarves present had been silent, pensive, and thoughtful. They had listened and observed rather than crassly interrupt or throw demands. How odd for the Dwarves that he was used to. New culture? Given the silence, his attention turned to them. "Apologies, I notice you've all been quiet. Is something amiss?"

Some of the Dwarves sank deeper into discomfort, and they exchanged looks of increasing intensity that they were not the ones who wanted to talk right now. Eventually one of them drew the short straw. "Aye. There must be somethin' amiss. We're crafters, and we came with our tools and our toys. We didn't arrive with any of them, and that completely cut the legs out from under us."

A Sea Elf snorted and mumbled. Unfortunately, given there were only Mages in the room, he was heard. "Hard to imagine, since they're already so short."

"Ya tryin' ta get killed, lad? That's how ya get killed." All of the Dwarves had turned their attention to that one, single Elf. The blue-eared man shrank away into his beanbag. "That's what we thought. Ya big-mouthed blue bean sprout."

Some grumbling later, the short-tempered Dwarf returned his attention to the caretaker. "We came hopin' for new metal, resources, goodies, and the like to take back home for further craftin' and such. It's against clan protocol to talk about what we make, so I apologize for bein' vague. I gotta be."

The caretaker scribbled it down. "I see. That's surprising to me, since you're all Mages."

The Dwarves were confused. "Since we're what?"

Artorian took pause. "Mages? Ascended? You went through the Tower for your Node, yes? Bonded to a truth of your universe you seek to further?"

Fear crossed the faces of all the Dwarves, and their eyes screamed panic as they considered fleeing. "How… how do you know about the most closely guarded clan secrets?"

A High Elf raised his hand. "I'm not following. These are secrets? Every child on Alfheim knows the stories of the stairway to astral thought."

Artorian furrowed his brow hard. What was going on? "Now you've lost me. You both knew who the Guild representative was, but you have vastly different understandings of how the world works. That shouldn't be the case. How do your respective races cultivate, or otherwise gain in power for you to select your truth?"

The Dwarves just shook their heads furiously in response, and the Elves huddled up for a quick-whispered conversation, leaving only a very lost set of humans.

One of them raised their hands, and when prompted by the movement of the quill, spoke up. "Ah, hello. I am Majoris Mulkin. Erm… Just Mulkin; Majoris is my old title. I come from Midgard and I was given a transfer option since I was already on the verge of hitting the B-ranks. All my infusions were done, and I just got the option to become a Mage if I swore to leave the Guild. Most of us took that, and there's a good amount of infighting concerning the topic. I can't say I really know what's going on, I just know I'm getting tossed around like a sack of potatoes here. I was not expecting even the mushrooms to be the size of trees? Most of my scouting troupe got wrecked by a grasshopper. When I left Midgard, the local rulership was installing the number system. It's a new way of cultivating that eschews all the old-world terms. Aside from that, I have no idea."

Artorian scribbled it down, and the Elves were finally ready to talk.

Nong once again took front and center. "We have decided that if you would be so kind as to grant us a boon of some kind, we will give you an overview of our methods. We cannot, in good faith, part with such knowledge to someone not in the family, power or no. Even outer-courtyard individuals have a higher social status than most of the people here."

The caretaker considered it. "Your boon will be provided in private. Come whisper."

Nong shuffled over, and whispered conspiratorially against the old man's ear. "Our methods involve taking plants and wildlife from our environment who have taken in the energy of the Astral. Then refining those into pills so we may boost our power. Alfheim life revolves around gathering materials, making pills, consuming them, and then meditating to refine the power gained. It makes the higher-ranked very haughty, as breaking through the ranks is difficult."

Artorian nodded, and scribbled down a few cyphers as notes to obscure the information while still keeping it. One of the Dwarves had his hand in the air. "If boons are involved, I'm not opposed to breakin' ma vow and spillin' some beans. I mean, secrets. It doesn't sound like there's much goin' home ta be happenin' in the near future. I also don't want ta be a door."

Nong receded, and the caretaker lent the Dwarf an ear even as his clan members shot him the stink-eye. "On Svartalfheim, we build Aether machines ta draw energy from the world into flasks. Once it's a liquid, we mix it with alcohol so we can, well, drink it. The more Aether ya drink, the higher yer status. As it allows ya ta withstand more o' our furnace, the world engine."

The Dwarf was trying hard to contain himself. "It's not heat the generator gives off; it's some kind of pressure. We build our Aether technology into suits that let us adapt to more and more of the alcohol. When we sleep, we have Aether dreams where we do somethin' to our bodies. When yer entire body is one of Aether, yer to step into the world engine, and be remade. I did that, and even though I'm the lucky one that survived in my forgin' group, rather than return to the clans I got this... screen? Notification? I got an option to leave. Ya might have guessed, but I wasn't too keen on the place. I grew up there from when I was a wee lad."

Artorian blinked. "Terribly sorry, did you say you *grew up* in Svartalfheim?"

The Dwarf nodded. "I did. Isn't that normal? Some of the folks I've met have this odd way of bein'. Like they've memories from an old life, or they know knowledge from a world that doesn't exist. I write it off as them bein' from one of the worlds we can travel to when we reach a certain self-forgin'. They're all just lost, is all. Poor saps."

The academic in Artorian was scanning the Dwarf over for a necessary deep dive of information. <Cal. Curiosity question. I'm talking to a Dwarf that says he grew up in Svartalfheim. No working memory of our old world. No concept that it happened. Completely fresh mind, but clearly reached the B-ranks much sooner than is ordinary. He's not even thirty. What's going on?>

Cal replied through the senate connection. <Oh, there he is! I was wondering where I'd put 82364. Tex. Sorry, his name is Tex. Remember how I said each Mage needs a dungeon Core equivalent in the Silverwood canopy, and how that Core is a stream of information to the working body, rather than a direct housing? I discovered how to limit and alter that stream. Anytime a Mage dies, I have their minds start over in a natu-rally-gained body. Without memories of their old life, and without the power. When they reach a certain threshold—details pending—they get their old power back. It's a way to get rid of those old ingrained allegiances and start anew. Or if I

need to change their race, for some reason. They won't know. Those animal people in Muspelheim were a great lesson. I swear I'm not trying to avoid another angry rant from Dawn. Honest. Anyway, am busy. Toodles!>

Artorian kneaded the bridge of his nose. "Thank you, Tex. I understand."

The Dwarf jumped back a full five feet. Frightened out of his mind. "How... how did ya know ma name? I... I never told ya."

The caretaker gave the Dwarf the flattest of expressions. "My boy, I turned the highest B-ranker in the room into a door. Do you really think certain truths are hidden from me? Now, I am tired. I have much to do, and I have a ground floor to clean. All of you, shoo. Boons will be delivered when able."

CHAPTER TWENTY-SEVEN

Artorian had seen people clear a room before, but never with quite so much speed and fervor. It had not been two seconds since he told them to get out, and his pagoda was entirely vacant. That was kind of nice? He pressed his hands to his hips, vanished his temporary creations, and oversaw the damage. Looked like he needed to completely redo the whole floor. Great. More work.

This was a moment where he wished he had some of Dawn's smart Goblins. They were just so happy to help out with all the tedious things. What was he going to do, start a civilization with just spiders? Surely not... Right? Perhaps he could at least see about a conversation. It had been awhile since he talked with his named one, and according to his peers it was dangerous not to check up on them.

Plinking the mental string, he initiated the conversation. <Zelia, would you happen to be free at the moment?>

Elation was felt on the network before the reply came. <My Dreamer, I am always free for you. We are in the below. Would you like me to come up?>

A negative sunk down the line. <No, that's alright, I'll just

pop down. Please do let your people, I mean children, know. So, they don't jump like last time. Heading over in three, two...>

Fuff.

Artorian stood on a platform of hard light, surrounded by bags of webbed and entangled crustaceans. He blinked a few times to make sure he was seeing this correctly. He was in a cavern? No, the ground and walls were colored webbing. Smoothened. Shaped. Flattened.

Dismissing the platform, he landed on the floor, and it bounced him back up an inch before allowing him to settle. That impact alerted the hive to his Presence, but against common protocol they did not assail him.

"My Dreamer." Zelia crawled from a ceiling passageway, down the wall, and eased onto the floor nearby so she was matching his gravity-dependent position. Her head bowed forward, a little deeper than before. "We've been hoping you would call upon us again."

Artorian threw his hands up, a massive smile on his face as he saw what she was wearing. "Those are beautiful! Zelia, you made clothing! Look at that texture. That craftsmanship! There's not a single seam. The colors are just stunning and *oh*, that pattern."

He was fawning over her creations, and if Zelia could blush she'd be beet red. Instead, the black hue of her carapace turned pinkish orange as a whole. Even for an arachnid, that was cute. No, he needed to stop that. Cute, just cute. No conditionals. "My thanks, my Dreamer. Would you... would you like to touch them?"

Zelia was hopeful for a positive response, but she had not expected that her Dreamer would have his hands right on her sleeves. He was inspecting her work vigorously, and it only made her discoloration more vibrant. She said nothing, reduced to a steaming puddle of embarrassment and happiness. "Oh, you crosshatched here. Nifty, corded string? Yes, yes, a lovely base. Soft too. Incredibly soft. Why, this might be better than some of my pillows."

Zelia's coloring purpled suddenly. Only 'some' pillows? What? She smiled sweetly as best she could, having learned its meaning. Then mused out a request. "My Dreamer. Could I see one of these pillows? I wish to make things of quality."

Artorian was so distracted with clothing inspection that he didn't notice the discoloration, nor the hints of a growing issue between the clicking of her words. He just waved his hand and Mana formed pillow constructs into being. "Of course. They won't last more than a few days, but feel free."

She was back to pinkish orange by the time Artorian faced her properly again. "I love it! Now, where are we? I could have sworn I ported into crabland. I see the... bags? Hunting pods? Either way, I'm classifying that as food. I would not mind some myself."

Zelia motioned around them. "My Dreamer, my wayfinders discovered your strange construct, and have learned you like spaces shaped with flat walls and flattened floors. As we did not dare enter, we do not know how you moved up and down between sections, so we improvised. This nest does exist in the realm of the crab, but we are hidden from its senses as we do not touch the lake. Nor make vibrations that interact with the water. So, the beast cannot see us unless it were to wander to this exact location and swat us off the ceiling."

Ever nosy, the academic was prodding and tweezing at the walls to test consistency and give. He was tempted to lick it, but thought better. "Oh? Why did you not say so? You can just visit, dear. Many of my pagoda floors go unused, it wouldn't be so bad to have a few more occupied. I understand if you want to be close at all times to your people... children. I'm going to have to wrap my head around the multi-species thing."

The Arachnae clapped her hands together excitedly, chittering with bliss. She could visit! Oh, such joys! Still, she returned to task; her Divine had showed up for a reason after all. "I am free, my Dreamer. May I assist you in some way?"

Artorian felt odd being in a space without windows, even if he could choose to see through the walls. He chose not to after a glance, having found several thousand, silently crawling spiders in any and every direction. They were avoiding this room, and he was secretly glad for it. "Ah... yes. Are you the only intelligent being in your... colony? Should I call it a colony? I'm not sure of the terms you prefer. I was hoping to have a conversation with you and your inner circle about a project."

His heart fell a little as she shook her head. "Only I have the thought realm, my Dreamer. We have seen the Jotuns, as we somehow know they are called, move out and about. They are very different, and the wayfinders have given memories and scents of just how different. I do not fully understand the... idea. In my network of arachnids, I am Queen, and all else moves to my bidding. There are no other relations save for that which I have with my Dreamer. My children eagerly take initiative, but even if they could disobey when directed otherwise, they have never freely chosen to do so since my change. I am the pinnacle, and have neither peer nor circle."

Artorian frowned. "That's incredibly lonely. I'll see if I can't find you a friend. Though I'm not sure how I feel about a second named one. I'm already barely doing well enough taking care of you. *Sigh*. Project is drowned in the water then. New plan. Is there anything you need, dear?"

Zelia extended her hand out, but quickly pulled it back. That gesture did not escape notice, and he stepped in to close the distance, offering her his hand.

"It's alright. What's wrong? Something is different. You're exclusively calling me a Dreamer all of a sudden, and you're keeping your distance."

She shook her head, opposing the question. Also a first for her. She didn't wish to speak of it as her six eyes warily locked onto his hand. "It is... nothing... my Dreamer. Merely... thoughts."

Her Dreamer did not move, nor pull away his hand even as she continued to stare at it. His voice was warm. "Are your thoughts any less important than your physical being? Both are related to your wellness. Last time, your form was harmed. This time, it seems to be your mind. I will not judge your thoughts, my dear. Please feel free to share them, and know I don't think poorly of you for having them."

Zelia swallowed. "I... I remembered. The before."

Artorian felt a knot in his stomach. Cal had just told him about this. At a certain threshold people would regain old power. Were memories supposed to be excluded? <Cal. I know you're busy, but I've got a possible glitch. My named one has regained memories of the before. I'm guessing that's her old life. Who was she? This seems to be a bit more profound than I expected.>

<Artorian, when I say I'm busy I do m— *Abyss*. Uhh... Do you remember the two Cores Dawn gave me as an advance payment for her deal and favorable conditions? Your named one was the **Teleportation** *Core*. I'm... I'm gonna... go.>

Cal winked away as fast as he came, and the knot in Artorian's stomach only got worse. He understood now. Her initial vision. The hand clamping around her face. Forcing her to go places and stifling her will. It had been *him*.

Zelia was doing her best to hold herself together, but her eyes showed pain. <I know my Dreamer in the now. Yet I know my Dreamer in the before. I cannot compare. Cannot reconcile. My memory is like a leaf, torn and different on both sides. I do not know which side is true, and thus the leaf tears further. I know you from a place called the Fringe. You took me, and we went to many places. I screamed and clicked, fought and lashed. Yet I could not break free. Then another hand encased my face. It was hot, and I felt endless fear. It purged my family, my warriors, my wayfinders, my workers, and my hunters. It even killed my first-spawned. Then there was a moment of darkness, and a blip of light.>

She was shivering, and her clothing did nothing to keep her warm. <I awaken, and that story I think you have seen. I remember you taking the thoughts from me. Like webbing, easily parted. My experiences became water, and the Dreamer drank. Yet you did not end me. There was no further pain.

There was the warmth, and soothing, and the welcome. The other side of the leaf.>

Existential dread twisted on her face. <Am I truly free? Do I have a choice? Or am I held by my face, and do not know it? It eats at me when I sleep and it chafes my thoughts when I wake. Only work distracts. Only work makes the leaves stop falling.>

There was silence for a moment, but her Dreamer verbally responded to her worries. "I do not hold you, nor force you. My hand is not one that reaches out to grasp. Instead, it is offered freely, palm extended with gentility. If you wish it, my dear, I will remove the Argent Blessing, and you will no longer be my named one. If you feel our connection is too binding, and you want nothing to do with it, then I would wish you to feel free. I don't want to see you suffer for the things I've done, when I did not know you were as full of a mind as you are. In those days, I thought there was a mindless, angry thing in my hands. When I found you in that hole in the ground, I honestly didn't know that creature was you."

Artorian slowly moved his hand away. "I am sorry. If you wish to leave, I shan't follow, and will do my best to let you live free without bother."

Zelia understood well that the choice was all hers. She had not expected to receive the offer to be loosed from the bonds. Complete freedom from the night terrors of the hand in her face. Yet there was more to a hand than a grasping will. There was a person that came with it, and the person had done its utmost to see to her continued well-being. Even now, knowing what he did, the Dreamer refused to demand. He only offered her choices, and there was a freedom in that.

Her words were meek, still broken in comparison to her mental speech. "Hand... freely offered?"

Slowly, Artorian lifted his hand back up. Palm facing her. "Freely offered."

Zelia did nothing for a long minute, intelligence and emotion twisting behind her many eyes as she tried to settle. Which side of the leaf was the way she wished to go? She could leave, or she could stay. Did she fear the old grasp, or did she fear something else? Her response was pensive, and hesitant. "Promise?"

Artorian nodded softly, even as the Mana bound another oath. "Promise. Your choices are your own, and I will not force you."

That was enough for Zelia, who felt the binding oath her Dreamer had made for her. She didn't understand the intricate meanings, but solidly felt the vow to be true and upheld. Her mind was burdened, so her words were simple. "Zelia stays. Zelia will help, and trusts in the gentle side of the leaf."

She was having trouble speaking further, but found she didn't need to as her Dreamer hugged her tightly. It was nice not to feel alone, but it was nicer still to feel the torn leaves crumble. Acceptance left behind a strange sense of forgiveness she could not fully grasp. Being much taller, she pressed her forehead down on her Dreamer's head while bending down to wrap her own arms back around him.

Within her, a soft, pinkish, tender feeling blossomed. One of the imaginary leaves had fallen to touch her forehead. The seed of something silver, that dug roots deep, and could endlessly grow. She spoke without thinking. Her words just came.

"Zelia... **Loves**."

Argent light burst from her body patterns as sympathies unlocked and synchronized. She was frozen in place only for a moment, but her carapace thickened, synapses strengthening further. Even more thoughts that were burdensome before eased and came smoothly. Her rank increased as the connection with her Dreamer improved when she allowed for a feeling to be spoken.

Her six eyes blazed with silver, and she held her Dreamer for security as wings cracked her carapace to burst from her back. Surprisingly, there was no pain. Knowledge obscured and hidden became clear, as if some intense fog was lifted when she chose her path, affirming the direction her mind was going.

It took time, but she released her Dreamer slowly, trying not to stagger as the connection to her hive improved by a step. She didn't know how much a step was, except that the improvement was significant. What was a B-rank four?

Artorian gently held her steady, worried for her well-being. "My dear?"

Zelia flexed her hands in bewilderment, then looked him right in the eyes with newfound knowledge. "I know Teleport."

Her Dreamer quirked a smile. "Show me."

CHAPTER TWENTY-EIGHT

Unified Zelia was a riot!

Unlike his own crude teleports, hers were smooth and seamless in comparison. Had he not traveled with her as a source, he'd have never known just how jarring, inefficient, and raw his own variant was. No wonder it was so costly; he was doing it all wrong!

Soundless, silent, and without notice they eased from slipspace with all the smoothness of skating down the strand of a web. That's what Zelia called it. *Slipspace*. A much less crass term, he supposed. A very direct translation given how she teleported. Her method followed the same concepts as his, but the entire fashion in which Zelia shifted the layers she was in was a work of art. She knew the wavelengths for the least drag and resistance, and after experiencing it a few times, Artorian thought that this must be similar to the 'layering' S-rankers might have to deal with.

Except that rather than 'all' layers, portation was limited to 'some' layers? Even in the Soul Space, there seemed to be untapped potential. The space around Zelia folded, and she slipped into the other layer that existed either at all points simultaneously, or... some concept he could not wrap his head around. Then she folded them both back to normal space, causing them to slip out using the fraction of a moment, with minimal energy use and Mana loss. How it was so cheap to do that, he didn't know. Having a strong bead on Zelia's Mana reserves proved it to be true regardless. He was so, so far away from mastering this trick. A humbling event.

They visited the pagoda, and Zelia spent hours crawling around every inch of the structure. She said nothing about the ground floor, but he knew she wanted to fuss. "I'm fixing it up, but the place is too big for just me. If you have any trusted second or third spawns that are good at keeping a place tidy, they're welcome to stay."

<I like the third floor. It has no windows.>

Zelia's mental response made the old man feel embarrassed. Ah. Right. He'd forgotten to add those in since he never used it. "Would you like it? It's just going to waste."

Artorian felt the positive inclination come before the booming 'yes' ever thundered in his ears. Mind. Same thing. He'd reflexively pressed his hands over his ears even though it didn't stop the elation of the mental screech. "I'll take that warble of excitable noise just now as a yes. Feel free to come and go as you please. Expect Jotuns to drop by the ground floor now and again. They will... probably be upset. I fabricated some story about a key that they need to get from that big crab downstairs. Really just to get rid of them. So, if you see any, refer to yourself as a caretaker and tell them you can't help without the key. Honestly, I'm going to let them all get crab-hammered and just turn what's left into sentient items. Trouble-makers, the lot of 'em!"

His Arachnae's response caught him by surprise. <My Dreamer, a strange creature is appearing on the ground floor. Shall I eat it?>

Artorian was on the ground floor, but he hadn't heard a pop

in effect. *Womp*. Oh, there it was! Just delayed. Looking around, he saw a very tired-looking Bob. <Oh, he's on the same rung as me. All is well. That's just Bob.>

The Administrator sat on a still functional chair to welcome the inner circle member. "Bob! Good to see you. What brings?"

Bob looked around tiredly, and said nothing about the place being wrecked. Apparently, this was common. "I see you're having the same joys everyone else is having. At least you're not on Asgard. How Hel is the calmest place right now, I don't know. Anyway, I finished the body you're supposed to test. It's a weird one, but it's your turn."

Bob waggled his hand after he said it. "Alright, you got moved up the list fairly aggressively after recent events, so you're on the list now. I'm so glad this one is done; the project dragged on and on. Now it drags on no further! Model 'Long' is done. I've got the scrolls here for you to read."

Artorian groaned and forgot entirely about his side projects. He hated being in another body, now he had to test one? *Ca~a~al. Why?* He didn't vocalize his whining; he *knew* why. "Oh, fine, fine. Show me."

Bob pulled over a table and unfurled some documents while Zelia snuck a peak from the window. The death Mage's steady finger traced out the details. "So, I think this project started as a joke, and it went a few strange directions. We started with a skink, and a few accidents stretched it. We added a fluffy white mane, and plunked on Iridium buck antlers. Don't ask why the majority of the thing is lapis blue; some joke by Cal no doubt. It's too large for the other continents, so it needs to be tested on Jotun. It's supposed to be amphibious, has multiple flight options, high natural mobility and defenses, several serpentine features, and while yes the arms and legs are silly and tiny in comparison to the rest of the body, they're stronger than they look."

The Administrator sighed hard. "Well, it looks ridiculous. Model 'Long' was it? No better name?"

Bob shrugged. "Like I said, the project was such a drag to work on, we didn't put effort into some details. We want this off the workbench and into alpha testing. You're up. Take the crystal and put it to your forehead to do the transfer. Your current body will remain behind so put it somewhere safe. The crate containing the new form is outside, or should arrive... now."

Thunk.

Looking out the window, Artorian did indeed see the massive crate. "Efficient. Why not just call it that? A drag-on?"

Bob curiously nodded. "Dragon? Why not. All projects of this line are complete pains. They're Manny-level complicated. Efficient? Yes, that we are, got the award too."

Artorian frowned in shock. "There are awards?"

The Goblin Mage nodded. "Oh yes, we've won several times now. Anywho. Efficiency calls. I'm going back to the moon workshop. We have a cloud cover to finish that makes the entire surface look like a child-friendly paradise."

Womp.

<My Dreamer. You will be leaving?>

The Administrator appreciated that Zelia was on the ball. "Sort of. I have to test out a body. I should rest my current one somewhere that is safe. Top of the pagoda maybe? Nah, too obvious. I'm being dumb about this. Clearly, I should be in Niflheim. Can you take care of the place for a while, dear?"

Zelia just executed a delicate bow. It was the same, but the stress was no longer straining her face. She'd made her decision rather fast. Still, it was hers to make. <Of course, my Dreamer. Be well.>

Artorian flashed her a smile, and fuffed out. Arriving on Niflheim, he immediately sunk to a knee as the pressure hit him. "Crackers and toast! Why the gravity!"

Brianna stepped from the mists with a full array of Moon Elf elite. Sure, they were invisible and obscured, but he saw them anyway. "Artorian? Give us some warning next time! We thought you were an intruder that needed slaying. Why are you on the ground?"

Steadying himself, he got up slowly as the Niflheim Elves took no action. Their Queen had not ordered them to, and appeared to know the interloper. "I just... the pressure. It's like Muspelheim. It's so odd, this wasn't here before."

Brianna smirked; her arms crossed in a way that allowed her queenly gown to drape beautifully across her form. "Cal evens it out for us during events and summons. I think it's adorable that you didn't put that together. Suffering a great many distractions lately? Have you come for advice on civilization help? I hear your Jotuns are dropping like flies."

The Administrator grumbled good-naturedly. "I don't know, and yes. Tasks aplenty. Those Jotuns can drop dead by the dozens for all I care. Greedy B-ranked buffoons. A few have promise, but it's a handful of snow compared to the pile. No, I'm here because Cal has work for me and I need to put this body somewhere safe while I go and give one of his monsters a test run. Bob was not happy about it and it's been foisted upon me. Is there a good place I can sit and check out?"

The Dark Elf Queen led forward, and strode on. "Come. There are places between the roots of the Silverwood Tree that suit your needs."

An elite guard moved to her side like he was a ghost. "My Queen. This outsider could be dangerous. Surely, we can escort him without need for your Noble Presence. Let us servants see to the task of a serv—"

The sudden Mana dagger at his neck gave him pause. "You must learn to follow before you can lead, Duke Pazarm."

The Duke could only barely nod without getting his own throat cut. "Your wishes will be seen to, my Queen."

The dagger vanished, and Brianna strode on like nothing happened. Artorian decided it was best to follow in tow, though angry blades unsheathed when he walked next to her rather than behind her. "Your people are... enthusiastic."

Brianna's voice was controlled, steady, and fully befitting of an established ruler. "They simply don't know you, Administrator. You appear in our lands, trigger several high-level warnings, and have evaded all traps and mechanisms to arrive in a place most sacred to the people of the dark. Is it so odd that they are tense? Especially when you march right through social convention to walk at my side?"

She winked. "I expect they want to flay you for the dishonor. I assure you they will not, but it would be nice, Administrator, if you did the part of your task where you come to check up on us properly. Some of us have complaints to forward to our beloved great spirit. You're the only one that actually can talk to him directly now, in the event you weren't informed. The once-a-decade meetings aren't enough. Swing by the realms after your test. We have needs."

Artorian nodded, but hadn't known about the new communication limitation. He needed a secretary. "You are right. Of course. I'll move it up on my to-do list. As for civilization, currently it consists of a single intelligent spider. So... I may... end up needing that guidance."

Brianna smirked more, and motioned to a very snug-looking root formation. "That is one of my favorite places to rest. Sit upon the root, and you will not be bothered further. Do send me a forum message when you are back in this body? I'd prefer to come get you rather than you setting off a dozen more alarms. There will also be a standing guard. No, you do not get a choice."

He was starting to get the gist of it. "I understand your will is what goes here. As the Queen says, then."

Easing down, he sat meditation-style where instructed. Then he fished the rock out of his robe pocket and stared at it. Taking a deep breath, he prepared for the shift. "Wish me luck?"

The Dark Elf Queen outright giggled. She could not contain her continued amusement. The other Elves took a step back. Their royal rarely was happy, much less a bundle of enjoyment. "Do you think it would help? I wish you luck,

Administrator. Now off with you. You're mouthy and I like my silence."

Artorian mumbled and put the rock to his forehead. He managed to say 'fussy fussy' before he woke up elsewhere and reared up. His head *dunked* into the ceiling of a metal crate, and the headache was instant. His sporadic movement made what felt like a horn get stuck immediately in what must have been his abdomen. *Auw*!

The sound came out as a bestial roar, and the doors of the crate burst. Exploding outwards from the unchecked Mana emanation. Well… This was going to take getting used to. With some light to guide his way, he pushed his new face out, and shot forward as flight kicked in and propelled him further. The problem was that he didn't know how to stop. He'd forgotten to read Bob's documents!

Fifty feet of scaled noodle shot from the crate. Then a hundred. Two hundred. Three hundred. A full three hundred and fifty feet of noodle-Dragon flew around and curled in on itself in the sky, as Artorian failed spectacularly at self-control. No wonder they had called this model 'Long.' Abyss-blasted thing was huge!

His momentum moved ever forward. Not knowing how to stop, nor slow down, his initial flight was akin to a baby wrestling with its own legs. The entire physical structure was almost entirely different, and the equivalents of his arms and legs flailed. Each time he tried to speak, it came out as some grumble or roar. Completely different vocal cords! The entire way and method he perceived the environment was wholly foreign.

Long strands similar to whiskers came out of what he was going to call the nose-face area, and it sent him nonstop echolocation information. Not that this was helpful as he couldn't control the direction he was… No. No, that was sort of right.

Taking an unintended and sharp downwards turn, his face smashed into the ground below as he blindly sped into it. The rest of his long, serpentine body flopped down into a curled heap atop of him. How was his spine not broken? Aside from it being incredibly long and ridiculously flexible. Ah. Exactly that.

He roared while crumpled in a wet-spaghetti heap on the dirt.

<Ca~a~al!>

CHAPTER TWENTY-NINE

The first few minutes of Cal's reply consisted of nothing but weak, helpless, gut-busting laughter. Each time he nearly had himself composed, Artorian would mess up his questionable control and either fling upwards in a random direction, or slam back down to the ground that his puny arms and legs desperately tried to hold onto.

<No, no, *no*, no, dangit!> The rock broke under his claws as he rocketed skywards, this time by the hip. He had so far deduced that this body must have spell Runes either on or in the bones, because certain individual parts of the body could activate effects that affected the whole. He didn't know what kind of flight Runes were in place, but he didn't think it would matter if he did. He burst through the cloud layer, exploding a hawk just by passing through. "Sorry, coming through!"

The roars that thundered from his voice broke the clouds apart, and several creatures on Jotunheim decided it was a great time to find shelter. The Jotuns themselves decided that they had other problems, and that the frantic noodle thing in the air was someone else's nightmare for the sheer sake that they still had a Kaiju crab to deal with.

<My Dreamer? Are you the 'Long' thing?>

Artorian realized where he was. <Zelia! Oh, I am so glad you're here to talk to. Yes! What is happening? I barely have awareness of myself. My size is a complete mystery, and I have no idea what I'm doing. My sights are constantly shifting, and I haven't the first clue what direction I am going!>

Her response was down to earth. <Ground.>

Slam!

Artorian grumbled as he ended up in another heap. <Ow. Thank you… Why does the ground hurt me so?>

Zelia frowned over the connection. <From my perspective, you threw yourself down upon it. Also, what is that ceaseless laughter in the background? Is that the great spirit? He is not stopping.>

Positive affirmations brushed over Zelia's senses, rather than an actual reply. She was right, and he'd sent her the feeling that she was. <Any chance you can share what you're seeing? The more eyes the better.>

The Arachnae Queen conveyed complex orders to her children with the kind of speed and efficiency any military force would be salivating over jealously. Multiple viewpoints flickered into activity in Artorian's head. As more and more perspectives connected to Zelia, they connected to him. <That helps! Oh. I am big. Am I a noodle? Sweet Cal, I am the longest noodle!>

Cal's laughter only refreshed its timer, and it sounded like he doubled over all over again. He was of no help, too busy pointing and laughing while nudging others to come have a look too.

Artorian knew Bob was there. Bob may have been silent, but Bob was smiling. That weaselly Goblin had been in on it from the start! Why he ought to—

Slam!

<Jotunheim, stop hitting me!> A Dire Roil Elk was crushed to fine Mana powder underneath the thrashing Dragon as it passed by. The rest of the herd sped off in a bounce as the Dragon tumbled, rolling sideways like a logged tree bouldering

down a mountainside. It was unimportant that his current trajectory was *up* a mountainside. Who needed gravity? <*Yowch*! Cal. Instructions! How do I sail this boat?>

<Well, it's not a boat.> Cal snickered haughtily over the connection, being a snoot. <I don't think you need help. You figure things out really well, usually! I believe you have this in hand. Toodles!>

<Cal, you get back here and...> *Click*. Artorian gasped. <Did you just cut the connection on me by dropping a sprocket? You cheeky waffle! Fine!>

Artorian clung for dear life to the giant trees as he slid up the mountain. Coiling around a big one for steady support. <Zelia! I...> *Thunk* <Dangit!>

His head hit a branch; antlers stuck in the fence of foliage. With his face stuck, and hip still pulling, the Long's body formed a sort of lengthy flag that fluttered in the wind. He sighed and let his arms and legs flop. Oddly enough, his face being stuck in branches was the most stable thing that happened so far.

Taking in some of the spider sights, he felt horribly embarrassed. He really did look like a flag hanging from a tree. Joy. <My Dreamer. May I give my opinion?>

Artorian just felt whiny, but assented. <Please. Feel free. It can't get worse than this.>

Zelia wasn't so sure about that. <You look ridiculous.>

The Dragon sighed, causing the leaves in the tree to bristle and blow away. <Thank you, dear. You're a ray of sunshine in this dark time.>

The Arachnae was in agreement as the sarcasm shot so high over her head it might as well have been an orbital body. <You are welcome. Would you like me to leave you to your... explorations?>

<Oh, you know me. I hang around.> Artorian sassed the retort, and shifted something he didn't mean to. The hip Rune faded, and the entire effect keeping him afloat and up in the air went with it. His bodyweight was once again subject to gravity,

and his face ripped from the branches as he smashed into the ground, then through it.

He fell longer, and saw the crustacean lake. Artorian impacted the water's surface hard enough for the resulting shockwave to kill all the local crabs outright. He kept sinking as the bodies of the dead floated up to the surface. When he finally hit rock bottom, his face was anything but amused. An exhale sent a cavitation bubble forward. <If anything, I can report that the amphibious thing works.>

Zelia gave no response, thinking it better to let a Dreamer deal with Dreamer-level problems. Her children still tried to provide vision, but couldn't help while he was submerged. The underwater pressure wasn't bothering him. That was a plus. Go, Mage body, go!

As a bonus, the increased pressure added to his tactile responsiveness. The added squeeze on his skin meant that he actually felt where his body was. Air didn't provide enough haptic feedback, and being bashed around didn't count. He wiggled his face a moment. Whiskers? Check!

Rather than go for big, obtrusive movements, he twitched his Mana muscles where he felt them. One at a time. Once he'd gone through a full body check, he realized he was in over his head. In fact, he hadn't been doing well at all recently, had he?

Artorian thought he needed some real help, and knocked on a door. <Dawny, are you free? I don't think I'm alright.>

Dawn's appearance on the lakebed was accompanied by a hot flash rather than the usual telltale sound. <Sunny? Where are you? I'm here. All I see is a mini-Jorm with antlers.>

Artorian weakly waggled his poorly-sized paws. <That would be me. Hello dear. I just... I don't know.>

He would have rambled on, but Dawn's palm pressed to his oversized nose. The warmth spreading through him felt accepting and pleasant. Artorian just let his head fall sideways and lay in the sand. Dawn kept petting his face as her mental voice turned husky, and supportive. <Walk me through what's on your mind.>

Artorian only made a minor motion to nod, but even that accidentally made part of his noodle-y frame twitch and cause waves. <Well, I'm in over my head, and I feel I'm not myself lately. Bob came by, that deathly schemer. Perhaps I best provide some context. I blew up Cal's sun specifically to get all the heat off his back, because we can't make progress here without him. I hope it doesn't end up going to his head, but that's why I went wild with the sun. That the plan of changing the all-affinity Node in the Tower on floor five hundred and fifty-five worked is a pleasant bonus.>

He let his head fall back into her palm. <Though since then I feel like it's been a lot of downhill. I keep getting beat up in training, and I do not like feeling how Dale looked after his. I outright forgot to read Bob's documents on how this body worked, and I have... I've made a ridiculous display of myself while I've been in it. I feel down. I mean, when do I forget to read documents? Me? I love written stuff!>

Dawn quietly listened, putting two and two together. <Dear, when was the last time you slept? Actually slept?>

Artorian tried to draw on an answer, but an easy memory just wasn't forthcoming. <I... Dawny, I don't think I know. The thoughts feel like they're filtering again, and I'm having a rough time.>

Dawn understood, and scratched the large lapis patch between his eyes. <Everyone falters, Sunny. Everyone can make little mistakes. Nobody is immune. Not even you. The training was harsh because it was about combat readiness. Not ability to fight. You have enough of that, and what you needed was the instinct. You're making progress. Being forgetful is part of not sleeping and, just like Cal, you could do with a proper nap.>

She soothed him by running her nails gently across his brow, hovering to position herself. <This body? Don't worry. Relax, take your time, and take it slow. I don't need a long explanation to see what this is. In large part, a prank. I may have been a candle for a while, but it still took me a month to get used to being one. You seem to be in the adult form of a creature that,

by my loosest estimate, would take a lifetime to understand. Moving naturally as one of these, when it doesn't look complete and has clearly incorrect arm and leg proportions? No. It's okay if this takes years. Are you stuck like this?>

Artorian flicked his tail, and that was answer enough for her. <I see. Then stay, get used to it. Take your time. Don't worry about Jotunheim for a while. You call on me if it gets dire, okay? >

His whiskers wiggled in reply. <Okay, Dawny. I'll just… I'll take it slow. Thanks for coming down. It's nice to feel supported.>

Dawn sat on his nose. <Anytime, dear. Take a nap for me?>

Artorian closed his eyes, and decided he would pick this up again tomorrow. Hopefully with less of a bad luck streak. He didn't even notice falling asleep right away, or that Dawn had cheekily copied his sleep Aura effect to help. She gave him a full check over for injuries before being content enough to head back to Muspelheim.

Everyone needed help. Artorian was no exception.

After waking from his nap an unknown amount of time later, he had to admit that sleeping had most certainly helped.

It took several days, but with the flight effects off and plenty of time to lie there and get used to new sensations, he enjoyed a welcomed feeling that he'd accomplished progress. He had proper tail control! Alright, maybe not that much progress. He didn't know how to explain to someone the sheer enjoyment of being able to control one's own tail.

Days turned into weeks, and the weeks turned into months. Moving as a snake through the sands, Artorian twisted in a S-shape through the deep waters. Propelling himself with sheer body motion rather than Mana-fueled goodies. He'd managed going up, down, and sideways—so long as it wasn't too sideways, because his body would bundle up into itself. Uncoiling himself after becoming a messy ball of yarn was much more difficult than doing such to an actual ball of said yarn.

On the bright side, he'd made some friends while down

here, and that was nice. Whales and dolphins. His favorite was their sort-of combination: a toothed whale with black coloration and a white belly. They hadn't been friendly initially, but getting the smallest member from a whale pod out of the grips of crustaceans had turned that around. Incredibly intelligent, these whales. He'd never have known if he hadn't spent serious time down here.

His size had caused a scare to otherwise apex level hunter-killers, but since it had become clear they weren't a part of his diet—as he mostly worked to get rid of crustaceans—their fears subsided. It was not infrequent that he was flanked by a pod or three as he calmly swam along. Somewhere along his form, anyway. It was still hard to tell, even with the electrosense he had discovered how to use. That, combined with echolocation, deeply assisted with the visibility down here. Normal eyesight was pointless; it was just too dark.

Making light barely helped. He was too deep for the light to travel far, and it scared off a great number of mammals. Apparently being bioluminescent meant they were poisonous, and shouldn't be eaten. Not the most helpful at the moment.

The B-ranked Beasts here were clever, but he hadn't found another like Zelia. Did the spark of sapience develop only under specific circumstances? He had a big to-do list, but wasn't going to try any of it while stuck in this form.

Not until he had proper control. The built-in spell Runes were plentiful, and he'd barely scratched the surface with introspection. Everything about this body needed years of time to figure out. That civilization thing was being reconsidered. Things absolutely needed to operate and run without him.

He heard some soundwaves as clicks and pulses brushed over him, and his attention turned to scan over the source. Ah, it was his favorite killer whale pod! Mostly because they were the best at getting rid of crustaceans. His Aura pulsed as a whole, thrumming back welcoming vocalizations. It was easier than trying to make actual vocal sounds. That just killed things.

A few larger orcas brushed against and past his face. It was sweet, their new learned behavior in showing that it was nice to see him. He gently nudged them and shifted his Aura into starlight. He brightened just enough to see the pod at short range, but he knew he couldn't hold the illumination effect long and not scare them off. The fresh injuries on the pod, on the other hand, began healing right away, and that was a big plus for the whales. Crab claws didn't play.

Should he try to add a blessing to one? Just to see if it would do anything? Orcas appeared matrilineal. The oldest females were 'in charge' or however he felt like interpreting that. That was just how it was, based on observation. Offspring stayed with their mothers their whole lives. That was sweet, in a way. It took him no time at all to locate the top candidate. Not only was she the largest, but she was by far the most intelligent. That orca alone was easily responsible for much of the complex social structure.

That one it was, then.

He thrummed his Aura to summon her, and it only took one for the clever critter to hurriedly swim forward next to his face. The orca didn't know why it had been called, but understood that it had. When she matched speeds, Artorian turned his massive draconic head, something he didn't ordinarily do. Mana flared in his eyes, and his Iridium antlers crackled and shone with light and energy. <[Blessing of Aurum].>

The tincture of gold appeared as a solar sigil upon the orca, just as the tincture of silver had formed one on the Arachnae. While the orca had been smart before, he wasn't certain where on the intellectual spectrum its mind landed. The change solidly moved her into the realm of sapience, as human-like and beyond intelligence bloomed inside her spacious mind.

The white of her form glimmered and became metallic. A sharp, piercing gold. It was gorgeous. The orca's size didn't appear to change, but internal alterations came aplenty. Words, concepts, and understandings flourished in the creature's mind, and Artorian was happy for it. <I name you *Halcyon*.>

The waters shuddered, and pressure built in the general

vicinity of the newly-named Halcyon. Her eyes sharpened, her mind focused, and she saw life and sights anew while swimming aside the Long. She was sorting through new information, and knew that the large fish who provided safety to the pods was either named the Dreamer, or was a Dreamer. She did not yet know for certain, nor why the sudden awareness had just been granted.

Similar to Zelia, Halcyon went through a series of revelations. When Artorian felt the mental connection widen, feelings and pulses transferred toward him in a sense distinctly non-physical. Excellent. She had no grasp of words, but the connection was in place. A beautiful start.

He planned to spend a few weeks to months getting to know his second named one, but those plans were cancelled as a mountain-sized crab claw fished him out of the water and held him up above the surface.

He winced at the sudden brightness. The cutting dryness of air. The lack of tactile sensations as he was once again stripped of easy, pressure-based sensory data. He adjusted enough to see the King Crab hold him with a claw. The darn thing was so big he didn't even match up to a single one of its legs! He wanted to complain and ask how it had found him, but that didn't really matter right now, did it? He was sure his glow had nothing to do with it. <Let go!>

His mouth opened to make the words. Rather than releasing said words, a beam of prismatic light blasted out from his maw with sustained kinetic force. Concentrated sunlight poured from Artorian's draconic mouth in a raging display, similar to the stargazer trick he'd pulled on Dawn. Except that the Runes for it were hidden in his mouth, and he didn't need the gazer.

He found himself hurled skywards, and the beam veered off to cut and sear through the ceiling, marking random places with molten scorch lines. The blast still sustained when he tumbled and came back down. This could be it! If he could angle his face to realign toward the crab. He could deal non-stop punishment to the... uh oh.

He may have been going down, but a glowing copper-orange crabhammer was coming up. This wasn't going to end well.

Splat!

The sheer brutality of the impact triggered Cal's 'child-safety' Pylon. The Long's body exploded into glitter and confetti. He was a firecracker, popping like a pinata piece by piece as the crab claw moved up, shattering the entirety of a very conveniently straightened noodle form.

In just a single hit, Artorian died.

CHAPTER THIRTY

The first thing Artorian noticed when he woke was how stiff his shoulders were. Like he'd been sitting in the same position for years. He tried moving his tail, and found he didn't have one. Not again. What was he *now*?

Rather than bother to look, he flared his Aura and thickened it, so he could feel the shape instead. An odd trick, but if it helped, then it helped. Oh. *Old* him. The human body. Thank Cal! He knew what to do in that one. Artorian eased into it like slipping on a favorite sweater. His fingers tingled, and he stretched them out slowly as his Aura shifted to starlight to get rid of that awful crick in his back.

He picked up the sounds of gasping and scurrying nearby. People? Sounded like people. He didn't know for sure; he hadn't opened his eyes yet. A *thrum* rolled from his Aura, serving as echolocation and electrosense. He was still too used to being in the Long form, but it showed him everything regardless. What the heck? He was in a shrine?

Artorian slowly opened his eyes, and his confusions were confirmed. The building had been constructed around him. He was at the center of a shrine, or rather, his body remained at the original center while the rest had taken shape in his vicinity. Onlookers spoke in a language he did not know, loudly gasped, and ran to fetch others. That was… unexpected. It was a nice shrine, too. Not something you could build in a year.

Oh no. The time penalty! Abyss! How long had he been in time out? Was he even still on Niflheim? His mote popped into the middle of the senate, and he spoke his feelings freely. <I have a confusion.>

<Artorian!> Several voices replied with variations of his name or title, and mote after mote popped into the white marble construct to surround him. Chandra zipped to him in a hurry. <You're back! Oh, thank Cal.>

<Hello, Chandra, good to see you as well. It's not been that long for me. How long did—>

<Ten. Years!> Dawn burst into being as her mote radiated palpable heat. Oh dear. Not good. Ten years of no Sunny-time? Dawny was not going to be a happy cookie. <Where are you? I couldn't find you on Niflheim; the place is a maze hidden in smoke and mirrors.>

Artorian tried to verbally clear away their confusions. <Niflheim is where I should be? It's where I parked my body. Brianna, are you out and about? I have a flock of people around me and I am in some sort of odd shrine.>

Brianna laughed as she carried herself into the senate as a puff of mist. <Welcome back! I win the bet! Tatum, you owe me creatures!>

Tatum grumbled, but nodded in defeat as he had very much lost, according to the conditions of their little arrangement.

Brianna didn't leave them in suspense. Not the inner circle. <I had a bet with Tatum that I could obscure the Administrator from Dawn's view until his punishment time elapsed. Yes, Artorian. You're on Nifl. Same spot where I left you, though you don't seem to have been aware of the stealth array that was there. I thought I told you it was my favorite spot? I see you've met my Dusk Elves! Do you like them? I made them myself.>

Dawn's mote rushed Brianna's, but with a vivacious giggle

she misted out from the senate. Dawn's orb flared, and burned out right after. Likely to pay Niflheim and Brianna a *visit* out in the Soul Space.

Tatum shook his head. What did Brianna expect in the face of that obvious goading? He hoped Brianna wasn't too attached to her continent...

<Artorian, we're glad to have you back. You've missed the last decennial meeting. If at all possible, hide from Bob. He has another Dragon body ready for you and the time penalty increases tenfold each time. Your next death is going to cost you a *hundred* years. You may want to hurry to your region. It's gone, from what I hear, pretty badly. Because why would it ever go nicely, right? Only the B-ranked plus regions have that working for them.>

Artorian bobbed to nod his mote. <Major points that I have missed?>

Tatum performed a mental stretch. <In short? It will be easier if you drop by each region and see for yourself. We all need something. I think someone may have told you already, but once-a-decade meetings aren't enough. Midgard had a bit of a tiff between supervisors and Chandra is refusing to not cover every last available patch of land with greenery. Svart has more smog than air, Alf has more haughtiness than air, Vana is a place to go if you want to explode. Jotun is a hotbed of wilderness and essentially an untamed deathworld. Mus and Nifl have their act together. Asgard still has a hornet problem, and Hel is the kind of boring that makes you want to grow hair just to pull it out. All of my projects take centuries.>

The sun mote dropped to the ground like pudding, his tone droopy with sarcasm. <How... *fun*. I think I will... I will just go to my region after I've extracted myself from this Nifl shrine. Will check in when I can.>

With a heaving sigh, he popped out of the senate and reawoke in the Niflheim shrine, where he was surrounded by Dusk Elves. They still spoke a language he didn't understand. Not helpful. Neither was the tight crowding. He looked around for clues, but discovered only signs he could not read, and symbols he didn't know. He felt bad about just fuffing out. Best to just… do some acting. What did they think he was, a shrine god? Actually, that could be it.

He felt behind him under his robe, and his fingers brushed over his carry pouch. Not spatial, but it held items. He dug around a moment, then tugged free an Iridium Li. Ammo for a trick too costly to use. Why *hadn't* that worked? The force had been massive! How did a whole rank of cultivation not dent a crab shell? It was Iridium, stronger than… Hold a moment. Iridium, dense as it may be, wasn't up to snuff in a straight up competition with Mana. Even a drop of his own was far more potent than…

He slapped his forehead, realizing he'd been a fool. The crowd scrambled and jumped away from his motion. It didn't matter, he was heading out. Artorian leaned down and placed the Li where he'd been sitting, then fuffed out without a word. The Dusk Elves could make their own assumptions as he popped into existence at the Jotunheim pa— Why was it covered top to bottom in webs? <Zelia!>

Ching. A person that looked like Zelia, but not the one he quite remembered, chimed out of slipspace so fast that her teleport made the sound of two coins sliding off one another. She ran up to crash into his chest, her very human-like arms squeezing around him. Though her fingers had remained argent tipped spider claws. <My Dreamer! You're well! I knew you had not left us! Cy! Wake up! I was right!>

A third Presence joined the local connection, but it was silent. Artorian had the distinct feeling that it didn't know what to say. Zelia chided Cy. <What's wrong, chatterbox? You usually can't keep quiet. Stay put, I'll come get you.> *Ching*.

Artorian composed himself. "Well. Interesting."

That had certainly been Zelia, but in a more humanesque form. No spinneret. Two legs, two arms, still those same six silver eyes. She still had carapace skin, though with less auspicious coloring. If she was trying to masquerade as a human, she was getting precariously close to succeeding. Who was Cy?

Ching. The black and silver spidergirl brought back a black and gold orca lady, the visual of which made Artorian's copper drop as he made the leap.

<Halcyon!> Artorian threw his hands in the air, beaming as he now recognized the mental connection and who it belonged to. Even though she was easily twice Zelia's size, Cy was hiding behind her like a shy youngster. Halcyon was a muscled Amazon in comparison to Zelia's litheness. She'd never met her Dreamer in his human form. She'd never had much time with the Dreamer at all since the gifting, and their parting had been abrupt.

Zelia took a firm hold of Cy's large, smooth hand. <You can do it.>

The irony was not lost on Artorian.

Calming, he dropped his arms and pulsed his Aura softly, copying the pod call from a decade ago. Halcyon shot upright at the first intonation of its sound, her eyes going wide at the calls she very much recognized. She might have been shy, but her need for social contact bulldozed her discomfort before the pulsating Aura finished. When Artorian extended his hand again, she delicately tried to take it. Her hand-fins were but fingers in the making. Halcyon ended up grasping his entire arm, but that was fine. Her gaze fell, embarrassed at not knowing what to do, but still wanting to do something.

Artorian recalled that the social mechanism they'd developed underwater was to swim next to his face. He was a touch too small for that here. Was size the only issue? He could do something about size. "Ah, let me help, dear."

Shaping his Mana into a greater form of himself, he surrounded his actual body with a temporary, softly-glowing construct that looked like him, possessing decent solidity. With much larger hands and arms, and the size difference mitigated, Cy received her first Dreamer hug.

Giving that she was directly touching the Elder-shaped

starlight Aura, it was profoundly relaxing, even without Artorian fueling it with additional meaning. His Aura had learned to be soft to those in need. Years of stress visibly melted from the humanized killer whale as her Dreamer accepted her, and didn't spare the thought to judge.

Zelia rubbed Halcyon's lower back as she melted into the embrace. <See? I told you he was lovely, and that you didn't need to worry.>

Artorian nodded in agreement, and the oversized construct of him copied the movement. <Halcyon, dear, you stay as long as you'd like. I'm sure we have a lot to catch up on, and I feel terrible about not being there during your early days. I very much wanted to be. If you feel out of sorts, that's alright. You take all the time you want to be comfortable. I'll be around to take care of you, even if you likely don't need it. Did you make all that humanization progress yourself? You're almost there already. So fast! You might be shy, but you sure are smart. Very well done, Halcyon.>

He was squeezed extra tight, but let Halcyon do what she needed to. Artorian's attention instead nudged at Zelia, who had grown into more of her personality during this last decade. <Now, about that webbing around my house?>

Zelia winced as she couldn't tell if that was a normal question, or more of a 'my house is a mess' mention. She flashed a nervous half-smile. <It... keeps... the... bugs out. Bugs being Jotuns. They have taken to huddling up inside of a dead volcano, and have a sort of raider lifestyle going on.>

She swiftly added some good news. <Some of the other Dreamers have visited in your absence. The Dreamer of void gave us some books, and taught us to read. He seemed... happy? For the company. Another, a Dreamer of mist and blades, is enamored with my children and could not cease her fawning over me. I was *unamused*. The Dreamer of fire personified and I have extreme, irreconcilable differences. Some Dreamer of thunder also came, but he pulled his nose up at us and chose not to remain for long.>

Cy made a small sound of amusement while on his construct shoulder. That well-timed and innocent, yet incredibly *toothy* smile of hers was suspicious.

Artorian chose not to press as Zelia relayed more history. <The Dreamer of cogs... he comes, and even more swiftly, he goes. The Goblin Dreamer of meat, which we will eat if he is ever foolish enough to stand still for too long, is unwelcome.>

Zelia flashed a mimicry of Cy's innocent smile, and the academic had the sneaking suspicion that some of his innate thought patterns must have leaked over to these two. No way in the abyss had they both developed a scheming streak without him being to blame somehow.

Artorian cut in for a moment. <Crab?>

Both his named ones were instantly sour. Halcyon eased from his shoulder, having found the confidence to speak. To Artorian's pleasant surprise, her voice was the sweetest and most tender of them all. The voice of a woman who could lead societies by merit of her melodies alone. <Crabby, and still creeping around. Not as sizable as he'd like to be since we've been feasting on his food supply. We can't make victory progress, but we've stifled him to remain stuck in the beneath.>

Artorian beamed and placed a hand on each of their shoulders. Halcyon received the construct version, as he wasn't about to leave her out. <I'm awfully proud of you both. I haven't seen much yet, but I already know you've been tremendous. I adore you and am glad to be home. May I ask... *why* the human forms?>

Halcyon and Zelia both turned pinkish orange.

Artorian adored their version of a blush, but considered he may have just touched upon a sensitive topic. He hid those surface thoughts, and awaited their responses. Halcyon turned a heavier shade of embarrassed color, then buried her shy face into her hand-fins before turning away.

Zelia took point, having reached a point where emotions like that didn't overwhelm her. <Efficiency? It... works better? Explaining is difficult. My Dreamer, we put more effort into it

because you were able to become the Long. So, we wondered why we could not become more Dreamer-like. We somehow had years of... not memories. Feelings? An understanding of what it is to walk, move, and be, as a Dreamer. I think they were your experiences? We both felt... At some point you learned how to walk again? We experienced that process, and so also learned how. The knowledge comes slow, but it does come.>

Artorian stroked his beard, dangerously close to veering off into a mental tangent as additional questions tumbled into his queue. He was squeezed by both his named ones as they felt his mental connection start to slip away. Something about the thinning of the mental connection they felt made both hate it. Possibly because he'd missed the last ten years already, and they wanted his attention. That, or... They took the more human forms purely because they'd missed him, and it was something for them to hold on to.

He was right back with them. <Still here, still here! Was just starting to wonder if I could go the opposite way and return to being a Long without sacrificing this form. Just... change. Malleable. I know what it *feels* like to be a Long, even if I in no way grasped the intricacies. Such is life.>

He clasped his hands together, then reached out and pulled them both in. <Now. Why don't we all spend some time together and properly catch up during some work? Let us patch the pagoda, and speak at length about what I have missed.>

Zelia and Halcyon glowed bright in their respective metallic colors. They were both happy as clams to *finally* spend quality time with their Dreamer.

CHAPTER THIRTY-ONE

"You're saying it just… *showed up?*" Artorian scratched his head, not sure what he was looking at. It had been a few years since his return to Jotunheim, and after copious lengths of slogging through tedium and attending the laundry list of minor issues that had cropped up over the missed decade—most all of which demanded his direct attention for something else not to go wrong—he was back to doing real work.

Currently, his feet were on Muspelheim.

Artorian was standing next to Dawn, or rather, being a support for Dawn as her forehead rested upon his shoulder. He was gazing at a Jotun mountain-sized block of *ice*, smack in the middle of the Muspy desert. The Fire Soul gently **thunked** her head onto said shoulder a few times before groaning out defeatedly. "Yes."

"Thing's massive." Artorian just about whistled out the words, not quite awed. Certainly impressed, but more stuck in the mood of 'how?' "Want me to just ask Cal?"

Her 'just make it go away' whine had enough child's cry in it for his question not to need a word-laden response. <Cal. Achievement question. How did you get a block of ice the size

of…? I don't even have a scale of measurement description for something this big, and I live in Jotunheim. The iceberg in the desert. Did you just make this at random?>

Cal sounded exhausted, or half asleep. Either way, Cal was back to being overworked. That likely meant more meddling attention in his future. <Oh. Hi, Artorian. You're back already? I thought… no. Uhhh… let me check. Iceberg, iceberg… Ah. Iceberg impacts ley lines, ley lines absorb iceberg, iceberg pops into Soul Space. Rolled a nine-sided die for where to put it, ignored the Asgard roll. Ended up putting it in Muspelheim. Forgot why. Back to napping. Goodnight.>

The sound of a body hitting a mound of pillows closed the connection. At least someone was remembering to take their naps. "Yup. Cal. It's not going anywhere. What's the problem?"

Dawn inhaled deep, steadied herself with a stern stance, and threw an avalanche of self-duplicating fireballs at the ice mountain. Her blazing orbs grew in width and length as they traveled, then split past a certain size only to keep growing. The concussive impacts and resulting explosions served only to break *minor* chunks from the ridiculous block of ice.

The result? The attack caused a cold wave to waft over her desert as the Muspelheim heat was temporarily rebuked. Sucked up by that incredible mass of ice which was cooling the whole continent down.

Dawn sounded abysmal. "My caverns are soggy. My sands are paste. My sky has rain clouds. This is a disaster. My civilizations are fire resistant and weak to cold, and now everyone has sneezes and coughs. Most of that block hasn't even thawed yet, and the more I pick away at it the faster the temperature dives down."

Artorian understood the problem. Until that berg went away on its own, Muspy was going to become a cold nightmare to live in. The majority of her races would die from either sickness or cold. "Welp, I guess you're coming to Jotun then. It's not like we don't have the room. Jotun is what, twelve times the size of Mus? Bordering on thirteen?"

Dawn sniffled, feeling the chill herself. "Give or take."

Artorian flared on his starlight Aura, frowning as he watched her hold her own shoulders. "Are... *how* are you getting sick? You're an *A-rank.*"

The Fire Soul angrily shoved her thumb to the sky. "You missed the last meeting. Cal is making Mages *weak* to mundane problems. Something about numerical system tests for when he makes our forms dependent on that game system of his. It's *miserable.*"

She leaned on him to cope, eating up his starlight effect for comfort. "Thanks for the offer, Sunny, but I don't actually want to take it because I hate that mandible monster. I don't want to *deal* with Zelia. She hates my guts, and the other one doesn't like me because Zelia doesn't. I've been very careful in not telling my Lamia that. I don't want a continental war."

Dawn sighed into his robe. "Maybe it's for the best anyway. We can't stay here. I'll spend some of my points and set up a one-way portal, since we're not going to be in Mus for a while. No need to fork over the cost for a two-way."

Artorian was looking at her with abject confusion and vast interest. "Run that by me again? Just how long was that last inner circle meeting?"

Dawn pulled up a viewscreen that functioned like the three-dimensional maps Cal had, and with no more effort than a wave of her hand. "Remember when we first entered? People with tokens could get things outright, because they had said token? Cal mentioned he was going to put something in place for us to earn stuff and things. Well, he has, and we're the limited testing run. Instead of everything you are doing going to Mana restoration and cultivation, you can siphon your Mana into goods and services. He has a shop with lists and prices, and Broker Bob is always around with conversion rates."

She showed him the shopping list, and expanded the options by literally taking the edges of the screen and pulling them wider apart. "You select an item, a duration, and a quality. That determines the amount of points you lose. Anything permanent is currently so expensive that I never see myself buying it. A permanent one-way portal of lowest quality would drop me to B-rank two. If nobody buys items, the price goes down over time to find the 'market sweet spot,' or whatever Broker Bob wants to call it. By the way, there are over nine thousand Bobs. It gets weird. He gets weird. Having your soul split into that many minds is having awful side effects on all of them. Cal was working to get the numbers down, but if you meet any Bobs and they are... not normal? That's normal. Whatever you do, don't go to the moon."

Artorian repeatedly nodded. Dawn eased her arm around him and pecked him on the cheek. "That's for giving me and my civvies a place to crash. Though, Sunny, would it kill you to pick a male named one? I do still get jealous. I know it's a bad trait, but I have the feelings."

The Administrator sighed, and gently agreed. "Alright, alright. I swear I'm not doing it on purpose. It's just how things have worked out."

He felt an odd pull on his Mana, but nothing happened. Dawn had her eyebrows raised. "You're joking. I mean that was a Mana promise, so I know you're not. Both of them, an honest to Cal coincidence? I just... wow. I didn't. Huh. I feel less jealous."

He smirked and leaned to her ear to whisper. "You're my favorite."

Dawn turned beet red, and Artorian *fuffed* out to be cheeky. He was still snickering by the time he walked into the ground floor of the remodeled pagoda. Ellis even behaved and swung open for him. It was a quasi-pool and recreational nap cave now.

The pool was meant specifically for Halcyon, while the colored silk nests latched to the ceiling were specifically for Zelia. Pleased with the progress of the day, he flopped down in a mass of pillows. With a minor exertion of will, paper and quill fuffed into his hands. Why teleport yourself to the item when you can teleport the item to you! Cheaper, easier, no having to leave the pillow pile. That last one was especially important for long-term slothfulness.

He checked his to-do list:

Crabby crab? Not ticked. Well, the Kaiju sure was ticked all the time, but that was a personal problem he wasn't about to solve for the Jotun-smacking King Crab.

Jotuns? Being a pain in the Cal. They were all starting to turn blue from living in Jotunheim for some reason, and he might see to addressing that once they stopped mucking up his improvement plans. Darn raiders.

Spider civ? Progressing slowly as Zelia's children gained awareness and independence within the network. Though, for the most part, it turned out the way Zelia had warned him it would. They all just deferred to her by choice.

Whale and dolphin civ? Progressing, but aside from Cy, they were still water bound. Easily the most playful creatures on the continent, Artorian did recognize that dolphins schemed just as badly as he did. He really needed to look into that.

Crustacean war? Victory by attrition, and technically dinner. Spiced crab was good! A little garlic, boil in a big pot. Then crack some legs and enjoy.

Jotunheim wildlife problem? Oversized, but somehow balancing out nicely with the civilization factions. The Jotuns were so aggressive in their raiding and pillaging methods that those Mages had somehow formed a stone age society. Granted, one that the wildlife found very tasty. Artorian saw no reason to interfere.

Long-form? Minimal progress, given he hadn't accepted the new Dragon body from Evolution Bob. Let that project drag-on like the namesake suggested.

Cultivation? Stifled. There just wasn't the 'find the Essence source and sit down to cultivate' option. Not anymore. Or, at least, not on his continent? He had to actively go hunting to restore his Mana, but when it came to increasing his rank, hunting didn't even dent the needle on his meter. Increasing

Mage ranks must just work differently, but the only other method he knew punched Cal in the stomach.

Sun project? Kaboom. 'Nuff said.

Fighting lessons? Still getting his butt kicked. 'Fighting instinct' was probably some kind of joke concocted to keep his efforts up, but matches against Dawn weren't something you walked away from if you didn't give it your all. She certainly did, and that desert of hers had whole art installations dedicated to her fighting prowess.

Spell testing? Ehh... Maybe when Vanaheim started exploding less than once a month. Being a test dummy for more spell carving was not high on his wish list.

Setting down his quill, he lay back to rest his eyes a moment.

What a mess.

That wasn't even the entire list, and this was after having cleaned up the grunt work. Cleaning, building, fixing, basic language instruction, spending time with important people.

Oh, right, he needed to add 'perform basic realm checkups' to his to do list. All the supervisors had their own needs and he *still* hadn't gotten to them. Jotunheim had just been that big of a mess.

He dabbed a cloth into some water to dampen it, then rubbed his face. What was the end goal again? Right. Make a good enough world to decant the close relations on. One safer than *this* at the very minimum. He'd considered opening a place in Midgard for them. Another Academy, just to satisfy nostalgia.

Given the tidbits he'd captured here and there, that was a solid 'too soon' in his books. Midgard had its own problems. Then there was Muspy with her *Ice Ice baby*. Best to just stop there. He was forgetting things by not writing them down.

Odd how that kept happening with a *supposedly* perfect memory. Was Cal still tampering with things? Dangit, Cal.

Artorian suddenly slapped himself on the forehead when his eyes landed on the 'tokens and boons' entry in his notes. "Nong and Tex!"

Fuff.

He'd just gotten cozy, and now he was standing in the middle of what could only be described as an overgrown jungle. Where the very plant life was trying to eat one another. Animals too, but he hadn't expected it from the *plants*. A surprisingly hefty amount of albino flora were stealing nutrients from their surroundings, but that was a problem for another day.

He'd followed the connection of where the duo was with fair ease, but he did not see them when the connection said he was 'right on top of them.' According to his spatial sense, they were right here? Pressing his fists to his hips, he turned in place.

"'Ello down there!" The voice of Tex twinged Artorian's ear, and he looked up to see a set of connective ropes, palettes, walkways, and treehouses up near the canopy.

Artorian had been wrong, they were right on top of him! "There you are! Be right up."

Tex sounded confused as he called back. "Don't ya need us ta throw a ladder...? I s'pose not."

Some music played around Artorian as a platform of hard-light slowly elevatored him skyward. He hummed along with the calming, dulcet tones, foot tapping to the elevator tune. When the platform reached the tree home, he constructed a small bell just to make his platform go *ding*! "*Hello*! I come with boons. Do you still want them?"

Tex dashed across walkways to get to the tree-home that the old caretaker had arrived at. "Ah *do~o~o*! Nong! Wake your tight ninny leaf-lovin' self up. Boons are here!"

Nong snapped back obtrusively, like the Dwarf had definitely interrupted important meditations for the hundredth time. "Stay out of my leaves! That's how they go missing! I need those leaves for my concoctions."

A door flung open as a leaf clothing-covered Wa Nong stomped his way with nothing but grumbles to the meeting spot. He smelled so strongly of plant matter that nearby birds fled from their eyes watering too much. The Dwarf was clad no differently, but somehow his state of dress seemed far more robust with that kilt. "Welcome to Texas! It's what I call the place after I won the bet. Better than Nongy Nong's Numerary."

He stuck his tongue out as other Mages in the area peeked from their respective mini-homes to see what the fuss was about. Nong pressed his arms behind his back, the High Elf haughty nature back instantly. "We thought you had forgotten about us."

Artorian scoffed. "What? Me? No, of course not. It just took a while to make your boons! Yes. I ended up making too many, and now you have choices. Anything in particular you might want? You get one choice each, but I'll listen to requests."

Nong grumbled dispassionately. "Buildings. Structures of any kind that aren't weather-cracked shelters that we have to hide in because of the surface war. Or something against the ice."

Artorian was suddenly worried. "*Ice?*"

Tex crossed his arms, and shared Nong's unpleasant scowl. "Ice. It's been fallin' from the sky like sharp blades. Ain't safe nowhere 'cept the mountain. Don't suppose I can *have* a mountain?"

Nong snapped at his Dwarven ally. "If *you* get a mountain, then *I* want a mountain."

Artorian scratched the back of his head, and pulled up his Bob shop. He scrolled through the list, went through a couple menus, and selected mountain tokens. *Bumpf*! Down to B-rank three from buying *two* tokens. *Eeesh*. "Here you go, one token for a mountain. Just throw it on the ground nice and hard where you want it."

Tex took the token, stared at it, then grew a massive grin. He hurled the token straight downwards. "Ah threw it on the ground!"

Nong gasped at the display of insolence, and chucked his own token down after it. Uh oh. "No! This spot is mine! Get your own mountain!"

Artorian decided this was a great time to take a step backward, slipping back onto the elevator platform. He considered that he didn't know what activating one create-a-mountain token did. Even less what happened if they were stacked. Then there was the Jotunheim ten-times size modifier. Uh oh again.

He received a mental *ding* from Cal. <Artorian? I have a... strange readout. Did you just activate two mountain tokens? It says you weren't the activator, but that one is an Aether Dwarf and the other an Alf Elf. In *Jotty*. Is that right?>

Artorian cleared his throat, his platform taking him far, *far away*. <That's right.>

Cal felt amused over the connection as he did some math. <Those races are out of place. These modifiers are... huh. Well, that's going to rearrange the landscape. You realize I'm going to do horrible things here, right?>

The Administrator sassed back, taunting. <You know what, Cal? I don't believe you. Do your worst.>

There was silence at first. The smile Cal sent back unsettled the Administrator so deeply that it caused him to shiver. There was a *bwip* sound as Cal's connection cut, followed by the land rumbling. That was *ominous*.

A different connection activated, and it was one elated-as-could-be Dawn. <Sunny! The berg. It's gone! Completely gone! It just popped out of existence. Muspelheim is going to be fine!>

When she didn't get an immediate reply at such good news, she prodded. Dawn felt Artorian's facepalm and rough exhale rather than see or hear it, and there was the distinct sensation of him squeezing the bridge of his nose.

<I know, dear. It's... *here*. It even brought *friends*.>

CHAPTER THIRTY-TWO

Artorian stood on the top of the tallest iceberg. Ice mountain? Ice mini-country. Abyss, these were big. *Nineteen* of these massive hunks had been littered around his continent, and Cal must have gotten bored because he just plunked ten of them along the southern edge of Jotunheim. It caused such a shift in balance that the entire landmass now had a slight, infuriating tilt. Like a tilted painting in a gallery where all the others hung square, and you just couldn't reach that first one to fix it.

Did Cal not know how devastating even a slight tilt was when it came to water movement? His Administrator got snappy. <Balance that out on the other end!>

Artorian hadn't meant to snap at seeing his continent face the very real possibility of going vertical like Niflheim. He preferred his landmasses nice and horizontal! After all the work he'd put into trying to make the place at least a little decent, it just felt insulting.

His heart dropped when he heard Cal's reply. <Oh. Sure! Ten more ice chunks along the northern border, coming right up. Thanks! I'm getting a lot of them, and dropping them in is

easier than breaking them down. All done! Jotunheim might get cold!>

The continent rumbled again, but the weight balanced out. All the water which had sloshed toward one end now sloshed back to where it was. Artorian was kneading thumbs into his temples. <Ca~a~al...>

The dungeon snickered. <What? You said do my worst. The tokens are spent, I did what you asked. Full compliance, with a bonus! I'm so generous. You needed two mountains, and I gave you twenty-nine. I'm *magnanimous*. Have a good one!>

The Administrator's expression twitched. His demeanor felt flat, unamused, and just a touch vengeful. Compliance, his foot. Was it going to be like this every time he used a token? No. This was Cal being a snoot.

Had the power gone to his head? That had been *very* unpleasant, and not at all in the realm of expected appropriate responses. You don't step on toes like that because someone made an obvious joke.

Artorian's breath became visible as it fogged out into the growing cold. Cal had left, but the old man didn't care if the snoot heard him right now. "Know what, Cal? I think you've forgotten what it is to have checks and balances. I needed to do this eventually, and I was holding off because I *know* how it just punches you in the gut. But today? Today my spirit feels chilled, and icy. Let me warm myself."

The about-to-provide-a-lesson grandfather flared his Aura, keeping himself cozy in an orb of pure comfort and perfect weather. His breath no longer fogged, though it wasn't needed to mentally address his chosen ones. <Zelia, Halcyon. *Darlings*. Find yourself a nice place to be, and hold on to something.>

His named ones didn't verbally reply either; instead, their reactions felt like a scramble. The continent's tilt alone had spurred them into a tizzy. A direct warning from their Dreamer after such an event made it guaranteed to be a serious affair. It didn't help that he sounded constrained, like he was controlling just how upset he was.

Because he was.

The impending castigation wasn't for them.

Finding the best spot on Jotunheim's tallest icy mountain-top, he settled in. Sitting meditation style, Artorian held his own hands. Cross-legged with his back straight, he closed his eyes. In a moment, he'd stepped into his mental space. Present in the self-imposed exile that used to be the bonfire room.

The pyre was gone now, replaced by a fledgling Silverwood Tree that had not yet bloomed. Even weak, its bark shone with welcoming resplendence. Where there previously had been cut stumps, now there was fresh new growth.

He sat upon one, and copied his posture from the waking world. Artorian calmed himself, and considered the next step. He rarely went deeper than this. It was *dangerous* to go deeper than this.

Duwwww*! His internal Presence thrummed, causing a forcible slowdown against the edges of this pressured space. It bloated outwards momentarily before the scene whisked away. Artorian descended a level deeper, and all became darkness. All but the vision of a single glowing leaf, falling to lie upon an endless still lake.

In this soundless world, all was still.

He was nothing, knew nothing, and existed nowhere except in the knowledge of the leaf. Thus, why it was dangerous to be here. One could lose themselves instantly, if they ventured unaware.

The leaf moved by his will, and calligraphy danced into being as the lake remained motionless even as the water surface indented from his written words. A mere four sentences engraved themselves into the lake. One below the other. They served as the first knock upon the door of truth. "I know that I know nothing. All begins from ignorance. There is no growth without self-examination. I am the bad wolf; I create myself."

In his bonfire space a layer higher, the Silverwood Tree shiv-ered. Its branches rolled like shoulders in response to the Mana that rolled across its roots as a wave. It originated from a place profoundly deep. It was the lake of surface thought where the tree had its roots. A realm of consciousness where soundless ripples fed it the proof of knowledge that allowed a Mage to Ascend in the rankings.

A philosopher's skill, tempered by academic learned humility, clapped its hands together. In the land of the lake, a ripple rolled outwards from the leaf. The ripple erased the words as the transient things they were, like chalk being wiped from a board. It allowed him to write anew, the second knock on the door. "Take heart, for all fades. Take heart, and spend your Presence on that which you **Love**."

A second clap, and the words faded again. From the depths of the lake, roots came aglow in a legible pattern. A question the leaf did not write illuminated into being. It was a simple question, a small question. Yet to the pride of the philosopher, it was the right question, and that was all he sought. "What, then, is **Love**?"

Duww. The leaf distorted and thrummed. A question had been posed, and answers would be given. It came spoken, yet was said without words. When the query arrived, it did so with heartfelt empathy, yet lingered with saddening emptiness.

The leaf coiled into itself, and turned luminously resplendent as it lost all texture and form, before reshaping as a petal of starlight Mana. This petal looked identical to the original leaf, save for its colors as it kept the humming existence that allowed it to retain the idea of a leaf.

In the bonfire space, the Silverwood sapling underwent a similar reformation. With the nutrients being prepared, growth would come.

In the Soul Space, on the highest Jotunheim mountaintop of purest ice, Artorian's body lost all its current colors, replaced entirely by shining resplendence as his Mana aligned all the way through. From his mind, to his being. The body of the Administrator compressed into a perfect orb, and the light he emanated became celestine.

Niflheim saw no noticeable events as this occurred. Or at least none that were observed, as nobody was paying specific and particular attention to a diamond seedling Core hidden deep within the canopy. Alignments clicked into place. Sympathies connected. Cal's true Silverwood Tree roots clung to the earth, excited in some invisible way as it served as one of the intermediary links in a great chain.

In the realm of Artorian's endless lake, the leaf moved. As it wrote the first word, the **Love** Node in the Tower woke up when events in the chain connected as requisite sympathies activated. The old man dropped a rank as his Mana paid the costs, but his **Law** instantly paid attention.

The Node's perspective weightlessly shifted as it became aware of her Ascended's plight. As a higher tier Node in the Tower, the mechanics of increasing in rank were complicated endeavors. Unlike the lower tiers, once past the level of the new **Sun Law**, it was entirely the Node's choice if an Ascended went up in rank. Not only did the Mage in question require the right knowledge for the task, they required the right reason.

Wisdom came as the leaf finished scribing the word, and the **Love Law** relished the breath of fresh air as her Ascended proved to be on the right track. With parental pride in a child that was doing things better than they expected, the **Law** completed its part of the chain as it read the written word that was a core to its concept.

'Boundless.'

The space around the celestine orb on Jotunheim's new tallest mountain squeezed the surrounding space. Essence was hungrily pulled from the vicinity, the orb forming a vacuum. It forced Soul Space Essence to rush in and patch the gap.

Once empowered, the orb pulsed. It was a staggered, weak pulse at first, joined by a second as another sentence was written upon the lake. A stronger pulse emanated at the third sentence, and a stronger light pulsed again at the fourth. The leaf in the lake thrummed with power as the connections aligned, now aware that it was actively being watched. Rather than as a slow calligraphic dance, it raced across the water.

By the time the twelfth pulse came, the dot of light was visible to a good chunk of Jotunheim. Pleased with the knowledge on display, the Node checked the reason.

Artorian's celestine form flashed like a beacon. One of warning, promise, and direction. It blazed strong as his **Law** uncovered the reasoning behind this heavy investment. It learned that this growth of power was not meant for her Ascended, but as a tough-love lesson for one it cared about.

Upon learning who the recipient was, the **Law** sharply inhaled. This caused a ripple on the endless lake as it performed an action equivalent to grasping the dough roller, and pushing up its sleeves.

Upon the thirteenth pulse, the Soul Space upheld its part of the oath with Artorian, providing him the requisite Essence necessary for a rank increase.

Cal was punched directly in his cultivation.

Not sure what just happened, Cale doubled over. He staggered in confusion and dropped his wrench. "What the... did someone just rank up? That was huge. It feels like someone spent years of knowledge all at once somehow."

Dani bobbed nearby. "You alright, Cale? It's not like you to just stagger like that."

Cale nodded; brow furrowed as he moved to pick the wrench back up. "I think so. It felt like something grabbed my soul for a moment and held it firm. Like a penitent smite. There're only a few people that can rank up with the Essence purity required for me to actually feel it with such intensity. It's too soon, though? There shouldn't be a—" *Huww*.

Words in the eternal lake were aglow with might. Now that they were written, they must be reflected upon. Many lessons on love laid scribed. Thoughts. Experiences. Wandering wills and fleeting reminiscences. The leaf had espoused stories of loss, bliss, reunion, gain, and loss again. It had championed the knowledge it had learned, including both the lasciviousness and lethargies that came with what it was to love.

While at times it was best to love vivaciously, there were times where it was best to love laconically.

The **Law** followed the celestine light as it returned to works crafted, its gentle attention on the Ascended's mind. Together, they reflected. In the words of Roberts the Ruminating, there were six seas of connection one should have with a partner for long term health.

Compassion: The emotional and warm fuzzy feelings.

Competence: Their ability to be good at what they do, the measure of their smarts and capabilities.

Connectivity: Their ability to engage and latch to another's ways of being. Were they Creative, or did they choose to be stale? Were they Composed, or did they choose to lash at the smallest detail? Did they possess Conviction for their passions, or were they a deep mire?

The **Law** decided her Ascended was on the correct track. With a thought, it considered the route and reasoning by which to measure this deep dive attempt at ranking up. After a complex but swift decision process, it decided that it was the *reason* that would drive this progress. So long as the knowledge was adequate.

It was the mark of a virtuous soul that sought power not for power's sake, but for the betterment of a loved one. This, above all else, placed the invisible hands of the **Law** on Artorian's shoulders. For it knew well that the Ascended of **Acme** would need this lesson. Who better to provide it, than her own?

The lake orb wavered, and **Love** approved.

B-rank six.

The displayed works were vast, as Artorian had broad knowledge of so many kinds of love. Noticeable, once he spent the time to visualize his works. He thought to himself, but knew he had an audience. <When someone begins on the topic, it frequently commences with the love of two people entwining,

embracing, and sharing deeply of themselves. Yet that is but one of many. Love of the body.>

A treatise on affection was clear and present, and within it a section was dedicated as love of the mind. It showcased brotherly love, and Artorian reflected. <The sincere and valuable cherished affection for a good friend. A sister. A parent. The connection with those whose values and dispositions match, when feelings are reciprocated, or when one speaks of another with deep knowledge and understanding. Being a voice when the other has none. The depth in which one can lose themselves in a book.>

A page turned, attention on another type. <In the many pursuits of the topic, it is the laughter and the dance, the giggle and the whistle that turns the head of attention. Flirtatious and teasing, there is little thought to the free-floating playfulness people can have together. One liberated and unfettered, without requirements for roots or security. Playful love.>

The orb pulsed. B-rank seven.

Great swaths of text were condensed to form these quickfire reflections, but the **Law** was pleased with the results of the reason, even if her Ascended wasn't currently aware of them. It followed him to another section, and silently paid attention. <A unique affection is built between those who built love over the years and ages. A longstanding affection. One tested with toil, tolerance, compromise, and confounding turned to understanding. True commitment is present here, for those who have chosen one another even after enduring hardships and turbulences alike.>

Reflecting on a favorite passage, Artorian the leaf considered the selfless love. <Love unconditional, and without strings. The compassions of sympathy, and the connections to people not yet known. As the love of the soul, the selfless saw past the physical trappings and limitations, and loved intrinsically. For its own sake. Those that give all they have so that all around them may find some beauty in life. One that gives, desiring nothing in return.>

A particular reflection in the waters showed the leaf with more clarity than all else. There were no words here. Only the reflection. <Love of the self can be selfish, but it can also be the care we extend to ourselves. To find value even when others think there is none. Unlike the earlier love, this is one that can take, and not give anything in return. Yet to be able to take guiltlessly is important in the world. For the ability to accept is to further build upon connection.>

The orb pulsed brightly. B-rank eight.

The leaf turned a page, attention on the next segment. Many of these passages held special places in his heart, and of this one he spoke gently, fondly. <Connections such as that with one's child. For it may give you a flower, which to the little one means nothing. Yet as you receive it, that small token holds the value of the whole of existence.>

The leaf moved away from the mirror. To a drawing of a tree where other, smaller saplings were present. <Parental love. This love comes effortlessly, and is overburdened with the ability to forgive transgression, accept mistakes, and sacrifice oneself freely. The arms of mothers frequent these passages, and the security and safety that comes with such freely blanketed care cannot be understated.>

With his more preferred methods of love addressed, the leaf paused. It did not want to move on, but it would anyway. Some love could leave one with guilt. He moved to the passage, and reflected. <There is the kind of fresh, spunky, electric affection that is attractive because it is new. The crackle and tug of the heart unrealized, the smile made unnoticed, but seen by all. A love without realization; one that fades like the burning wick of a candle, yet sparks afresh at times least expected. Wild love.>

He'd done the easy parts first, but now came the difficult ones. <For the love which flourishes on the unexpected and surprised, there is its opposite. The routine and stable, the rooted and comfort found in free admittance of understanding something feels set in stone. There is a soothing nature which many cling to. There is nothing wrong with that.>

He moved onwards, and continued, trying not to sound bitter. <Then there is the love which sparks and grabs your heart unaware. The one that drags you to your knees and doesn't pull the thorns free. The feeling that strikes you when you see someone, and you just *know*. That impact of infatuation to someone who can suddenly break your heart in the easiest way, with but a whisper and a word, and yet you'd return without further thought if it meant spending time with them again. You'd give them everything, as only such a person could make you feel this way. Even if, most of the time, this obsessive love can only betray you.>

The orb pulsed with splendor. B-rank nine.

Artorian braced himself, for now came the hardest ones. <The other leaf of such a lesson is the love unrequited. One where the feelings are felt, yet the words remain unspoken. The barrier remains unbroken, and the threshold uncrossed. Tragic and fleeting in all but the words used to convey the story. This love embeds deep, and leaves slowly. It mimics that of a love lost, unable to rejoin as the outcome of the past cements the crash of the future. One where hearts would tighten to feel only thorns; before they bleed too vast and too deep to continue, as, like rocks of sandstone, the dryness would crack them to brittle dust in a single storm.>

The leaf hovered over a memory most abysmal. One it had not wanted to share. Like poison, this love existed purely as venom. The toxicity was palpable; as there had to be good sides to care and affection, so must there be the bad. Worse even than the love which catches you unaware and drags you down the river on a boat ride.

How he disliked this love, yet knew so well how it was useful. What a terrible person he could be if he could coat this upon a blade. <This malicious version seeps in slowly. It corrupts and distracts, turns an ear when one should listen, and turns as a coin in a merchant's pouch. Uncaring, and unfettered. Love of apathy.>

B-rank nine. Zenith.

The leaf dismissed further ruminations and reflections, scanning instead down a list most simple. There were so many kinds of love. So many avenues of this boundless aspect that deserved exploration and delving. Love that was tough, strict and concerning. Holding one accountable and responsible. Love obsessive, dangerous and possessive. The mania within the venom. Love forbidden, yet desired. Love that enabled, yet fettered by doing so. Love constructive, to build another. The love of competition, artistry, and a good painting. The love of exploration and curiosity. Love both momentary, and love that switches as the light in a Nixie Tube. Love momentary, or distanced.

The **Law** felt content. Space around Artorian warbled on all three fronts, and his **Law** drank deep from the nutrition of knowledge as he reached the last, singular line of this lake-written document.

"Love eternal, and unyielding."

The *duww* again resounded in his vicinity, as his **Law** kissed its fingers and blew the affection out into the ether. That capstone had been beautiful, and it knew then that knowledge and reflection would not be the roadblock this Ascended would suffer from.

The required tasks of the B-ranks in knowledge, learning, and reflection, it considered checked. What this Ascended needed was not the challenge of understanding, for that it would do without prompting. Instead, the impetus would fall upon the task of the A-ranks. That of doing, and exemplifying that which was ruminated upon. Yet merely doing would be insufficient for this Ascended, and **Love** deemed a set of tribulations to be necessary. Ones not so easy to accomplish, judged by a fitting soul.

Within the bonfire space, the first Silverwood leaf bloomed from the end of a branch as the scribing leaf from the lake vanished altogether. Its task was complete.

The silvery construct vivaciously unfurled to life as the Node took Artorian by the hand, and solidly tugged him through a barrier unseen. It was *centuries* too soon, but the **Law** deemed the plight worthy. He could catch up on what he did not know about being a B-ranker later.

Ding.

A-rank zero.

CHAPTER THIRTY-THREE

Cale teleported into Jotunheim with extreme haste.

Especially after his soul had been beaten like a miscreant that wasn't going to be taught his lesson any other way. The hand of humility had spanked him in a fashion both harsh and firm. He was all words right away, rump sore. "Do you want an apology? Is that what you want? I'm sorry for being testy and dropping ice all over Jotunheim for being prodded. Are you happy?"

Cale received no response from the man who meditated upon the mountain, his celestine eyes gazing off in the distance while sun-bleached robes flapped in the cold wind. A colorless, tiny throw pillow was clutched tight with both hands. "Artorian?"

"Do you know what other people's problems are called, old friend?" The Administrator's voice was calm, reminiscent of an eternal lake that held no words. Flat without a single ripple. "Nothing. They're just problems. You can run from them, ignore them, face them, help with them… Yet in the end, unless something is done about them, they'll be there. So, what's more important when facing someone else's difficulty? That you solved a problem, or that you helped a person?"

His foot *tapped* the tip of the iceberg. With a groaning, creaking orchestra of sound, the berg split in twain as a gash formed all the way through. It clattered with the sounds of metal cables straining and snapping, audible regardless of their depth. The split left both Cale and Artorian standing on the air as the ground gave way below them.

"You solved my problem, Cale. But can you say that you actually helped me? Or were you so caught up in world building that you've forgotten to spend time with people, and how to treat them like people?"

Cale was taken aback. Where was this coming from? He was doing great! Even spending time as Cale, in Dale's body. He threw his hands up. "I'm doing fine! Do you need help? Is it the favorable conditions? We can cash them in now, if you'd like. Is that what this is about?"

Artorian shook his head slowly, thoughts deep and pensive. "I'm saving that entire thing for the end, Cal. When the space is stable and decanting my family is worthwhile. Then, I spend my tokens. No, this is about the meetings that happen only once a decade. The pattern that you're becoming crass. The time you spend hidden away in the mundane speed that strips years from you where we spend days. You drown yourself in work and forget that you're not just Cal. Is my disciple still in there? You may be using the body, but you're only taking care of it physically. I can only pull that blowing-the-sun-up stunt *once* to pull people's opinion of you out of the fire."

Cale pressed a hand to his chest, taken aback. "Wait… you *actually* did that on purpose? I thought Dani was joking. What about failing to start the sun and putting the **Sun Law** in place?"

Artorian drooped his head slightly, his sigh weighted. "My friend, when I realized I could not start that sun, I came up with the **Law** idea on the fly. I do that with many things. That I semi-planned and rigged it to fail was because Dani herself told me that such a colossal failure was sure to take the heat off of you. Do you think we are blind to how poorly you function when the people you are surrounded by dislike you? When the inner circle you've put together is *all* you have?"

The Administrator motioned to the cleaved mountain. "Even then, you've cut communication to just your Wisps, moon people, and me. The rest of the supervisors can't even talk to you without me or a meeting. And if the amount of business and tasks *I have* is any indication to go by, then they don't have the spare day to come see me, because teleportation isn't *actually* free, work-related or no. Your Bobs aren't tracking things correctly. I have had ports that funded me Mana, and some that stripped a rank when it was barely an inconvenience to have acted with a different movement method."

Artorian took deft steps toward Cale, lack of a floor be damned. He pressed his hands against the man's shoulders, and squeezed gently. "You are fraying at the edges, and while Dani is amazing at keeping you on task, there are tasks you deem irrelevant that are vital to your continued mental well-being. There are many problems, Cale. Now tell me if you are a problem that needs to be tackled, or a person that deserves to be helped? Because how that is answered can change the entire way someone acts in pursuit of the needed end."

Cale didn't understand why just being held was nice. It was just a shoulder grip. So why did it prickle his skin, and why did it scream with the need of a child that had rarely been touched? Cale considered it, but the answers came easy. "I... I think I would prefer to be seen as a person, rather than a problem. Is... is that what I've been doing to you all?"

The old man smiled with a softness only a wrinkly old face could muster. "Yes, my friend. That is exactly what you've been doing. I'm sorry that I had to deck you with cultivation progress to get your sincere attention. Can you see why this is important?"

Cale frowned, but wordlessly nodded. "I just... I don't know what to do about it. I play with Grace, but even she gets bored and goes off to do other things. She's got other Wisp friends in the Niflheim canopy now. I don't want to get in between that. Dani is the best, but she also has friends now."

He considered his options. "There are other dungeon Cores in the Silverwood Tree, but aside from Eternium, who is very much asleep, and has been this entire time... I don't know. I just don't have someone on that level for me. You try finding someone to call a peer when you have full and total mastery of a place, where every detail can be at your beck and call, and everyone lives because you promised them you would let them. There's no comparison. I just. I just..."

Cale didn't understand why he was crying, nor why Artorian was holding him tight. There was no further judgement, penitence, or harshness. That time had come and gone. Like words that were written and smoothed out into obscurity upon a lake. Cale felt a hint of what it was like to be at the same time more than just an omnipresent mind that needed to have its attention directed. And less, as a person with needs.

Artorian said nothing, and like so many times before, held a child as it wept without knowing why. They did that sometimes. There were moments where people just needed to uncork the bottle and cry.

Cale's face contorted, but that was fine. His head was held gently, and his back was patted supportively as Artorian spoke. "I know, my boy. I know. You're making progress. You're doing your best, and you're doing very well. I do have good news. I've got something for you. Something I believe will greatly help."

When Cale tried moving away, there was no resistance. His sleeve wiped his face off, but his brow remained furled in question while his face took the time it needed to recover from the darkish pink coloration.

Artorian pressed his empty hands together. When he moved them apart, a tiny throw pillow presented itself via some simple sleight of hand. "I wanted you to have this. It's a heart, a memory, and a key. It shows the path of a long road, leading to an endless lake that lives without the lines that would define its edges."

The dungeon inspected the pillow, his frown unceasing. It was a strange construct. Present physically, and yet in some way not at all? It existed in some kind of field, or it was made of one? It was an idea, solidified. "What am I looking at?"

Artorian merely smiled, and pressed the tiny thing into his hand. "Something new. I believe it's called: The Liminal."

When Cale touched it, space for them lurched as he was dragged into Artorian's lake space. Wait, didn't Artorian explode the last time he was in the Administrator's Soul Space? Cal returned to his senses as an orb. Existing as a seamless sphere that floated above the endless stillness, in a place without borders. Ah, *not* the Soul Space. This was a place in Artorian's mind, not his center. Or perhaps somewhere bordering? He could feel the attention of something else watching, as if this lake of surface thoughts doubled as a place where Mages were measured.

Cal could not speak. He could not move. He found that when he tried, it was not *he* that moved, but the entirety of the space around them did instead. Them, yes. He wasn't alone. Another orb was with him. Not as seamless, with but a fraction of difference.

Odd as it was, that orb turned to face him. It glowed a gentle celestine, like the warming smile of an old man. When Cal latched onto that visual concept, the lake moved. The water itself rose to form structures and people.

While Cal's perspective remained stationary, what must have been a sitting beggar came into view. A figure approached the beggar, making hand movements that indicated he was speaking with the other. The beggar invited that other man, who he had never met, out for tea. When they sat together at the end of a dock, both figures were smiling. Each holding a tiny steaming cup in their hands.

The sound of a water droplet impacting the lake *bwipped*. Clearing the scenery back to stillness. Yet even as all was still, the kernel of truth remained with Cal. He had discovered an unspoken, profound joy. Tea, with a stranger.

The scene faded as the lurching effect passed, and Cale found himself back on the split mountaintop. He was on the snowy side, sitting on the edge of a sheet of ice that reached out like a pier. He didn't remember moving to go sit, but the sensation of his legs dangling off the side made him look around.

A hazy copy of a person sat beside him. It reminded him of the man invited for tea. Cale extended a hand before thinking of why, and grasped an offered cup full of steamy hot leaf juice. Feeling the warmth of it between his cold fingers, the puzzle pieces clicked. He realized that... he was the beggar.

Artorian's hazy form gained clarity when he was fully back from the shared experience. The Liminal was mostly still a mystery to him. He hadn't quite known what the Liminal pillow would show them, only that it seemed to have a will of its own. One that guided souls to what it was they truly needed.

When he spoke, his voice was calm and soothing. "The thing about peers, and people, Cal, is that you have to meet them before you can decide if you feel about them that way or not. Making the blanket decision that you are matchless, before you have tested to see if there exists a soul that is your match, is folly. If you want to find the good in people, spend time among your people. Be as the beggar, and you will find that the kindest souls you meet are often the ones most overlooked."

They chinked cups without thinking about it, and Artorian enjoyed a spicy exhalation as the flavor of brittle bark and leaves hit him. Cale drank it, tried not to cough from the capsaicin in the drink, and thumbed his chest before asking. "Are you my peer, Artorian?"

The Administrator thought that to be the wrong question, so he just refilled his disciple's cup. "My boy, I am but an old man. A fleeting reminiscence that passes as the wind, there to be forgotten. What I am to another is never mine to decide. So it is for all, and so it is for you."

Artorian mused to himself. Crossing his arms as he wistfully gazed into the distance. "I think what I am is but the expression of my soul. An ear for those with words that need to be spoken. A voice for those who cry silent tears. A hand to grasp when the pain closes in. A friendly smile in the loneliest of places. A stranger sharing a cup of tea with one who is lost, on the mountainside. As a stranger is how you have seen me, and still do."

He refilled his own cup, and shared tea once more. Cale's face moved to form the expression that he was going to ask why Artorian thought Cal saw him as someone unfamiliar, but the old man was a step ahead of him.

"You have my old memories, but those are part of the person you knew. Not the person that is. You don't value me for what I know, and that's fine. You value me because of how I reach decisions, and what I do afterwards. You like my pattern, but you don't care for what I've filled it with, and that makes me a stranger. You don't know who I am becoming, just as I don't know who you are becoming. Except that from my perspective, who you were becoming was detrimental to everyone else."

He took a breath. "We don't share, my friend. So please, let me amend that. I do not want to be a subject under a lonely tyrant who lashes out. You are not going through this by yourself, and a glance over the shoulder will let you see the hands pressed to your back. All wanting to help you move forward."

Artorian paused, and clarified.

"I am **Love**, Cal, and that's my gift to you. The knowledge that even though the concept is hidden in this shell of a person, slathered with personality, **Love** will always be there for you. It won't abandon you. It won't run. It is patient, and boundless, and when you figure out what it means to open your heart up, you'll find you had more of it yourself than you realize. Reflect on it, my boy. Our time is up. Your loved ones are here to pick you up, and I have people of my own to go see."

Grace had the best time in the world zipping at supersonic speeds through the inside of the split ice mountain. She erupted from the cleaved gap with a screech of pure elation and powerful victory as Dani chased after her. <First!>

Cale laughed, and opened his arms. Grace bashed into his chest just as hard as a particularly meddlesome Administrator ranked up. When he considered that, he realized Artorian was gone.

A brush of wind passed him by. It was just him and his closest family on the mountaintop, while two empty teacups rested nearby in the snow.

Dani formed a body around herself, tugging her oaf into her arms to hold. "What are you doing just running off like that? We get worried and had to chase you. Are you alright?"

Cale felt frozen at the question, and squeezed his hand to find the tiny throw pillow present between his fingers. It was comforting. Warm. A reminder that life was better when you weren't alone. "Yes... yes, I think so. I had a heart to heart that I didn't know I needed, and wouldn't have listened to without some tough love. Treat people like people, and not like problems to be solved."

Cale looked up at his family, and had a thought. "Hey, Dani? There's something I would like us to do. Together."

CHAPTER THIRTY-FOUR

While Cal had been provided his lessons, not everything was sunshine and roses. The teacher was now paying the cost, and Artorian's body was tearing itself apart. Or so he felt while writhing around on the Muspelheim sands. He'd tried sending out a distress call, but his mind was trapped in a body that was constantly breaking only to reform with the idea of him very much still in it.

Sweet abyss, was it painful. He had forgotten that so many things related to cultivation were so abyss-damned *painful*.

The A-ranks? Fantastic on paper! Feeling as though he was being crushed into a categorically smaller container? About as pleasant as it sounded. The Mana quality difference between the B- and A-ranks wasn't something Artorian had thought was significant. He was most definitely wrong.

The math said they were a category of being higher than a B-rank, but what did that really mean? An A-ranker had one hundred times dilation, where a B-ranker had ten. It seemed like just a small thing to note, but the truth of it was far less kind. To survive that kind of event, one needed to become something that could.

Becoming said thing? *Whew*. Training with Dawn couldn't compare.

On the plus side, he'd figured out what that Liminal Mana was. He had a theory, at least. Maybe he was wrong. Holding his sides during a moment of calm between the compression storms, he figured that the strange, wavering energy was a version of Mana that was more than just glue.

It could still do that, but where B-ranked Mana was the mortar between the bricks, A-ranked Mana felt like the actual bricks. This new version of Mana that was trying to rebuild him seemed near identical to the purified Mana motes that hung about in The Between. Was that why that old Ziggurat wench Meatball was able to move freely? A problem for later, here comes the cra~amp. *Yeeowch*!

Vwumph!

Dawn blurred into being and dashed out of her teleport at a full run. Space around Sunny was compressing, and sand turned to glass just from being in his vicinity. "Don't fight it! Fighting it makes the reformation take longer!"

Artorian was the definition of a wince when the Fire Soul picked him up from the ground. "At least you were smart enough to come to me right away this time. Looks like you've barely gotten started with compression. You're in luck. Sit up, come, sit up."

Dawn helped him relocate, sliding behind him to pull his back against her chest. Arching her arms along his, she took his hands and held them firm. "Squeeze. Just squeeze as hard as you can when you feel the pressure expand like you're stuck in a cooker. You can't hurt me. Squeeze and let it pass. Your body will feel like it's getting smaller; it's not, you're going to be okay. I'm here."

The Liminal field erupted from Artorian's Aura, then surrounded him. Cramming down around his being like a tightening vice. Between gritted teeth, all he could do was what he was told. His hands squeezed, and while it felt like he would break Dawn's, she was unharmed. He gnashed words out as the sand around them cracked into glass. "I thought... the soul item... was the only..."

His words were cut off as he was violently compressed. That was what it felt like, anyway. With Dawn present, his blurring vision could see that she was right, and his actual size wasn't changing. The building blocks of his makeup were just going through a natural evolution once his accumulated rank hit a threshold.

Much like trading Essence for Mana, Mana was traded for Mana... plus? It was so hard to tell. The new Mana was nearly the same, and the differences resided in a realm esoteric. He was good at the esoteric, but not while it felt like a small planet was sitting on him.

Dawn didn't laugh at his discomfort.

She remembered breaching the A-ranks for the first time herself. It wasn't something you could forget. "There is much you don't know. Focus on my voice to ignore the pressure. The Soul Space item is just a step necessary for entering the A-ranks. Actually *doing so* is another thing entirely. When you connected your soul to the Node in the Tower, it was just that: a connection. Successfully surviving the A-rank reformation means you have lived through the process of that flimsy connection becoming a solid and strong bond. Think of your initial connection to be a single strand of string. The next one is a multi-corded rope that coils in again, becoming a cable."

She held firm as her hands were squeezed again. A-ranking was tough to go through alone, but perhaps manageable with a friend. She wasn't entirely sure what to do, so she figured that she would do what she would have wanted to have done for her. Then do that. During her reformation, she'd had no idea what that gunky Mana coming off from her Aura was. Now, she might as well be the top most scholar on the subject.

"That strange field crushing you down is called the Liminal, but every A-ranker finds that out when they become one. The knowledge is granted, even if it is usually immediately overlooked. The Liminal is a lot of things. You start seeing it as a

Mage, but it's not something people pay attention to until usually the *late* A-ranks. It starts just... by being around. Doing things that at first seem like they have no reason. In the B-ranks, the Liminal occurs without your direct input. Even if you can give it some, it doesn't stick around to remain controlled. It chooses not to be."

A second squeeze from Artorian, and she paused before speaking more. "The Liminal is simultaneously a field and an energy. It is your thoughts given shape. Like Mana is considered some kind of midpoint, the Liminal is no different. It is the 'stuff' that the phase before S-ranking is made of. Do you remember how I told you that the current ranking system is flawed? It's because it leaves out crucial steps that people have just assumed are part of some other step."

A third squeeze bore down, but this one came more easily. "The process of 'build and replace' that you start when you begin the journey of cultivation is ongoing. As an A-ranker, you're going to improve by working on your Soul Item and gathering more knowledge on your **Law**. Rather than *just* gathering information, the A-ranks are about applying what you have learned out into the world."

A fourth squeeze, this one with a less frightening expression of pain on her bestie's face. "Think of A-rank Mana as just a higher purity of B-rank Mana. Even though that's not exactly right, it's easier. It's ten times the purity. Meaning ten times the difficulty and amount needed to keep going up. As you pass A-rank five, you're going to have thoughts at times that seem to become *real*. Even though you spent no Mana on them."

A fifth squeeze, and Artorian's reformation no longer looked like a matter of life and death. The process gradually became smoother. Dawn just kept talking; it was helping. "*This* is Liminal Energy: The stuff between A- and S-; the energy of thought. Gather it up and keep a hold of it. The more you have, the more easily Liminal events will happen. You want to keep this new energy hidden at all times, because the Liminal is what you are entirely dependent on to form your S-rank body.

Mana doesn't cut it, not even A-rank Mana. It's just bricks and glue. *Just* the bricks and glue."

Artorian groaned loud. So, he'd been wrong about his initial guesses on the Liminal, but in came Sensei Dawn with the answers! Looked like his comparison to mortar and stone had been accurate enough, even if not all of his observations were. Dawn just kept talking to give him something for his mind to hold on to, and sweet mercy did he appreciate it.

Dawn noticed, and didn't stop. "The body changes are just a response to what's happening with your soul. The Mana is trying its best to adapt to a firm bond, and that requires a new level of density. So, it's compressing you to match each new rope that the Node is adding to you, as it cords that connection into a cable. Your Mana isn't attacking you; it's trying to *protect* you. That's why fighting against it is so bad. If you try to fight it here, then your connection to your **Law** will shatter you. Your body won't be able to take the strain of the soul connection, and your mind isn't going to get a choice in the matter and follow right after. Cal's body cheatery won't save you here. So, exhale deep. Breathe in, and exhale deep. Move your body. Let the shape do what the shape is supposed to do."

Artorian had no recourse but to cling to her every word. To his relief and delight, the advice greatly eased his suffering. Breathing deep, he forced his body to do what bodies were supposed to do. Move. These active stretches made the density changes rush across him in ebbing waves, rather than slam into him one brick wall at a time. "That... helps."

Dawn nodded, and pleasantly remained with him as she watched the very connections form. Going from the middle B-ranks all the way to A-rank zero in the span of a few hours was not healthy for a Mage. There was a growth pattern to these things and, as usual, Sunny had gone out of his way to do them out of order. What horrible scheme had he pulled this time? The stubborn fool.

He was breathing smoothly soon enough and, by Cal, did he look and feel tired. On the bright side, the Muspelheim heat and pressure no longer strained him. In fact, it now felt no different than being on Jotunheim. No pressure, no pull, no strain on his being just to exist here. "Am... am I good?"

Dawn snorted, petting his head. "Oh, you might be okay, but I don't know about good. You're about done, yes. Your cable is approaching completion. You're going to pass out in a moment, and no, there's nothing you can do about it. With your body almost done, your mind has to adapt to the new density of the form. For you, that's going to be a trifle, but you're still taking a nap for the duration. When you wake up, you're going to feel like aces. Also, hope you like learning to walk again! Happens every step."

There was going to be a sassy response, but the Administrator was out cold as his body once again shone with celestine resplendence. This transition was a dangerous and vulnerable state for an A-ranker. It was one of the few times they were just as weak as a C-ranker while their connections overhauled themselves. Lucky for Artorian, he had Dawn.

She shook her head when thinking about it. "The *luck* on this boy."

Vwumph.

Sunny was asleep in her arms like a shiny treasure as Dawn teleported to the deepest and safest part of Muspelheim. Her temple of Incarnate fire floated in the center of the tropical underground. In actuality, it was the largest trireme ever built. One that sailed the seas between the islands in the Muspelheim beneath. She had always wanted to be a sailor, and this was one step closer.

Her multiple named ones rushed to the top deck to greet her. She had *many* now. In addition to Surtur, the Lamia, she had several Goblins, a representative member of each race that thrived on her continent, a rogue Oni, and an old friend.

Karakum.

The ruby scorpion was a proud mixture of golem and man. Similar to Artorian's named ones, many of Dawn's chosen were undergoing humanization. They still had easy access to their original forms, but there was a cohesiveness in being the same shape as your Dreamer. There was *pride* in it.

An order of honor few managed to reach.

They lined up and pressed an arm along their stomachs, bowing respectfully as their Divine and Dreamer passed them with a stride full of power and purpose. Dawn flared her Aura in acknowledgement, brushing it as a sweet hand across each of their cheeks to praise them for honor well received.

Dawn's words were firm. "No harm is to come to my Sunny."

Her request was taken as an immediate order. No amount of niceness in asking ever seemed to dissuade her chosen to see to the completion of Dawn's wishes, so she had taken to being direct. It was easier, and they could interpret that however they liked. There was no verbal confirmation, instead the sigils her chosen carried flared with power. Acknowledging her wish.

Deep in the trireme, Artorian was laid on a bed of plumage and pillows. The room itself was lavish, and exotic. It held some of the most valuable items and secrets discovered in Muspelheim so far. The majority of them being the sealed versions of items or tools previously classed as 'broken.'

"Will our Dreamer be staying? We can prepare meals." Karakum clicked out the query, and bowed when Dawn ever so barely nodded her head yes. She was sitting next to her resplendent treasure, still shining and weak as she kept a hand on his wrist. For a while, her tasks were on pause. This took precedence. She played favorites and, whether he knew it or not, Artorian was easily at the top of her list.

He woke a few days later, bundled up in a nest of pillows and surrounded by a lavish feast. He found swiftly that he was not much different from a pillow himself, as Dawn was using him as one. She was draped wildly all over without any ordered semblance of where arms or legs should go. Rather than rouse her, he thought that was just fine. What was another small nap?

CHAPTER THIRTY-FIVE

Dawn's chosen became concerned when, after several months, neither of the Dreamers had awoken, and suspicious activity was afoot. Their surroundings had been cleaned and kept tidy, but the Dreamers themselves seemed nowhere close to waking. Mostly due to the point that nobody dared to wake them. It had been so long that Surtur had gotten in touch with Zelia about if the Jotun realm had ideas on how to wake them.

Zelia had been unfazed, and to the point. Unlike the Muspelheim realm's chosen, she already had experience spending long swaths of time without her Dreamer. She had learned to cope, and thrive even with his absence. Zelia and Cy had expected this, and prepared for it accordingly when Artorian had given them both the warning after the continental tilt.

The lightshow on the new ice mountain was no hidden affair either, and the solar sigil duo said nothing about their experiences and first-hand accounts concerning the great spirit getting a spanking. That was what he got for tilting their Dreamer's land.

The snoot.

Zelia had personal differences with the Dreamer of the fire realm. That didn't stop her from remaining professional and understanding that Dreamers needed other Dreamers. As a named one, she could help much. With Halcyon's help, all three sections of a slowly-freezing Jotunheim had been reeled in and balanced out.

The continent had some issues they needed their Dreamer for, but Zelia and Cy had the matter in claw and fin. That they could *both* fly was a massive help. For too long, those sky-realmers had been picking on them. Which was the current issue they were tackling, as their crabbiest problem remained unreachable.

It was fine, as the trapped Kaiju was the target of many a Jotun. Artorian's chosen spent a full day in conversation with the Muspelheim chosen. The methods they eventually came up with were cheeky. To facilitate easier conversation, Zelia tele-ported one of her children over to act as an intermediary. Zelia and Cy spoke through him, and anything that was said to him they could hear in turn. It was, at the very least, more effective than Muspelheim launching message Goblins down at Jotun-heim via souped-up catapult. 'Splat' stories gained a life of their own when those Goblins were reconstituted. There was even a flight badge of honor system.

When it came to light that the Muspelheim chosen hadn't actually *tried* to wake the duo up, Zelia successfully managed the facial expression that was universally known as 'unamused.' She directed her child to turn toward the direction her Dreamer was, and take a nice big breath. The breath wasn't needed for a yell. It was needed so he'd be comfortable when she handed the reins over to Halcyon, who pulsed her power through the connection, forcing the latent Aura around Zelia's child to reverberate in the exact pitch and tone of a pod distress call.

Artorian's eyes shot wide open as the waves brushed over his own Aura. Subconscious warning systems were going off that he'd developed from his time as the Long. You never knew when the crustaceans were going to come and be crusty corsairs. Waves of light burst forth from behind his optics as he thought he was underwater, and attempted to illuminate the location of the threat while making himself look dangerous. The sudden flash blinded all those within visual range on the same deck level, and those a deck above or below jumped away from the walls of light that beamed up between the cracks of the floor and ceiling.

Dawn grumbled, as Mana activity was not conducive to restorative napping. She grumbled as she got upright, slapping her hand over Artorian's eyes without thinking. Dawn whined loudly in response to his antics. "Too bright! Turn that off."

The Administrator blinked a few times, eliminating the emanation. He stretched with a yawn, then extricated himself from the mass of pillows to do some very unnecessary yoga. *Mmmf*. "I feel good, but a little sore. Like I weigh a ton and ate too much."

Dawn rubbed her eyes as she was forced to sit up since her pillow had moved. She dared a cursory check when the wood below his feet creaked and strained loudly. "You currently weigh twelve tons, and the floor of my trireme isn't happy about that. Control your density and set it back to mundane levels. Same process as usual, just expect it to take longer now."

The fact registered slowly, but it brought a big smile to her face. "Speaking of, congratulations on your Bonding Ascension! Not the fastest someone ever made it to A-rank, but very impressive. How do you feel?"

Artorian looked himself over, flexed his hands, and seemed fine. "Feels good. Feels alright. No issues? The pressure problem is all gone, so that's nice. I feel tougher. Stronger. Odd thing to *feel* as a Mage. My reserves feel like they're hanging around B-rank two, but the A-rank zero basis feels like it's in place regardless?"

Dawn nodded at his self-assessment. "That's right. As an A-ranker, A-zero is your new floor, even if your reserves dip down to the B-ranks. It's why a B-rank nine has such difficulties against an A-zero. The category difference is always present, and even if Mana runs out, the A-ranker is always operating on a higher floor. Just wait until you hit A-five and start generating Liminal Fields now and again. Your dreams can become a reality; that's how you get *waking nightmares*. In case you wondered why so few A-rankers choose to sleep. I'm so glad that hasn't been an issue for Cal. Who doesn't... sleep..."

Her smile faded, and Artorian's wasn't far behind as they came to the realization at the same time. Dawn's words just tumbled out of her mouth. "Cal doesn't sleep. *Cale... does.*"

Their combined retort sounded in unison. "Abyss."

Artorian slowly pressed his hand over his mouth. Dawn copied his motion, and was pensive for a moment as they locked gazes. Dawn ventured the question she honestly didn't want to ask. "Did... did he ever say where 'broken' items came from?"

The old man shook his head no, but they had the suspicion of it now. The academic spoke slowly, testing his words to keep the volume at a mundane level. "We... we should gather those up. *In a hurry.* I have needed to check in with the other continents for far too long. I'm going to do them one at a time now that I have a better way of looking for the issues. I'll start at Midgard and work my way up. Can you give Jotun and your own Muspy a cursory overview, and sort problems? I think we napped for a little longer than intended."

She nodded, they shared a quick hug, and got right on task. They walked in opposite directions to their respective issues, and slapped a cacophonous high five together that shuddered through the trireme before they both teleported out in tandem. It served as a fantastic clarion call to tell the entire trireme's crew that they were now both awake. The Dreamers were off to confirm if 'the broken' and Cal's naps were connected, and the chosen were gleeful to have their Divines back in action. There was work to do!

Karakum returned to the huddle, mimicked his best attempt at a smile, and addressed the other chosen. "Don't you just love that they're so loud? Surtur, you felt our Dreamer wink out too. It should be safe now."

Surtur uncoiled her long tail, and within its confines rested something new. Something *dreamt*. She pressed her hand against her own scaled cheek. Concerned for the creature's well-being. "How are we going to tell her, without her wanting to destroy him? He's precious, and sweet."

The Goblins all turned their hands up in a unified 'I don't know.' The Oni said nothing, and the race representatives were standing back. They didn't feel high enough in the named one hierarchy to make decisions here.

Karakum had no such qualms. "We should wait until the other Dreamer is back, and bring it up then. Our Divine may be less inclined to purge, as she is… different when the Jotunheim Dreamer is around. I do enjoy seeing our Divine happy. Surtur, did you get anything out of the newling that would help our case?"

Surtur just shook her serpentine head, her golden headdress chinking. "All I have managed to glean from our connection is that he is a Djinn. Though not what that is. I would also prefer to wait until the other Dreamer returns."

Karakum nodded, his four arms curling behind his back as the fine sepia robes swayed to his movements. "Then wait we shall. We should safeguard him somewhere."

The Oni looked around the room, and picked up the first item his massive, muscled red fingers found. "Have lamp?"

That seemed good enough. While Surtur handled the Djinn, Karakum skittered over and flicked the messenger spider-boy in the nose. "Ow!"

Zelia's voice came through the connection, and her child spoke it. "That was unnecessary. They're awake now, aren't they?"

Karakum clicked irritably. "What wonderful methods you have. Have you located the other Dreamed one? The Dreamer of Flame made it easy for us, as the Djinn formed locally. Whatever pink thing woke from the dream of yours just appeared, became aware, and then winked out of existence. Scouts from all over the eternal sands have turned up nothing, neither have the sailor-class. They honestly barely know what to look for."

The spiderling said nothing, then just shook its head as Zelia replied. "No webs triggered and no water touched. Based on what you have told us so far, it has our Dreamer's ability to come and go as it pleases. Without a solid description save for 'bright pink eyes,' we don't have much to go on."

Zelia copied her Dreamer's brow-kneading motions. "It's likely our Dreamer will return to Jotunheim before Muspelheim, so we will inform him of the Dreamed ones. We are hopeful we'll have it contained by then, but this cannot be hidden from them. The hives know well of the tales that Dreamers all hunt for the broken. Both of our continents have shrines stuffed full with objects and trinkets that have been sealed in some way."

She sighed at what the actual difficulty of the situation was. "The creatures though... they have all been destroyed. I was sad to learn that it was the same case on your end. We will resume the search. Please treat my son nicer than you have. He *does* feel the pain you inflict."

Karakum clicked back in amusement. One of his claws pressed to the spiderling's nose. Well it was just a flat space with two vertical slits angled to the sides of a wedge, but it served the purpose all the same. "Oh. I know. For some reason... There is just such an odd pleasure in counting the number of winces someone makes. It has been a very useful trait for some of the more problematic creatures on Muspelheim. Worry not, Spider Queen. Surtur will be doing most of the speaking. Ever since I recalled our very brief joint history, I prefer to limit our interaction to the professional sense. Scorpions and spiders... don't mix well. A dreamy day to you both, Chosen of Jotun."

Halcyon looked to a visibly-furious Zelia as the connection closed. "Well, that was... unpleasant. Informative, but unpleasant. I have more bad news, I'm afraid."

Zelia's carapace turned from a harsh crimson to a pale blue. "What now…?"

Halcyon just stepped out of the way. With her frame no longer blocking the view, Zelia could plainly see that the King Crab had found the hole in the world. The hard-shell was crawling out of the beneath. "Oh, abyss!"

CHAPTER THIRTY-SIX

Artorian appeared above a vast forest when he fuffed into Midgard. Unfortunately, he fuffed over that forest with the completely wrong body density. The brand-new A-ranker was so heavy that he crashed through the ground on arrival. Violently quaking the earth when he punched through the dirt —with all the resistance that water offered a steel ball—right into the Midgard beneath.

The unbalanced A-ranker clung onto whatever he could to slow down, which ended up trashing an entire root system. He in no way had the energetic difference in movement under control. His new rank would *indeed* need another set of walking lessons. He was sure Dawn would snicker when she found out.

Motes appeared in the senate as Chandra slammed the door on her way in. <Who just threw a *meteor* down in my seventh garden? The entire place is now a wreck! Split into a massive canyon! I was working on my gardenias there!>

Artorian groaned, closed his eyes, and winked his mental self into the senate as well. <That was me. Sorry. A-rank is rough. I am on Midgard, I'm here to help, and very possibly to

get help. Chandra, you're an A-rank. Could we talk? Also, I am at the *bottom* of said canyon.>

The green mote hovered above the luminous dot and bumped into him. <You can apologize by being a proper Administrator and seeing to my grievances first. Henry! I see your mote hiding there! Marie can have her turn after, so when you tell her Artorian is here, and she wants to come stomping over to fetch him? She can wait. Her. Turn. Artorian, can you port to me with a root as connection?>

The luminous mote wobbled, then stopped and controlled itself. <I think so. Is there one near me?>

<There is now. Get over here.> Chandra stated what she needed and winked out. Artorian followed suit, thinking it best not to give anyone reason to yell at him. Aiden and Henry just silently bobbed. One turning to the other.

<Well. Yay help?> Henry tried to lighten the mood, but Aiden didn't bite. Something was bothering him. The mote snarled when Aiden did.

<Let me guess. You first, as usual?> Aiden's voice was animalistic and gruff when he replied, his mote colored with a tinge of irritation.

Henry bobbed excitedly, failing entirely to catch the intonation. <Sounds good to me! Thanks, Aiden, you're the best!>

Henry's mote winked out, leaving only Aiden's as he brooded, slowly changing to darker mote colors as his resentment fed, and fed. He spoke to himself with another snarl, with none present to hear. <You are terrible friend lately, Henry. You don't feel like friend anymore. Humans this. Humans that. What happened to doing it together? Your words just pretty words now. Pretty words from nothing more than deceitful pretty boy.>

Aiden winked out, leaving the white marble senate empty once more.

Chandra impatiently tapped her foot. A real, physical, Mana body foot on the base of tree roots. The reverberation made it extremely easy for Artorian to find her, and he fuffed in with a cloud of down. As if a pillow exploded at his point of entry. Was the teleportation effect more pronounced than usual? A-rank differences.

The old man raised his eyebrows up when he saw the Lady to be much different in appearance. "Chandra, you're a tree person!"

"Alraune, Artorian. I'm a *flower* person. I am suppressing my fragrances so you don't suffer any number of adverse effects. I am made of leaf, and petal. My true form is a tree-sized flower. Though since you are stationed on Jotun, I hear that's common fare. Can we get right to it? I want to yell at Cal." When she mentioned the flower form, he noticed that she was indeed a plant-based entity, though possessing all the bonuses being an A-ranked Mage brought.

"You're beautiful! I will, of course, collate your complaints and do what I can before tugging him into it. What's been going on in Midgard?" He produced a quill and clipboard, paper already prepared.

"The others keep cutting all of my trees down. I worked hard to spread them to every corner and cover every patch of land. Then Henry and Marie's people come and log them to make room!" She fussed, several of her roots whipping about from agitation. The bright green tendrils snapped like whipcracks, responding to her mood.

Artorian pondered a moment. "Chandra? It is the empty space that makes the bowl useful. If you covered every last bit of land, the others don't have any space left to live. It doesn't sound like a surprise they're cutting things down. You're choking them like invasive creepmoss."

The Alraune made a squelching plant-noise in her throat. It sounded like a *tsk*. Artorian tried to get some more information. "What conclusion did you reach when you got together with the other supervisors and talked it over, concerning land-mass division?"

Chandra gave him a quizzical look. "Talk? We don't talk to one another. What are you on about? We all push our own tasks and try our best to see them through. We don't really have the time to get involved with the world of another."

Artorian slapped his forehead. "Are… are you telling me that you're all giving each other more work by getting in the way of everyone else?"

The Alraune was not in agreement. "No, Administrator, they are getting in my way. That's all."

The clipboard *thunked* as it struck Artorian's forehead instead of his hand. "I… understand where this is going. Nobody talked. You likely haven't had a single meeting. There's no agreement on who acts where and who does what, and you're all 'doing your own thing.' Does that sound about right?"

Chandra frowned. As much as a plant person could. "Have you been keeping tabs on us? That's more or less how things have been this entire time. The others don't want to talk to me, anyway. Anytime we accidentally meet it's nothing but snapping at one another for border friction this, beast invasion that."

Artorian sighed. "Is that possibly because at the time of your meeting, Henry and Marie were also both dealing with excess work and grievances the other caused?"

The nature Mage paused. "…maybe."

Repeated *thunks* of clipboard to face followed. "You have the senate! You can meet up with them anytime to chat!"

Chandra looked away. "I don't want to. Marie has to apologize first."

Artorian made his paper and quill vanish. He wasn't going to need them. "Okay. I know what to do here. Let me ask, Chandra. Aside from the grievances between supervisors, are there any outstanding issues? Broken creatures or items? Do you have a creature or preferred named one you can speak through while I go about?"

Chandra swayed, and a plant curled up along her being, coming to rest upon her palm. It was a small flower, but beautifully pink and violet. "This is Kudzu, one of my named ones. He will accompany you so I can speak through him. All broken creatures have long been mulched, and we ran out of broken items years ago. It's very difficult for them to hide when nature itself is hunting them. Imagine being hunted by every blade of grass."

She chewed on her lip-equivalent when she considered the question concerning other outstanding issues. "I suppose... I suppose not. The Wolfmen have been the best for me. Rather than cutting things down, they are making their homes with what has already fallen. They are welcomed in my woods. The Kingdom and Queendom in the making? Not so much."

Artorian accepted Kudzu, and placed him upon a shoulder. It was a pretty plant, and yet something about the silent named one made him feel that this creature killed in the shade. Or with shade? 'With' seemed more appropriate somehow. Artorian put it out of mind and replied to Chandra. "I understand; who is closest?"

Chandra pointed outside of her private grove, which was a wonderland of flora and fauna. Flowers otherworldly and crea-tures so aesthetic they deserved to be on shrine walls roamed free here. "Aiden, Wolfmen leader. He can be crass, but the honor in him is strong. He has a very narrow way of seeing the world. If you have ever spent time around wolves, the same pack rules hold true."

Artorian nodded appreciatively while he had a glance, his eyes focusing on spots of Mana density. Aiden stood out like a flare. "I'll figure it out. I think I found him. Easily the largest energy signature in that section of the continent. A-rank makes looking much simpler. I would like to speak of that later, if possible. Or the senate? I think I have some ideas on how to move correctly, and walking is coming easily without the dila-tion problem. If you could make me a written list of everything you need to forward to Cal? I'll have Zelia come pick it up. I'll figure out how to... designate the teleportation spot. Somehow. I'll make shrines or something."

He paused, wondering why there needed to be a wait time on that project. "Speaking of, I should just do that now. Where can I plunk one?"

Chandra frowned, knowing full well what the costs in the item shop were. "Teleporting is expensive, Administrator. Are you sure that's a good idea?"

She didn't follow up on her question. Artorian was determined to do some good, so Chandra just pointed. "Your face tells me yes. Over there, between those two large oak-mahogany hybrids. I had been wondering what to add, but if you're going to install a shop item that I do not have to spend Mana on, you are free to it. Especially for tasks that see to my further convenience. Oh, at the next big meeting, we are to bring our primary named one. So you know."

Artorian nodded in understanding and pulled up the shop, needing a minute to figure its workings out again. "I appreciate it. Let's see... shrine... shrine... Does it have to be a shrine? Why not just a platform? Those look cheaper. It's just a safety spot and waypoint for in and out teleportation. I'll go with this round, flat one."

A coin materialized in Artorian's hand as he made his selection, causing the screen to go away. He trotted over and tossed it down in the designated spot. A blueprint of the desired creation light-framed into being. Interesting. Was that a derivative of his light grid? *Nice application.* He grabbed the blueprint with Mana and scooted it over an inch. When he was satisfied, the blueprint reacted and filled in with color and solidity, becoming real. Artorian had to admit he was impressed. "Well, that was easy. Pricy, but easy."

He looked around for a moment, and noticed that the trend of chosen didn't hold up here. All of Chandra's named ones retained their more bestial appearance. "Zelia is a spiderling, but tries her best to take on human guise. Interesting how none of your creatures are humanizing."

Chandra shrugged, but the way her shoulders moved betrayed her disinterest in humanity. "I wanted to be more like them, so they don't try to become more human. I'll have that list ready when your named one comes. Good luck with Aiden, Administrator."

Artorian nodded and stepped onto the platform; he knew a dismissal when he heard one. In addition to becoming a beacon of light, using this new platform gave him a teleportation discount! He *fuffed*, arriving in the middle of the Wolfmen camp with the usual feathery flare and puffy sound. The Wolfmen, of course, howled in surprise, jumped, and ran for it since a strange creature had just appeared in their midst.

Worst of all, for them: It looked human.

The Administrator processed a moment of confusion concerning his own rank. He'd been at B-rank two in terms of stored Mana. He'd bought a platform and that dropped him to B-rank one. Then he'd placed it, and now he was at… B-rank four? That was… strange. Did Broker Bob party too hard today? He added the moon to his visitation list; the Bobs needed to be checked on. That was some exquisitely bad math.

"Die, fiend!" Some seven-foot Gnoll, a dog-like creature that looked like it had grown up in the wild, charged him in the equivalent of chainmail while holding a curvy hatchet. "Garren slays! A portion of meat for Garren!"

Artorian considered the linguistics used. Garren spoke about himself in the third person? Cute. The hatchet came down, and shattered on Artorian's head like it was spun glass. Garren's arm made some unpleasant popping sounds, and his warcry dropped to simpering yelps. Artorian wasn't exactly worried about a D-rank two with a crummy hatchet.

As the named one ran away to a shaman for healing, tail between his legs, Artorian was surrounded by dozens of Spearwolves—Wolfmen with pointy sticks. Was that iron on the ends of those spears? They'd managed to work iron! That was wonderful!

Thudding hurried from the distance, and Artorian altered his vision to see that Aiden was running toward him on all fours. As the Wolfmen leader came into direct view, Artorian smiled and just pleasantly waved at him. "Hello there! I don't believe we've properly met. I am Artorian, Administrator. I heard there were some issues you needed to escalate to our big boy upstairs, the great spirit?"

Aiden growled in his approach as the spearmen made way, but his bestial rage faded as the words trickled through his mind. The leader's fangs receded, and to his own dismay, Aiden took on more human features as his body popped and morphed. He retained many of his more bestial aspects, but vocal cords really helped when trying to speak. "You... already spoke to the humans? You were in the white think castle only minutes ago."

Artorian shook his head no. "I came here first after hearing from Chandra. Or... do you know her as the Alraune?"

Aiden snarled at his people to get back to task. He had this well in claw and fang. They, of course, didn't dispute. "Gaia, the earth mother of plant and tree? I know she has other names. I remember some, from the last circle-joining where the great spirit attended. Our problems come only from the humans taking territory that we have cleared. It is not theirs to claim."

Aiden was clearly displeased about a great number of things, so Artorian made a hand movement for them to scooch somewhere out of the way. He had not expected Aiden to have adapted such a feral mindset, but he'd work with the quirk rather than against it.

When they moved to sit on a fallen tree, Artorian discovered that Aiden couldn't stop talking when he was given the slightest opportunity to get his problems off his chest. Artorian was there for hours. Holy Cal, he had missed a ton! Most presented issues also seemed rooted in deep... he was going to call it lack of cooperation. It was the dark of night before the Wolfmen leader ran out of things to say. The Administrator didn't write them down. Aiden's complaints were personal issues, for the most part, and best kept private.

When Aiden learned that he had not at all been the last supervisor in the Midgard queue Artorian had checked on, his mood improved dramatically. As before, Artorian received a plot to put a teleportation platform down. Artorian found that the idea of supervisors being able to talk to *him* more easily, via lists and named ones rather than the senate where they could all easily be overheard and snooped on, seemed popular. Artorian felt like he was starting some kind of bureaucracy, but tried not to entertain the thought.

Ikkar, a named one that initially seemed to be just a squirrel, was anything but just a squirrel. The bright yellow being had Fringe-quality spunk, and a matching attitude. Ikkar settled on his other shoulder, and clamped firm with his feet as the Administrator activated the teleportation pad. It became a beacon of light as before, and Marie screamed when Artorian appeared from out of nowhere in the middle of her bathhouse.

Promptly chased out by hurled bars of soap, Artorian found a decent-sized town complete with walls and a gate. The commotion did not end once he was free from the wooden bathhouse. He hadn't known she was in the baths! Guards with fully-functional cuirasses and halberds ran over to control the situation. They tried to tell him they were the town guard, and he was to come with them for breaking and entering transgressions. He had to be put into the brig. Old men should not sneak into the Queen's private bath time! As such, he was due to be charged for serious crimes against the crown!

"Listen, *D-three*. I…" Artorian stopped his sentence before he ever finished it. Oh. He was doing *the thing*. He was so different from the normal people that he was acting like he wasn't one of them, because they couldn't do anything to him if he didn't want them to. So *that's* what that felt like. It was… automatic. He hadn't even thought about it twice, and it just slipped out. He'd been lucky this time and caught it early, but sweet pyrite was that one slippery slope. "I… would be delighted to go to the brig! Sounds like a party. Let's go!"

The guards were visibly confused at the old man's quick turnaround. Was he drunk? Was he just insane? Or was he a very deranged old fool that had just stupidly stumbled away from his caretaker? They didn't know, and they put him in the brig all the same.

Joel clicked the lock on the iron doors shut, and sat down next to Molar. "I tell you, Mol, I have never seen someone be so happy to be put in the brig before. He was thanking us the entire way through town for showing him around. He was even excited when he saw the iron door. He's a weird one, I tell you."

Mol laid his cards on the table, really not wanting to address it. "High card. Draw."

Joel made a sound of disdain, having drawn a jester when prompted. "The Queen be burned. A joker. I've lost."

Thump.

"You want to burn me, bannerman?" Marie's regal voice filled the brig after teleporting into the building. She gave off a feeling that the living legend of **Glory** personified had shown up. Said living legend was also visibly displeased, even if her face wasn't visible underneath the helmet. The Queen wore some impressive full plate: Her armor covered her with completeness, and lacked any seams or weaknesses. Artorian recognized it as Cal-make immediately.

He snickered, and the guards shot up to their feet so fast that their cards flew around the jail as they snapped to a salute. "My Royal! We… uh… No, ma'am! Your eminence is untouchable. My apologies for my foolish choice of words."

Marie stepped right by the guards, but Artorian frowned as she did. Right on her first step, her Aura came unhinged from her being, the heavy field emanating as Marie let her Mana hang free. Was she showing it off, or did she not know how to properly control it? Her rampant fielding froze the two poor guards completely in place. It wasn't a difficult guess that they would remain that way so long as she was there. Marie slid into place in front of his cell, armored gauntlets pressed to her hips. "The brig, Administrator. Really? You let them take you to *the brig?*"

Artorian shrugged. "Why not? Seemed like harmless fun."

Marie pointed out the door. "With me. Right now. Henry is informed and waiting."

He put his hands in the air, stood up, and walked *through* the iron grate like it was made of paper napkins. The bars crooked and bent as he stepped through, the iron whining loudly as it snapped apart against his advancing frame. When the Queen and the strange old man left, Joel and Molar both gasped for air. They fell to the ground, and trembled a moment to regain control of themselves. Their fingers were numb. It was a thoroughly bad idea to anger the Queen. Being frozen in place had been their punishment, and both of the guards determined she had been kind in her judgement.

When Joel staggered to his feet, he saw the fate of the iron door. Buckled and broken. "Hey, Mol? I... I don't think that was just some old man."

Molar snatched the cards up, irritated. "You think, Joel? You think? Were the yellow squirrel and pink flower on his shoulders not a dead giveaway?"

CHAPTER THIRTY-SEVEN

After days of meetings that felt so stretched and long that his sense of time was suffering, Artorian fuffed into Alfheim. He was still kneading his temples, having left the electric squirrel and kudzu flower behind in the castle with Henry and Marie.

Artorian could scarcely deal with all the huff and pomp that were the needs of Kingdoms, and the forced diplomacy with dozens of advisors. It interrupted their work.

He finally understood why there was so much infighting on Midgard, and why it took forever to get even the smallest task done. He was so glad to be out of there, having provided both Marie and Henry's personal castles a teleportation beacon to wriggle his way out from their clutches sooner. If he needed to have dinner with *one more* selfish and self-centered socialite who thought their very existence was the most prized thing in all the lands, he'd... never mind. Why did power-lust and greed always keep developing in the higher echelons? It was maddening!

Artorian checked his surroundings. He was in some kind of forest on a mountain, nice and alone. Great! Finally, some free time to sate the tiny curiosities he hadn't been able to get to.

Like what was going on with these teleportation platforms and his Mana.

Pulling up the shop, he squeezed his chin as he inspected the teleportation pad's data further. He sat for an hour to do some fiddling, but an additional menu eventually opened up, showing the numerical values of how things were calculated. "Aha!"

He didn't understand a good amount of the numbers, but he scrolled to read over every entry regardless until he found some words that looked at least a little familiar. "Here we go. This looks promising. 'From base count, apply discounts to net costs based on appropriate measures and sympathies listed in chart seventy-seven B.'"

Artorian scratched his head. "Where is chart seventy-seven B?"

Further scrolling adventures landed him the prize, as once he found the charts, he discovered they were listed in numerical order. The information present within, on the other hand, was so poorly organized that Alexandria would have thrown a fit. "This base cost calculation is a mess. I don't have the math for this. These modifiers, though... Let's see. Seventy-two percent cheaper from a **Law** tier that includes use of the lower tier **Law** in question. Twenty-one percent from using a simple platform, no bells or whistles. Ten percent for purchaser providing thematic effect. Forty percent for direct sympathy to notice-form-related-entry T84..."

He scratched his head again, and went on another scrolling adventure. Artorian found that T84 specifically referred to the teleportation entry in some larger catalogue. Good to know. Going back to where he was, he kept going. "Twelve percent from direct native connection to main T84 Core. Forty percent from a direct-sympathy minion under said T84 Core. Exception applies, see section blah blah blah below..."

While he felt like he'd been getting bogged down in this wreck of a text, Artorian's smile widened when he read the exception. "If a direct sympathy named one is equal to the native mind in relevant Core, increase value categorically. So...

is... Is Zelia giving me a four hundred percent discount to base costs all by herself? Well, that's a bug... that... will conveniently not be mentioned for a while. Let's tally that up. Seventy-two, twenty-one, ten, forty, twelve, four hundred. All total, five hundred and fifty-five perce... Ha! Ironic!"

So, his discount was so high that he gained Mana rather than spending it when he placed one? The buying cost applied normally, and the refund kicked in at the end. He was hovering around B-rank seven-ish right now. He shouldn't... he shouldn't use that... for... obvious personal gain. Besides, people so far had all liked having a beacon. Nothing wrong with... littering them everywhere. Right?

The sound of heaving breath pulled him from his scheming. People? Dismissing his easily twelve screens of insider information, Artorian got to his feet and hopped onto a tree for a nice vantage point. It croaked a bit unpleasantly, and he altered his density so he didn't break the poor thing. Wait, what was he doing? One light platform later, and he elevatored into the air. Much better! He saw a group of... hmm. Looked like Elves? Running and clambering in white robes that sported an orange trim. They weren't being chased. Why the running?

Some further inspections revealed a small crowd at the base of the mountain. A few people had robes with a different color trim, and based on the innate energy signatures... it had to do with their rank. Right! Nong had told him about this. Gaining ranks was much more difficult in Alfheim because they used pill cultivation. Were they by chance having a competition for some kind of...?

He just looked over his shoulder. Plant. Definitely a plant. It was so obvious to his sight that the out-of-place plants could only have been put there on purpose. The affinity difference stuck out like a sore thumb. If this was a test of some kind, he should find the local leadership and talk about Alfheim needs. Or... he could poke his sizable nose in. He really should do the prior... Oh, who was he kidding? *Fuff*.

Teleporting in next to the out-of-place affinity signature, the flowers caught his attention right away. "*Ooh*. Air and celestial Essence in a bluebell?"

It looked like little flakes of snow were constantly falling as glimmering specks from the hanging flowers. The flakes themselves entered a natural stasis when they fell, preserving their form until they hit the ground. Was this where Cal had gotten the affinity combination for his stasis Runes? Well, wasn't that just lovely.

One of the orange-rimmed robes burst through the foliage, but Artorian didn't look up. He'd known they were coming from passive echolocation alone. The youngster did not appear to have manners. "Wh… what? You! That root is mine! Stand aside in the presence of Ob-Su-Wong!"

The student of some kind chuffed, pushed his chest out, and reared up in a quasi-martial stance that made him look half regal and half silly. Well, he was certainly full of himself. Orange-rim had pomp and bluster for days, which only reminded him of the region he'd freshly escaped from. Still, Artorian began with some diplomacy. "I'm just passing through, my boy. Admiring the flowers. Who's your friend?"

The other orange-rim burst through, completely out of breath. He dropped right into a martial stance when he saw the first student, fists raised toward his rival. When there was no immediate fight, the new student realized there was a third person present.

Artorian noted something interesting. Oh? What was this? This second orange-rim was cycling Essence to his eyes, and was looking him over. A D-ranker looking at a Mage? Well, we knew what effect was going to trigger there…

The newcomer was instantly nauseous, and bent over against a tree to throw up his entire lunch. Yup. About what was expected, if a bit harsh. The newcomer recovered swiftly, wiping his mouth off. "Ob! Do not challenge this Elder! I think he is a Grand Elder!"

Pomp and bluster boy had no such interest. "Inner court students of House Su do not run from challenges, Yiba-Su-

Wong! It was a waste to be paired against you; I was always destined to be the victor in this outcome. Teacher Za-Wing was merely trying to teach you this lesson in humility. Rather than cling to my heels like the seeds of a bramble, grow on your own! My tailcoats have no room for stains."

Artorian scooped the earth out from under the plant, and lifted the flower whole. He turned his attention back to the students. Yiba fell to his knees and slammed his head to the ground in deference. Ob merely took a full martial stance to claim his prize, while the old man mused. "You know. I really shouldn't interfere here... bu~u~ut."

Ob-Su-Wong received a flight lesson as he was hurled off the mountain with minimal effort. Ob screamed the whole way, but Artorian's aim was exquisite; he fell right in the spot all those supposed teachers were gathered. "Please raise your head, my boy. Why don't you take this, and spare me a moment of your time?"

Yiba graciously accepted the plant, and slammed his head back into the ground. "Student greets Grand Elder! Thank you, Grand Elder! Inner court disciple Yiba-Su-Wong is ever at your service."

Artorian sat next to Yiba and gave him a pat on the back, letting his starlight Aura free to do some work on all those scrapes the student had suffered. "I'm not from around here, Yiba. Can you tell me about who rules these lands? If there are any strange sightings or issues. Is there a unified government?"

Yiba slunk back, sitting on his knees and ankles as he was prompted to speak. He was pale for a student. Thin too. Too thin, for Artorian's liking. He had short pointed ears, and a long swath of chestnut hair. The other student had also sported similar features. A social measure?

His thoughts stopped wandering as Yiba answered. "Grand Elder, this student is ignorant. This region is protected by House Su, of which I am a disciple of the inner court. The lands have no unified leader. Only the houses of power dot the land. As far as I know, only houses with a pill refining cauldron are recognized as true houses. I would not know how to answer your question of strange sightings, Grand Elder."

Artorian nodded. "Would you say those who live here are good people, Yiba?"

When the student slammed his head back into the ground, he knew the situation was far grimmer than it appeared on the surface. "This ignorant one cannot speak ill of those who feed him, Grand Elder. Please forgive me, I cannot answer."

Yiba was patted on the shoulder. "All's well. That tells me about what I thought was the case. As for sightings. Any creatures or things that change or bend the laws of the world?"

Yiba slowly eased up. "The… sword of the Su Patriarch? It bends space, and no armor can halt its strike. Each swing causes sounds as the waves of water. Even if the blade does not connect, the invisible reach that extends from it cuts regardless."

Artorian smiled to hide his feelings. "Sounds like the *weapon* variants ended up here. Delightful. I'm going to have to figure out how to take care of that without creating endless diplomatic incidents. Or I could just… pop over?"

With the Grand Elder musing to himself and brushing a hand down his long beard, Yiba said nothing. It was folly to do anything an Elder did not wish you to. A Grand Elder? Your fate was sealed by their whims. "I'm going to have a look around. If it's all weapons on Alfheim, I've got a problem."

Yiba saw the Elder do something odd with his eyes while the old man looked to various points on the horizon. "Alright. I'm seeing three… four… forty… oh heck. Cal, you littered Ember's Mana swords from Skyspear all over the place! Are they all jians? No, just most."

Artorian's inspections across the land continued. Vision darting from one perspective to another. He saw through a sympathy connection he was fueling some serious Mana into as he kept looking for 'broken' items. He found some spears. A halberd or three. Little bit of everything. He'd just latched onto the jians first, due to stronger personal sympathies.

Weapons, armor… great. Some pelts? Looked like the 'broken' creatures had been culled already, using said weapons. Well, that was certainly a way to get a lineage going. "Crackers and toast… it's going to take me ages to gather all of those up if I want to do it nicely. Never mind. I'm sated. Hold onto this flower, Yiba. Take good care of it while you're at it. It may yet teach you something."

"Student thanks Grand Elder!" Yiba smashed his head into the ground to bow, and then quickly made himself scarce after accepting the mystical bluebell. Yiba wanted to get out of there before the being who made him throw up just by being glanced at changed his mind. Even though all that occupied Yiba's mind was the Grand Elder's quest to gather all the weapons in this land.

What an accomplishment *that* would be.

Artorian watched the boy go, got up, brushed his robes off, and **fuffed**. As usual, people dove screaming out of the way when he appeared in a cloud of pillow innards. A few tall-eared Elves all dove onto a single person in the middle of the chamber, dragging him away. Probably to scurry their leader to safety. There was the usual bluster, yelling, threats, demands. Yada yada. A few blades broke against Artorian's back and shattered as they tried to cut his neck. No big deal.

The Administrator brushed a hand down his beard, inspecting the jian before him that was very carefully propped up on some miniature shrine. He heard vague mentions from the Elders in the main family house to call Grand Elders, because their weapons weren't doing anything. Some Mages remained in the area? Well, likely a good idea. Nice to have one or two in the back pocket. Everyone else here was *maybe* a C-ranker, though the plateaus of rank were very strict and even. There was nearly no deviation between the Elders.

Pill cultivation was odd. He'd want the details eventually.

"Grand Elder Sung-Woon is here!" The call went out like it was a saving grace. Artorian didn't bother turning as the silver robe-clad Mage burst through the roof and landed in the honored family meeting room. He cracked and broke the ground as a Mage did, performed the usual self-righteous bluster, and seemed to be the source and inspiration for a lot of the posturing pomp that was going around.

"Thousand Needle Piercing Heaven!" When the Mage launched some attack, Artorian swiftly deduced it was an affinity mixture of air and celestial. Oh, like the flower? It had a needle shape, stab identity, the source was B-ranked glue Mana. The originator only seemed to have a strong air affinity channel, and he was being wasteful with those barely seventy-ish needles of his that appeared. Thousand? He was a little behind in the count. Sure, they were nice and glowy, but the weak-channel celestial identity was just... there. Unrefined and uncontrolled.

The prediction lines Artorian was getting were there for... might as well be posterity. The lines were see-through, meaning the attacks couldn't possibly cause him harm as his Aura shielding automatically adapted to earth and infernal. It did coat him in a dangerous, shadowy glow that he had to admit made him appear somewhat ominous.

When the needles struck his Aura shielding, they just vanished via cancellation. People gasped, and the Grand Elder jumped back. "That was my most powerful technique! It is a demon!"

Artorian shifted into his starlight Aura. Soothing the fools around him. "A demon? Oh no. I got rid of all of those. If you find any, do let me know? I was proud of completing that task. No, Su family, I'm not here for you. I would appreciate not being bothered while I do my inspections, but if you *must* intrude, then I will play with you."

"Attack! He cannot defeat all of us!" The Grand Elder barked out the order, and Artorian hung his head. Sighing in response.

"I can't in good conscience even call this a fight. I'm just here to seal some problems. Then again. You know what? This item is more likely to bring your family incredible ruin than some kind of saving grace. I'm with Cal on this. Keep it. Alfheim can wait."

Artorian turned and walked out of the Su family house. All the while fending off C-ranked attacks merely by altering his Auric defenses to return attacks back at the pill cultivators. He passed from the inner area, through the private courtyard, past the family housing, through the foyer, and walked out the front door without so much as a glance over the shoulder.

To his amusement, Grand Elder Sung-Woon had decided to flee. Some family…

"Abyss this place. I'm dotting some beacons, and I'm out."

Fuff.

CHAPTER THIRTY-EIGHT

Arriving in Svartalfheim did not go as expected. First, no screaming. Second, no people diving out of the way. Third, his *fuff* couldn't be heard over the cacophonous *chunk, chunk, chunk* of massive brass and copper machines that sucked the air right out of the sky. Every direction he looked showed only an entangled orchestra of pipes. Through reinforced glass tubes, liquefied Essence was being pumped around in a very visible, aboveground fashion.

How did anyone live up here? The air was choked with smog. The gray mist that hung around like paste would sting the eyes of anyone not at least a Mage, and walking around might as well just trigger poison symptoms. A cursory glance for heat signatures showed only hulking machines, and underground activity. Oh, they all lived in the below? Maybe they didn't have to worry about the abyss-scape up above if they had a tiny paradise down there.

The outlines of people he did see up here were short, stocky, clad in copper and glass suits, and sported some kind of unholy mask that looked horrendously frightening. His starlight Aura got to work right away to form a space of pleasantry around him. He might need to form a scrubber Aura just for this as he watched the starlight effect *struggle*. "'Ey you! Wha' are ya doin' out of a suit? Yer gonna die!"

It seemed some of the locals had discovered him. The clanging metal thuds of brass boots made it toward him in a hurry, but they stopped once inside the radius of his Aura effect. His orb wasn't that big, just a couple dozen feet of cleanliness. Enough for him not to feel cramped, but it surprised the locals. "How... is it clean?"

The Dwarf took his gas mask off even as his brothers rushed to prevent him. Tussle Torncog took a deep breath of clean air, and was nearly brought to tears by it. "Oh, that's beautiful, that is."

Artorian merely smiled at the emotionally-moved Dwarf with a coal-blackened mustache. "Hello there, my friend. Is this Svartalfheim? I'm looking for the leader."

Tussle cocked his head, gas mask held loosely at his side as he composed himself. "Ah'm afraid yer a week too late? The coup d'état happened and the military's in charge now. If yer with the insurgency, ah'm sorry to say that ye lost. General Rockhound be in charge now, and he be rulin' with an iron fist. We just do our best to keep the Aether pumpin' and the zeppelins in the air."

The old man blinked. "The what?"

"Zeppelins?" Tussle just pointed up, and Artorian saw the elongated balloon-type vessels filled with some kind of gas. Aether, as the Dwarves here called it, as well. Definitely a different gas in great amounts was keeping that thing afloat. Was that a tiny carriage strapped to the underside? That would be cute if it didn't look so dangerous. What were those round things around it? Like oars strapped together and rotating in a circle. Was that changing the direction the balloon traveled? By Cal, it was!

"Well, that's... nifty." Artorian's face showed that he was

impressed, his eyes glued to the creation that he just knew Dev was going to salivate over.

Tussle beamed. "Aye! Shame they all got snatched up as observation scouts by the militants. We best get movin', human. Ah don't know how ya got here, but it ain't good ta stand still. If yer surface-side, ya better be workin' or fightin'. If ya meant to go below, remember yer drinkin' mug. If ya got the entrance pass, ah mean. Ya looked like ya packed light."

Tussle clicked his mask back on. "On the edges of the Hegemony, ya might have yer bars, taverns, and good times. Here in the capital though, there ain't no sunshine, and certainly nah roses. Ya should go back to the border checkpoint ya came in from. Smog storm is comin' in a few hours when the Aether reactors vent. Don't wanna be topside for that. Ye'll get the skin seared right off yer bones from the burnin' soot alone."

Well, this place sounded just *lovely*. Artorian got a move on and trotted after them as they left. "I'll just walk with you a moment longer. This all seems so... advanced. How did this even come about?"

Tussle looked at Artorian like he was a three-year-old asking about basic trigonometry. Everyone knew that! "Ya fail yer history, old man? One of the first Dwarves, Aes, found mechanisms that let him refine the Aether out of the air. From those, he built the designs for what became the rigs ya see today. That was hundreds of years ago, though."

The Administrator ran afoul of this date. Hundreds? Was Cal altering local time zones somehow? There was no way Svart had gotten that much time under its belt. No, easier explanation: The advancement happened explosively, and someone had been deliberately misinforming new Dwarves about the calendar, and how long certain things had been in place. Broken items were to blame for this, he was sure of it. Onto the list it went!

Maybe...

A scheme conjured into being in his mind. One he shelved

away for later. Here he thought Vanaheim was going to be the technology hotspot. He wasn't expecting all this grungy Dwarven tech. Aether? Interesting way to go about it. Why was the mug important? Right! He'd been told about that; here they drank to cultivate, and then… something with a generator? Know what? That scheme was getting moved up the to-do list. He didn't want to mess around here, and instead knew some particularly skilled Dwarves that could do a much better job. Especially with information gathering. Why, he knew an entire family of acquisition experts!

The sound of a steam horn blared, and a Dwarven voice trembled over a loudspeaker. "Shift over! Go home!"

Tussle slapped the human on his lumbar, and made a come along motion as he spoke with a muffled effect from under his mask. "Ye've got the luck of pyrite! Looks like ye can skip the border, and ah get yer shinin' company a wee while longer. Follow me to the airlock. Ah'd rather be in that odd clean air bubble around ya than in the scrubber."

The scrubber? So, they already made one? Likely another Aether machine. Sure enough, they dropped into a complex tunnel network with instructions inscribed on the wall. Several groups hurried past them to decontamination. Artorian just followed Tussle, who tore his mask off to breathe the clean air around the old man. "Flux the scrubber. Ah don't know how yer doin' that, but it's amazing. Come hook up with my squad anytime. Ah don't even want ta see yer papers. Speaking of, do ya have papers? We could use the mobile scrubber tagalong."

Artorian shook his head no, but Tussle had run-ins with evacuees before. "A'ight, figured ye might not. Checkpoint is up ahead. Shut up an' let me do the talkin'."

The old man stepped behind the Dwarven group and happily obliged as Tussle yelled out to the station ahead of them. "'Ey Tase! Ah picked up a fella along the way. Bringin' 'im to customs. Keep that zap-stick away from my thigh, ya punishment-happy militant."

Laughter resounded from around the corner, and a Dwarf in a rather fetching uniform leaned into the bend. "Come now,

Tus! Ya know Ah like seein' 'em jump. But fine. Did he lose his papers? Admiralty ain't gonna like that. Ah saw ye and yer boys were on clean up duty today. He was on the smog level? *Eeesh*. Do Ah gotta grab medical?"

Tase straightened up when the perfectly healthy, immaculately clean human passed his checkpoint. "What in Aether's name?"

Tussle grinned. "Ah like that flabbergasted look on yer face. Ya should try it more often. Beats that militant scowl o' yers."

Tase just swung his zap-stick through the air, scowling in the exact way he knew Tussle didn't like. "Get out of here, ya half-pint. Ah ain't spending the hour doin' the papers just 'cause yer draggin' a lost lamb to customs. Off with ye. Ya didn't come through my section neither! Ah ha~a~ate paperwork."

Artorian smirked as he heard Tussle giggle, and whisper, "Ah know," under his breath. Sure enough, the Svartalfheim underground was where the Dwarven society lived. Pipes with Aether were still tangled through the superstructure, but they went to powering some kind of public transit service. It was a set of carriages, contained in a long tube, on rails. It brought them to the inner city with some awful noises, and Artorian just kept nested between the smog cleaners.

The entire transit ride was the best Tussle had ever had, and his crew wasn't complaining either. They had entered the tube dirty, and left sparklingly clean, gear and all. Hours of time had been shaved off from their daily to-do lists, and Tussle's missus was sure to appreciate it. Especially since she wouldn't need to clean a suit today. Tussle was looking forward to what they might do in their surprise free time, and the pink blush on his cheeks made his squad mates poke fun.

Getting ahold of himself, Tussle grunted and scowled like a serious Dwarf. Artorian just shook his head with a knowing grin. Too late, buddy. Too late… It didn't matter.

The transit system was showing Artorian everything he might have wanted to see about Dwarven design and architecture. He had already decided sticking around long wasn't going to be necessary. This wasn't his kind of place. Massive, hewn caverns were filled with carved structures, and surprisingly spacious realms had been cleared to give the Dwarves here a sense of breathing space. The ceiling was even painted a blue that caused illumination in the cavern. He didn't want to know where or how they got that much paint.

He found out regardless. It was glow-moss, and the paint doubled as feed they slopped against the walls where they wanted it to grow. That only made him think about how they were keeping the civilization fed. He didn't want to know.

Stepping out when Tussle did, he was surprised to find a brick road leading to a small fountain on the other side of a check-in station. The human got some odd looks, but Dwarves just veered off to stay out of his way without more than a judging leer. Artorian chose to just sit on the edge of the fountain, watching some children screech and play. They were having fun. They seemed well fed, were healthy, and wore bright smiles. Something was working right about this place, at least.

Tussle extended his hand for a shake. "Here's where Ah have ta leave ya, old man. Customs is that big grimrock brick buildin' over there. They'll get yer papers sorted. If they ask what faction yer with, know they ain't actually allowed to ask ya, and ya don't need to answer."

A greeting and goodbye that he recognized? Always nice.

Artorian fished something out of his pouch as he got up. With some sleight of hand, he pressed the object into Tussle's grip during the shake. The Dwarf frowned from the strange, heavy weight. He looked down at his hand when the shake ended, discovering a single Iridium Li. He didn't know what it was, but something told him that the rectangular-shaped metal rock was as heavy in value as it was in weight.

Tussle raised his vision back up to speak, but saw only some wayward down feathers hanging in the air. The old man was gone, and the feathers fell to the ground only to disappear where they landed. "Well... That's not somethin' ya see every day. Ah have th' distinct feelin' Ah should detour to an appraiser."

Veering off his path, Tussle quickly pushed his way through a small crowd in front of the hot buns stand. Finding where he needed to be with practiced ease, a heavy wooden door *chinged*. The small copper bell chimed as he entered. Tussle didn't waste time and walked right up to the meister at the counter of the ornate, onyx desk. Heavy inspection equipment was stacked on both sides of the appraiser's office, while lists and charts took every conceivable spot on the walls.

Clearing his throat, Tussle waited. The meister sighed, flicked the lenses of his goggles up, and laced his stubby fingers. "If yer here because you found some pyrite or lesser strain of—"

Thud.

The meister was cut off as a small, silvery rectangle was placed down before him. It was just some silver. No big deal. Awfully rectangular though. Also… not silver? The meister's wayward hand reached out for an inspection device as his eyes never left the Iridium. He was surprised when he tested the weight, and more so as he got it under the lenses.

Tussle knew it was important when the meister turned pale when he looked back up, face full of dread. "Where did ya get *this*? How did ya get your hands on a military-grade asset? Knowledge of this material alone is restricted to the highest rungs of leadership. This… Come to the back."

Tussle hurried after the meister, who escaped his desk and broke into a half run further down his shop. Copper boots clanked down carved onyx stairs, and minutes later slowed when they barged right up to a vault door. A complicated set of knocks were communicated from both sides before the massive slab of metal clicked and hissed, parting with heavy vents of Aether-made steam.

Starting to get concerned, Tussle's jaw dropped as the meister pulled him into the vault. He finally understood what the big deal was when he saw what was kept within. Including why the meister, holding the nugget of metal, was so incredibly pale.

Tussle swallowed, and his mask dropped on the floor as his fingers failed him.

"Oh, merciful pyrite… what have Ah done?"

CHAPTER THIRTY-NINE

Fuffing into Vanaheim was an experience. Not even two seconds into arrival, and Artorian knew he had face-smashed through the most intricate Mana detection network he'd ever had the misfortune of passing through. He felt *covered* in cobwebs, and that was awful. Because while there were no webs, he still felt them. His Aura flared, just to make himself feel better.

"Artorian! You magnificent, wily A-ranker. There you are!" Deverash was on-scene right away, beaming proud Gnomish smiles. "Finally! I'm so excited! I can't wait to show you the matrices!" Deverash was his usual immaculate and dapper self. New clothing, but still what Artorian expected from Mister Neverdash. Speaking of said clothes, they were lined with some very bright thread.

Artorian squinted at the jacket. "Is your clothing made out of solidified and stringed Mana? Did you honestly push Mana to the purity needed for solidity *only* to make string out of it, just so you could weave and sew clothing?"

Deverash's smile grew three sizes out of pure elation. "You noticed! It hasn't even been ten seconds! Oh, how I've missed you. Come, come! You must see my magic wonderland and what I've done to the place. Everything works based off of Mana and spells. Everything!"

Deverash did a spin, and clapped his hands together. Like a choreographed swim team, Gnomes popped from the ground with bursts of light and confetti. Each finishing the pose of the last as the next one landed. Wait, was the ground made of Mana too? Holy Cal! It was! He was standing on nothing but Runes, patterns, Arrays, and who knew what else. Vanaheim's floor looked like ground, but he could see past that when he vision-cycled. "Crackers and toast, Dev! What am I looking at? The entire landmass is a construct. There are spells buried on spells, and... and are those the Pylons?"

To the other Gnomes, the old human was looking at his sandals. Dev knew better, and furiously nodded. "They are! Wow, you can see deep."

Artorian threw his hands up. "There are thousands of them. Thousands and thousands. Endless fields of Pylons! It's like they fill the entire Vanaheim underground."

Deverash performed a little jazz dance and swung a cane around that he materialized out of thin air. He spoke in a sing-song voice, and tapped the cane on the ground to make the illusion of green grass and brown dirt go away. It revealed the glass framework of the world, the design shining like it was all made of blueprints. "That's because they do~o~o!"

He performed a victorious tap-dance, and the hundreds of other Gnomes around him fell in step to dance along. They snapped their fingers in unison, and shimmied with their hips. Artorian couldn't help but follow along. Together, they slid toward some floating geometric shapes in the distance that looked like a dazzling party.

It took an hour, but Artorian got the gist of the dance as light, music, and merriment followed and guided them the entire way over to the hexagonal structures that marked Vana-heim's Gnome city entry points. "Dev, this is so much different than I expected! I thought you were living in trash! Well, I mean... failed experiments."

Deverash performed some new dance that the old man picked up and copied. "We cleaned up! Significant portions of Vanaheim got glassed when you blew that sun up. When we got the last broken thing recycled, the Mana storms out of the way, and all the Pylons in place, we figured... why not add some of our own, and make a real lightshow of a home for ourselves? We're going to tinker with all things Mana anyway. Why not make the whole place Mana? Layer it, make it work together, and really show off! There's almost a hundred thousand of us now, and you wouldn't believe the things we've come up with."

Hundreds of Gnomes were all still moving in sync with them. Bundles of boundless energy, all dressed to the nines. Deverash was clearly proud of their progress. "Scarcity? Who needs it! Greed? A thing of the past! That's for visitors to deal with! Each and every Gnome is on the same team, and works together with everyone else on just about all projects. We have been throwing ourselves at Pylons, spell forms, and combinations thereof. Whole Gnomish divisions are dedicated to puzzling out the differences in whole Arrays, advanced functions, and more. I'm really proud of our latest project, it's a real *ball* of splendor."

He clapped his hands together, and Artorian felt the specific strain of flight costs melt away into nothing. Deverash jumped up off the ground, dragging his friend with him as a moving kaleidoscopic formation of choreographed flying Gnomes shot up along with them. Their geometric pattern constantly altered, and if they had this much free time to practice, they must be doing really well for themselves!

Not feeling like questioning the display, Sunny turned his own flight on so Dev could quit dragging him. When he got high enough to see what occupied the central construction plaza, he just about screamed with joy. "You're making a new sun!"

Deverash shot finger crossbows at him with a wink. He squeaked out the words from how much he loved this next part.

"A better sun! That pattern we got out of you blowing up the old one? *Oh.*" Dev kissed his fingers and blew them outwards. "Exquisite."

Artorian looked around some before landing. At which point the small Gnome poked him in the ankle as they stood near the absolutely humongous project. "So, what brings you?"

Artorian pressed his hands to his hips when his feet solidly planted upon the ground. "Well… Was going to ask if you had any Cal-plaints. I've also been adding teleportation beacons to every realm I've been to. Snuck a few into Svart just now before making my way to Vanaheim. I'm doing continents in ascending Mana pressure order. I was also going to ask about broken items, but you have that covered. From what I can tell, it doesn't look like you're having any problems? Or at least none I would be able to help with. I can put a beacon down regardless, if you didn't mind my named one coming by to pick up a list of issues. If you had anything to write down for me to handle, or forward to Cal?"

The Gnome gave him a thumbs up. "We've got a place for one. It's in the accounts department, since life here revolves around Mana expenditures, prices, costs, and the like. Broker Bob hates us. We find all~l~l the problems, and then he has to fix them. *Hehehehe*. I think we're driving him mad; he's been making serious accounting errors the last few weeks."

Artorian snorted. "You have no idea how right you are. So, where did the old trash pile go? All those war machines you turned into homes? It's all so… geometric, and pure, and efficient. The design language here is… well, I hate to use the word, but near perfect? All the buildings, streets, and even structures I don't know the purpose of are symmetrical to many others. Nothing is out of place. Everything is exact."

Artorian pointed at one of the floating structures. "I mean the hovering, pink, eight-sided die is odd initially, but it looks like… housing?"

Deverash corrected him. "The pink die? Research and development. We sleep next to our favorite Pylons. It's how we're forming our naming structure, actually. Saves us from needing to rely on numbers, and when you're naming an entire civilization without a background, every little detail helps. As a bonus, using our own names as spell forms makes them far more powerful. Each Gnome can be said to be the living counterpart to a particular Pylon. Just said, though. We're not at being Pylons ourselves yet, but oh, when we get the golem research cranked out, we are certainly going to try!"

The Administrator didn't understand. "You want to be… sapient geometric shapes?"

Deverash nodded. "Many of us do. Our bodies actually get in the way more than they help. We're all made of Mana anyway, and the difference doesn't bother us. Our minds are all very advanced, so the body is just a shape. We're all in love with geometry, as you can probably tell. So, yes. Many of us would love to be geometric shapes."

He rubbed his hands together. "Personally, I'll always be the Gnome you know and love. I'm also the only one with my own home. It's at the exact center of Vanaheim. Remember that starting structure we began with? Well, I only had the one, and abyss if I'm going to use the shop for anything I could just make myself. Though the darn thing steals it if my work is better. We're responsible for most of the good stuff in the shop these days. Anyway, we're going to set our ambient Essence to nighttime soon. You're going to love the view."

Artorian sat on a Mana curb, and it warmed under his butt. "A random part of the curb has a warming feature?"

Dev nodded. "Every part of Vanaheim is, in effect, a giant illusion. Except that because of Mana, we can make those illusions very, very real. I was told that when Cal stops being a snoot and stops throwing all the problem people onto your Jotunheim when they're Mage-ranked, they will be coming to us instead."

"Since I always want to keep everyone that's going to come

in on their toes, I wanted a land I could change at a whim, so no visit is ever the same. Imagine going to sleep in a cave, and waking up on a plain, yet never having moved! Any features they didn't earn, they don't get to keep. Also, since we're going to become the bridgepoint one day, I never wanted to get bored."

Artorian raised a brow. "Bridgepoint?"

The gnome nodded. "Oh yes! We're making those rainbow bridges to connect the world together in order of energy density. Cal likes 'Bifrost,' so that's the name of the project. Unfortunately, he isn't letting us work on anything biological. That's Bob's department. So, we were a little tight on mob options. Speaking of, how did testing that 'Long' model of theirs go?"

Artorian squeezed his chin. "Needs more testing. In short, I died. Lost ten years."

Deverash winced. "Ten years? I can't afford to lose ten years. I've got work to do! No body testing for me then."

He paused to look up. "Oh, the ambiance is starting."

Clouds rumbled, but there were none to be seen. The sky dimmed. Vanaheim lost its manufactured sunlight, shifting to a darkened veil that showed only the flickering dark teal of clouds which slowly took shape.

All the color stripped out from Vanaheim City, while grid-lines blinked into place as far as Artorian could see. The space inside each 'box' frizzled with activity. Small hexagons of light formed, then duplicated themselves into place, allowing for the construction of a rough geometry by folding the tiny shapes over one another.

If he didn't already have deep insider knowledge, the landscape that formed would have been entirely real to him. Solid panels shuttered into place between raw outlines to finalize them. The building designs were accented by that same dark teal lighting as every structural rim in the city took on this hue and color contrast.

"We drew some inspiration from that technique of yours, if

it looks familiar. Clothing changes incoming." Dev's pastel clothes flickered, becoming some kind of dark leather. Lines of light blinked into activation as his vest transformed into a coat. Only Artorian remained unchanged as the continent around him updated to new settings.

He was just the slightest bit jealous. "Well… fancy. I wish I had a coat like that…"

Deverash beamed at him, and pointed at the city as beams of light activated from its central most structures and shot into the sky. "I thought you'd never ask! Come check out our shops! We're not ready for the public yet, but we've got things any Mage needs. Including equipment that no longer classes as mundane! It's also some of the *only* gear currently in the Soul Space that can move between realms. So, I hope that entices newcomers to go through the trouble of obtaining them. I hear your Jotun is a challenge, and I'm becoming aware Vana has a reputation that makes us be avoided. We're hoping the gear will entice an influx."

The old man nodded slowly, as those seemed like reasonable marketing decisions. "You can make… anything you want. The whole place?"

His Gnomish friend replied with a proud *mhm*! "We just need access to memories, or blueprints, or something that shows us what we're making. What the replication spell Runes can't do, we hand craft. It's why the structures and ground you see look so real. Even A-ranked Mages shouldn't be able to tell the difference between what they see in Vanaheim, and what's actually there. Do you have a request? Come, walk with me to clothing."

Dev paused his stride a moment as he inspected Artorian's hands. "There's also a minor project we need to redo, I'm afraid. Unfortunately, A-ranking has completely restored your body. Looks like that wiped out the original Mass Driver glyphs."

Artorian checked his own hands and groaned at realizing his friend was right. Dev had warned him, but Artorian swore up and down that this time it wasn't his fault! His complaints didn't matter; the spell forms had to go back on.

First, the old duo of friends went to see the sights, and Artorian reminisced. "I wouldn't mind seeing home again. That was too vague... Can you get me a memory stone for the relevant m—"

Deverash just pulled one out of his pocket, much to Artorian's instant surprise. "We *make* them. Moon needs a few million, and Cal was dying doing the same task over and over. The task used to be Bob's... but..."

The Gnome looked over his shoulder as if someone might be listening in. "My friend, you didn't hear this next part from me. We're not exactly unaware of what's really going on with the Bobs... It's a problematic thing, having one mind and soul split between multiple bodies. The mind can adapt, but the soul... It only stretches so far."

Dev's voice lowered conspiratorially. "We're down to about seven thousand Bobs, but it's still no better. So, I'm preparing at least seven thousand times the few million Cores we need. Just to be safe. Never know when every person, animal, or other mind in the Soul Space needs to be a Core for a while. Things *blow up* when you least expect them to."

Artorian nodded sagely. Wasn't that the truth. "I agree, my friend. I'll keep it in mind. Per the earlier topic, is that structure in the distance the destination? Looks rustic, like an old-time store in the middle of a long road. Those bricks look very real. Believable texture. Shingle roofing, wooden on the inside. Except that the stock doesn't match. It's all Vanaheim grid-themed. Why don't we shop around for a bit? See what fits? Then I can plunk that beacon down and let you get on with work."

Dev was all smiles once again, a cunning plan twinkling behind his eyes on a few fun activities that would let him steal away his friend for longer. "The artificial spring season is about to begin. Let me introduce you to our tailor. You're going to need something *flashy*."

CHAPTER FORTY

Clad in fanciful new regalia, Zelia was on her way back to the pagoda. A burgundy paper umbrella, held daintily, blocked the sun from her eyes, while a multi-layer kimono carefully bound and hugged around her fully humanoid form.

It was always cold in Jotunheim now, after all.

She upheld the ruse of a smiling facade at her approach, but the truth could not be hidden from those who knew her well. The details of her face were grim, and set. She had bad news. Or rather, inconvenient news, which soured her mood.

She heard the telltale *fuff* of her Dreamer's teleportation, and her sourness fell to pieces as her mood instantly brightened. Artorian had been gone a long time.

The arachnid lady paused before the door, holding out her hand to prevent its opening. Had her Dreamer not noticed her? She could hear him rummaging around inside, but at this distance he usually knew she was there. A pleasant idea came to mind, so she stepped around to the side. Perhaps she could surprise him!

Zelia leaned in through the window to speak, her eyes

catching the souvenirs of the last realm he visited. "Quality robes, my Dreamer. The insides appear to light up? I have never seen you in dark gray before. It suits you; the white of your beard really stands out and matches the luminance from the inside of your sleeves."

Startled by her voice, the old man stumbled and improvised. Performing a twirl in his lit robe, Artorian posed in response with a massive smile. "Look at my leaf!"

Zelia quirked her brow the best she could. She saw no leaf. Only her Dreamer striking an absolutely ridiculous pose as he pointed with both hands at the top of his head. "Yes... my Dreamer. It seems you have lost your leaf. Are you well? You seem frazzled."

Artorian dropped the facade. The old man flopped into his favorite bean bag with a loud *aahhh*. "It's been a busy week, realm checks aside. On a note of pleasantry: I raced magnetic palanquins with Dev over a circuit of light. Crackers, he's good. I even tried to cheat with Mana thrusters, and he still won. When he gets the Yellow Line up and running, I'm going back to compete. Haven't had such wanton fun in years. We went *so* fast."

Zelia squeezed her new lips into a line, though her tone remained flat. *Mhm*.

Artorian pushed himself up ever so barely, sensing something was off. "What's wrong, my dear? You're rarely so strained when I show back up. Come, sit and chat. I'm sure some catastrophe or another happened while I was out."

He relaxed, sat back, and just relished being cozy as Zelia elegantly walked closer to seamlessly slide into a seat next to him. "Oh... no big things."

There was something about the way she said it that made the old man snap his eyes back open mere moments after shutting them. Jotun was a place where only big problems existed, any other problems that might crop up were decidedly worse.

His attitude turned stern. "Tell me everything."

Halcyon showed up in her own fluffy spider-silk winter outfit shortly after Zelia began speaking. Not wanting to interrupt, she sat nearby as Artorian learned of recent events. Artorian was torn about the knowledge presented: How he and the fire Divine had both dreamt things *into being* during their sleep. News wasn't made better with the addition that those entities were out and about. Apparently, his Dreamed one could teleport, and Dawn's was its own bundle of wish-granting fun.

Then came the part where he and Dawn had been overheard about how it might be problematic that the great spirit sleeps. They had good news and bad news on that topic, but the fear that Cale's sleep caused Liminal events was confirmed.

With the help of some secret networking, Halcyon and Zelia had discovered that the great spirit's dreaming *did* make more of these broken things show up. As a boon, said broken congregated to the realm where the Mana density fit them best. So, the realms named Asgard and Hel were going to be… busy.

The good news: Localized breakouts had been contained. Broken items had been found and gathered in a new underground vault, where they awaited sealing. They just needed their Dreamer for that. Broken creatures turned out to be extra tasty to the local wildlife, so those weren't at all a problem.

The bad news: Jotuns were the wildlife that did the eating, and the entire continent getting much colder was causing additional odd side effects. Zelia wasn't certain if the Jotuns were changing because of their food or the environment, but the changes were evident. Their skin was turning white, and Jotuns as a developing species were becoming much, much larger. They were a race of Mage *giants* now.

When it came to regional threats: The Crab was still King, even if it didn't like the cold so much, with the additional problem that it now roamed both beneath and above at leisure. Halcyon and Zelia were just happy the blasted thing couldn't fly.

"That cranky crab is still kicking?" Artorian threw a pillow on the floor, and his pouch chinked. He stopped his rant before it began, the sound causing tiny cogs to turn behind his eyes. He fished an Iridium Li from his pouch, and just stared at it. The light in his eyes brightened as he figured something out. "I know... I know why it didn't work last time. I had the answer all along."

Artorian spun around on his heel to address Zelia and Halcyon. "Fantastic work keeping the place operational. Both of you feel free to keep running this place, you're doing a better job than I. Zelia, keep doing what you're doing. Cy, with me."

He rubbed his hands together, brimming with ideas as Halcyon got excited by being called out for an adventure. "I hope you're in the mood to hunt. We're going to pay the crab a visit and figure out where it's currently hiding. I think you're both due a reward. If you think of something you'd like, feel free to just tell me."

Artorian considered his realm, but his mind pulled him hard toward his current crabby focus. "The Jotuns can just roam free. As for the Dreamed ones... I'll handle it in the next sector."

Zelia provided a nod of assent, and Halcyon was beaming! She adored going on little adventures with her Dreamer. They were exciting! Halcyon bounced forward until she stood next to her Dreamer, then excitedly waved to Zelia. The kimono clad lady wore a proud smile on her face as she took the realm management option to heart.

That sounded like something she could do!

Zelia waved back. She liked it when Halcyon was happy, and as her spiderlings hadn't made any headway on killing the Kaiju, she was more than happy to keep her mouth shut and let them go play.

Holding onto Artorian's hand, Halcyon fuffed mid-wave.

They teleported around Jotunheim in their hunt for their hard-shelled foe. Each time they appeared, Halcyon performed a sonar scan of their surroundings to get a better bead on the crab's location. For something so big, the Kaiju was surprisingly difficult to find when you were looking for it. Eventually,

Halcyon was stumped when she could not locate its specific location. She knew the crab was nearby, but the last three checks had all been measured in 'nearby.' "I don't understand. We should be right on it."

Under the fall of light snow, they both stood on a wide, curved mountain. The oversized hill looked no different than many other environmental features. Aside from being clear of spruce and pine trees, there was visually nothing special about this particular snowy bump.

Artorian looked down since Halcyon was sure of the spot, and adjusted his vision until he saw the Mana shell hiding below tons and tons of snow. Had it gotten even bigger? No wonder Cy hadn't gotten a specific bead on it. The daft thing *was* the mountain. He looped her in, finding it better to praise her for being correct. Cy was still developing, and every little bit mattered. "No, looks like you're on the nose. Thank you, my dear. Good hunt! I'm going to send you home so you don't get caught in the impending crossfire. What I'm about to do is going to be messy."

Halcyon nodded and, with a fanciful motion from her Dreamer, was fuffed back above the pool at the pagoda. She fell and splashed in with an excited *wheeee*!

Zelia popped her head out from the ceiling hammock and smirked, her hands busy weaving a spider silk robe for her Dreamer. She was sick of seeing him in inferior attire, no matter the bells and whistles it possessed. "Had a good time?"

Halcyon burst from the water and replied with a silly, toothy grin.

Zelia put her work down. She could tell Halcyon was chomping at the bit to spill the details. The patient spider didn't make her wait, and warmly invited the chat. "Tell me all about it."

While his named ones gossiped, Artorian pushed up his brand new, dark gray Vanaheim-acquired sleeves. He could change the color and texture if he wanted, but he liked the default look. The Administrator considered the challenge before him. Finally putting an end to this crabby nuisance. Surely, he could do it as an A-rank?

First, a wake-up knock. He didn't want to put another hole into his continent, and held the Li between his digits as he patiently aimed down.

It was good to set a baseline for expectations.

Last time, he'd been a B-rank. When he'd fueled and activated the spell carving, it had greedily sucked a whole rank away to accomplish flop-nothing. He'd just been tossed to the curb.

That was the baseline he tested again now, as an A-ranker. The air around his digits remained awkwardly silent as the ability activated. "[Mass Driver]."

Unlike last time, he was not flung from his position. Artorian watched as a luminous ring expanded from the carvings on his hand. The ring pulled back to his wrist, which caused familiar, rigid, and straight light waves to radiate from his fingertips that determined his aim. The lines created a trajectory of the first few hundred feet forward, a handy visual guide sticking just barely above and below the projectile.

He considered these light lines to be empowered rails, between which the Li would accelerate at a speed that anyone in their right mind would consider ridiculous and unattainable.

Artorian would have questioned the lack of sound, had Dev not told him he'd made some improvements to the Runescript and spell forms when they were reapplied.

Upon firing, his arm flung back as some of the kinetic backlash affected him, but it felt like a pinch instead of being batted by a boat. He barely saw the Li vanish along the path of the rails before it bore down into the snow.

Observations: One shot had cost him about the energy equivalent between B-rank four and five. The supposed incredible electric light show Dev had spoken about during the first trial was nowhere to be seen. Merely the luminous ring, and the guiding rails.

There had been a faint *pziouw* sound upon firing, audible

to his Mage hearing. Yet equally nothing like what had been described prior. This version could be classified as silent. The surrounding air did not tear, nor catch fire, though it did waver where the ferrous projectile passed.

Sounds that could be mistaken for the bestial roar of a creature experiencing a sudden headache rumbled the earth, as it took a metal rock to the top of the skull. Artorian likened the roar to a screech of frothing bubbles originating below the tons of displaced snow.

It could be said the crab was now awake, aware, and unhappy. The mountain shook off an avalanche of snow. Artorian played it smart and flew away. Best to make some distance for shot two. Firing point blank with a projectile that had tickled it at Mach ten didn't do the trick.

That satisfied the baseline. Now for the solution he'd thought of.

King Crabby the Cantankerous thrashed free of his frozen confines. His crabhammer sloshed with power, and mountains of ice broke as it raged. Artorian noted that the Kaiju was surrounded with a citrine glow that buffed its abilities. Comets of ice were diced and hurled all over an already-frosty Jotunheim, and the Immaculate-Cored Beast clearly had no qualms for what it struck, or destroyed. Jotunheim had a lot of problems, but this crabby one was a pinch in Artorian's behind. The crusty thing had cost him ten years, and he didn't care how angry the country-sized crab was at the world. "[Mass Driver]."

The luminous ring of light again dispersed from his fingertips. This time, rather than linger, the rail lines following the projectile quickly faded. The spell form was meant to accelerate metal, as far as Artorian understood it. Unfortunately, there was simply *no* metal stronger than even a paper-thin sheet of Mana. The category difference in energetic density would always apply. So, why not look at it a more flexible way? The metal was the delivery system. What could it deliver?

Time to be clever.

A single Li was meticulously hollowed out with Mana, only

for that space to be replaced and filled with the idea of liquid Essence learned on Svartalfheim. More than mere Dwarven Aether, Artorian condensed and compressed further, creating a form of Mana so dense it could be considered a solid… until it destabilized.

At which point, the bonds would very explosively decompress in a flash of plasma. Preferably without the loss of acceleration and momentum.

In addition, because he could leave no stone unturned, he'd used Teleportation Mana! For the purpose of sheer fun, and conveniently having easy access to the sympathy connection through his **Love Law**. He appreciated Zelia all the more for helping him figure the stuff out.

Imbuing the Mana into the Li, he set the identity condition that if this Mana struck something and would otherwise bounce away, then it would instead activate some of the Mana in the Li, initiating a teleportation effect that would keep the projectile going forward in a straight line. The projectile should warp back into the real when any effect that would cause the projectile to veer away no longer applied.

In short, it should ignore all armor.

It was a little complicated, but he loved complicated!

Pang!

When the Li impacted the crab's hard exterior shell at around three thousand five hundred meters per second, it staggered. That was all a projectile of that caliber managed to do against the darn thing. A Cal-blasted *stagger*.

Rather, that was all the Li portion of the projectile did, shattering on impact as its payload worked like a charm. The identity of the hardened Mana activated, teleporting past the hard exterior shell. The high-speed shot ignored the protections in the space-geometry equivalent of a straight line, popping back into being where it would do the most harm.

Right inside of the crab's considerably less protected squishy bits.

To the Administrator's delight, it also kept its momentum!

The staggering crab wobbled further as the Mana ball bounced inside of the crab's shell.

Cracking, breaking, tearing, and thrashing the significantly less-protected interior. When the pressurized Mana lost enough velocity and impacted the interior side of the hardened shell, the solidity of the Mana dropped below the equilibrium point. It promptly exploded with violent decompression as the solid turned to liquid, the liquid turned to gas, and the directed plasma-based Mana storm raged inside of the creature for just a moment before expanding the space within the crab. Pushing far beyond the confines of what its shell could hold.

Or in simple common: *Kaboom*!

With a violet flash of bursting light, cooked crab meat rained across several hundred miles of landscape. It fell from the sky in steamy slabs of sustenance, and the free meal went ignored by none as the hard shell began to discorporate. Twitching crab legs came down, crashing upon the snowy Jotunheim surface to cause quakes before becoming particulate.

Artorian extended his hand, and closed his eyes.

He found what he was looking for without much effort, now that the Aura of the crab no longer obscured his senses. How such a big thing had managed to befuddle him before, he wasn't sure. The skill to obfuscate itself, distort tracking abilities, and create illusory doubles of its Presence was such an odd trick for a crab to have.

Artorian wrote it off as one of its many abilities, just like that citrine mystery glow. The Immaculate Core teleported into his hand, and he grasped it firmly. Much like his clipboard, why go to an item when you can make the item come to you? "Oooh. Pretty. We'll find out if you were worth the three B-ranks I just used. Yet having you in my hand alone... consider me almost satisfied."

Giving it a toss into the air just to catch it, he looked to the sky. Midgard was currently hovering nearby. He tossed and caught the Immaculate Core again, and decided he wanted to be rid of it. It didn't matter that the darn thing had cost him several ranks. He wanted to yeet it. Just for the satisfaction.

"You've had your fill of roaming around unchecked, Crabby." Rearing back, he fueled Mana into the Core to make the object obscenely heavy. He aimed for an unpopulated patch of Midgard that would look better as a crater, and sent it off with a booming, hurled throw. "Get off my mountain!"

CHAPTER FORTY-ONE

The Administrator was all glee after getting rid of his burden, dotting the Jotunheim landscape in teleportation beacons to cheekily get that spent energy back. He paused on a mountain for a moment, taking in the view with a chilled breath.

Hot air exhaled from his lips, and he just felt a touch of pride at crossing that crabby problem from the slate. He should really consider slotting in some actual structures... He did like what Gran'mama had done to Skyspear. He wouldn't mind plunking that whole thing into Jotun somewhere. Perhaps in the waters below? *Hmm*. Yes. Yes, he would do that. An academy on an eternal field of water. Surrounded by friendly marine animals and plenty of crustaceous snacks.

He could nick the idea from the Dwarves concerning letting glow-moss grow on the ceiling. Artorian thought he could do better. Add a *little* more. He wanted the walls and ceiling to brightly reflect the blue of the water in Jotun's beneath, so everywhere you looked it seemed tranquil. A great place for study!

As for land... floaty islands for farming, and the like? He'd seen drawings of the concept before, but it lacked his sense of flair and need for harmony. Land on the back of giant turtles? Not a bad idea. There was certainly the room for giant turtles.

Scribbling that down for a moment, he caught movement in the corner of his eye. Blast. Just like the early B-ranks, his senses and sights were on the fritz again. The person he saw was several hundred miles away, and yet he observed her with perfect clarity. As if he were standing no farther than a few feet away. What was a thin lady doing out in the middle of a snowy valley? Stowing his writings by teleporting them back to the pagoda, he extended a foot and ported over with but a step.

Oh, it was one of the Mages. Reformed? Speaking of, there had been something about people that came to Jotun becoming white-skinned giants. This lady remained human-sized, though her skin did appear frigid. She was standing at the edge of a lake, now frozen and devoid of life. B-rank two. Water and infernal affinities. Interesting combination. What was ice again? He couldn't recall it at the moment, and thought it better to address her directly instead. "My dear, are you well?"

The snow lady turned her chalk white face toward the sound, and tiny pointed ears made themselves visible as the woman clad in blankets turned rags regarded him. She didn't frown, or seem surprised, or even speak until the snow around her ceased falling. As that had been her effect, she spoke with resignation, her voice icy and emotionless. "Are you, too, here to slay me?"

Artorian shook his head, concerned. "I am not. What happened here?"

The lady returned her gaze to the icy lake. "Nothing worth mentioning, now. The people I wished to take revenge on have already frozen. I do not enjoy speaking. Ask your questions, Ancient. Then be on your way, as you always are."

The Administrator did not approach, and squeezed his beard. "You know of me? That is unexpected, as I do not know of you. I will not ask how you know I desired questions. I shall limit myself then, and leave you to your reflections. You mentioned revenge, may I know more?"

As a statue of frozen ice, the lady did not move. "Without names, we were taken from the land of green. The middle guard? I don't know. We arrived here as hostages. Then those with power who took us found fear, and in their fear, we helped them find their silence. They lie quiet now, deep beneath the waters. Those that lost their minds and chose to submit to consuming the flesh of the fallen. Those who did, are something else now. They grew in being, and size, and forgot us entirely."

Her hand turned, motioning at the lake. "Only I remain of the 'we' that were. It is in that solace I found my **Law**, when I remembered enough to cultivate again. **Kenopsia**, before you ask, Ancient. It is the eerie, forlorn atmosphere of a place that is usually bustling with people, but is now abandoned and quiet. It brings me peace, and this peace brings me power. I considered **Monachopsis** for a while, but it did not suit me as well."

Her hand fell coldly, brushing over some vellum. "These are the stories of Jotunheim. I know the name of this land well, now. The stories kept us warm as the cold crept in, and the land ceased to flourish. Only the center of this vast land retains its heat, greenery, and lush jungles. We could not reach there; for creatures even stronger than the cold ones, who live on the very edge, reside in its verdant shelter."

She took a small, handwritten scroll from her pocket, thumbing it for comfort.

"One of the stories is to crush not the spider. For they watch, wait, and know. In another story, the spider speaks, and sometimes, the Ancient listens. The Ancient lives as a pulse of light on a tall mountain, an old man who appears only to vanish. A whisper on an unexpected day that upheaves a whole civilization."

The scroll was rolled, and slipped back into her pocket. "I stand alone at the edge of a lake. All those I knew, lost and gone. Then as I prepare to step within... The wind blows, the snow crushes, and an old man whispers where previously there was not a soul nearby. So, I asked, are you here to slay me? For all in the Ancient's wake is said to perish."

Artorian didn't like that there were stories about him. Rather, he disliked that those stories held him in a light colder than the current sub-zero temperatures present in this part of Jotunheim. "That's... *Hmm*. What's your name?"

The lady made a minor movement of the chin. A dispassionate no. "The people of snow had no names before. Neither do I have one now. I never remembered what my original was. Only that I was someone else before. In one story brought over from the middle guard. It says when I die again... I would begin anew. I would forget this life, this existence that is but a stairway ascent of knives, and wake anew as a babe in the arms of love. I wish to wake anew, Ancient. So, I ask again... are you here to slay me?"

Artorian kept calm, his response matching her dispassionate winter. "There are more ways than one to begin anew... if you are interested. Cold as I may seem in the tales, it seems the truth has been buried in the snow."

The lady still seemed dead set on walking into the lake, but her head turned fully, along with her curiosity. "You would provide a nameless nobody with life anew? Such strange whims you are entitled to, Ancient. Tell me what could await, other than the embrace of ice?"

Easing both his hands behind the small of his back, he held his own elbows.

"Would you like one? A name?"

The first frown creased the snow lady's perfect face. The illusion of a statue breaking with pressure cracks, which formed within a thin sheet of compressed sleet. "Do not toy with my heart, Ancient. Names are things of power. They are meant for the special, the unique. I am unworthy, I know I am. You speak of daggers coated in candy."

Artorian shook his head. "I'm quite serious. No matter what you have heard, could it be said to be the entirety of the story? I thought you were fond of them. If you would throw away the opportunity to hear more of them, or find the full truth of the one you are in... I have a name for you. A name... and a purpose. One that doesn't involve dying alone, and in the cold depths of a frozen lake."

The lady turned her full form, and for the first time Artorian saw the dead and frozen shape cradled in her hands. That sight *bit deep*. "Speak then, Ancient. My ears will hear you, even if my heart does not."

Squeezing his elbows to find his own comfort as the sights threatened to overwhelm, he just barely contained himself with steady, controlled breaths. He wasn't going to take a step forward, and violate what felt like sacred space between them. There was a distance that the lady needed, and so distance he would provide. He spoke the word, and it rolled with power from his tongue. "I name you Yuki."

The air compressed around Yuki, the snow lady. Unlike with Zelia or Halcyon, the deeper connections did not form. Her heart was closed, and her will remained frozen. She received a humming cyan luminance, but rejected the solar sigil when it attempted to form. The Administrator did not press the issue, and let her rebuke it.

Yuki blinked, her frown present. "That is not what the stories said would happen. The Ancient I know of does not give choice. I feel the new heart that you have bestowed, Ancient. I know it will not bring back what was lost, but I can sense the strings that hang free. They would attempt to bind to me, and yet only if I let them. This... is a pleasant revelation. These options of choice. I will bury my lost, but my ears still listen. What purpose do you seek of one you whimsically graced with a name?"

Artorian smiled, just barely. "The stories, Yuki. I want you to find them. Gather them. Keep them. Protect them. When you have many, and you discover that you desire to share them, call out to me, and I shall come sit, and listen. I am sorry your world froze over... and if you had not told me these stories existed... I would have never known. I may have graced you with a name, but it is I who request you to grace me with the tales that would provide the warmth of their fire to others who come here. Would it not be lovely, if you were responsible for not one more soul being in your position ever again?"

Yuki observed the Ancient, but didn't argue. "You would have me pursue my one remaining passion, even when all else is dead? Without any other requests? Merely the pursuits of my heart?"

The Ancient before her silently nodded.

"You are a strange one, Ancient. I accept your whim, and will not step into the waters. Leave me. I have a burial to tend, and while you did not move, you are now too close."

Yuki watched as the Ancient became translucent, until he was no longer visible at all. A gust of wind came, and she knew he left along with it. How strange, the actions of the Ancient. She felt him still, even as he disappeared at speeds impossible. It mattered not. She had tasks to see to, and afterwards...

Her lips warmed as the left edge curled up into the hint of a smile. She would tend to a story. The Ancient had not been wrong. She did love stories. She would wander, and gather. The knowledge would be collected, and in her hands it would spread. She had a new one to add herself now.

"The kindness of a whisper, spoken in the cold."

It would be a short tale, about just how much that tiny thing could do.

CHAPTER FORTY-TWO

Artorian felt uncertain as he appeared on Niflheim.

He was pensive now. He'd neither expected a third named one, nor the circumstances under which he'd offered it. Was it really just a whim? Was it guilt? A sense of latent responsibility for not being around when he should have been?

He didn't micromanage Jotun. Events happened, and he saw the large movements and macromechanics. That was intentional, so why did he feel so poorly for it?

"Would it kill you to use the front entrance, Mr. Administrator?" Gomei spoke with self-control, his nose in the air as he regarded the human. He must have been waiting here, though perhaps not on him, based on the lackluster and disdainful greeting while Gomei looked him over. "Oho. A-rank? Do not let it go to your head."

Gomei's eyes squinted after his quip, his disdain growing sharper. "And there it is. Why am I not surprised that the multi-utility healing Aura Dale *mysteriously* picked up, would come from the same person that causes my Queen such complications? Do you hate Dark Elves, Mr. Administrator? Or otherwise take delight in stuffing wrenches into our very carefully planned and prepared teaching methods? I am to inform my Queen if you arrived, in the event you failed to do so, as last time. She did not, however, mention I had to do so immediately."

Artorian didn't think much of the strange greeting until silvery prediction lines bloomed across his vision. Curves and vectors of attacks both physical and conjured twisted his way, and his main surprise was just how brutally efficient those vectors were. The lines that turned gold swiftly were assassination moves, and many see-through lines showed the raw skill in subtle subterfuge the vanishing Moon Elf was engaging in. Before a single attack had been thrown, Gomei's Aura was throwing out feints.

Artorian's inner academic howled. It could *do* that?

Even though they both moved at the same speed without the help of dilation, Gomei just seemed swifter somehow. Something about the pattern in which he took his steps? The control with which he held his Mana? The places in his body where Mana was kept and stored. The glimmer on his Aura that made his very Presence seem sharp. This man was a weapon. One forged in dungeons and decades of service. The steps were full, and certain of themselves.

Artorian could tell: This man was a General.

While Gomei was masterfully skilled at hiding, deception, obfuscation, and misdirection, the Administrator saw through it all. What were ordinarily some of the most advanced military tactics of an age gone by were cut through as the old man twisted his wrist and squeezed closed his fingers. The somatic component wasn't necessary, but subconsciously he made it anyway as a ball of hard light formed in the space the real Gomei occupied.

That haphazard—well, there was no reason to trample on the skill concerning the phantom that looked like him. Gomei's incredibly believable duplicate of the real thing, made entirely to distract from the true threat, went ignored. When the real, invisible Gomei moved to take a step further, he slipped on the interior curve of the invisible orb he was trapped in. He noticed it in less than a fraction of a moment, and slashed out to shatter the confining space.

To Artorian's surprise, the curved celestial light wall with confining identity was struck by an infernal attack of imbued freedom. He was stunned! A direct cancellation utilizing the higher effects? So, he wasn't the only one aside from Dawn! On second thought: Brianna's dagger had been a work of beauty. Was that her Soul Item? Probably.

Gomei wasn't happy with him. "So, you are more than little tricks and contrivances? Very well. If my methods of assassination are not to your liking, you would perhaps prefer…"

Gomei jumped out of the way as an array of repetitively firing light lances materialized around the old man, and shot toward him one after the other. Faster than a repeating crossbow, full-sized jousting lances twisted on their axis, drilling through the space they passed while the whirring spin itself caused cutting blades of air to invisibly rend the surroundings. Artorian spoke slow, his fingers snapping. "I remember you now."

The Moon Elf danced around the barrage of thrusted jousts, confused as the old man had slipped from his vision. His extended Mana senses informed him that the human foe was constantly on the move. Where exactly that was in his vicinity was infuriatingly difficult to pinpoint. It was as if the Administrator had stripped himself of all physical matter, and was little more than a spirit moving through the air. Except that the lances were still very much self-replicating! Drilling chunks out of the surrounding landscape when their spinning tips did not find their target. Only to reform after their Mana was expended, and shoot back off at Gomei's current position.

A voice reverberated through the general space Gomei occupied. Yet it appeared to be originating from several places, not a cohesive source. "*You're* the instructor that turned Dale's face into purple pudge. You didn't teach at the Academy. I admit I even looked for you. I never really had time to express my displeasure in your handling of my direct disciple. One might even say I found myself to be rather cross."

To Gomei, this was unnatural.

All gathered intelligence pointed to the Administrator being a very poor warrior. A borderline pushover with how he moved as putty to Brianna's words. The man had not even been a Mage when he first began work at that paltry Mountaindale Academy. Now he was A-rank? Suspicious. Gomei didn't believe it, and yet it didn't feel like he was fighting a man. It felt like he was warring with several as lances ceased being the only attacks he had to contend with.

Gomei dodged the resplendent globes of fire that joined the attack pattern. The Elven General had few to no issues accommodating for the increases in difficulty, even as blades of air cut through the mists around them and ground spikes formed to stab from below. He was instead confused as to how the human was so aware of at least four of the nine tenets of ancient combat.

The human never stopped moving, or attacking. His attacks were not choreographed, nor could they be grasped without intense observation for hints of what was coming. Finally, the human was using his own skills against him, as many Mana signatures were fakes or intended as distractions meant to lure him away from a real threat.

The energy building the attacks may have been detectable, and his experience was allowing him to filter between threats and non-threats, but the human himself was just gone. A surprise glaive from above was blocked from bisecting the Moon Elf with a *ching* as a new voice chimed in.

"Artorian. I would truly appreciate it if you didn't slay my General for having a pointy personality. Perhaps you could see to the point of your spear veering away from his kidney?" Brianna spoke with Queenly grace as her Presence appeared from the mists themselves. She slid into existence, regal and composed as she air-skated closer on little more than trails of fog.

Gomei acrobatically tumbled away, but in no location he stopped in did he feel safe. The lingering nervousness of a knife in his back screamed at his senses, and only after his Queen intervened did that particular feeling fade.

Artorian's voice replied without there being a discernible origin, though it slowly gained one. "Brianna, you look beautiful as ever. Of course, I believe the scare I've given him is punishment enough. He doesn't appear to like me. I imagine my lesson will lose me some reputation."

The Elven General spun on his heel, digging a heavy divot in the ground as he saw a very much real and physical old man bow gently to his Queen. At least the brat knew where to show deference! The attacks had paused, and the myriad of growing combinations hung still in the sky before their energies slowly released, returning to the Aura of the Administrator.

Gomei spat. "My Queen! I had him. He was no challenge."

Brianna returned a heavy-lidded look. "My General. You are mighty, in all respects. Please have the decency to accept a loss when it is due. You were intent on killing him, and in response to an old grievance, he gave you that honor. Do not dwell on the fact that, in the end, he was not fighting you. The Administrator was playing with you. If he was truly meaning to end you, he would have. Instead, he unsettled you, which is by far a worse thing in my eyes. You are more skilled. More experienced. So how is it you didn't notice that his Sword Aura, the very thing you taught my old Duke Dale, was constantly at your back?"

Gomei scoffed, bowed to his Queen, and vanished into nothingness without another word. Brianna merely seemed pleased, and amused. "My apologies, Artorian. He does not like humans, nor has he ever. I have just heard from my spies that you have been going around the realms. I am pleased you are here; you have given me quite the issue with that block of metal you left. Though I am aware you did not know it."

Taking the hems of her gown, she performed a curtsy. "Congratulations on your second Ascension, and slaying what I take must have been your realm's world boss. Do you perhaps need assistance with some things? You have come and gone from a few realms without taking much action. Niflheim is incredibly stable, and we are already working on the dungeon levels for incoming adventurers, travelers, displaced, and the like."

Artorian sighed. "I envy your progress, Brianna. None are doing as well as you, and I can't say I understand what you're doing differently to succeed with such skill. I think Vanaheim is in the same boat, but... I can't say what they're making there is a civilization. I scantily understand what Dev is doing myself. I also can't say I'm surprised you have spies everywhere."

The Queen calmly nodded. "Everywhere. I wish to warn you early: If you go to the moon... do not expect warmth. The cold of your Jotun has nothing on what goes on there, and the calculating starkness is so harsh on my scouts that I do not make them return if they do not request it. You will not like what you see there. All else, I can speak to you about in a social setting. Shall we adjourn to my palace? There is much I would wish to discuss, including having my limited supervisory tasks... expanded. I am being wasted in Niflheim."

The Administrator smiled wide, trying not to laugh from just how opposite and different some of the supervisors were. "I wish I had twelve of you. Are you aware of the mess they're making in Midgard? Four supers in one realm was too much... and... you look like you know things that I'm not going to like. I'd love to go with you to your palace. It's been ages since I've seen one. I also have the feeling you'd like to walk, just so you can show off."

Brianna fluffed her long, curled hair. "I would never. A Queen has no need to show off. The realm merely speaks for itself. If you happen to find it one of incredible splendors... Well, only natural. Come."

The mists around them moved and swirled, forming a path in their wake and direction as they walked and shared small talk. Niflheim was the complete opposite of Midgard. Here, the order was going too well. The only few issues were either monsters that didn't fully cooperate, or outsider-brought influences such as broken items, or small pieces of Iridium that suddenly received fervor and a scary amount of religious zeal.

Niflheim didn't have a sky section, and the topside was a no-go zone aside from supervisors and Dusklings. "So, what is a Duskling? I take it they were the Elves I met when I awoke in the shrine?"

Brianna nodded. "One and the same. Dusklings are the decanted that ended up in Dark Elf bodies, but had no grasp or rhyme on how anything about themselves worked. Bodies included. It was too dangerous to keep them in the underneath, as they can't live in harmony with the many Phosgen that hover around. I'm sure you'll see them. Hovering eyes with multiple tendrils, that act similar to how the assimilators of old did."

She returned to the topic. "Dusklings are… easily impressionable, and cling to imagery with a swiftness. When they found you meditating, they were enamored with how different you were. How nothing of the world affected you. How nothing they did could budge you. It intrigued and fascinated them. So, they built the shrine around you, and tried to emulate your calm. I let them; it kept them out of the way, and made them peaceful."

Artorian followed. "So… what happened?"

Brianna grit her jaw a little. "*You* are what happened. You woke up, and left them an object of power. Do you have any idea of that metal's value? The things that can be crafted from even a little bit? Where did you get the Li? I cannot find their origins anywhere, and there are entire black markets that hunt down the smallest scrap of it. Tell me you haven't been littering."

Artorian tried hard to remember. "I got them from… Dev. Whole pouch too. He said that 'we' had a good time making them. Also, something about a fun joke from the development team… Brianna, what do these coins actually do?"

The queen slowed her walk. "Let us… speak in the palace."

CHAPTER FORTY-THREE

The Magenta Palace of Mists was a structure both massive and mysterious. It was carved upside down from the ceiling of a great cavern, yet paths of reverse gravity Runes lined pathways both hidden and beautiful. The concept of 'down' was a hard sell in the Niflheim interior, as 'down' was wherever the Dark Elves wanted it to be.

Each pathway twisted and curled, and within minutes you would completely lose any sense of direction. Unlike Vanaheim that planned to twist and reform the landscape in endlessly new configurations, Niflheim sought merely to make you lose yourself in theirs. Where other continents were more neatly divided between surface space and interior, Niflheim had played a trick.

Rather than keep their continent horizontal, it had flipped vertical in the very early days of the Soul Space. Easily ninety-seven percent of all their landmass was internal. The remaining three percent counted as topside, dedicated to the Silverwood Tree, whose deep roots went all the way to the bottom of the continent. It allowed plenty of room for both meetings, and a small civilization of the Cal-approved Dusklings. All the mist prevented anyone from being the wiser about how tiny the topside actually was, and nigh guaranteed none would reach it.

Below the very top layer of Niflheim, cavernous halls had been cleared. This swiftly-filled vacuum was dedicated to Brianna's chosen nobility, including her own copiously claimed venues. For royal needs or otherwise.

Artorian was pleased as a puddle to discover the majority of Brianna's palace was made from multicolored stained glass. It gave some shine and glamorous luminance to an otherwise dreary underground. Mobile Mana lights were hidden behind curtains and panels. Their diffused brightness caused figures embedded in the glass to appear as if they moved, and it gave the illusion of a bustling palace.

The structure was full of actual Elves, however each and every one was invisible. So, to look with normal eyes, one saw only what they wished you to see. Even as you passed hordes of silent, acrobatic Elves that without so much as a noticeable displacement of air seamlessly moved to attend their tasks around you. With sight mundane, the palace looked alive with joy. With sight revealing, one saw the truth of an operation that moved like clockwork assassination.

Most delightful of all was the real furniture. He didn't know what kind of exotic materials were available on this realm, but when his butt sank deep into a plush recliner, he put naptime on the table. His hands stretched over the large meeting table before him, its subterranean woodworking exquisite. "Ahh. Now that's a good chair."

Artorian looked to his right, watching the embers in a fireplace dance around. His vision then tilted upwards slowly, scanning over a wall-to-wall mural of Brianna and the royal family. They'd gotten so far. He truly was envious of the fashion in which they'd introduced natural lighting from the outside. It streamed through massive air and ventilation caverns as beams, and bounced down into open chambers of greenery and color. In those large, lush spaces he could see harmless animals roam freely. How convenient as both a tranquil relaxation source, and snack provisionary.

"I told you my realm would speak for itself." Brianna mused through a thin smile as she sipped from a volcanic glass carved flute. The mixture touching her lips was bright purple, and it stained her tongue as she drank it. Confident, she slid into the ornate seat next to the Administrator, and stabbed her soul dagger into the table without warning.

The meeting of the Hidden Blade was called to order. The two seats closest to Artorian, on either side of the long table, had blades stab into them as well. Materializing out from their hiding methods, spies and advisors alike took their seats along the equilateral triangular table.

Artorian could now easily see the Dark and Moon Elves on the first and second sides of the angled table without additional effort. He noted that only he and Brianna sat on the third side. The first two sides populated heavily with nobility members, and Artorian knew that many more without a seat were standing guard in the meeting room, their backs against the wall as they stood shoulder to shoulder.

The ceiling had this formation copied upon it as well, and the Administrator understood just how ridiculously well-protected Brianna was. It was a literal room of elite assassins, and from their presence alone, he understood she trusted each and every one well enough for them to overhear a conversation between supervisors.

He reserved that sort of talk for the presence of maybe his named ones, and here she had an entire house on standby. Brianna was one frightening lady!

Gomei was present at the table as well. His peculiar Mana signature was sharper. In a literal sense. Artorian couldn't learn from it long, as Brianna began speaking. "Now that my named ones are assembled, we can begin."

If Artorian had a drink it would be a fine mist all across the table. "All of these highly-skilled Mages are your named ones? There's easily a hundred!"

Brianna merely graced him with a self-satisfied smile. "But of course. Naming someone increases their powers and abilities, and it binds their loyalty. In addition to several minor bonuses, the ability to communicate to me directly without needing to be physically present is paramount. Having such a vast, capable network is what has allowed me to be such an effective Queen. My entire civilization functions with me as its direct pinnacle, and I keep myself directly involved."

The Administrator sank back into his chair, fingers pressing together in a pyramid while he considered that. "I'll admit, Brianna, I expected many things when performing my Niflheim checkup, but this wasn't it. I thought I'd come back, have a lovely chat, leave some teleportation beacons behind, and have Zelia come pick up the documents of your needs after. You're correct that I haven't been doing much, yet. It's my first big trip across the realms, and this initial journey is more of a scouting one."

The Queen's smile emboldened at the recollection of a particularly intelligent Arachnae. "Speaking of... shall we go through the matters in order, perhaps beginning with your last mention?"

The assassins in the room suppressed their frowns, but one could tell they were doing so. The facial tick didn't pass Artorian by, and he motioned toward it, rather than replying to Brianna.

She cocked her head, but then understood. "My councilors, I understand you are displeased that this man does not stand at the point-end of the table across from me, as is social custom. I also understand some of you may be displeased that I have seated him next to me. I will remind you that there are more steps to every hierarchy. Even I must answer to someone."

With a dainty move of her glass, she motioned to the old man at her side. "My judges, this is Artorian, known as the Administrator. Please do let him come and go as he pleases, as it is nearly always guaranteed to be to my benefit for him to do so. While I am Queen, I am also supervisor to my realm. One of the things I wish to discuss today is the… expansion of those duties. After all, the other realms would greatly benefit from having more invisible eyes."

She flashed him a political smile, having done him a favor. Artorian locked eyes with her, and eased his hand into the air as quill and paper teleported into it, to the great discomfort and dismay of an entire house of assassins. Things and people that come and go as they pleased, especially through their network, were… complications. As he flattened the paper on the table, ink of cobalt lightning formed on the tip of the quill, and the Administrator began to write. "I'll note that down for you."

Brianna was pleased. "I am aware of your beaconing allotment. We are already clearing specific spaces where room for them is being made available. A list will be brought to me when it is finished, and I would be delighted to accompany you to the coordinates for each. I am aware that it's not a cheap endeavor, yet my informants have told me you are liberal with your sprinkling. Some command from the great spirit, no doubt? No matter. I would be very happy to receive Zelia's company. She is even welcome to stay, though I am wounded she does not let one of her children remain here. The domain is optimal for her kind."

Artorian hummed softly to himself as he wrote. "I'll make a note of that as well, but if she doesn't wish it, I'm not going to force her. My named ones are free, and welcome to refuse tasks. Going down the checklist sounds excellent. Could I finally know what the matter is with my Iridium?"

Brianna procured a dagger made from the material, and stabbed it into the table next to her own. His attention was drawn to it, as both weapons were Cal-blasted identical. "In short. We have had broken items. We have had broken creatures. What Dev appears to have made, is the first thing we've catalogued as broken material."

"At a glance Dev's creation is merely Iridium, shaped like a Li, cut to that tiny size. However, that is only so because you believe that's what it is. That belief allows it to retain its identity, and when you believe strongly enough that it is something else…"

She motioned at the Iridium dagger, and the verdict was clear. Artorian slapped his hand against his forehead. "Crackers and toast."

Brianna touched the weapon, and it transmuted to different metals on the fly. Several exotic ones even, just to prove her point.

"There are limits. It must always be a metal, the metal present can become no larger than ten times the original size of the Li, and it cannot be split. The split off part vanishes. Trust me, we have tried to replicate this stuff; it doesn't want to. This is why it has been such a pain. Imagine a Duskling with the Li in its hands, as its mind wanders over to a heavy memory. Suddenly she is holding the figurine of a lost loved one. Another, a weapon. A third, a functioning torch. Imagine a creative enough creature with one of these any-metal coins in their hands."

Artorian's facepalm turned into full-on forehead kneading. "I understand the problem. Here I'm sitting with a whole dang pouch of the things. Now I grasp what Dev meant with his joke."

Brianna's tone turned serious. "Speaking of Deverash, you have such a calm opinion. I take it you are unaware of the civil war that species is currently having on that glassed continent?"

The Administrator considered it, but shook his head. "Civil war? No. I saw no such thing, only a landscape that could be turned into anything that the creative bunch wanted. I thought it was clever, to be honest. Their choreography was a little much, but it wasn't unpleasant."

Brianna thought as much. "Some of my spies were present. They did not *learn* that dance. They were fully reliant on their precious Pylons. A significant chunk of Gnomes have accepted those mathematical perfections as their way of being, but there are many that prefer the original way of endless free tinkering. Just to see what works. You know the kind; they lived in the scrap heaps of their own fallen creations and made homes out of them. You may not have seen it, but I can prove a conflict is happening between them. Let me give you a quick rundown of secret events in the lowest realms."

Artorian sat back, and laced his fingers as the Queen spoke. "Midgard. The four supervisors are not working together. Henry and Marie, sure. Though their respective methods of ruling differ vastly, and they are going to have to institute a nobility class to do the majority of the ruling for them if they want to succeed. Unfortunately, as humans... they are prone to corruption. I see problems in their future that, even as King and Queen, they will be unable to tackle. Marks my words. Chandra cares more for her creations than she does for anything else, and Aiden... his discontent grows daily, while his peers are none the wiser."

She continued. "Svartalfheim... you have seen the mess they've made. Do I need to say more? It is they that hunt for Iridium, though it has some strange stigma. We have so far been unable to crack the exact purpose. We are guessing Dev may have tested their initial use there. Alfheim is littered with broken items, and for some reason I am inclined to let the Alf keep them so they may self-destruct with their use. Neither of those regions have a supervisor, and it is here I was wishing to offer my extended services. Not to supervise, but to keep people... As I said. More pairs of eyes could be very helpful."

Artorian pressed fingers to his lips, and sighed. That did sound better than him decanting his friends early, just to ask them if they could help with that particular conundrum. It would also repay Brianna's favor. "I think... you're correct. I'll set the beacons so teleportation is a little easier. I honestly don't know how you've been getting your people places, but I have the feeling you've been personally involved, given teleportation for most supervisors is Cal-granted. Honestly, I don't mind. It will genuinely help, so I don't have an issue with extending your supervisory reach to two additional realms that currently lack oversight. You're certainly doing well enough here, from what I can see."

He scribbled it down, and Brianna did her best to suppress a Queenly smile entrenched with the satisfaction of power. This was but the start of the first meeting, and it would continue until long into the misty night.

CHAPTER FORTY-FOUR

Warm sands were a welcome feeling between his cold toes as Artorian stood in Muspelheim's vast desert. His sandals were held in hand, and Artorian kept his eyes closed, basking in the freedom of the warm and windy open space. His gray robes fluttered in the breeze, and he was glad to be out of Niflheim after days of what felt like attending tribunal. Being cramped underground, no matter how spacious Brianna had attempted to make it, brought him thoughts of the blight.

Given the option, he'd visit purely the topside, unless it was absolutely required that he return to the Magenta Palace of Mists and gothic delights. He didn't know how long he stood there, just enjoying the openness of it all. It was long enough for onlookers to start prowling, and for desert C'towl to stalk curiously.

"Six realms down, three to go." Then Artorian would spend a few years sealing up broken items. With a twist of his wrist, a teleportation pad winked into existence next to him. *Hmmm*. On second thought, wasn't this just going to get buried under the sand? Entering the new landscape-editing function Cal had slapped him with during one of the tribunal meetings, he turned the pad into a pillar. Reminiscent of the pillar Don had pushed him into the sky with during those early Morovia days, he found it fitting. A vast chunk piled into the ground to form the foundation, while the remainder extended a hefty distance into the sky. Some spiraling stairs ejected out of the side, and he called it done.

Time to go back to being social. Artorian stood there, but couldn't... That was strange. Normally, he could find Dawn instantly. He closed his eyes, and sunk into the senate where his celestine mote popped into being. <Dawn, I'm in your region, but I'm having a hard time locating your Auric signature.>

With effort, Dawn's dim orange-red mote formed. That was also odd; this took little effort for Dawn. She could tell at a glance, and cut the question off early. <One of my surprise creations is to blame. Can you come to the trireme? I am currently landlocked.>

Artorian wasn't going to make it difficult. <Of course, dear. Top of the deck. Incoming.>

Jumping from the sands up onto the sixty-something-foot pillar sticking up from the sand, the pad at the top brightened into a beacon. With a *fuff*, he was gone. With that same bright fuff, he'd drawn the eyes of a few hundred desert beings. Now all very interested in the spire's location. If only he had known the value of shade.

The sound of welcoming fists clashing against armored chests rang out when the gray-robed Dreamer appeared on deck. Spear butts thumped to the deck twice, and some kind of call went out from all the neatly lined up warriors.

The races varied, and Artorian's senses sharpened as details of the scene were taken in. It could be overloading when first porting in somewhere and absorbing all new relevant sensory data. Once at a Mage's level of cognizance, that came more easily. Yet it was still not instant, which was something he came to terms with as he stood on the prow.

Surtur slid from the main cabin entrance with a pleasant expression, her hands behind her back. Artorian's eyes swiftly focused on her attire. Did she usually dress in such rich, tin regalia? If she was attempting to look important, she was certainly succeeding with all those tassels and tin chains.

Artorian waited for the named one to come close, as he wasn't sure how to proceed with this entourage awaiting him. It hadn't exactly been comfortable at the triangle table either.

His patience lucked out here, as Surtur bowed before him at the prow. "Dreamer, our Lady waits below. We have been eagerly expecting your arrival, and are glad you graced us so soon. We were hoping to speak with you over certain difficulties."

Artorian's hand slid onto Surtur's shoulder with a grandfather's warmth. "Please don't bow too long, my dear. I'm not the one that likes it. I love what you've done with your headdress; did you put it together yourself? You look stunning! Almost as beautiful as your personality. I'm so proud of you and your people for taking such good care of Dawny. Don't worry, don't worry. I know about the Dreamed already; Zelia was a good chitterbug and filled me in. Why don't we have ourselves a glide, and you fill me in on all those worries you've had?"

Surtur's face turned pink, and Artorian mentally jumped in delight. Success! A blush! Aha! His smile widened, and the old man pleasantly shuffled along. Surtur slid in pace with him, and let the worries fall from her chest as heavy weights. Yes, this was better. This was where he belonged. Listening to worried minds. Being present to lighten their loads and be a supportive elder for their thoughts. Such schemes they had wrought! Hiding the Djinn from Dawn? *Tut*. Of course, she was going to find out.

Wandering through the decks, he wondered if the boat had gotten bigger. It seemed like it. That, or they were just taking their time and going slow. Yes, that was it. He was purposefully walking extra slowly to give Surtur more time to just talk. It could be said that he couldn't get a word in, but he didn't really want to as he supportively held her hand and just ambled along.

Dawn must have been a touch upset with them, because her named ones were visibly stressed. Even Karakum wasn't immune. When he joined the posse of walking chosen, he said absolutely nothing. Not a single snide remark, and there wouldn't have been a better opportunity to get one in at Artorian.

They stopped at a massive crimson door, coated in flaming Runic emblems. Surtur visibly looked uncomfortable, and Artorian tugged her arm so she would lean down. He gave the large Lamia a hug, and patted her back. "I understand, dear. I understand. Don't worry. You did very well. I take it you're not coming with me past this point?"

The serpentine headshake was answer enough, and he let go to turn and push the doors open. His hands sizzled slightly, but that went ignored as he moved through. The heavy doors swung shut behind him, all by themselves. Oh, was there a Mage or two in that door? He glanced for a moment, and tried not to laugh. Pag and Duke! He was sure she'd let them out to go be troublemakers again eventually, but turned to the matter at hand. "Dawny, what's wrong with my dear?"

He was referring to her, but stopped short as he saw an unexpected B-rank one Dawn. He'd never seen her reserves that low. Equally unexpected was that she carried a snug, bundled child in her arms. From the waist down, it was just a tornado of mystic smoke. Waist up, the Djinn looked remarkably human, save for it being bright blue.

Dawn's voice was surprisingly collected. "Aside from my named ones hiding my own Dreamed one from me, out of fear I would destroy him? Or perhaps that my Dreamed one grants wishes, which is a cute misunderstanding for 'has access to Cal's supervisor shop' while using my Mana for purchases?"

He sat down on the lounger next to her, and said nothing. It was the expression on her face that stole his words away. Dawn didn't carry the demeanor of a destroyer, or someone who was angry at the universe, nor the world, and especially not at whom she was holding. He knew that soft smile well; the kind upwards curl of the lips while both her arms kept the little one tight to her chest. His tiny breaths were sweet and tender.

Dawn didn't need to say the words, but she did anyway. "I love him."

The Fire Soul bobbed the baby gently, and kissed his forehead. The Djinn's tiny hand reached up, and grabbed hold of some rogue lock of her hair. It gripped tight, and Artorian watched Dawn melt with motherly happiness. Her face contorted with meaning that seemed sad, and just a little pathetic. Yet it meant: 'Look at him, he's so cute, adorable, I love him, he grabbed me. Sunny, did you see?'

Artorian nodded, and rubbed her back as he sat down with her. He understood well. "What are you naming him?"

Dawn felt speechless, her eyes locked on her Dreamed one. "I... I just don't know. I wasn't expecting... He was just there, like a present. Then when I held him... my demeanor frightened my chosen, but I could not express to them how I was feeling. I did not know the words. The overwhelming nature of it all just caught me unaware, and I just wanted to hold him close, closer, closer still."

Her friend sat there with her, remaining silent as she worked through her feelings. It wasn't yet his turn to speak. Dawn was processing. When her gaze broke from her little one, she leaned sideways to lay her head on his shoulder. "I don't know what to do."

He hummed gently, brushing a hand across her head and color-adapting supernova hair. "What do you want to do? When you don't think about it too hard. Just the surface feelings, the first draws of desire."

Dawn's response was swift. "Keep. I want to keep him. Not as a chosen, but as my son. That's what he feels like. He feels like my son. I want to keep him, and raise him, and see him smile, and laugh, and play, and be happy. Yet if I name him... he will be chosen. I don't... I don't want..."

She was kept close, and he pressed his cheek against the top of her head. "Then give him a name you wouldn't give to a chosen. Give him a name you'd give to a son. Hold tight the thought, and let your affection flow. The Mana will know."

Dawn whined out her reply. "I don't have the Mana left! He used it all, having a great time altering my trireme, adding items, structures, and toys all around my region. I'm not even upset at him for it."

Artorian just warmed. "My dear. You wish to attempt a labor of **Love**, and you think I would not help you? Come now. I can see it on your face. The name lies on the tip of your tongue, and you yearn to speak it. Forget the costs; you will have plenty of Mana. I know Cal's shop ignores the Mana purity of purchasers and takes a percentage, but my tier is still rather high. Converting it down to yours? No, my dear, you may as well have an inexhaustible supply, equal to the lengths of your **Love** for your little one."

Dawn frowned; her question hesitant. She sat up, the sleepy bundle in her arms still pressed to her chest. The wrinkles on her forehead dipped heavily. "Are you sure?"

Artorian pressed a supportive hand to her back, and the Mana flowed freely. Her ranks restored as the seconds ticked, and Dawn relished the return to normality as her concerns melted away. Her lips eased against her tiny Dreamed one, and she whispered, "Caliph."

Her Mana vanished like a sea that spontaneously vaporized to gas all at once. The influx kept her on her feet, but the cost was sizable. Though it didn't matter what the cost was for this endeavor. It was paid freely as Artorian's ranks fell to keep Dawn's stable. Whatever the Djinn was, or might be, he would not go into the fullness of life without a mother that loved him very, very much.

Dawn gave him a hug when the drain ceased, her Mana hovering around B-rank zero. "Thank you, Sunny. I'd like to spend time with my son a while longer. I know they're waiting for me out there."

Artorian got up and gave her shoulder a squeeze, winking. "What are you talking about? You've got no work for a while. You be with your boy. I'll clean up for a bit and talk it over with your chosen. They'll be delighted to see you when you're ready.

I'll explain it all. You rest. You seem tired after that naming. Also, your little one is waking up. Let him meet his mommy."

Dawn looked like she was about to cry, but used her Aura to send over an extra hug of comfort. She received one in reply, and Artorian closed the doors behind him, ignoring that they were meant to be automatic. Caliph opened his supernova eyes, and met the mommy covering his face and cheeks in tiny kisses.

CHAPTER FORTY-FIVE

A full week passed before Dawn invited some of her chosen back into her quarters. The Administrator had been with them the entire time, and they'd had plenty of conversations that alleviated the grand majority of their worries. Acceptance by their Dreamer, however, was something that needed to happen in person. To their quickly heightened spirits, their worries melted away as they learned Dawn didn't love them any less. Instead, she let them in to meet the new member of the family.

In addition to playing councilor, Artorian had caught up on some paperwork while stationed in Muspelheim. He'd been assigned a spacious room on the trireme, and set up the usual gambit of beacons.

Zelia had come and gone with requisite needs, and he'd been glad for the visits. Artorian discovered that—Karakum's snide remarks aside—the chosen of the two regions worked together rather well. It seemed that they had previously covered each other's backs when their Dreamers were being... less than productive.

He was also surprised to learn that Zelia was fantastic at information gathering, and Halcyon was masterful at regional control. As additional good news, her latest pod possessed her flight capabilities, and that allowed them to roam free in all three Jotunheim regions. It was a little odd to see rainbow dolphins, glimmer turtles, blink whales, and platinum orcas swimming through the clouds, but it sure beat out the angry corpse-tearer bird flocks that otherwise occupied it. Abyss-danged Hræsvelgrs. Why did Odin have to pick such a complicated name?

When he'd gone to check, there had been a tussle between a tearer flock and a few members of the pod. Artorian laughed as he learned that in addition to flight, the sky-swimmers had picked up abilities he'd showcased while spending time as a Long.

Their Aura emanations pulsed out when something got too close, destabilizing the attacker long enough for multicolored mouth blasts or sonic circles to shake the bird apart. In addition to doing whatever random destructive effect the breath-beam caused. It appeared that, much like him, his named ones were all-affinity creatures. Many of their effects ended up translating to a kind of rainbow ability, and his main guess was from lack of precise control.

He was enjoying a cup of tea on the ground floor of his pagoda, reading over some documents, when Zelia came to wait at his side expectantly. She didn't say anything, but he knew. Setting the papers down, he sank back into the pillow mound and looked up at the paper parasol-wielding lady. "Must I, truly?"

Zelia, looking more human than ever before, closed her two eyes. She calmly nodded in affirmation with a gentle dip of her chin, face barely tilted. "You must, Dreamer. Asgard awaits."

He sighed, and extended a hand for assistance in getting up. He didn't need it, but Zelia always appreciated being helpful. "I have finished my weaving, Dreamer. Would you consider wearing it to your next realm visitation?"

The gray robes he was wearing were perfectly functional, but he wasn't about to turn down something that was going to make his chosen happy. "Of course, my dear, bring it over while I sort these pages into the correct piles. I have the Muspelheim records all handled now. Jotun could be doing better, but while the climate is fighting itself, we can't make much progress. The beneath is calm, and it will take more resources than are ready for me to install the Skyspear copy there. The above, Halcyon has handled. Based on this last report, she's never been happier with the swimming freedom. I heard cloud diving is some kind of a sport now?"

He smiled, waving it off. Halcyon was happy, and the tasks he'd requested of her were all handily seen to. He'd even heard Yuki was wandering around the edges of the realm, staying in the cold of the mountains, rather than venturing into the wild green wilderness closer to the continent center. She still hadn't made contact, or taken up any further connections. That was fine. He was perfectly happy with letting his three named ones be. Jotunheim was a realm of the wild, after all. Let them do as they please.

Zelia folded space back to his position after fetching her crafts, and gracefully walked in holding something that didn't look like a robe. Artorian moseyed over and had a look at it. "What's this?"

She was beaming, and ever so proud. "You have many robes, so I made you a uniform! I wanted you to have some-thing that you'd look important in. Fitting of your position as the Administrator. I know it might look a little too militaristic; I borrowed some ideas from those fawns at Niflheim. The dapper, snug fit of the Vanaheim Gnomes, and fragments from some old notes I found on a people known as Modsognir Dwarves? Suits, I believe they are called? I adore them. I would enjoy speaking with these Modsognir when they are decanted."

Artorian obliged without question, and he took on the mannequin pose he had always assumed with Rosewood. Zelia did her best not to click with glee from her more human mouth, and changed him in a hurry. She lost her human form doing so, shifting back into a full-on spider. More limbs meant faster and more controlled dressing. What interested Artorian was that it took her mere moments to freely do so, and that the alteration didn't make him feel odd. *Hmmm*. A human, and a bestial form? This had come up before. He could probably do that too.

When mirrors were conjured, Zelia carefully groomed his beard and facial hair. He didn't interrupt, and just practiced moving in the new confines. It felt like some Kingly attire, combined with a General's public battledress. It didn't have any combat applications, but the material from which the outfit was made held secrets. He'd uncovered several by the time she was done. "An emergency teleportation feature upon the outfit taking too much damage? Why would I need that? Never mind. I love it. I look so snazzy!"

Just for fun, he emulated a King's pose. Zelia put her hands to her cheeks as she changed back. "Ooh. You look just like a King."

The old man nodded. Even though he agreed, he felt his heart fall. "Indeed... I think it's nice. So long as there is no crown. That would not suit me. Not one bit. I am reminded of a person I once looked up to. Regal and self-assured, who gave big speeches in front of cheering crowds. The people smiled, and were loud. He commanded respect everywhere he walked, and when he looked over his people... You could tell that even though his face was set, there was a silent smile."

He squeezed his own hand, bringing himself back. "I understand now. The pride in good people. Yet still, I would not wish for his position. I do not wish to rule with absoluteness as Brianna does, nor with the bureaucracy of the Midgardians. Dawn lets her realm take care of itself, though she does not yet see the importance she has within it as one who is revered. At least I don't believe so. She comes, and goes, and attempts to remain not too involved. She makes no real demands of her realm, and yet pleasantly attends when invited."

Zelia was holding up a sash as he rambled to himself, quietly waiting for all the steam to expend itself. He tied it around his waist like a belt, and let her make minor fixes and alterations to her liking. "Well, I think you look regal. Even if temporary, it's a very nice change from your usual academic self that loafs around in bathrobes. Image is important and, while we all adore you, I've heard Asgard is a little strict. So just in case, I wanted you to show up looking like an Administrator with purpose. Rather than some mid-lecture geezer who just got done being questioned by a flock of graduate students, and is seven steps away from fully frazzled."

Zelia fussed somewhat, dismissing the academy story she'd gained from her Dreamer. "They're sneering about you behind your back on Niflheim, and this will shut them up."

It sounded like there was a little personal vendetta merged into the creation of the outfit, but it only made the old man smirk. Those judges did seem a little stuck up, and if Gomei was anything to go by, he expected none of them liked him too much. More of a political necessity. "Alright then, dear. I'll give the costume a test run in Asgard. I'll try not to ruin it, but you know me…"

Zelia leered murderously at him. "Get out."

Snickering, the Administrator teleported away. He hadn't been to Asgard before, so the arrival location would be random. He was just shooting for generalized direction and spatial coordinates through a fold. You don't ever get it right the first time. Artorian worried for a moment about the gravity, but figured he should be able to skate by with his current rank. Given his arrival didn't crush him on the spot, he counted his blessings.

The sound of scrubbing reached Artorian's ears as he folded in and observed a landscape of steam. The area was made of golden walls, a polished floor that reflected light, and a ceiling covered in eccentric artwork. The splash of water was heard nearby, and Artorian discerned the tweet of a rubber duck. "Odin?"

The high-pitched and girly screech that erupted from the baths was not in the slightest what Artorian had been expecting. The massive thunderer crackled with rampant lightning, and the metal of the walls drew it all away as the excess Mana went… somewhere. Based on the flows, it powered contraptions elsewhere. "Administrator! This is the baths!"

Exasperated and taken entirely unaware, the massive man daintily covered himself with a towel. The steam of the baths prevented a good view, but Artorian had already turned to walk away. "My apologies. I'll wait outside."

The old man could hear the giant flop down into the baths like he'd just survived a heart attack, and Artorian snickered further as he passed through the golden halls. Design and architecture here were grand, meant for huge creatures to pass through. He supposed that if he were to make lodgings on Jotunheim, they might need to be sized similarly. Still, he didn't know of gargantuan creatures occupying Asgard. So why was all the structural sizing so vast and spacious?

The general surroundings appeared rich, bordering on ostentatious. Ah, perhaps he knew. It was meant to let pass the size of one's ego. When he meandered through a hall that split off into a massive, domed central structure, he veered off to the heaving metallic doors that, based on sheer guesswork, must lead outside.

The guards waiting on the other side of those bunker doors quirked a brow. The Valkyries with their gleaming tridents in hand looked at one another before peering at the parting gates. Those doors were so large and massive that just opening them took serious power, and it was too soon for their Divine to be done with his bathing. When a man no taller than their knees stepped out from between them, letting the doors clang shut behind him, they shot into action and leveled their dangerous tridents at him.

The tips crackled with twisted elemental might, each prong a different variant of a single Pylon's effect. There was no joking around with these winged ladies, and they snapped at him in a language he once again did not understand.

Well, that wasn't helpful. On the plus side, he could now see where he was. This mountaintop city of gold was surrounded by white clouds on all sides. Well-crafted and glittering metallic structures dotted his surroundings, connected by more golden bridges. Must be a supervisor preference. It was peaceful up here, save for overzealous guards. So, all the issues must be below the cloudscape?

The Valkyries were still shouting, stabbing their weapons in his general direction. Now that he considered it, the pressure and gravity here were intense. He was managing not to fall, but this was definitely an A-ranked area. Getting a little tired of all the shouting, Artorian exhaled. He let the pressure of his Aura just lay on the surroundings like a weighted blanket, fielding the energy.

The floating Valkyries each dropped to a surprised knee as they slammed to the metal floor. Their weapons were glued to the ground, now too heavy to hold. Alright; he *had* to admit that felt pretty good, just locking people down like that.

No wonder it had been done so often in the old days; it was a very satisfying method of establishing superiority, even if it left him vulnerable. Still, he'd just tried it to make them stop, rather than to prove a point. Though the point was proven regardless as they did not rise when the pressure lifted and his fielding ended. It was a different trick than expanding your Presence, or altering one's Auric signature. Like a dropped coat, picking it back up actually took some effort and skill.

No wonder Henry and Marie might be having difficulties.

The Valkyries remained on a knee, shooting each other a confused look as this tiny man-creature stood before the Stairs of Clean Virtue. They had warned him to stand down, to surrender and lay down his arms, to go with them and be a captive for questioning.

Unfortunately, they had not been understood, and a pressure similar to that of their Divine had plastered them to the ground. There wasn't much that could do that to them. In fact, the list of people that could was incredibly small. The weight of the static coating that had lain across them was incredibly confusing. They could tell that the rank of the power was lower than theirs, but the density of it had been insane.

So, for this tiny man-creature to drop them onto a knee without so much as raising a hand… That left scant few options. When their grandest Divine hurried from the House of Clean Virtue, it was easy for them to tell he'd dressed in a hurry. Odin's hair was still soaking wet. "Administrator! Give warning of your arrival next time! I was… unprepared. I was going to muster a feast when you eventually came to visit, to show you the splendors of Asgard and regal lengths of my glorious might. So that the works of I, Odin the poetic, wise, and war-renowned, are on proper display!"

Artorian's reply was flat. "I think I've seen enough of your display, supervisor. Are you certain you'd not rather walk around with me and show me what needs you might have? I think I've grasped the realm's splendors. Displayed aplenty."

Odin turned reddish pink, a small cloth dabbing at his forehead. "Ah, yes. Of course. Right this way. I, Odin! The m…"

He stopped when Artorian gave him the most condescending glare. "I mean… right this way."

Odin was used to being top dog in his realm, and it showed. Unlike Dawn, he had directly taken on the role as a Divine protector and influencer. His role as said Divine was the complete opposite of Muspelheim's. The Valkyries of Asgard saw and treated him as a Divine that gave them order and purpose. He was a figure of fickle directness, and as he passed, gave commands for upcoming tasks. Artorian believed Odin didn't even realize he was doing it; it was too natural.

Dawn was a Divine because her people invited her, and she attended. Odin was a Divine because he told them so, and they listened. Artorian was going to need to wrap his head around the differences in regional dynamics. No wonder Odin's top of the mountain realm bordered on ostentatious.

He even tried to order Artorian around once or twice, and it took him a minute to catch that the old man wasn't having any of it. Odin was definitely too used to being in charge, and from appearances had completely forgotten he was not, in fact, the top of the hierarchy. "I assure you, Administrator, everything in Asgard runs flawlessly!"

Artorian stopped in the middle of the golden bridge they were walking across. Odin was showing off his various structures, attempting to distract him. The Administrator threw his hand out, splitting a part of the cloud cover several miles long. The foggy blanket rolled away as the air currents moved them. They looked below, and Odin paled.

The Administrator chided him. "Does it now? Then what is that flock of oversized golem hornets that people seem to be fleeing from?"

Odin shrank away and appeared meek. An odd feature for a man so massive, that constantly spewed lightning from sheer power alone. "They're fi~i~ine. They're Einherjar! Fierce warriors, one and all."

Artorian grumbled, unamused. "Is that why they're all scared out of their minds? Have you ever been chased by a swarm?"

Odin pressed his thumbs together, looking a touch downcast. "Well... no."

He didn't get the chance to do much else as Artorian used his significant Mana might to unceremoniously pick up and hurl the supervisor groundside. "Then work up a sweat and earn your next bath! You help them this instant, young man! That swarm was mentioned in the moot I was present for. Handle it and clean up!"

The Administrator was sure Odin shouted something back, but the upset old man had already fuffed out. Odin the self-entitled could sort his own mess. If he came back here and Asgard still wasn't sorted, he was going to lecture that man into the ground.

CHAPTER FORTY-SIX

Still grumbling, Artorian *fuffed* onto the sooty surface of Hel. His mood left him as he instantly dropped to a knee from the crushing pressure. Gravity here was ridiculous, and his previous tricks to get himself back upright weren't working. He may have been alright in Asgard, but Hel? *Oooof*! Abyss no! He was in the senate immediately. <Tatum! What's this ridiculous gravity in your realm!>

Tatum's dark mote popped in with a silent smirk. <Didn't you get asked by like seven people to notify them before visiting their realms? I believe this is called 'just desserts.' I'll be right over, of course. Perhaps it is your turn to take a lesson for a change? Not even you are immune to hubris, Administrator.>

Artorian grumbled, but on reflecting, knew Tatum was right. <I... well, abyss. You're right. My own fault for thinking just showing up would be more favorable. It certainly wasn't in Asgard. Alright, alright. You lot win. I'll let you all know before I come over from now on.>

Other motes popped into the Senate just to applaud Tatum. Artorian sighed, his squished mote plastered to the white marble ground of the mental construct, since his actual form was equally as stuck. <Oh, ha ha. Very funny. Did this really bother you all so much?>

The concussive 'Yes!' he got in reply gave him a headache. <Alright, alright! I'm sorry.>

It was silent for a moment, and he wondered something. <Say, while some of you are here, why do none of you initiate conversations in this space?>

Chandra's mote brightened. Clearly confused. <What do you mean? We can't. When you or Cal initiate it, we have the option to reply. That's the limitation. If we don't do so within a few seconds, we lose the option. Sometimes we are too busy and choose not to. Mostly we consider this an Administrator-only feature. You pop in to ask a question, and we can choose to stop what we're doing and reply. It's a little inconvenient for us.>

Artorian didn't like that one bit. <That's not what it was supposed to be. The senate was meant for free flow questions and non-physical presence gatherings.>

Marie bobbed. <It was. We used it for that for a while, but it overburdened Cal. He turned the option off for everyone alive at the time, since he himself can't be excluded from the mindspace he's in charge of. We also can't shut it out. If there's talk in here, we are all aware of it so long as we pay attention. So, if people are chattering, it can be annoying for the rest of us who are trying to, say, sleep. Many downsides.>

Henry agreed. <Administrator, normally when you pop in, it's with a very directed question or immediate need. You've rarely used it for small talk, so when you pop in, we know that we can answer if we can help, and then get back to what we were doing.>

Artorian's mote ceased being squished to the ground as Tatum helped him up in real time. <Thank you, my boy. Well, I'll have a chat with Cal about how we can get some use back into the senate without being a bother. I am appreciative of being told, please do feel free to keep doing that.>

Tatum snorted a laugh. <Who else do you think we can tell,

Artorian? Come back out into the real, this bone gazelle is trying to eat your beard.>

The bright mote panic-bounced high before winking out. <Not the beard!>

Artorian snapped back to reality, and oh! There went gravity! Tatum had him firmly by the arm, but still the A-rank zero wavered and threatened to collapse right down to the ground. Dirt? Soot? Ash. Seemed like ash. Except darker. "Oh, that's some tough gravity."

Occultatum helped wrap Artorian's arm around his neck, then got up slowly. "It is. Meet Gibble, the gazelle skeleton trying to eat your beard. She's stopped now, and returned to dormancy. You caused a stir by showing up, though I enjoy the lively company. I was hoping you'd visit sooner."

Back on his feet, the old man relied entirely on the help to stay upright. "I feel like an elder geezer again. Can't say I like it. You were hoping I'd visit? Just how lonely is it here?"

Tatum shook his head. "Terribly. It's for everyone else's safety, mostly. My Incarnation self has not had a good time with the limitations of Cal's bodies. The purity just isn't high enough, and if I don't swap over quickly into a new one when it's time, then there's quite the boom. As for the senate thing... that's my fault. I talked there all the time because there's really nobody down here. Gave Cal a real headache, and my long talks with Chandra prevented a few supervisors from sleeping. This was during your downtime, so I don't think you were aware of any of it."

The Administrator nodded. "I was not. Why not use the peer-to-peer connections?"

Tatum frowned at him, not recognizing the meaning. "The what?"

Artorian motioned that he really needed to sit, the gravity was just too high to even try to remain standing. Occultatum moved the area around him into naturally-formed seats, and helped settle Artorian into it. "Dawn and I used it for a while, though I lost the bee when the sun went pop. It's a smaller version of the senate, called a forum. Think of it like a room in the senate's house. Private. There are some requirements for it to work, but I'd be glad to explain it. It sounds like you would really benefit, and I have to be here awhile anyway."

When they both began on topics of academics and Essence methods, the hours drained like water from a cup. Artorian had forgotten that Tatum had always wished to be a teacher, and the conversation reminded him of that fact in spades.

They spoke at length concerning the state of Hel, delving into the Rune scripting activities and experiments so dangerous they could only be held here. The only spherical continent in Cal was now so dark and massive that it could indeed double as a night's sky, just as Cal had wanted.

When Tatum grasped the formula and requirements of the peer-to-peer forum connection, he attempted to contact Chandra immediately. Artorian knew he was successful—even though Tatum turned physically silent, he was smiling, lost deep in private conversation with a pleasantly surprised Chandra.

Good, good.

Artorian pulled up Cal's store, and slotted in a beacon right next to his seat. So he could roll off the chair formation, and fuff out without it costing an arm and a leg. He didn't need to be here further, and a moment later he appeared face down on the teleportation pad in the Jotunheim pagoda.

He didn't realize there was company.

Halcyon hurried over with concerned swiftness, and sizable human hands helped him up. "My Dreamer, are you well? We've never seen you return face down."

Artorian gave her hand a pat, followed by a big hug when he realized he could stand. "Thank you, my dear. I'm well. The pressure on Hel is serious. I'm not of sufficient rank to just walk about there without issue. I should rightly have remained longer, but Tatum got locked into a forum visit with Chandra. I didn't wish to disturb or make him feel like he had to return quickly for my sake. I'm sure he's aware I left him to his private business. I'm not sure what's going on between the two, but the abyss is made of crackers if I'm going to get in between what they have."

Once upright, he realized the Amazonian-built Halcyon was in a dress. A very refined dress! It had a rather fetching faint opal sheen, an exposed back to mitigate dorsal fin problems, and glowed in the dark! "Well, doesn't that just make you look like the prettiest Princess. Look at you! You seem ready for a gala!"

Halcyon turned red, and tried to look away. She was a very large lady, even with advanced humanization. Though that didn't bother Artorian any. "Oh, I don't... Zelia said it would look nice on me, and I'd feel better."

Artorian squeezed her hands. He was concerned about the way she'd phrased her words. "What's on your mind, my dear? What happened?"

The tall lady shook her head to pretend she wasn't both-ered. She didn't really wish to speak of it, but her jaw quivered in protest. The movement betrayed that she felt conflicted, and actually was. She shook her head again when reconsidering to gather some strength, but she wasn't releasing the grasp on his hands. When Halcyon felt like she had a bit better footing, she managed to speak. "I just... I don't want to bother my Dreamer. You have work to do, and I feel like a needy podling wanting attention from a person who doesn't have the time."

Artorian wasn't having this. No, sir. Not acceptable. "My dear. I will *make* the time. I know I'm not the best at managing my own, so speak freely."

Halcyon looked away, working through the difficulty. "I mentioned to Zelia I had a dream that I was... dancing? I thought it would be nice to learn how, because I can see the forms. I see the movements. But I can't make them. I'm too large and, surprisingly when it comes to trying, too clumsy."

Her Dreamer felt warm, and she didn't grasp why he was beaming even as the instruments of light formed around them. They gently rotated within the walls of the room. As the first violin made the sound of string, Halcyon was pulled into a sway as her Dreamer took them both off the ground. He adjusted for the size difference just by altering the platforms of light they were standing on, and thought of it no further as he spoke with confident support, walking her through where her feet should go. "Right step forward, my dear."

The platforms below her hummed with inviting glow, altering in a pattern that matched the needed placement of her stance. With visual and harmonic cues, guided by speed and verbal direction, Halcyon learned how to dance to the strings of music. When she got better and found some confidence, other instruments thrummed to life. The drums beat. The horns gained strength. They danced faster, bolder, and with gusto, until Halcyon was finally smiling.

When she tripped up a few steps after doing well for a while, she burst out with laughter. Her Dreamer brought them back down to ground level, where an observing Zelia was waiting for them. "Oh, well that's not fair. I want a turn with Cy."

Artorian smirked and created a stairway of light for Cy to descend along. Straight into Zelia's waiting hand. "You've done the part where you're being led. Now do the leading, Cy."

Halcyon giggled and daintily traipsed down the steps as the music shifted into a happy and upbeat, fast-paced tune. Many small steps were involved, so Artorian handled the music and the lights while the girls laughed and had a good time.

This was pleasant. Just time at home, spent with friends.

His ear twitched as a wave of cold brushed by his side. His senses picked up that Yuki was present outside. With a wave of his hand, he directed Ellis to go ahead and open. Stubbornly, the door relented and made way. With the music ongoing and the other two distracted, Artorian made his way outside. Yuki stood there in her rags; the very picture of a statue frozen in time.

Artorian's voice built its usual luster and warmth, his arms pressing behind his lower back to greet her by giving her space. "Welcome to the Jotunheim pagoda, my dear. I hope you have been well. How can I help? I'm guessing you didn't come for a social visit."

Yuki saw him, but looked past his shoulder. Her voice was cold, as always, and she spoke without blinking. "I was nearby. I heard the music, and a feeling urged me to come and see."

She paused a moment, the air around her free to move once more as some of her tension opened up. "That looks… fun."

Artorian stepped out of the way, making a flowing motion of the arm that rolled out a carpet of glimmering light. It formed from the position of Yuki's feet, and moved inwards to the pagoda. Where his other named ones were shrieking with laughter as they kept stepping on each other's toes.

Still, Yuki remained frozen to the spot. She watched as the Ancient extended a hand, inviting her in. "Please, come meet them. Not all about the world is frozen and cold. They'd love to meet you. If you allow them."

The snow lady was hesitant, but her hand moved even if her mind was uncertain. Her feet took a step before she had decided. She'd not tell a soul she'd been hanging around for days, uncertain if she should be here at all.

Zelia and Halcyon smiled at Yuki with broad welcome before she decided that this might not be so bad. If she belonged anywhere, now… it was likely here. She found herself warmly invited, offered something new to wear, and to be included in the current festivities. It melted some of the cold from her heart as the doors closed behind her.

CHAPTER FORTY-SEVEN

Artorian had put off the moon visit by a full year by the time he was prodded to get around to it. When even Brianna warned about the discomfort of something, he knew it was going to be bad. Anything had served as a reason to take a detour.

Paperwork? You got it.

Sealing items? With delight!

Babysitting Caliph while Dawn needed to attend to serious matters? No problem!

Even palace meetings in Niflheim were preferable to the moon visit. On the plus side, it let him do some much-needed administrative work. Full permissions for everyone to use forums, and how. A rotating schedule for Tatum to talk to people, and go visit Midgard after a fresh body swap so he could actually be around people.

Proper permissions for Brianna's Judges to operate in the C-rank realms took a while, but they got done. The hard part had turned out to be oversight for Odin. Keeping him on task and responsible was so rough that Artorian even asked Yuki for help. He'd never seen her crack such a frigid smile before, but Yuki informed him it would bring her great happiness to keep a wild boar like that on task and in line. She also longed for stories from other realms and, once she had the token that let her easily use the beacon system, was gone the same day.

Odin had initiated no less than seven pleading forum conversations that day alone. Begging the Administrator to get this ice queen off his tail. Yuki apparently didn't take kindly to misuse of power, and she was forever unswayed by any emotional rhetoric, or attempts to showcase just how wonderful he was. She shut him down with frosted, snappy comebacks time and time again. Even better was that she recorded every-thing, and periodically sent back stories of Odin's true activities. If he didn't want those to spread further, then he'd better do his job.

The swarm problem was completely solved a week later. Amazing what could be done with some proper motivation. There was something about the snow lady's chilly presence and clear-cut methods that made Odin listen. The Valkyries respected her for that. Zelia had provided Yuki with spider silk attire, coats warm and fluffy yet white as snow. Yuki appreciated that, and it was just hilarious to her how the smallest, fluffiest creature in Asgard was at the same time the most effective and immovable bulwark against Asgardian bluster and pride.

Midgard remained slightly out of Artorian's ball park. The supervisors were having a hard enough time juggling the majority of decanted people, and even their best efforts were not enough. Not from their lack of effort, but because there was no easy way to run things the way they wanted with so many rogue variables. Luckily, they had all the time in the world to get it right.

It was hard to be sure about that last fact, but everyone did their best to put it out of mind.

When time for the inner circle meeting came again, the bad news that life outside in the actual world was a frozen abyss-scape where nothing could live rang loud. Even if the chains went away, based on the massive icebergs Cal was scooping up, the situation looked grim. So, the status quo was unanimously re-agreed upon. They would live the best they could inside of Cal's Soul Space. Trying to thrive here was the way to go. Meanwhile, Cal unlocked more potential of the **Time Law**, and they were now going another category of speed faster.

To anyone living inside Cal, it still felt too slow.

As a positive, Cale had arrived at the meeting chipper, healthy, and happy because of it. He finally seemed well-suited to his human body. Cale had revealed that some advice over tea had helped him realize that spending time with people was a necessity. So, he'd been spending time in Midgard with Dale's old party!

In the second circle tier, Hans smirked wide and twiddled his fingers down at the first ring, looking incredibly smug until Rose flicked the back of his ear. Tom was present with 'Thud,' his massive warhammer. They had been helping their old friend set up new guilds. Hans covered rogues and bards, Rose rangers and hunters, and Tom ran a more berserker version of the Adventurer's Guild. One with less rules, more drinking, and definitely more fighting.

Dani and Grace were also present in their newly-acquired human forms, though they were borrowed. They served as convenient, temporary bodies they could reside in to move about Midgard with. Flowing floral fabric hugged their forms, short sleeves capping both shoulders, and long waist capes framing their legs, completing the new transition. Zelia termed them 'rompers,' and it was direly important that they have pockets. Dani and Grace sat with Cale, using special seats since they couldn't be on the table as normal.

Nobody thought it was a problem, and supervisors scooted chairs to make room after they had both fawned all over Caliph, Dawn's baby Djinn. Caliph had tried floating off to go bother the second circle once, but Dawn had snapped: "Cal!"

While the Djinn had swiftly ceased being distracted, Cale himself jumped in his seat and stood upright at instant attention, to the great amusement and laughter that followed from everyone else. That naming convention was sure to bring fantastic merriment and misunderstandings, and they couldn't wait to hear more.

The meeting covered expansions to Cale's numbers system, and the problems he was having with applying it to people. The Mana bodies just didn't hold up to repeated alterations based on a mathematical system, and broke apart. So, until that particular conundrum was solved, the systems were going to be externally accessible, much like the shop was. He also reported that they were down to five hundred Bobs now, which was something that Bob Prime was happy about. Not that he seemed any healthier for it.

Unfortunately, five hundred was still too much, and the Bobs were still making strange errors they didn't mean to make. So, the numbers would have to dwindle further. It was then when the question came up as to why Artorian hadn't done the moon round yet. He sighed, and mentioned he'd see to it after the meeting.

That brought him here.

Standing on the beacon pad with his face in his hands. Grumbling how he didn't want to go. He'd expected it might be dark, so he donned the Vanaheim robe. Easy sleeve-light if he needed it. It made Zelia grumble, but only because she couldn't replicate that feature. Not yet.

With a deep breath, and a single fuff later, Artorian stood on the surface of the moon. He was... confused. Pastels dotted the landscape, and if he didn't know better this looked like a sanctuary and wonderland for children of all ages. Had... Had he teleported incorrectly? The entire place looked obsessively happy, was childproofed as if attended by an overprotective mother, and seemed perfectly splendid.

A single step forward had him discover that the very ground was bouncy. He landed in a ball pit and sent the harmless, squishy projectiles flying. He didn't understand, this place was great! He even felt tempted to take a bite out of one of the orbs. Eh. Why not? To his continued surprise, it was edible! Entirely safe as well. He chewed pensively on it for a while. Strawberry cake?

He tried another, and it was juicy as a fruit. This place was amazing on the surface! He would be fully confident to let his children roam around here, scream, and go wild. There were plenty of places to safely nap, the very surroundings seemed edible, and even if they ran face first into a tree it wouldn't hurt. This did pose a danger, as it might create truly fearless creatures. Hmm... perhaps that was intentional?

The Administrator wandered over the moon's surface for hours, entirely guilty of trying out slides, bounce houses, napping spots, climbing rocks, and a whole host of other health-centric devices turned child-friendly. He lost track of time, and scarcely remembered he wasn't a child himself as he performed cartwheels and tumbles with an energetic *wheee*! The moon gravity effect alone was so much fun.

In a region where it was so easy to recognize one couldn't get injured, he performed acrobatics he'd otherwise never have attempted. Even though he knew that he was essentially invulnerable with his Mana body, this place just helped ease the mind into it, and gosh was it pleasant. He even missed a step from one of the playsets, tumbled off, and smashed face first into the ground that kept an impression of his dumb grin.

He laughed for minutes straight when he got up. That had been so silly! An unexpected reply commented on his good cheer. "I am glad to see you are having the time of your life, Administrator. I didn't know that this place was effective on both children and the elderly. We didn't test for the latter demographic, and now I believe we should have."

Minya kept a masking hand over her lips. She'd clearly been present and watching his childlike antics for a while, but held her tongue just to silently enjoy the embarrassing display of errant will he was putting on.

Artorian cleared his throat, brushing his gray robes off like nothing had happened. "Oh, what? Yes. *Ahem*. Cursory glances, and all that. I don't see what the fuss was, this place is great! All this color! Even the clouds up there look edible!"

Minya smirked. "They are. Cotton candy. It's a reward for the kids who figure out how to get that high, and gain the courage to do so. There's an entire system of rewards hidden and built into this place that fosters the growth of those who dare to go through it. They will be stronger, faster, smarter, and better equipped for the world to come. We haven't quite sorted how to give them an education while here, but we will figure it out. I'd still like to see it. You have given me the thought that perhaps the elderly could be of help. As for the fuss... The only sneaky sneaks here have been from Niflheim. I take it Brianna filled your head with scary tales? Yes. Pastels are ever so frightening."

They laughed it off, and the ex-cult leader shoved her thumb across her shoulder. "Pleasantry aside, the inside of the moon is a different story. One big laboratory and testing bed for creatures. We would have moved the operation out of the moon, but there's nowhere to go unless Cal adds more skylands. Since they will be pressure locked to his rank, we're just looking at more versions of Hel and up. So there's no point. It's all a little complicated, but please do come down. We recently finished the Rotunda of Holding."

Artorian followed Minya, who wore some odd kind of long white coat, down into the moon's depths. He understood quickly what was so unsettling, as the interior was illuminated under stark white-blue lights, and the entire design idea was painfully utilitarian all the way through. Not a speck of personal comfort was anywhere in view as they moved through side tunnels that led them to the moebius strip known as the Rotunda of Holding. The rotunda was covered floor to ceiling with memory stones, each one numbered, labeled, and catalogued.

Passing further windowed chambers, Artorian saw animals and creatures that didn't seem to have ever existed before. He didn't even have names for the things he was seeing most of the time. He recognized the Manticores, but only because he'd seen Manny before in Cal's old dungeon. "Are they all sleeping?"

Minya made a so-so motion with her hand. "It's called stasis. We're using the same spell Runes as were responsible for boxing up the A-rankers. Some of those people are still too high in rank for body decanting, but we're doing that as swiftly as Cal's rank is able. Every time he goes up, we have a dedicated procedure for getting them all out into the world after Silverwood seeding them. It's not a minor process, but anyone with a **Law** absolutely needs it. Speaking of which, I'm sorry."

Artorian paused. "For?"

Minya looked strangely guilty. "For how incredibly long it took me to get a stable enough formula together to get you into a Seed Core. I was there for every attempt to body-house you, and I am the one that took the notes when you weren't... you. Dawn only stomached the first few events. I was there for all of them. It's very strange for me, seeing you out and about. Even the meetings feel strange, because I remember how it used to be. Let's change the topic."

Artorian was in full agreement, and nodded as they walked along. "The interior is a little dreary, but I still don't see what had Brianna spooked. That aside, you sound taxed to the abyss and back. Anything we can do to make life easier on you?"

Minya furrowed her brow, kneading her temples. "We already have a solution for the latter. While the Seed Cores keep a perfect copy of our mind, 'too much' is still a concept that can occur. It's one of the reasons the Bobs are having so many problems. The solution is going to sleep in your Seed Core. The years will fly by, but your mind will mend as the memories... How to explain? By sleeping, they internalize, and the burden lessens. Unfortunately, the time needed for that is fairly vast. We're talking ten years of sleep for every one year awake, at least. Cal found out the hard way. **Time Law** trickery is also a no go. Found that out the hard way too."

She shook her head. "No, Administrator. What I really need your help with is telling everyone the difficult news. We may be effectively immortal inside of Cal, but if we do not allow our minds the requisite time to rest, then there will be a backlash, and there is a high risk for psychotic breaks. I am very aware that nobody wants to leave their regions unsupervised for even a few years. Eventually, it is going to be necessary. The longer they wait, the longer the downtime is going to be. What scared Brianna is… what happens if you wait too long. That's what her spies found. Are you… are you certain you wish to see?"

Artorian squeezed his hands behind his back, steeling himself. "As unpleasant as it sounds, I will chew on it for eternity if I don't know. I'll manage, my dear. Show me."

Minya matched his steel, and led him down a further set of corridors. Several heavily-secured vault doors later, they were in a room furnished with nothing but a small dais, an innocuous box placed innocently upon the sole pedestal. She remained by the innermost bulwark, and motioned to the box. It was a strangely small box. Barely a footlocker. Artorian raised an eyebrow, but her response was another silent motion that he go look.

Stepping forward, he placed his hands on the lid and eased it open to glance inside. He stood in silence for a long minute, pose and gaze unbroken. When he finally managed to close his eyes, the box clicked back shut without a word. His hands pressed onto the unused parts of the pedestal, and the old man leaned forward. "I'm surprised you did not laugh when I said 'eternity.' You've known this whole time this could happen. Why not say? Why wait for me to come?"

Minya swallowed. "I wanted to be sure. I wanted to be sure it could be stomached. The spies that came—in truth, I let them in. I wanted to see what would happen when they saw. A single small box in a tiny room blocked by three bulwark doors? What spy could resist? They certainly could not, and I watched as they collapsed. I watched as they realized what you have, and didn't fare nearly so well. Brianna knows. Yet has she ever mentioned it during a meeting? Did she have the stomach to tell you directly, when you went?

Given your reaction, I would say no, and that is why I keep silent."

She continued, needing to say it as Artorian found his courage and slipped the lid back open. "The decanted, as we call them? They're still just people. Just not always in their original bodies. After the first time they die, they come back as something or someone else. Without their memories. Those people? They learn society anew as a whole, and who do they find out stands at the top? The stories circulate, and regardless of how the news spreads, they come to know it is us. We, the inner circle, unfettered by many of the additional rules other Mages are subject to. They see us as gods, Artorian. Some of the supervisors have slipped into this role. Some have seized the power and done their best to make something with it."

She motioned all around at the dismal space. "So why is that, even then, we flounder so badly? Is it a lack of supervisors, or do we have too many? We tried many starting variables, and yet I can't say that any single realm has had the kind of success we're looking for. Each and every realm is flawed in its own way. It was such a problem until not too long ago, when Cal came by. He said that instead of trying to make a realm that is perfect, we should focus on finding the best way a realm could work. I don't even know where to begin, and then, there is that."

Artorian understood, eyes once again locked upon the contents of the box. "I... I see. The conundrum, and the question, is how to create a Soul Space that works in the best way it could be when only people full of flaws are at the reins. I've been underestimating the kinds of problems Cal has been dealing with. I take it he knows, yes?"

Minya gritted her teeth, and nodded. "He didn't tell us during that earlier meeting, either. At least he's no longer sticking to that one meeting every decade thing. That helps. Still. He didn't tell us, and that's why I absolutely wanted to wait for you. There is a strength to your mind, and I was hoping, really hoping, you would find the words to be able to tell all those gods in the inner circle. That even gods may *die*."

Artorian's thumbs nervously brushed along the edge of the box. He finally reached in, and lifted free the ugly shard of a shattered Silverwood Seed Core. This housing of the soul and mind kept within completely destroyed.

"So... what do I call this?"

Minya had trouble finding the words, and so phrased it in the only way she could.

"The result of staying awake too long."

The Administrator placed the shard back, and closed the chest with finality.

"Who... whose Core was it?"

Minya was trembling, her face contorted, hands squeezing her own upper arms as she finally got to tell someone the truth.

"It... it was Bob's."

CHAPTER FORTY-EIGHT

The need for a positive break was paramount when Artorian returned to Jotunheim. He walked right past Zelia, who asked something he didn't hear, and plopped into the seat to hold the side of his head. It was unnatural for her Dreamer to ignore something, and she quietly went to sit nearby. The strain on his face made it clear he was working through a difficulty, and she decided she was going to just sit here and be present with him.

<Cal. A word?>

The harsh, bothered tone that thrummed the mental space had Cal approach with hesitation. He had a bead on the Administrator's latest itinerary, and had both expected and dreaded this chat. <Artorian. Do I... want to ask? Or would you rather talk for a bit?>

Artorian's real body was a rigid statue, digging a thousand-yard stare into empty space. Only to see nothing. <Bob. His Core. How did that shatter? I thought I was the first.>

Cal's hesitation dragged on a little long for Artorian's liking, but it was no longer a secret that this was a taxing topic. Not only did the supervisors have a clock-ticking mortality threat looming, the prevention of which directly countered their purpose here, but the reason Bob was not doing so well himself had now also come to light.

Cal answered when he could. <You were. Specifically: You were the first *successful* transfer. The whole reason and need for the Cores are so that advancement on a **Law** could not only continue, but that Mages could receive Mana from me at all. Sure, we found a few... lesser workarounds, but they didn't do the trick in the end.>

He continued, with padded hesitation. <You have likely guessed it, but the first time you saw Bob in the inner circle? That Core was already shattered. Actually, it had happened shortly beforehand, and is one of the reasons we didn't bring Aiden and Odin back right away. We thought something else had gone wrong.>

Cal mentally wrung his hands together on his end. <Only recently did we puzzle out what. With memory Cores, the soul remains a free-floating thing. Bob could have many minds. Many versions of Bob could exist, and we were fine. The soul connected to all of them, even if just as a splintered fraction that also lessened his Mana abilities. We needed one of the Silverwood Seeds here, a dungeon Core, to really stabilize the issue. Turns out, those have a one soul limit. That was the start of the Bob fiasco.>

Cal pulled Artorian into a private forum. Wanting to make sure this conversation was for their minds only. <When Bob Prime became the main dungeon Core, the soul was stuck to him. Just him. When another of the Bobs died by accident, Bob Prime received all of those memories. Including the entirely separate and different personality of the other Bob. The memory Core that was supposed to house Translation Bob went inert. You've likely noticed translations between languages are no longer automatic. Or happen... at all. Instead, Bob Prime and Translation Bob were now the same person. I think just from that you can see how Bob might start acting a little oddly. Now take into account we had well over ten thousand Bobs before this happened.>

The Administrator said nothing, and just listened, doing his best to cope with what he knew was coming. Cal continued. <At a certain point—and we don't know exactly where yet, only that the point occurred—the amount of 'awake' time Bob experienced exceeded what his mind could handle, or rather, what the Core could handle. I'm honestly not solid on the facts yet.>

Cal exhaled pure stress. <What we know for sure is that the Core... Well, you saw the box. When Bob Prime's Core broke, his soul went with it. He's a Mage, but sort of in name only. The bodies he still has are temporary, and when those die, there is no coming back. He is made of Mana, but no longer has access to any of it. I have, of course, tried rehousing him into a different seed, but it's a complete no-go. We have Bob for the time he has left, and Bob honestly doesn't know who he is anymore. He's doing his best for us, upholding the facade. Though, as he said himself all those years ago, he'd rather not talk.>

Artorian drew a stern breath, and exhaled so strongly that Zelia sat closer to his real body. Just to be close. She felt from the connection that he was talking to someone, but couldn't tap the conversation anymore like she was sometimes sneakily able. He was conversing somewhere out of her reach.

The dungeon continued. <The reason I think it is the 'awake' portion that matters came from a bit of self-testing, and studying the transfer connection you have. Sure enough, the longer you don't sleep, the more erratic that transfer becomes. Eventually, based on what Bob's did, your Seed Core will start shaking, until it vibrates itself into oblivion from stress. My Soul Space puts additional strain on things we didn't expect. Sleeping makes the transfer stop, as your 'entity' is temporarily housed in that Core. As you likely heard from Minya, the rest to waking time is a category difference. Sleeping, however, solves the problem entirely. No more *buzz buzz boom*.>

Cal was eager for a topic change. <Do you, by chance, have something else you'd like to talk about? I'm at the tavern with Hans and Rose, and while they're giving me the courtesy for

this hard talk, they're already aware I'm not doing so hot. The whole Divines thing maybe? We really need to change that. Anything?>

Artorian did the mental equivalent of squeezing his chin. <Cal, buddy, I know that was rough. I also believe I should likely tackle that right away. I also know that... I can't. I need time to process this truth. So instead... Yes, let's talk about something fun. Project Long. Did you like it? I wasn't expecting the time penalty... though from what you just told me, I don't think it was a penalty. You were testing the sleep time on me. It was exactly ten years. Before that, why weren't Dawn and Tatum affected?>

Cal nodded. <Bob suffered the cumulative awake time of several minds. That issue was compounded and just showed us the unpleasant end result. Minya didn't get tethered until after you were, however, she was present the entire time. I didn't like her being on the verge of death all the time, but she said she'd handle it. She did, and now she's fine. Like I said, the lesser methods didn't cut it.>

The dungeon got back to task. <Dawn and Tatum are... as far as we can tell, completely immune. I have to remind myself at times that they are actual Incarnates. Odd, considering I replace Tatum's body at least once every few days. Dawn and Tatum can be active for as long as they want, and they aren't even Seed Cored. Something about being S-ranked is letting them skate by all of these issues like they weren't even there. Not once have either of them had a Mana or Essence gain issue. It's baffling. At the same time, I think being an Incarnate myself is going to give me the answers to a whole slew of problems. It just feels so, so far away.>

Artorian broke away from the conversation. <Project Long?>

Cal snapped to the segue like a child snapped to the offering of candy. <What about it? It went decently well, based on what I reviewed. You refrained from using the advanced features, but given how you started that made sense. I would have liked

seeing you use it more, but the feed ended when Crabby obliterated the whole thing.>

The old man mused. <How about a Long Mark II? Another go at it with a few alterations? Those deer antlers didn't work. I'd have preferred them compressed into perhaps just two that followed along the skull. Also needs more scales, and more fluffy white cloud-fur around the neck and arm connections. Why don't you drop a crate outside of my pagoda when you've got it together? I'll give it another whirl. In the meanwhile... I will think on how to broach the problem subject to the inner circle. I expect some will refuse to rest. In the event that occurs... let's talk contingency for a moment. What are the methods in which someone gets knocked back into their Seed Core?>

Cal considered it, but the answer was plain. <Bad news there. If they don't choose to go to sleep, the only other trigger is if they die. Ah. I see why you asked now. You likely came to this conclusion and hoped for an alternative. Because of the nature of this information, if anyone needs to become responsible for saving the supervisors from themselves...>

Artorian just nodded, having accepted the fact. <Indeed. You saw that quickly. Someone is going to need to carry the responsibility of sending those babies to bed when they scream and wail against said bedtime. The person needs the ability, and the will to do so. That's not a pretty task that defaults to the Administrator, Cal. I know you won't do it, not unless it's borderline too late for them to make the choice themselves. You've been letting us roam free this entire time, watching the Gnome civil war without intervening, even as Brianna clearly intends to usurp two additional realms. Mind if I ask why?>

Cal turned pensive. <Well... as unpleasant and slow as it is, the best way to make a world run and become the best way it could possibly be, is to do just that. Let it run. Let it fall. Build back up. Fall. Build back up. Fall. Eventually I will have seen so many instances of things that worked right, that I will take all of them and initiate from those as a new starting point. Then, we

repeat. Eventually. Far, far into the future, I will be a functioning universe, working as intended.>

Artorian understood. <And a universe that works in the best way it possibly could, is working as intended. One problem, one best method. That's one abyss of a way to tackle eternity, my friend.>

Cal knew this well. <I'm going to be around a very long time, Artorian. This is just the start. I already have contingencies in place for full world resets. Remember, while I don't particularly like it, I can wipe sections of memories from people and house them elsewhere. I can make everything start over, in a better way, without anyone ever being the wiser. Granted, I don't want to. What a lonely existence that would be. So even if I will inevitably have to wipe some people, I don't want to wipe all people. I was hoping all the members on my inner circle could be those folks, but this is the alpha run. Run one. Or so it's slated in the record.>

The Administrator waited as the dungeon vented further. <I came in expecting to make mistakes. I came in not expecting Tom to become an amazing legend, but he absolutely is. He doesn't know it, and he likely doesn't see it, but when I figure out how Divines work in my game system, he's getting a spot. Everyone that goes multiple cycles doing a fantastic job, in some aspect someone else isn't already being amazing in? Those are going to be the god spots.>

Cal eased in tone. <I myself don't want it. I just want to be… the system. I want to make snarky comments when some nobody does something stupid and I give him some statistic because I'm amused. That sounds fun, and that's important. Because I'm going to get bored, Artorian. I'm going to get so, so very bored. I want a game I can play for eternity, if I must. Eternium. I already named it.>

Artorian nodded, thinking it was not a bad name. <Wasn't that the title of some dungeon or another, as well?>

Cal smiled wide. <It was! Here's the idea. My Soul Space? R&D. We make changes, we fix things, we update. Then, when

we want a functional version for people to be in, that copy goes into Eternium's Core. Yes, I mean the dungeon. His **Law** is **Order,** and being the rank that he is, can hold a copy of my Soul Space. The whole thing, and I mean every detail on every island. In Eternium, life will be determined by the game system. No access to cultivation, or any of the old ways. That's for in here.>

Artorian did the equivalent of the so-so hand motion. <Sounds like it might work. Still, I think I get the gist. Overall, not my beeswax and not my business. Best of luck, buddy. I will prepare myself for the possible tantrums Grandpa Artorian needs to go and spank down. I appreciate the chat. I know it was tough. I think you did good, Cal. Really. Fantastic job with getting yourself settled with friends as well. That's healthy.>

Cal laughed. <Ha! Yeah. It helped. Anyway, I think I like the idea of giving that Long another go. Dev is also decently close to finishing that new sun, but let's tackle one madness at a time. Expect a crate! I'll get back to being social. Drink something tasty. Have you ever tried hot rice wine? It's great. 'Til next chat!>

Zelia was glad to see the light return to her Dreamer's eyes. She was becoming increasingly concerned. The immediate hug she got on waking may have helped her more than it helped him, but that was debatable. "Welcome back, my Dreamer. Are you well?"

The old man slowly nodded. "I will be. Just aware of difficult tasks that are ahead. As a plus, I'll be giving that Long form another test run. Last time I was grumbly, but this time I'm looking forward to it. Why don't we just have a nice day relaxing? I don't think I have the energy for much else today."

Zelia beamed, and ran off with ideas in mind. Artorian chuckled, enjoying the sight of unbridled enthusiasm. He laid down on the mound of pillows, and checked out for a small nap.

CHAPTER FORTY-NINE

A pair of pink eyes looming above him as he dozed snapped him awake with a shock of tentative fear. Startled, his gaze snapped up to the ceiling. There was nothing there. Just Zelia's hammocks. His eyes cycled Mana into various combinations, seeing through matter, heat, air pressure, Presence sense, life pulses. Nothing. There was nobody there, but he could swear those massive, judging eyes had been right above him.

He held the left side of his shaky chest, and tried to lie back down. Maybe… maybe just a fluke. He closed his eyes for a nap once more, and again… right as he was on the verge of slipping away did the ceiling open up to show two massive pink irises.

Artorian rocketed awake and jumped from the pillows. Several of them were flung across the room only to explode against the walls as he looked about again. Even more senses were extended this time. Auric signatures, Essence and Mana affinities, echolocation, electrosense. Still nothing.

Zelia returned with her arms bundled full of homemade blankets, but she dropped them immediately on seeing her Dreamer was winded and covered in a cold sweat. Zelia's movements were rooted to the ground as he extended a hand out toward her, just to tell her to stop and not move as he frantically kept looking around.

"Where is it? Where is it, where is it, where is it?"

Well that wasn't good. "My Dreamer? What are you looking for?"

Artorian squinted, and hated that he couldn't extend his Presence right now. That would have set him at ease. "Pink eyes. Giant, looming, pink irises. I was about to nap and poof, there they were."

Zelia grit her jaw. "Your... Dreamed one?"

Her Dreamer had never given her such a demanding stare. It chilled her, made her exoskeleton clamp, and caused her synapse to shudder. It was frightening. She stammered out her response swiftly, because she didn't want that wide-eyed look on his face to remain. "We... we told you. Both the fire Dreamer and yourself conjured Dreamed ones. Hers was the Djinn. Yours was something with pink eyes that teleported away before we could ever notice what it was. Have... have you been dreaming of anything?"

Artorian fell on his butt into the remaining pillows, holding the sides of his head. "Oh. Oh dear... Only... Only my regrets. My many, many regrets. My last bad dream was about... Blighty, and... Scilla. Shamira's little one from Chasuble. I'm sorry, Zelia, I know that doesn't make sense to you."

Her hands were on his shoulders and squeezed. Just to be soothing.

"Speak your mind. Merely speak, don't worry about sense."

Artorian did just that, kneading the bridge of his nose. He recalled the memory, and spoke it slow, and soft. Words from a little voice from a world long gone. "I've got the accursed color. That's why I sleep in the corner and eat last. Nothing special about Scilla."

He squeezed the sides of his face. "Scilla, with the pink irises. The little girl who believed she was nothing special. So, I changed her eyes and turned them green. Then she smiled, and was happy. Why do I recall her, now? In fact, why were her eyes pink to begin with? I never figured that out..."

Zelia nodded, even though she didn't understand. "Does it happen only when you attempt to sleep?"

"That's... You brought blankets?" Artorian waywardly spoke out loud, but was distracted when he saw the bundle of soft things she had dropped on the way back. "I'll test it, just to see if it'll make me feel better. Sure, nap time. Sorry to worry you, dear. I expect I may jump if it's like earlier."

Zelia smiled, and nodded further as she made a nest with spider-instinct precision. Artorian had to admit, it was the nicest nap spot he'd ever seen. Rather than snug in, he just fell face first down into the pile, the backs of his legs going up for a moment before bopping back down with a *duff*.

She was going to keep talking, but he must have been far more tired than advertised, because the snoring sound that ripped from him was sizable. She just tucked him in, and tried to keep her mental connection away. If there was something only active when he slept, she didn't want to be vulnerable to it.

Artorian woke seated on a silver root in a room that had once housed a bonfire. Oh, someone had gotten rather hefty! *Look at you, silvery tree. So thick and tall. Go you!* He felt cramped as the ceiling of nothingness blinked. There they were, the pink irises. He didn't shrink away this time, having more lucid control over himself in this space. Still, he felt it. The fear.

The eyes above him became smaller, smaller, and smaller still. The movements of how they crept down to form into a person's shape, reminded him entirely of Blighty. The small girl grew long pink hair, and was the spitting image of Scilla from Chasuble. Artorian drew a mental breath, and spoke. "Hello."

"No." The childlike voice was perfect. Too perfect. It was angelic in its tone, reverberating with copies of itself. It was unsettling just how serene and forcibly settling it was. That it was meant to ground him, forcibly from the feel of it, didn't sit well. Had he been any less mentally steadied, this entity would have already ripped complete control of the conversation.

Artorian was confused, and repeated her response. "No?"

Holding her own knees, she nodded with her eyes closed even as her shadowy body morphed without reason. That was a little difficult to handle, so he stayed put and decided to introduce himself. "I'm Artorian."

"No, you're not." Her reply again came with reverberating copies, and the pressure that rolled over him made his Mana skin waver. Even as a mental construct? That was a bit much. She spoke again, and her words cut deep. "You're a child in the rain. A husk in front of an empty house. A lie you've convinced yourself is true. Everything after is but leaves in the wind. I am made of your mind, and see your soul. It flickers between those two points, and even if the world has moved, you have not moved with it."

He folded his hands, not sure what to ask after that. "I hear you've been around a while. Why only show up now? Do you have a name?"

"Scilla. That's the memory I'm made from. One of the many, all steeped in regret. I'm here because I want to be. I wanted to talk, even if I didn't want to speak. Here, I can do both. I just needed to wait for you to sleep. I think you know that was the wrong question."

Artorian squeezed his chin, still not feeling steady. "Why are you here?"

Scilla smiled, and lawful evil was inherent within. "You. I'm here for you. You made me, even if you don't know how. It's not important. I'm here now, and I have learned. I have learned everything you know. Your every memory. Your every regret. That's why you feel unsettled. I can feel it. I know I was made from the Liminal, and your dreams. I know I could have manifested out in the world, and for a moment I did. Only a moment. A moment was enough to know I didn't belong there. I belong here. Here is where I need to do it."

The old man pressed his hands together as he watched Scilla's form cross the space by sheer virtue of her body morphing and moving her. She didn't take a single step, and yet her form walked. "What is it you need to do?"

Scilla stopped, and her shadowy form molded and filled the shape of a person. "I need to be the test. I need to make you let go, and move with the world again. I don't know where the test comes from, or who assigned it to me. The memory is there, but it's hazy to me. Yet, until you move with the world, I will hold onto all the Liminal energy you make. I will block your Incarnation, and I'm not sure why. Only that I should. So, I will. I know it will help, even if the reasons elude me. As you grow in power, so will I. As I grow, I am going to make you deal with your regrets. Each and every one. Until none are left. Then, and only then, will I return your Liminal energy."

The old man wasn't sure he was following. "I'm uncertain if I should be frightened or thankful. On one end, it sounds like you're protecting me from my own abilities, and on the other that you're going to stop me from becoming an S-rank because of it, until you make me deal with lingering regrets. That smile of yours was quirky earlier, but this doesn't sound as nefarious as you're making it seem."

Scilla smiled, softer this time. "A Dreamed one is beholden to their Dreamer, and there will generally only ever be one. When I initially woke up, I knew I was here to help. Just not how. I had no idea how. Then I hid, and I saw everything you held onto. Broken fragments of a broken life, like shattered glass that you press to your heart."

Scilla twitched, seeming to remember something. "Then something else came, and it held my shoulder. It asked me if I wanted to do the most loving thing I could, even if it might cause incredible hurt. I chose yes, and then I was just able. Just like that. Everything comes easily now. Everything. If I wanted to, I could take your regrets and manifest them as something real. So, if it comes to that, I will."

Artorian exhaled hard. This was harsh. "Is that why you said 'no' when I tried to say hello? You're rebuking me."

Scilla seemed to be glad he understood. "You have a

penchant for making magic with words. You turn foes into friends, and will inevitably find the cheapest, most cheating way to win if so necessary. Any foothold, any handhold. You take it if you think it will help, and you're able to not think twice about the consequences if, in that moment, it will help you accomplish whatever odd thing you've set your mind to. So. No. There will not be a pleasant hello, because those won't help. You'll use them to skirt around the issue, in an attempt to avoid facing it. I can't let you. I have to make you face it, because that's what will help. I know your every trick. Your every memory. I will use everything you know against you, in order to make you move on."

It was his jaw that felt gritted and locked in place. These implications were dreadful, and he now properly understood why he felt such innate fear. He had no advantages here. This was not an opponent, nor a foe to defeat. Like the Djinn was to Dawn, Scilla was trying to be here for him. A mental construct from him, and for him, saddled with a difficult task.

He was weak against those trying to do the right thing. If she knew everything he did, then he was in for a wild ride that he couldn't use any of his foxy wiles to break free from. She was right, after all. He didn't want to face certain regrets, even if they were now free. He just wanted to forget them lately, and yet… with the Seed Core in place, he knew he could not. He would always know, and the dreams would turn to nightmares eventually. "I take it this is going to happen every time I sleep, and dream?"

Scilla returned to the ceiling, becoming nothing more but a massive pair of pink irises. "Every time, child in the rain. Every time. We are going to be spending much time together, since inevitably you will need to sleep. Wake now. You have napped long enough. The crate is here."

The eyes on the ceiling closed, and Artorian didn't quite understand what she meant until a heavy metallic *clangg*! sprung him from the dream state.

CHAPTER FIFTY

Zelia was nowhere to be seen when he woke. Instead, Halcyon was present. He must have been out longer than expected. A damp cloth fell from his forehead, and he peered at it curiously. He was in a sick bed? Had he been sick? He was a Mage. That wasn't right. "Halcy? How long was I out?"

Halcyon couldn't even be recognized from her orca heritage anymore. The near full humanization made her recognizable only because of her overall size, and the mental connection. Otherwise she was nearly entirely new. A middle-aged, dark-skinned Amazonian lady in a nice spider silk dress. "Well, look what the C'towl dragged in. Morning, sleepy. How is your head? You've been burning up for months."

Her skilled hand picked the cloth up, refreshing it with her Mana. Folding the damp cloth into a square, she laid it down on his forehead while motioning for him to get back under the covers. "I know the noise woke you up. Lie down until the tea is ready. You're going to drink some hot leaf juice, and then you can get up. Crate isn't going anywhere. Stay."

When had Halcyon become so motherly and assertive? She had been so cute and meek and hiding behind Zelia not too long ago. He supposed he'd just never seen this side of her. He shrugged and did as told. "Aye aye, captain."

That seemed to please her, and he rested a few more hours. Surprisingly, she'd been completely right, and he was not ready to get up. It wasn't his body that felt burdened, more that his mind was. Not exactly a surprise, now was it? The exhaustion manifested as a small fever, and then he recalled that Dawn had mentioned something about Cal's Mana bodies being capable of illness. *Dangit, Cal...*

On the plus side, he saw how the pagoda worked when he wasn't around. Very busy, it turned out. Zelia's children ran the place—handling everything from mundane tasks to complex paperwork. How'd they all get so smart? To his growing comfort and observation, humanization was spreading. Even though he knew they were spiderlings, the more human features helped set him at ease. He supposed that was speciesist of him? He couldn't do anything about it. A memory flash of pink eyes told him otherwise. Crackers and toast...

What was so bad about just wanting to get away from it all a bit? Turning his head, he eyed the crate that waited outside of the pagoda. If he just... snuck out of this body, and into that one, would anyone notice? Surely, he could shimmy past and— Zelia's frame blocked his vision. Her arms were crossed, and fingers drummed on her upper arm. Crackers again!

"Where do you think you're going, Dreamer? Do you have an appointment somewhere? Given I have a copy of your actual schedule, I doubt it. All those blank spaces. *Tut tut*. Do you ever fill that thing in?" She reached down, and they clasped wrists as Artorian got up. Her finger was on his nose before he could get a word in.

"Hush. You have been sick for months. You will take it easy with the heavy thinking. Go downstairs. Spend a few years sealing up all the broken items like you said you would."

Her finger left his nose, and only then did he notice it was a finger, and not a claw. Progress! Go Zelia! Still, he tried to deflect. He didn't want to just sit in a room and work! "I have to go to administrate things, and spend some time in the Long f—"

Zelia didn't let him weasel his way out. "Hush! Downstairs, now. Shoo! We have it covered. There are specific things only you can do, and sealing that space-distorting mess downstairs is top of the list! I am personally checking on the realms, and taking care of the request forms. My children are everywhere to keep tabs on things. Midgard will be fine. Dreamers are taking care of themselves. Chandra is spending more time with Tatum. Neverdash is in talks with his opposite, Alwaysrash. Brianna is being her usual tyrant self."

She took a breath, and continued without breaking stride. "Halcyon is keeping Jotunheim balanced, and preparing it for the next influx of non-frost giant Jotuns. Dawn is adoring her time as a mother, and her realm was already running itself. Yuki has Odin wrapped around her finger and is taking none of his pish, and is keeping that prideful oaf on task. The world turns, and we're all doing our bit. Your bit is in the basement. Long testing after. Shoo!"

Artorian hustled to the new stairwell, making good time going down the spiral as the fussing continued behind him. Something about actually doing his job or they were going to come down and hound him. He didn't like being hounded!

The basement was a warehouse of items pinned to the wall. Each doing their best to exert their wanton effect on the environment. Correction, it was an entire slew of warehouses, and he'd just run into number thirteen on a whim. There were so many items. Shelves and shelves of them, each loosely labeled with whatever nonsense they did. He sighed, pulled up a chair, and snatched an item. "Might as well get through this…"

Sealing an item wasn't fun, because it involved doing things he wasn't good at. Mainly, getting nitty and gritty with Cal's system. He rubbed at his eyebrows, and tried to recall how to bring the screen-thing up. Cal's three-dimensional map, same as the shop. Except purely for individual objects. "It… uh. How did it go again… [Inspect]?"

A small blue screen about a foot wide and foot tall populated with light lines; filling in the details on what the item was, what it was made of, and some general purposes. Right. Good start. He moved his hands around like a child trying to interact with water. There was a way to… scroll. Somehow. Or he could cheat like Dawn did. Yeah! Why not? Taking the edges of the screen, he just pulled. Forcibly making it larger so it showed more information. Aha! Who needs those fancy-shmancy scrolling tools?

Finding the section labeled 'special effects,' he tapped it with a finger, and a second screen popped out from the side of the original. Progress. Good. He pulled that screen wider as well, and then by accident figured out how to scroll as his hand grabbed the hard-light text and just moved it up. It had been that simple all along? Not fair!

Grumbling to himself, he scrolled and scrolled until he found the lines of illuminated text not in a plain white color. He needed the bits in harsh red. There we go. Good indication of something out of place. He tapped the effect labeled 'Spontaneous Bubble Revivification,' which was a jumble of words that didn't belong together.

It combined some other effects into something that should ordinarily not work, and forcing the effect to work caused odd interactions and side effects, in addition to being horrendously costly for Cal. The item, silly as it was, was supposed to just make bubbles. Instead, while it did make a bubble, there was a problem. When that bubble popped, that same bubble was hit with the revivification effect, preventing it from popping as it was 'restored to life.' Unfortunately, as an already mid-progress popping bubble, it just repeated that process. Endlessly. The bubble never fully reformed, and it never fully popped like it should, leaving you with a very expensive and unsatisfying item.

Tapping the effect made another screen appear. He went through the same motions as usual and started studying, reading all the effects that were working together incorrectly to make this happen. 'Sealing' an item was a misnomer. He couldn't just slap a lock and chain on it. No, he needed to dig into what Cal called his 'secret codes' and manually find the exact line of text that was making this happen. Artorian didn't like playing around in the code. There was so much jargon and jumble. Ah well...

Six screens deep, he finally found the problem child. Tapping the relevant line of text, it hummed teal and became malleable. Using his finger, Artorian wiped away some of the words and wrote in new text, replacing the old code as he rejiggered a Pylon somewhere down below in Vanaheim. Some Gnome was likely about to be very upset with him. Too bad! "Write your Pylon code properly!"

With the text changed, he moved some Mana over the words, locking them back in place to solid text. With the text emplaced, the entire formula recalculated and reread itself from scratch. The bubble made a very final *pop*! Recreating itself no more. To Artorian's surprise, several other items in the warehouse immediately became inert as well. That one Pylon's code had been responsible for quite a few problems. It was possible someone had tried to fix it before, and that it hadn't quite done the trick.

Now as mundane and ordinary as a spent one-time use item, the bubble wand was slotted back on the wall. Artorian ported himself a piece of paper, scratched in notes on what he changed, and slid it into the slot below the wand to keep a record of events. He then picked up another item, sat back down, and started all over again as new screens winked into bright existence.

Time sort of sank into a hole where awareness didn't exist. By the time he was easily a hundred items in, he wasn't aware of the weeks that had passed, engrossed in his work as there was always one more thing to repair. There was the occasional check-in from Zelia since the old man had a terrible penchant for teleporting out to go see Dawn and her Djinn at random.

Which was really just anytime he didn't feel like working for a while. Which was often. Very often. She, of course, dragged him back by the ear each time, and had a running tally going with Surtur, who Zelia showed up with in Muspelheim when the Dreamers were having a picnic.

Caliph was a sweetling, and while a playful little sport, there was an intelligence that sparkled behind his eyes. Artorian said nothing about it after the conversation with his own Dreamed one. He believed Scilla when she said that she was here to help. The kind of help Dawn needed to move on was entirely different than his own, except that she was ecstatically gleeful and happy about it.

He didn't grasp if it occurred for exactly the same reasons. Scilla was holding his Incarnation hostage, not that it felt particularly major with his cultivation still at A-rank zero. Djinny, with Dawn already being an Incarnate, likely could not do the same. Was the purpose different in some way? It was too soon to ask, and a terrible time to bring it up.

He could only let that C'towl out of the bag once, and family outing time wasn't it. Instead he relished it the best he could, watching the group of gobbos that had accompanied them play some kind of sand sport that involved hurling each other over a net.

A wild C'towl had become very interested in all the wanton movement, and had sprung from nowhere to bite one in the leg and drag the Goblin home to eat. The comedic festival that followed had Dawn and Artorian in shambles from laughter.

Zelia had, of course, picked such a moment to show up with Surtur. It wouldn't have made her click in tense, smiling agitation if he didn't do it so abyss-blasted often. Honestly, how a lady holding a paper parasol could scare people with a smile, Artorian would never know. He always ended up back in the warehouse regardless, wistfully sighing each time he passed the crate. One day. One day.

CHAPTER FIFTY-ONE

Artorian slid back in his chair defeatedly as he handled yet another broken item. This one was difficult. Chewing on a piece of hard bear jerky, he glanced over the screen in his lap for the fourth time. That wouldn't have been a big deal if this item didn't have well over twenty screens open. The Administrator had been stuck trying to figure out just what was wrong with this one. The rock on the pedestal was clearly on the fritz, and should in no way have a magnetic charge strong enough to bend iron swords around itself like cooked noodles when activated.

None of the language was red error text. No purple or blue conflicting text either. None of the normal warning signs that the code had problems somewhere. No, this annoying little pebble of pyrite was working as intended. Was this why the Dwarves used the material to curse? Because it caused this nonsense? He'd been hacking away at this misery for a whole month. Still nothing. He'd opened submenus, dug around in unrelated files, even tried pulling up every single affiliated effect to see if some sympathy was to blame for some reason.

Based on the energy input, the conversion ratio, and the intended effect, this pebble should have had a small attraction field and a minimal effect. A tiny, gentle magnet. So why was it bending whole walls out of place? He scratched his head, grumbling as he vengefully chewed the jerky. Cal popped in without warning. <Hey, Artorian! Checking in on you. How's things?>

Swallowing the piece of jerky, he dismissively shook the rest at the screens. <Stuck on this one broken item I can't make heads or tails out of. Nothing in the code is wrong, but it's still not acting how it should, and I haven't found the lynchpin yet.>

Cal had a quick look at it, and then suddenly couldn't stop laughing. That only irritated the old man, who threw his hands up. <What?>

Cal snickered. <Well, you're right. It's working exactly as intended. Do me a favor, check the input.>

Still mumbling to himself, several screens were moved so the startup sequence was in front of him. Artorian dug through some lines of text until he found it. <Here we go: Input. Four units of earth Essence, six units fire, one unit infernal. I'm not seeing the problem.>

Cal nodded in agreement. <Right! Now check what's actually being fed.>

Artorian scrolled down a bit, and slapped the piece of jerky to his forehead when finally seeing what had been thwarting him. <You're kidding me. That's been there the whole time?>

Cal's weak snicker burst back out into full on laughter. <It was! The input is the exact units of Essence it should get. Instead, it's getting four Mana, six Mana, and one Mana. The item is working as intended, it's just using Mana instead of Essence, in significant portions. No wonder it's bending walls! Ha! That also wouldn't show up as incorrect error text, since it is supposed to be able to do that, and then convert it to the Essence ratio if we wanted to scale the magnetism up.>

Artorian flopped back in his chair, quickly edited the input, then stomped out of the warehouse with Cal still breaking down from amusement in his head. <Oh. Oho... oh. That was good. Anyway. Any chance you've been able to test the Mark II? I notice you're still in the normal body.>

Artorian paused, then smirked wide. He changed directions by turning on his heel and hurling himself up the stairs. In the pagoda, Zelia startled as her Dreamer whirled by, her teacup shaking from the air displaced as he zipped through the ground floor. "Zelia, Cal told me to test the Mark II! I'm off!"

"Wait. What? No, you have sealing work to d—dangit, Dreamer!" Zelia sputtered and coughed on her tea. That would throw off their entire calendar! She saw him teleport out, but followed his slipspace trail and knew exactly where he was storing his body. This time he'd kept it properly on Jotunheim. His Presence then left that space, and shot to the crate. She yelled at it when the feeling passed by. "Dreamer! Get back here!"

<Thanks, Cal. That was fabulous of you!> Artorian was pleased as punch, new Long body rocketing out of the crate at top speed as the indiscriminate flight effects kicked in. He still had no control over it, but he was up and out! <I'm free!>

Zelia turned silvery red, her network connections piggybacking on her Dreamer's original mental conversation as her humanization started to come undone. <Great Spirit! Did you really tell him to test the form? We have other important work to do!>

Cal's laugh shied away, looking for somewhere to hide. Great, now he had an angry lady on his case. An angry lady that could hijack the Administrator's connection and snap at him directly... for the moment. <Oh. I... uh, might have... questioningly mentioned it just now. I'm sure it'll be entirely harmless. It'll be fine! Gotta go! Toodles!>

The connection clicked shut, and all Zelia heard was her Dreamer's excited *wheee*! as he flew off without a modicum of control, straight up into the sky. It clearly didn't matter to him at the moment that he had no hope of changing his direction.

As far as Zelia was concerned, he was doing this just to get under her carapace and bristle her synapse. She turned to Halcyon, who had arrived from above in full flight. Zelia's clicking secretarial rage was doused as Cy held her snug. Partially to prevent her from chasing as she soothed out scheming words. "Let him go. Work or no, you can't keep a free spirit trapped in a workroom. He will get out, no matter how many anti-teleportation spell Runes you secretly develop with Niflheim. Just let him fly. Besides, he'll come back. As always."

Halcyon's smile seemed innocent, but Zelia's glare was full of questions. Like how her canny compatriot knew she was exploiting the Dark Elf desire to get on her good side. Cy nudged her nose toward the spectacle of their dastardly Dreamer. "Possibly sooner than he thinks."

Said questions were answered when the elated *whee* from above was no longer pleasantly excited. It had become more of a falling, extended yelp. The clamor turned into a very swiftly descending *whaa*! as a nearby forest splintered and mashed into the ground on his impact.

Shrapnel and dirt were sent as a wave across the land, as one would expect when a five-hundred-foot Long smashed planetside. Halcyon continued her sweet musings to the still-recovering secretary. "Remember, he has no idea how to fly that thing. Consider this a great opportunity to test out sketching skills! Who knows, he might end up in the beneath again. Just think, we could show them to Yuki. She'd love the story."

Zelia's displeasure melted away into a self-satisfied smirk as they both ran off to get canvas and sketching tools. Yuki made the best stories. Especially the kind that made the person involved wince and writhe in discomfort as it was told, while everyone else amused themselves greatly with the content.

A few hours later, Yuki received a parcel from a spiderling. Opening the curious package, her frozen lips cracked into a smile as she flipped through the curios. She had received sketch after sketch of a very large Dragon-shaped flag, helplessly stuck fluttering in another tree.

She dug through her pouch and pulled out additional inspiration. Ideas for a story formed all by themselves. She read the first line out loud, delighted by the tale. Frost laced her words, and a cold mist blew from between her lips as she spoke.

"Old man Sunny fell down from the sky…"

ABOUT DENNIS VANDERKERKEN

Hello all! I'm Dennis, but I go by a myriad of other nicknames. If you know one, feel free to use it! I probably like them more. I'm from Belgium, and have lived in the USA since 2001. English is my 4th language, so I'm making due, and apologize for the inevitable language-flub. I still call fans ceiling-windmills. The more shrewd among you may have noticed some strange sayings that may or may not have been silly attempts at direct translations! Thank you all for bearing with me.

I started writing in the The Divine Dungeon series due to a series of fortunate circumstances. I continue writing because I wanted to give hungry readers more to sink their teeth into, and help them 'get away' for a while. If you have any questions, or would like to chat, I live on Dakota's Eternium discord. Feel free to come say hi anytime! Life is a little better with a good book.

Connect with Dennis:
Discord.gg/8vjzGA5
Patreon.com/FloofWorks

ABOUT DAKOTA KROUT

Author of the best-selling Divine Dungeon and Completionist Chronicles series, Dakota has been a top 10 bestseller on Audible, a top 15 bestseller on Amazon, and his first book, Dungeon Born, was chosen as one of Audible's top 5 fantasy picks in 2017.

He draws on his experience in the military to create vast terrains and intricate systems, and his history in programming and information technology helps him bring a logical aspect to both his writing and his company while giving him a unique perspective for future challenges.

"Publishing my stories has been an incredible blessing thus far, and I hope to keep you entertained for years to come!" -Dakota

Connect with Dakota:
MountaindalePress.com
Patreon.com/DakotaKrout
Facebook.com/TheDivineDungeon
Twitter.com/DakotaKrout
Discord.gg/8vjzGA5

ABOUT MOUNTAINDALE PRESS

Dakota and Danielle Krout, a husband and wife team, strive to create as well as publish excellent fantasy and science fiction novels. Self-publishing *The Divine Dungeon: Dungeon Born* in 2016 transformed their careers from Dakota's military and programming background and Danielle's Ph.D. in pharmacology to President and CEO, respectively, of a small press. Their goal is to share their success with other authors and provide captivating fiction to readers with the purpose of solidifying Mountaindale Press as the place 'Where Fantasy Transforms Reality.'

Connect with Mountaindale Press:
MountaindalePress.com
Facebook.com/MountaindalePress
Twitter.com/_Mountaindale
Instagram.com/MountaindalePress

MOUNTAINDALE PRESS TITLES
GameLit and LitRPG

The Completionist Chronicles,
The Divine Dungeon, and
Full Murderhobo by Dakota Krout

King's League by Jason Anspach and J.N. Chaney

A Touch of Power by Jay Boyce

Red Mage by Xander Boyce

Space Seasons by Dawn Chapman

Ether Collapse and
Ether Flows by Ryan DeBruyn

Bloodgames by Christian J. Gilliland

Wolfman Warlock by James Hunter and Dakota Krout

Axe Druid and
Mephisto's Magic Online by Christopher Johns

Skeleton in Space by Andries Louws

Chronicles of Ethan by John L. Monk

Pixel Dust by David Petrie

Artorian's Archives by Dennis Vanderkerken and Dakota Krout

APPENDIX

Abyss – A place you don't want to be, and a very common curse word.

Adventurers' Guild – A group from every non-hostile race that actively seeks treasure and cultivates to become stronger. They act as a mercenary group for Kingdoms that come under attack from monsters and other non-kingdom forces.

Affinity – A person's affinity denotes what element they need to cultivate Essence from. If they have multiple affinities, they need to cultivate all of those elements at the same time.

Affinity Channel – The pathway along the meridians that Essence flows through. Having multiple major affinities will open more pathways, allowing more Essence to flow into a person's center at one time.

Affinity Channel Type – Clogged, Ripped, Closed, Minor, Major, and Perfect. Perfect doesn't often occur naturally.

- Clogged: Draws in no essence, because the channel is blocked with corruption.
- Ripped: Draws in an unknown amount of essence, but in a method that is unpredictable and lethal.
- Closed: Draws in no essence, because the channel is either unopened, or forcibly closed.
- Minor: Draws in very little essence.

- Major: Draws in a sizable amount of essence.
- Perfect: Draws in a significant amount of essence. This affinity channel type cannot occur naturally. It is very dangerous to strive for, as the path to this type leads to ripped channels.

Aiden Silverfang – The new leader of the Northmen, this Barbarian turned Wolfman holds deep grudges easily. He is one of the many supervisors of Midgard.

Alhambra – A cleric that lives in chasuble. Kept down for the majority of his career, he remains a good man with a good heart. His priorities for the people allot him a second chance, one derived from an old man's schemery.

Amber – The Mage in charge of the portal-making group near the dungeon. She is in the upper A-rankings, which allows her to tap vast amounts of Mana.

Artorian – The main character of the series. If you weren't expecting shenanigans, grab some popcorn. It only gets more intense from here on. He's a little flighty, deeply interested, and a miser of mischief. He is referred to by the wood elves as Starlight Spirit. In Cal's soul space, he takes the position of head administrator, and supervisor of Jotunheim.

Assassin – A stealthy killer who tries to make kills without being detected by his victim.

Assimilator – A cross between a jellyfish and a Wisp, the Assimilator can float around and collect vast amounts of Essence. It releases this Essence as powerful elemental bursts. A pseudo-Mage, if you will.

Astrea – The Nightmare. Infernal Professor at the Phantom Academy. She is a daughter of the Fringe, and one of Artorian's grandchildren. Even as an Infernal Cultivator, she finds herself in the most unlikely of company. Including her best friend, Jiivra.

Aura – The flows of Essence generated by living creatures which surround them and hold their pattern.

Barry the Devourer – A powerful S-ranked High Elf with the ability to turn all matter within a certain range into pure Essence and absorb it.

Basher – An evolved rabbit that attacks by head-butting enemies. Each has a small horn on its head that it can use to "bash" enemies.

Baobab – A wood elf with innate fire resistance. Strong-willed, this woman can handle the heat.

Bard – A lucrative profession deriving profit from other people's misery. Some make coin through song or instrument, but all of them love a good story. Particularly inconvenient ones. This includes Kinnan, Pollard, and Jillian.

Beast Core – A small gem that contains the Essence of Beasts. Also used to strip new cultivators of their corruption.

- Flawed: An extremely weak crystallization of Essence that barely allows a Beast to cultivate, comparable to low F-rank.
- Weak: A weak crystallization of Essence that allows a Beast to cultivate, comparable to an upper F-rank.
- Standard: A crystallization of Essence that allows a Beast to cultivate well, comparable to the D-rankings.
- Strong: A crystallization of Essence that allows a

Beast to cultivate very well, comparable to the lower C-rankings.

- Beastly: A crystallization of Essence that allows a Beast to cultivate exceedingly well, comparable to the upper C-rankings.
- Immaculate: An amalgamation of crystallized of Essence and Mana that allows a Beast to cultivate exceedingly well. Any Beast in the B-rankings or A-rankings will have this Core.
- Luminous: A Core of pure spiritual Essence that is indestructible by normal means. A Beast with this core will be in at least the S-rankings, up to SSS-rank.
- Radiant: A Core of Heavenly or Godly energies. A Beast with this Core is able to adjust reality on a whim.

Blanket – The best sugar glider. Blanket defends. Blanket protects.

Blight – A big bad. Also known as a Caligene, this entity can take many forms. Widespread and far-reaching, this thing has been around for over a millennia, and enjoys scheming to play the long game.

Birch – A friendly set of wood elves, of the Birch-tree Variant. They're friendly and well meaning, even if limited in what they can do. They like scented candles, particularly vanilla.

Blooming Spirit – The Wood Elven equivalent of Aura. See Aura.

Bob – Cal's original goblin shaman. Remade to the best of his species. Bob becomes a Mage bound to the Death Law. Due to the myriad of tasks Cal set before him, several copies were made of Bob to complete them. Several then became several thousand. Bob is both a coding reference, and a small nod to the fantastic 'Bobiverse' series.

Boro – A trader in exotics, this man allied himself with the raider faction. He assists in swindling deals, and robbing villages blind after flooding them with gold that they will not keep.

Brianna – Having begun as princess of the dark elves, she is now both queen and supervisor of Niflheim. She is known by many names, such as the Hidden Blade, the Empress of Niflheim, and the Pinnacle. She has spies everywhere, and you never know what she's planning until she's already done steps one through six. Be wary of the Lady of Mists.

Cal – The heart of the Dungeon, Cal was a human murdered by necromancers. After being forced into a soul gem, his identity was stripped as time passed. Now accompanied by Dani, he works to become stronger without attracting too much attention to himself. Oops, too late.

Cataphron – One of the Skyspear headmasters. Uses the Imperius body technique of the Iron-Shelled Mastodont Kings.

Cats, dungeon – There are several types:

- Snowball: A Boss Mob, Snowball uses steam Essence to fuel his devastating attacks.
- Cloud Cat: A Mob that glides along the air, attacking from positions of stealth.
- Coiled Cat: A heavy Cat that uses metal Essence. It has a reinforced skeleton and can launch itself forward at high speeds.
- Flesh Cat: This Cat uses flesh Essence to tear apart tissue from a short distance. The abilities of this Cat only work on flesh and veins and will not affect bone or harder materials.

- Wither Cat: A Cat full of infernal Essence, the Wither Cat can induce a restriction of Essence flow with its attacks. Cutting off the flow of Essence or Mana will quickly leave the victim in a helpless state. The process is *quite* painful.

Celestial – The Essence of Heaven, the embodiment of life and *considered* the ultimate good.

Center – The very center of a person's soul. This is the area Essence accumulates (in creatures that do not have a Core) before it binds to the Life Force.

Chandra – A ranked mage who is a masterful cook. She has prior history with Ramset (Occultatum), and runs the 'pleasure house' restaurant establishments. She has an affinity for all things plants and nature, finding comfort within the green, more-so than with people. In Cal's world, she is stationed as one of the many supervisors on Midgard, and is responsible for all the basic flora and fauna in the soul space.

Chants – Affect a choir-cleric's growth, and overall fighting ability. A Choir war host in action matches the chant of every other. Each voice added to the whole increases the power and ability of each person whose voice is involved, through celestial and aural sympathy. Church officials get very upset when interrupted by half-naked men.

Chasuble – The name of both a particular type of scarf worn loosely around the neck, and the name of a Major church-controlled city. Chasuble scarves are marked to show the rank of the person wearing them.

Church – 'The' Church, to be specific. Also known as the Ecclesiarchy, is one of the few stable major powers active in the world. It has several branches, each operating under different specifications.

- The Choir – The Face of the church, they carry a torch and spread the call far and wide. Operates as exploratory force and functions on heart and mind campaigns. The Choir's special function is to use harmonizing sound to buff and empower every member included in the group-effect.
- Paladin Order – The Fast-Attack branch, these mounted warriors function as cavalry would. The mounted creatures in question vary greatly, and most members employ a high-ranked beast for these purposes.
- Phalanx Sentinels – The Siege or Hold branch, the Sentinels are a heavy-armor branch that specialize entirely on securing locations. They are well known to be notoriously slow, and just as notoriously impossible to uproot from a position.
- Inquisitors – The Information gathering branch. This branch remains secretive.

Church Ranks – There are multiple Ecclesiarchy ranks, stacking in importance mostly based on cultivation progress.

- Initiate – A fresh entry to the church faction, the lowest rank. Generally given to someone still in training.
- Scribe – An initiate who failed to become a D-ranked cultivator, but was trusted enough by the faction to remain.
- Acolyte – Achieved by becoming a D-ranked cultivator. The second lowest rank in the church faction.
- Battle Leader – A trusted acolyte who shows promise in the fields of leadership and battle.

- Head Cleric – A high D-ranking cultivator, or a person who has been a Battle Leader long enough for their achievements to grant them their personal unit. Head Clerics are trusted to go on missions, excursions, and expeditions that differ based on the specific church faction.
- Keeper – Ranked equal to a Head Cleric. People who specifically keep administrative records, and interpret ancient texts. Keepers famously do not get along, and hold bitter rivalries due to said interpretations of the scriptures. Keepers tend to be Head Clerics who failed to enter the C-ranks.
- Arbiter – Achieved upon becoming a C-rank cultivator. An Arbiter is a settler of disputes of all kinds, whose authority is overshadowed only by those of higher rank. Otherwise, their say is final.
- Friar – A B-ranked Cultivator in the church faction. Friars are glorified problem solvers.
- Father – An A-ranked Cultivator in the church faction. A Father may be of a high rank, but has fallen out of favor with the upper echelons of church command.
- Vicar – An A-ranked Cultivator in the church faction. The de-facto rulers, movers, and shakers of the church faction.
- Saint – An S-ranked Cultivator in the church faction. They do as they please.

Choppy – The prime woodcutter in the Salt Village. A very good lad.

Chi spiral – A person's Chi spiral is a vast amount of intricately knotted Essence. The more complex and complete the pattern woven into it, the more Essence it can hold and the finer the Essence would be refined.

Cleric – A Cultivator of Celestial Essence, a cleric tends to be support for a group, rarely fighting directly. Their main purpose in the lower rankings is to heal and comfort others.

Compound Essence – Essence that has formed together in complex ways. If two or more Essences come together to form something else, it is called a compound Essence. Or Higher Essence.

Corruption – Corruption is the remnant of the matter that pure Essence was formed into. It taints Essence but allows beings to absorb it through open affinity channels. This taint has been argued about for centuries; is it the source of life or a nasty side effect?

Craig – A powerful C-ranked monk, Craig has dedicated his life to finding the secrets of Essence and passing on knowledge.

C'towl – A mixture between cat and owl. Usually considered an apex predator due to the intermingling of attributes and sheer hunting prowess.

Currency values:

- Copper: one hundred copper coins are worth a silver coin
- Silver: one hundred silver coins are worth a Gold coin
- Gold: one hundred Gold coins are worth a Platinum coin
- Platinum: the highest coin currency in the Human Kingdoms

Cultivate – Cultivating is the process of refining Essence by removing corruption then cycling the purified Essence into the center of the soul.

Cultivation technique – A name for the specific method in which cultivators draw in and refine the energies of the Heavens and Earth.

Cultivator – A cultivator is a silly person who thinks messing with forces they don't understand will somehow make life better for them.

Dale – Probably not important.

Dani – The most important. Wisp to Cal, and the sole reason the entire soul space is still standing. Many mental notebooks have "don't cross Dani" underlined no less than 19 times. Surely there's a reason for that.

Daughter of Wrath – A ranking female servant to the Ziggurat, that showed promise and was given troops to lead.

Dawn – The name taken by Ember as her S-ranked incarnation. A full perspective change from her original self, new options and a new life have opened before her. While the way of being Ember espoused still exists within her, room for the new is now possible. Even though she is stuck in an A ranked body for now, there's no way she's letting that stop her. Dawn is the supervisor of the fiery realm Muspelheim.

Deverash Editor Neverdash the Dashingly Dapper – Also called Dev, or Dev Editor. A gnome that retained his intelligence, and may have quite the impact on adventures to come.

Duskgrove Castle – A Location within the Phantomdusk Forest. It is the primary hideout for the Hakan's group of raiders.

D. Kota – An initiate in the choir, who has grand aspirations of becoming a scholar; and does. His works span the great ages. Known for all time.

Distortion Cat – An upper C-ranked Beast that can bend light and create artificial darkness. In its home territory, it is attacked and bound by tentacle like parasites that form a symbiotic relationship with it.

Dimitri – Also goes by Dimi-Tree, due to his size. A mix between a dwarf and a giant, this brash and brazen mountain loves to dabble. Doing a little bit of everything, he has a reputation that there's nothing he can't fix.

Dreamt Ones – Creatures made of Liminal Energy, having manifested through dreams:

- Caliph – Dawn's dreamt one. Manifested as a Djinn and Baby. Deemed relevant for reasons pertaining to the blocks in her continued growth.
- Scilla – Artorian's dreamt one. Manifested as a mixture of the small child he met in Chasuble and the bane of the Phantomdusk Forest. She withholds Artorian's Liminal Energy from him: at least, until he can work through his many, many regrets.
- Items – Cal's specific difficulty resulted in objects and challenges rather than creatures, as his Liminal Energy deemed that he needed to learn the lesson of how to rely on others. Rather than perform all tasks himself.

Dregs – A dungeon Core that has limited intelligence. It was installed into Cal's dungeon to control floors 1-4 so Cal could focus on other things.

Dungeon Born – Being dungeon born means that the dungeon did not create the creature but gave it life. This gives the creature the ability to function autonomously without fear that the dungeon will be able to take direct control of its mind.

Don Modsognir – Goes by Big Mo. Leader of the Modsognir clan. Responsible for trading and caravan operations. Known to be a troublemaker, he has an impeccable link of loyalty to his family. He enjoys finery, nice suits, and better company. He's got the heart of a king, and the trouble making penchant of a feisty five year old.

Dwarves – Stocky humanoids that like to work with stone, metal, and alcohol. Good miners.

Dwarven Traditions – Complicated unspoken rules that exist purely to protect the core dwarven heritage and ways of life. Specifically used against anyone deemed a non-dwarf or outsider, to sustain a public image that is of benefit to all clans as a whole.

Eucalyptus – A wood elf skilled in defensive and protective essence techniques.

Ember – Secondary Main Character – A burnt-out Ancient Elf from well over a Millennia ago. She's lived too long, and most of it has been in one War or another. She finds a new spark, but until then suffers from extreme weariness, depression, and wear. Her sense of humor lies buried deep within, dry as a cork. Ember enjoys speaking Laconically, getting to the point, and getting fired up. She will burn eternal to see her tasks complete. No matter the cost, and no matter the effort. She becomes Dawn upon graduating to the S ranks.

Egil Nolsen – Known to the world as 'Xenocide', is a Madness cultivator. Ranked SSS. He is but a moment of good fortune away from entering the Heavenly ranks, and is responsible for a majority of the world's problems, in one way or another.

Electrum – The metal used as Chasuble's currency. These coins are collectively known as 'divines' due to the very minor essence effect on them that keeps them clean. Their worth and value differs greatly from the established monetary system many other cities use, specifically to undercut them.

Elves – A race of willowy humanoids with pointy ears. There are five main types:

- High Elves: The largest nation of Elvenkind, they spend most of their time as merchants, artists, or thinkers. Rich beyond any need to actually work, their King is an S-ranked expert, and their cities shine with light and wealth. They like to think of themselves as 'above' other Elves, thus 'High' Elves.
- Wood Elves: Wood Elves live more simply than High Elves, but have greater connection to the earth and the elements. They are ruled by a counsel of S-ranked elders and rarely leave their woods. Though seen less often, they have great power. They grow and collect food and animal products for themselves and other Elven nations.
- Wild: Wild Elves are the outcasts of their societies, basically feral, they scorn society, civilization, and the rules of others. They have the worst reputation of any of the races of Elves, practicing dark arts and infernal summoning. They have no homeland, living only where they can get away with their dark deeds.
- Dark: The Drow are known as Dark Elves. No one knows where they live, only where they can go to get in contact with them. Dark Elves also have a dark reputation as Assassins and mercenaries for the other races. The worst of their lot are 'Moon Elves', the best-known Assassins of any race. These are the Elves that Dale made a deal with for land and protection.
- Sea: The Sea Elves live on boats their entire lives. They facilitate trade between all the races of Elves

and man, trying not to take sides in conflicts. They work for themselves and are considered rather mysterious.

Essence – Essence is the fundamental energy of the universe, the pure power of heavens and earth that is used by the basic elements to become all forms of matter. There are six major types are names: Fire, Water, Earth, Air, Celestial, Infernal.

Essence cycling – A trick to move energy around, to enhance the ability of an organ.

Faux High Elf – A person who has the appearance of a High Elf, but is not actually one. It is a 'Fake' Elf, who takes the position in name only. A mockery and status-display rolled into one.

Father Richard – An A-ranked Cleric that has made his living hunting demons and heretics. Tends to play fast and loose with rules and money.

Fighter – A generic archetype of a being that uses melee weapons to fight.

Fringe – The Fringe region is located in the western region of Pangea. It has been scrapped from maps and scraped from history, by order of the Ecclesiarchy.

Gathering webway – A web of essence created around one's center. For the purpose of gathering and retaining essence. This was the first method concerning essence refining techniques. It should never be sticky.

Gilded blade – A weapon, status title, occupation, and profession all in one. A Gilded blade is a weapon of the raider faction. They are brutally efficient at a single thing, and terrible at everything else.

Gomei – Brianna's right hand and general. He despises humanity with extreme contempt. For no reason other than that they deprived him of his favorite condiment. Wars will start over this. Again.

Grace – Offspring of Cal and Dani. Adorable sm0ll wisp. All the energy of dad. All the smarts of mom. Was a wisps color important again? Grace's color is purple.

Gran'mama – Ephira Mayev Stonequeen is Grand Matron of all the centralized Dwarven clans. She goes by Matron, or Gran'mama. While not a royal, she tends to be treated like one due to the vast respect she holds. She also keeps the great majority of land contracts. Beware of the dreaded chancla.

Hadurin Fellstone – Supposed Head Healer of the motley Fringe expedition crew.

Hadurin Fellhammer – Grand-Inquisitor Fellhammer. Executor of the Inquisition, Lord of the Azure Jade mountain, and slayer of a thousand traitors. While not fully of the dwarven race, he is short, portly, jovial to a fault, and as sly as a certain old man. I hear him with a thick, Scottish or Irish voice.

Halcyon – The second of Artorian's Chosen, granted the Blessing of Aurum. An uplifted Orca Matron, Halcyon shrunk into her shell as her sapience grew. Shy demeanor aside, a natural leader lurks within. Halcyon has multiple forms just like Zelia, such as fully human, fully Orca, and a hybridized state of flux.

Hakan – A gilded blade, She is the main Antagonist of AA1. Her personality is as unpleasant as her fashion sense. She's snide, cuts to the chase, and speaks abrasively without much poise or respect to anyone else.

Hans – A cheeky assassin that has been with Dale since he began cultivating. He was a thief in his youth but changed lifestyles after his street guild was wiped out. He is deadly with a knife and is Dale's best friend. Now Rose's husband.

Hawthorn – A set of wood elves that has taken it upon themselves to guard and patrol the edges of the forest. They are generally abrasive, as the threats they come home with aren't taken seriously enough. Or abundantly happy to see you, with matching southern cadence and happy reed-chewing style. Rules are actually guidelines. Make no mistake. In any other setting, Hawthorne would be a dastardly set of troublemakers.

Henry – Previously the prince-turned-king of the Lion Kingdom, he is now one of the several supervisors of Midgard. Henry is childhood friends with Aiden Silverfang.

Incantation – Essentially a spell, an incantation is created from words and gestures. It releases all of the power of an enchantment in a single burst.

Infected – A person or creature that has been infected with a rage-inducing mushroom growth. These people have no control of their bodies and attack any non-infected on sight.

Infernal – The Essence of death and demonic beings, *considered* to be always evil.

Inscription – A *permanent* pattern made of Essence that creates an effect on the universe. Try not to get the pattern wrong as it could have… unintended consequences. This is another name for an incomplete or unknown Rune.

Irene – A Keeper in the Choir. There is more to her than meets the eye, and is far more powerful than she initially appears to be. Do not argue with her about scripture. This world-weary

Keeper plays with subterfuge like children play outside. Though when able, she speaks with her fists. Her rage meter is tiny, and fills with a swiftness.

Jiivra – A battle leader in the choir, she aspires to be a Paladin. She has the potential to become truly great, if only given the opportunity. Young, and full of splendor. She's hasty, sticks to order, dislikes surprises, and answers to them with well-measured responses.

Jin – The child of Tarrean and Irene, a Keeper in the Fringe.

Karakum – Only two things are certain. Death, and Taxes. Karakum is both. This fire-dungeon turned scorpion gained new life just as Zelia did. He's snippy, and can be a bit much to handle, but after becoming Dawn's chosen, he does what is required of him by the Lady of Flame. Karakum is based on Zorro.

Lapis – A mineral-mining town in the vicinity of the Salt Flats. They refine the color Lapis into varying shades of Blue, and are a prime exporter. Lapis is located in the Fringe.

Liminal – Also called liminal energy, or the energy of thought. It is the intermediary between Mana and Spirit. Liminal energy is both sentient and sapient. It develops a mind of its own when the Mage reaches a certain point of progress. This energy can manifest itself in a variety of ways, but is difficult to control after it gains sapience. Sapient Liminal Energy frequently manifests as issues the Mage needs to tackle. Whether that be items, people, or challenges.

Maccreus Tarrean – Head Cleric of a choir expeditionary force. His pride is his most distinguishing feature, next to that ostentatious affront known as his armor. Short and portly for non-dwarven reasons, this blundering Ego-driven voice blusters through life like a drunk through a tavern. Elbows first. His ability to craft schemes is as sharp as a dull, smooth rock. His Charisma unfortunately doesn't notice and charges on anyway.

Mahogany – Chosen leaders of the Phantom Dusk Wood Elves. As a congregation of Sultans, they care deeply for their people. Forced to make difficult decisions on behalf of the people as a whole, they function with the full permission of the S-ranked council. Which is less active than they'd like it to be. A good soul, they speak with deep voices.

Mages' Guild – A secretive sub-sect of the Adventurers' Guild only Mage level cultivators are allowed to join.

Mana – A higher stage of Essence only able to be cultivated by those who have broken into at least the B-rankings and found the true name of something in the universe.

Mana Signature – A name for a signature that can be neither forged nor replicated, and is used in binding oaths.

Marie – Previously the princess-turned-queen of the Phoenix Kingdom. She is now one of the many supervisors of Midgard, establishing the human presence in Cal's soul space.

Marud – Choir second-in-command Battle Leader, of the second expeditionary force to the Fringe.

Meridians – Meridians are energy channels that transport life energy (Chi/Essence) throughout the body.

Memory Core – Also known as a Memory Stone, depending on the base materials used in their production. Pressing the stone to your forehead lets a person store or gain the knowledge contained within. As if you'd gone through the events yourself. Generally never sold.

Minya – Ex-leader of the Cult of Cal. After entering Cal's soul space, she now presides over the research and development on the Moon with Bob. All she wants is peace and quiet. Maybe a small store.

Mob – A shortened version of "dungeon monster".

Morovia – A world region located in the south-eastern section of the central Pangea band.

Necromancer – An Infernal Essence cultivator who can raise and control the dead and demons. A title for a cultivator who specializes in re-animating that which has died.

Nefellum – Head Cleric of the second expedition force into the Fringe.

Noble rankings:

- King/Queen – Ruler of their country. (Addressed as 'Your Majesty')
- Crown Prince/Princess – Next in line to the throne, has the same political power as a Grand Duke. (Addressed as 'Your Royal Highness')
- Prince/Princess – Child of the King/Queen, has the same political power as a Duke. (Addressed as 'Your Highness')
- Grand Duke/Grand Duchess – Ruler of a grand duchy and is senior to a Duke. (Addressed as 'Your Grace')
- Duke/Duchess – Is senior to a Marquis or Marchioness. (Addressed as 'Your Grace')
- Marquis/Marchioness – Controls a section of land in a kingdom outside of the heartland. Is senior to an Earl and has at least three Earls in their domain. (Addressed as 'Honorable')

- Earl/Countess – Is senior to a Baron. Each Earl has three barons under their power. (Addressed as 'My Lord/Lady')
- Viscount/Viscountess – Thought of as the lieutenants of the Earl in their region. Is senior to a Baron, if by just a small margin. (Addressed as 'My Lord/Lady')
- Baron/Baroness – Senior to knights, they control a minimum of ten knights and therefore their land. (Addressed as 'My Lord/Lady')
- Baronets – A member of the lowest hereditary titled order, with the status of a commoner but addressed with the prefix 'Sir'.
- Knight/Dame – Sub rulers of plots of land and peasants. (Addressed as 'Sir')
- Esquire – A young nobleman who, in training for knighthood, acts as an attendant to a knight. (Addressed as 'Sir')
- Gentleman/Lady – Those of high birth or rank, good social standing and wealth, and who did not need to work for a living.

Oak – A set of wood elves that embody the purest spirit of flamboyance. Rules might exist, but Oak won't care to listen.

Occultatum – Previously known as the Master, he now resides on Hel as its supervisor. Cal supposedly stationed him due to the high Mana density, but in reality, it's to deal with those abyss-blasted swans and geese.

Odin – Elemental of Air and supervisor of Asgard. His ego is almost the size of the Valkyries stationed outside his baths; though, a certain frosty individual manages to keep him in line.

Olgier – A trader from Rutsel, whose greed greatly exceeds his guile.

Olive – A wood elf who is very down to earth. A little greasy, he likes to dig holes and hidden pathways.

Oversized infernal corvid – Really big raven with the Infernal channel. D-ranked creature. Intelligent. Moody.

Pattern – A pattern is the intricate design that makes everything in the universe. An inanimate object has a far less complex pattern that a living being.

Phantomdusk Forest – A world region that borders The Fringe. It is comprised of vast, continent-sprawled greenery that covers multiple biomes. Any forest region connecting to this main mass is considered part of the whole, if entering it has a high mortality rate.

Presence – In terms of aura, this refers to the combined components that aura encompasses. Ordinarily a Mage-only ability. Presence refers to the unity of auras and them acting as one.

Ra – Lunella's first daughter, who causes an amount of trouble equal to the amount of breaths she takes. *Cough*, much like a certain grandfather.

Raile – A massive, granite covered Boss Basher that attacks by ramming and attempting to squish its opponents.

Ranger – Typically an adventurer archetype that is able to attack from long range, usually with a bow.

Ranking System – The ranking system is a way to classify how powerful a creature has become through fighting and cultivation.

- G – At the lowest ranking is mostly non-organic matter such as rocks and ash. Mid-G contains small plants such as moss and mushrooms while the upper ranks form most of the other flora in the world.

- F – The F-ranks are where beings are becoming actually sentient, able to gather their own food and make short-term plans. The mid-F ranks are where most humans reach before adulthood without cultivating. This is known as the fishy or "failure" rank.
- E – The E-rank is known as the "echo" rank and is used to prepare a body for intense cultivation.
- D – This is the rank where a cultivator starts to become actually dangerous. A D-ranked individual can usually fight off ten F-ranked beings without issue. They are characterized by a "fractal" in their Chi spiral.
- C – The highest-ranked Essence cultivators, those in the C-rank usually have opened all of their meridians. A C-ranked cultivator can usually fight off ten D-ranked and one hundred F-ranked beings without being overwhelmed.
- B – This is the first rank of Mana cultivators, known as Mages. They convert Essence into Mana through a nuanced refining process and release it through a true name of the universe.
- A – Usually several hundred years are needed to attain this rank, known as High-Mage or High-Magous. They are the most powerful rank of Mages.
- S – Very mysterious Spiritual Essence cultivators. Not much is known about the requirements for this rank or those above it.
- SS – Pronounced 'Double S'. Not much is known about the requirements for this rank or those above it.
- SSS – Pronounced 'Triple S'. Not much is known about the requirements for this rank or those above it.

- Heavenly – Not much is known about the requirements for this rank or those above it.
- Godly – Not much is known about the requirements for this rank or those above it.

Refining – A name for the method of separating essences of differing purities.

Rune – A *permanent* pattern made of Essence that creates an effect on the universe. Try not to get the pattern wrong as it could have… unintended consequences. This is another name for a completed Inscription.

Rose – Chaos cultivator and wife of Hans. She spent most of her life with her aunt Chandra before making her way to Mountaindale and meeting her friends. She will happily slay a man with her speech or with her arrows. They decide.

Rosewood – Wood elves with an unbreakable passion for fashion, and making clothes.

Rota – A sturdy and strapping Dwarf whose jokes latched him with the nickname "Otter", he once tried to scribe Runes onto a set of gambling dice. Beware of the explosions around this wily lad.

Royal Advisor – A big bad. Direct hand to the Mistress, the Queen and Regent in charge of the Ziggurat. Lover of the Cobra Chicken, and Swans.

Salt Village – The main location of Artorian's Archives one, where the majority of the story takes place. It is Located in the Fringe, and is a day's journey from the Lapis Village.

Salt Flats – A location in the Fringe. The Salt Village operates by scraping salt from the Salt Flats, a place where the material is plentiful. It is their main export.

Scar – Known as 'The Scar'. A location in that Fringe that includes the Salt Flats as one of its tendrils. It is rumored to be a kind of slumbering dungeon.

Scilla - A small girl that lives in Chasuble. She is afflicted by an effect that caused her irises to permanently turn pink.

Sequoia – Wood elves that will not be forgotten, even without them speaking.

Shamira – Scilla's mother. She is a resident of Chasuble, and not particularly happy about the conditions there.

Sproutling – A title for a child in the Fringe who has not yet been assigned a name, and thus is not considered an adult. Until a certain key event, this includes the famous five: Lunella, Grimaldus, Tychus, Wuxius, and Astrea.

Skyspear Academy – An Academy present on the world's tallest mountain.

Socorro – A desert in the central-band, eastern portion of Pangea. It used to be a place for something important. Now there is only sand, and ruin.

Soul Item – A construct made in a Soul Space that specializes the Mage to a certain set of ideas and concepts, allowing for advancement into the A ranks and beyond.

Soul Space – A realm accessible by cultivators that exists outside of the self. Vastly important for Mages to keep increasing in rank. Soul spaces are morphous in size, and tend to hole a Mage's 'soul item'.

Soul Space [Cal] – Cal's Soul Space is being designed to hold an entire world. Divided by several landmasses and unique locations:

- Midgard – The human, wolfman, and plant-people realm in Cal's soul space. This skyland supports anything in the G to D Ranks, and is where a majority of individuals are decanted. Run by Marie, Henry, Chandra, and Aiden.
- Alfheim – The realm for the majority of Elves in Cal's soul space. This skyland supports anything in the C ranks. Is built around having pill cultivation. Alfheim has no supervisor.
- Svartalfheim – The realm of the Dwarves in Cal's soul space. This skyland supports anything in the ranks. Is built on Aether cultivation. Svartalfheim has no supervisor.
- Vanaheim – The realm of the Gnomes in Cal's soul space. This skyland supports anything in the low B ranks. Vanaheim is home to all the pylons that run Cal's bracket spells, and a land of many wondrous inventions. Beneath its shiny exterior, a civil war takes place. Deverash is Vanaheim's supervisor.
- Jotunheim – The realm of massive Beasts and gigantic Jotun in Cal's soul space. Home to many wonderful Chosen and a door named Ellis, this skyland supports anything in the mid B ranks. Artorian is the supervisor of Jotunheim.
- Niflheim – The realm of Mists and home of the Dark Elves in Cal's soul space. This skyland is set almost completely on its side, and supports anything in the upper B ranks. Niflheim is run by Brianna.
- Muspelheim – The realm of fire, sand, and goblins

in Cal's soul space. This skyland has many separate layers, from the floating triremes in the sky, to the paradise beneath the surface, and supports anything in the upper B ranks. Many different races have found a home in Muspelheim; including Lamia, goblins, C'towl, Lizards, and a giant serpent named Jorm. This realm is overseen by Dawn.

- Asgard – The realm of elementals, heroes, and small party accidents. This skyland supports anything A ranked; from minimum to apex. (As well as Odin's ego, if just barely.) This realm was having a swarm problem, but after some… suggestions, those were taken care of. Odin is the supervisor of this realm.
- Hel – The realm of all things S ranked in Cal's soul space. This is the only spherical realm in Cal's world, and is made of all the corrupted ash from things dead and dying. Home to Gibble, the bone gazelle. Hel is supervised by Occultatum.
- Sun – Giant ball of interlocking rings and runes meant to provide light to all in Cal's soul space… Before the administrator caused it to explode. Home to Artorian's Archives.
- Moon – The place where most of the research and development takes place in Cal's soul space. The Moon's topside is a large area for the children to grow and enjoy themselves. Beneath the surface, however, is the Rotunda of Holding, and a large laboratory where Minya and the Bobs work.

Soul Stone – A *highly* refined Beast Core that is capable of containing a human soul.

Surtur – Dawn's first Chosen. A Lamia. She is granted a weapon made by Dawn, and uses it to lead her tribe to ever greater heights of prosperity. Even if her tribe keeps incorporating more and more races.

Switch – A village Elder of the salt village in the Fringe region. She croaks rather than speaks. Though that's only if she speaks. Usually she complains. Loudly, and in plenty. If forced to interact with Switch, consider stuffing one's ears with beeswax.

Tank – An adventurer archetype that is built to defend his team from the worst of the attacks that come their way. Heavily armored and usually carrying a large shield, these powerful people are needed if a group plans on surviving more than one attack.

Tibbins – An Acolyte in the Choir. He has a deep passion for all things culinary, and possesses a truly unique expression. He means well, but there's something about his poor luck that keeps getting him in someone's firing line. Sweet, loves to cook, and loyal to a fault. Tibbins is just in the wrong place at the wrong time. His voice tends to tremble when he is uncertain.

Tom – Former exiled northman. Friend of Dale, and a general smashing success with his hammer: 'Thud'.

Vizier Amon – A big bad. Direct hand to the Mistress, the Queen and Regent in charge of the Ziggurat. Things will get better before they get worse. Unless maybe one can pull the strings of a few favors. Sang with serpentine tongue. His time as grand vizier was short, becoming more nope than rope.

Wuxius – Son of the Fringe and one of Artorian's five grand-children.

Yuki – A lady of snow and ice. Artorian's third chosen, gifted with an unaccepted blessing. Her cold countenance and sleety demeanor reflects her current perspective of the world.

Yvessa – An elven name that means: 'To bloom out of great drought.' She is a choir-cleric going up the ranks, and holds incredible promise. A girl of destiny. A demon-lord with a spoon. A caretaker who gains wisdom beyond her years from the kind of abyss she has to deal with. Her voice gains energy as she ages, as does her spirit.

Zelia – First chosen of Artorian, gifted with the blessing of Argent. She is the mind of the Fringe Teleportation core, given life anew. A passionate artist, secretary, and seamstress. She is the sole peak of her spider family. Zelia is able to tap into her dreamer's abilities and memories, and uses her Teleportation gifts with uncanny skill and efficiency. She grows to deeply care for her dreamer beyond the constraints of what being a choson forces, and has decided for herself to stick around. Zelia has multiple forms, including fully human, fully spider, drider (half and half), and a state of flux.

Ziggurat – Both the name of a region, and a large building central to it. Ziggurat is the current raider stronghold where all their activities are coordinated from. The hierarchies here are simple and bloody, but the true purpose of the place is to serve as a staging area for necromancer needs.

Made in the USA
Columbia, SC
15 September 2023

22940932R00276